GHOST STORIES

GHOST STORIES

36 Spine-Chilling Tales of Terror and the Supernatural

EDITED BY BILL BOWERS

Guilford, Connecticut

An imprint of The Rowman & Littlefield Publishing Group, Inc.
4501 Forbes Blvd., Ste. 200
Lanham, MD 20706
www.rowman.com

Distributed by NATIONAL BOOK NETWORK

British Library Cataloguing in Publication Information available

Library of Congress Cataloging-in-Publication Data

Names: Bowers, Bill, 1957- editor.
Title: Ghost stories : 36 spine-chilling tales of terror and the
  supernatural / edited by Bill Bowers.
Description: Guilford, Connecticut : Lyons Press, [2020] | Summary: "Ghost
  Stories is a ghoulish collection of true classics, both legendary and
  long-forgotten, with frightening stories from Washington Irving, Edgar
  Allan Poe, Bret Harte, Ambrose Bierce, Edith Wharton, Mark Twain,
  Harriett Beecher Stowe, O. Henry, Willa Cather, and many others. This
  ghostly collection delivers the ghastly, horrifying, and otherwise
  haunting tales of terror we love to read - late at night, with the
  lights off"—Provided by publisher.
Identifiers: LCCN 2020010416 (print) | LCCN 2020010417 (ebook) | ISBN
  9781493049165 (cloth) | ISBN 9781493057924 (epub)
Subjects: LCSH: Ghost stories.
Classification: LCC PN6071.G45 G46 2020 (print) | LCC PN6071.G45 (ebook)
  | DDC 808.83/8733—dc23
LC record available at https://lccn.loc.gov/2020010416
LC ebook record available at https://lccn.loc.gov/2020010417

♾™ The paper used in this publication meets the minimum requirements of American National Standard for Information Sciences—Permanence of Paper for Printed Library Materials, ANSI/NISO Z39.48-1992.

CONTENTS

Introduction

Let no ill dreams disturb my rest, No powers of darkness me molest.
—FROM THOMAS KEN'S "EVENING HYMN," CA. 1674

GHOST STORIES ARE AS ANCIENT AS HUMANKIND, AND THEIR APPEAL has never waned. Anthropologists tell us that all cultures worldwide have always believed in ghosts and supernatural beings. Fear of ghosts probably springs from the eternal mystery of death and our nearly universal dread of the unknown. Perhaps it's also tied with grief over departed loved ones—or lingering terror of departed enemies—and the hope, or fear, that their spirits may somehow continue to touch our earthly existence.

No doubt the first ghost stories were told or sung around nighttime campfires whose flickering light helped to keep the cold and mysterious darkness at bay. (The ancient Irish tale "Teig O'Kane and the Corpse" is one example.) With the advent of writing and, later, films and television, the means of telling supernatural tales has changed. But the darkness and the fear remain.

Like other cultures around the globe, American and Western European literature have fostered a rich tradition of ghost stories. But what exactly *is* a "ghost story," as opposed to a horror story or a mystery story? In assembling this volume, I wondered: Must I limit the selection strictly to tales of disembodied spirits? To do so seemed arbitrary and needlessly restrictive. Edgar Allan Poe (represented here by his classics "The Tell-Tale Heart" and "Ligeia") called his stories "tales of mystery and imagination." So this is what I have attempted to assemble here: some superb tales of mystery and imagination from the pens of some of the Western world's finest authors.

Many celebrated writers are included here, even though ghost stories may not be among their best-known works: Mark Twain, Washington Irving, H. G. Wells, Nathaniel Hawthorne, Robert Louis Stevenson, Joseph Conrad, Nobel Prize winner Rudyard Kipling, and Pulitzer Prize winners Edith Wharton, Willa Cather, and Amy Lowell. Lowell is best known for her poetry, and "The Cross-Roads" reads almost like a poem in prose.

Elia W. Peattie, Rebecca Harding Davis, M. R. James, and Ambrose Bierce are relatively little known today, though all were famous in their time. Bierce was renowned for his satire and his frighteningly realistic descriptions of his terrible battlefield experiences in the American Civil War. Henry van Dyke was a diplomat in the administration of President Woodrow Wilson, though few remember him today. He was also a supremely talented writer, as you will see when you read "The Night Call."

Wilbur Daniel Steele, Mary E. Wilkins Freeman, and George Washington Cable were celebrated in their time for their many supernatural stories, though they are little read today. Perhaps this modest volume will help to change that unfortunate situation! Gertrude Morton (possibly a pseudonym) is known for only a single ghostly short story, "Mistress Marian's Light," which I've gladly included here.

Whatever you do, don't miss Goethe's haunting poem "The Erl-King" or "Canon Alberic's Scrap-Book" by M. R. James or "The Body-Snatcher" by Robert Louis Stevenson. And I recommend reading W. F. Harvey's "August Heat" on a stifling, muggy summer night.

Here, then, are a few of my favorite tales of mystery and imagination. It is my hope that you will enjoy perusing them as much as I have enjoyed collecting them, and that they will provide you with many hours of reading enjoyment.

Did you hear a strange noise just now, from out there in the darkness?

Bill Bowers
Somewhere in New England

The Crime of Micah Rood

By Elia W. Peattie

IN THE EARLY PART OF THE LAST CENTURY THERE LIVED IN EASTERN Connecticut a man named Micah Rood. He was a solitary soul, and occupied a low, tumble-down house, in which he had seen his sisters and his brothers, his father and his mother, die. The mice used the bare floors for a play-ground; the swallows filled up the unused chimneys; in the cellar the gophers frolicked, and in the attic a hundred bats made their home. Micah Rood disturbed no living creature, unless now and then he killed a hare for his day's dinner, or cast bait for a glistening trout in the Shetucket. For the most part his food came from the garden and the orchard, which his father had planted and nurtured years before.

Into whatever disrepair the house had fallen, the garden bloomed and flourished like a western Eden. The brambles, with their luscious burden, clambered up the stone walls, sentineled by trim rows of English currants. The strawberry nestled among its wayward creepers, and on the trellises hung grapes of varied hues. In seemly rows, down the sunny expanse of the garden spot, grew every vegetable indigenous to the western world, or transplanted by colonial industry. Everything here took seed, and bore fruit with a prodigal exuberance. Beyond the garden lay the orchard, a labyrinth of flowers in the spring-time, a paradise of verdure in the summer, and in the season of fruition a miracle of plenty.

Often the master of the orchard stood by the gate in the crisp autumn mornings, with his hat filled with apples for the children as they passed to school. There was only one tree in the orchard of whose fruit he was chary. Consequently it was the bearings of this tree that the children most wanted.

"Prithee, Master Rood," they would say, "give us some of the gold apples?"

"I sell the gold apples for siller," he would say; "content ye with the red and green ones."

In all the region there grew no counterpart to this remarkable apple. Its skin was of the clearest amber, translucent and spotless, and the pulp was white as snow, mellow yet firm, and without a flaw from the glistening skin to the even brown seeds nestling like babies in their silken cradle. Its flavor was peculiar and piquant, with a suggestion of spiciness. The fame of Micah Rood's apple, as it was called, had extended far and wide, but all efforts to engraft it upon other trees failed utterly; and the envious farmers were fain to content themselves with the rare shoots.

If there dwelt any vanity in the heart of Micah Rood, it was in the possession of this apple tree, which took the prize at all the local fairs, and carried his name beyond the neighborhood where its owner lived. For the most part he was a modest man, averse to discussions of any sort, shrinking from men and their opinions. He talked more to his dog than to any human being. He fed his mind upon a few old books, and made Nature his religion. All things that made the woods their home were his friends. He possessed himself of their secrets, and insinuated himself into their confidences. But best of all he loved the children. When they told him their sorrows, the answering tears sprang to his eyes; when they told him of their delights, his laugh woke the echoes of the Shetucket as light and free as their own. He laughed frequently when with the children, throwing back his great head, while the tears of mirth ran from his merry blue eyes.

His teeth were like pearls, and constituted his chief charm. For the rest he was rugged and firmly knit. It seemed to the children, after a time, that some cloud was hanging over the serene spirit of their friend. After he had laughed he sighed, and they saw, as he walked down the green paths that led away from his place, that he would look lovingly back at the old homestead and shake his head again and again with a perplexed and melancholy air. The merchants, too, observed that he began to be closer in his bargains, and he barreled his apples so greedily that the birds and the children were quite robbed of their autumnal feast. A winter wore away and left Micah in this changed mood. He sat through the long, dull days brooding over his fire and smoking. He made his own simple meals of mush and bacon, kept his own counsels, and neither visited nor received the neighboring folk.

One day, in a heavy January rain, the boys noticed a strange man who rode rapidly through the village, and drew rein at Micah Rood's orchard gate. He passed through the leafless orchard, and up the muddy garden paths to the old dismantled house. The boys had time to learn by heart every good point of the chestnut mare fastened to the palings before the stranger emerged from the house. Micah followed him to the gate. The stranger swung himself upon the mare with a sort of jaunty flourish, while Micah stood heavily and moodily by, chewing the end of a straw.

"Well, Master Rood," the boys heard the stranger say, "thou'st till the first of next May, but not a day of grace more." He had a decisive, keen manner that took away the breath of the boys used to men of slow action and slow speech. "Mind ye," he snapped, like an angry cur, "not another day's grace." Micah said not a word, but stolidly chewed on his straw while the stranger cut his animal briskly with the whip, and mare and rider dashed away down the dreary road. The boys began to frisk about their old friend and pulled savagely at the tails of his coat, whooping and whistling to arouse him from his reverie. Micah looked up and roared:

"Off with ye! I'm in no mood for pranks."

As a pet dog slinks away in humiliation at a blow, so the boys, hurt and indignant, skulked down the road speechless at the cruelty of their old friend.

The April sunshine was bringing the dank odors from the earth when the village beauties were thrown into a flutter of excitement. Old Geoffry Peterkin, the peddler, came with such jewelry, such stuffs, and such laces as the maidens of Shetucket had never seen the like of before.

"You are getting rich, Geoffry," the men said to him.

"No, no!" and Geoffry shook his grizzled head with a flattered smile. "Not from your women-folk. There's no such bargain-drivers between here and Boston town."

"Thou'lt be a-setting up in Boston town, Geoffry," said another. "Thou'rt getting too fine to travel pack a-back amongst us simple country folk."

"Not a bit of it," protested Geoffry. "I couldn't let the pretty dears go without their beads and their ribbons. I come and go as reg'lar as the leaves, spring, summer, and autumn."

By twilight Geoffry had made his last visit, and with his pack somewhat lightened he tramped away in the raw dusk. He went straight down the road that led to the next village, until out of sight of the windows, then turned to his right and groped his way across the commons with his eye ever fixed on a deeper blackness in the gloom. This looming blackness was the orchard of Micah Rood. He found the gate, entered, and made his way to the dismantled house. A bat swept its wing against his face as he rapped his stick upon the door.

"What witchcraft's here?" he said, and pounded harder.

There were no cracks in the heavy oaken door through which a light might filter, and old Geoffry Peterkin was blinded like any owl when the door was flung open, and Micah Rood, with a forked candle-stick in his hands, appeared, recognized him, and bade him enter. The wind drove down the hallway, blew the flame an inch from the wicks, where it burned blue a moment, and then expired, leaving the men in darkness. Geoffry stepped in, and Micah threw his weight against the door, swung the bar into place, and led Geoffry into a large bare room lit up by a blazing hickory fire. When the candles were relit, Micah said:

"Hast thou supped this night, friend Peterkin?"

"That have I, and royally too, with Rogers the smith. No more for me."

Micah Rood stirred up the fire and produced a bottle of brandy from a cupboard. He filled a small glass and offered it to his guest. It was greedily quaffed by the peddler. Micah replaced the bottle, and took no liquor himself. Pipes were then lit. Micah smoked moodily and in silence. The peddler, too, was silent. He hugged his knee, puffed vigorously at his pipe, and stared at the blazing hickory. Micah spoke first.

"Thou hast prospered since thou sold milk-pans to my mother."

"I've made a fortune with that old pack," said the peddler, pointing to the corner where it lay. "Year after year I have trudged this road, and year after year has my pack been larger and my stops longer. My stuffs, too, have changed. I carry no more milk-pans. I leave that to others. I now have jewels and cloths. Why, man! There's a fortune even now in that old pack."

He arose and unstrapped the leathern bands that bound his burden. He drew from the pack a variety of jewel-cases and handed them to Micah. "I did not show these at the village," he continued, pointing over his shoulder. "I sell those in towns."

Micah clumsily opened one or two, and looked at their contents with restless eyes. There were rubies as red as a serpent's tongue; silver, carved as daintily as hoar-frost, gleaming with icy diamonds; pearls that nestled like precious eggs in fairy golden nests; turquois gleaming from beds of enamel, and bracelets of ebony capped with topaz balls.

"These," laughed Geoffry, dangling a translucent necklace of amber, "I keep to ward off ill-luck. She will be a witch indeed that gets me to sell these. But if thou'lt marry, good Master Rood, I'll give them to thy bride."

He chuckled, gasped, and gurgled mightily; but Micah checked his exuberance by looking up fiercely.

"There'll be never a bride for me," he said. "She'd be killed here with the rats and the damp rot. It takes gold to get a woman."

"Bah!" sneered Geoffry. "It takes youth, boy, blue eye, good laugh, and a strong leg. Why, if a bride could be had for gold, I've got that."

He unrolled a shimmering azure satin, and took from it two bags of soft, stout leather.

"There is where I keep my yellow boys shut up!" the old fellow cried in great glee; "and when I let them out, they'll bring me anything I want, Micah Rood, except a true heart. How have things prospered with thee?" he added, as he shot a shrewd glance at Micah from beneath his eyebrows.

"Bad," confessed Micah, "very bad. Everything has been against me of late."

"I say, boy," cried the peddler, suddenly, "I haven't been over this old house for years. Take the light and show us around."

"No," said Micah, shaking his head doggedly. "It is in bad shape and I would feel that I was showing a friend who was in rags."

"Nonsense!" cried the peddler, bursting into a hearty laugh. "Thou need'st not fear, I'll ne'er cut thy old friend."

He had replaced his stuffs, and now seized the branched candle-stick and waved his hand toward the door.

"Lead the way," he cried. "I want to see how things look," and Micah Rood sullenly obeyed.

From room to room they went in the miserable cold and the gloom. The candle threw a faint gleam through the unkept apartments, noxious with dust and decay. Not a flaw escaped the eye of the peddler. He ran his fingers into the cracks of the doors, he counted the panes of broken glass, he remarked the gaps in the plastering.

"The dry rot has got into the wainscoting," he said jauntily.

Micah Rood was burning with impotent anger. He tried to lead the peddler past one door, but the old man's keen eyes were too quick for him, and he kicked the door open with his foot.

"What have we here?" he cried.

It was the room where Micah and his brothers had slept when they were children. The little dismantled beds stood side by side. A work-bench with some miniature tools was by the curtainless window. Everything that met his gaze brought with it a flood of early recollections.

"Here's a rare lot of old truck," Geoffry cried. "The first thing I should do would be to pitch this out of doors."

Micah caught him by the arm and pushed him from the room.

"It happens that it is not thine to pitch," he said.

Geoffry Peterkin began to laugh a low, irritating chuckle. He laughed all the way back to the room where the fire was. He laughed still as Micah showed him his room—the room where he was to pass the night; chuckled and guffawed, and clapped Micah on the back as they finally bade each other good-night. The master of the house went back and stood before the dying fire alone.

"What can he mean, in God's name?" he asked himself. "Does he know of the mortgage?"

Micah knew that the peddler, who was well off, frequently negotiated and dealt in the commercial paper of farmers. Pride and anger tore at his heart like wild beasts. What would the neighbors say when they saw his father's son driven from the house that had belonged to the family for generations? How could he endure their surprise and contempt? What would the children say when they found a stranger in possession of the famous apple-tree? "I've got no more to pay it with," he cried in helpless anguish, "than I had the day the cursed lawyer came here with his threats."

He determined to find out what Peterkin knew of the matter. He spread a bear's skin before the fire and threw himself upon it and fell into a feverish sleep, which ended long before the purple dawn broke.

He cooked a breakfast of bacon and corn cake, made a cup of coffee, and aroused his guest. The peddler, clean, keen, and alert, noted slyly the sullen heaviness of Micah. The meal was eaten in silence, and when it was finished, Geoffry put on his cloak, adjusted his pack, and prepared to leave. Micah put on his hat, took a pruning-knife from a shelf, remarking as he did so:

"I go early about my work in the orchard," and followed the peddler to the door. The trees in the orchard had begun to shimmer with young green. The perfume, so familiar to Micah, so suggestive of the place that he held dearer than all the rest of the world beside, wrought upon him till his curiosity got the better of his discretion.

"It is hard work for one man to keep up a place like this and make it pay," he remarked.

Geoffry smiled slyly, but said nothing.

"Bad luck has got the start of me of late," the master continued with an attempt at real candor.

The peddler knocked the tops off some gaunt, dead weeds that stood by the path.

"So I have heard," he said.

"What else didst thou hear?" cried Micah, quickly, his face burning, and shame and anger flashing from his blue eyes.

"Well," said the peddler, with a great show of caution, "I heard the mortgage was a good investment for any one who wanted to buy."

"Perhaps thou know'st more about it than that," sneered Micah.

Peterkin blew on his hands and rubbed them with a knowing air.

"Well," he said, "I know what I know."

"D— you," cried Micah, clinching his fist, "out with it!"

The peddler was getting heated. He thrust his hand into his breast and drew out a paper.

"When May comes about, Master Rood, I'll ask thee to look at the face of this document."

"Thou art a sneak!" foamed Micah. "A white-livered, cowardly sneak!"

"Rough words to call a man on his own property," said the peddler, with a malicious grin.

The insult was the deepest he could have offered to the man before him. A flood of ungovernable emotions rushed over Micah. The impulse latent in all angry animals to strike, to crush, to kill, came over him. He rushed forward madly, then the passion ebbed, and he saw the peddler on the ground. The pruning-knife in his own hand was red with blood. He gazed in cold horror, then tried in a weak, trembling way to heap leaves upon the body to hide it from his sight. He could gather only small handfuls, and they fluttered away in the wind.

The light was getting brighter. People would soon be passing down the road. He walked up and down aimlessly for a time, and then ran to the garden. He returned with a spade and began digging furiously. He made a trench between the dead man and the tree under which he had fallen; and when it was finished he pushed the body in with his foot, not daring to touch it with his hands.

Of the peddler's death there was no doubt. The rigid face and the blood-drenched garments over the heart attested the fact. So copiously had the blood gushed forth that all the soil, and the dead leaves about the body, and the exposed roots of the tree were stained with it. Involuntarily Micah looked up at the tree. He uttered an exclamation of dismay. It was the tree of the gold apples.

After a moment's silence he recommenced his work and tossed back the earth in mad haste. He smoothed the earth so carefully that when he had finished not even a mound appeared. He scattered dead leaves over the freshly turned earth, and then walked slowly back to the house.

For the first time the shadow that hung over it, the gloom deep as despair that looked from its vacant windows, struck him. The gloss of familiarity had hidden from his eyes what had long been patent to others—the decay, the ruin, the solitude. It swept over him as an icy breaker sweeps over a drowning man. The rats ran from him as he entered the hall. He held the arm on which the blood was rapidly drying far from him, as if he feared to let it touch his body with its confession of crime. The sleeve had stiffened to the arm, and inspired him with a nervous horror, as if a reptile was twined about it. He flung off his coat, and finally, trembling and sick, divested himself of a flannel undergarment, and still from fingertip to elbow there were blotches and smears on his arm. He realized at once the necessity of destroying the garments; and, naked to the waist, he stirred up the dying embers of the fire and threw the garments on. The heavy flannel of the coat refused to burn, and he threw it deeper and deeper in with a poker till he saw with dismay that he had quenched the fire.

"It is fate!" he cried. "I can not destroy them."

He lit a fire three times, but his haste and his confused horror made him throw on the heavy garments every time and strangle the infant blaze. At last he took them to the garret and locked them in an old chest. Starting at the shadows among the rafters, and the creaking of the boards, he crept back through the biting chill of the vacant rooms to the one that he occupied, and washed his arm again and again, until the deep glow on it seemed like another blood-stain.

After that for weeks he worked in his garden by day, and at night slept on the floor with the candles burning, and his hand on his flint-lock.

Meanwhile in the orchard the leaves budded and spread, and the perfumed blossoms came. The branches of the tree of the gold apples grew pink with swelling buds. Near that spot Micah never went. He felt as if his feet would be grasped by spectral hands.

One night a swelling wind arose, strong, steady, warm, seeming palpable to the touch like a fabric. In the morning the orchard had flung all its banners to the air. It dazzled Micah's eyes as he looked upon the tossing clouds of pink and white fragrance. But as his eye roamed about the waving splendor he caught sight of a thing that riveted him to the spot with awe.

9

The tree of the gold apples had blossomed blood-red.

That day he did no work. He sat from early morning till the light waned in the west, gazing at the tree flaunting its blossoms red as blood against the shifting sky. Few neighbors came that way; and as the tree stood in the heart of the orchard, fewer yet noticed its accursed beauty. To those that did, Micah stammeringly gave a hint of some ingenious ingrafting, the secret of which was to make his fortune. But though the rest of the world wondered and wagged its head and doubted not that it was some witchcraft, the children were enraptured. They stole into the orchard and pilfered handfuls of the roseate flowers, and bore them away to school; the girls fastened them in their braids or wore them above their innocent hearts, and the boys trimmed their hat-bands and danced away in glee like youthful Corydons.

Spring-time passed and its promises of plenty were fulfilled. In the garden there grew a luxury of greenness; in the orchard the boughs lagged low. Micah Rood toiled day and night. He visited no house, he sought no company. If a neighbor saw him in the field and came for a chat, before he had reached the spot Micah had hidden himself.

"He used to be as ready for the news as the rest of us," said they to themselves, "and he had a laugh like a horse. His sweetheart has jilted him, most like."

When the purple on the grapes began to grow through the amber, and the mellowed apples dropped from their stems, the children began to flock about the orchard gate like buzzards about a battle-field. But they found the gate padlocked and the board fence prickling with pointed sticks. Micah they saw but seldom, and his face, once so sunny, was as terrible to them as the angel's with the flaming sword that kept guard over the gates of Eden. So the sinless little Adams and Eves had no choice but to turn away with empty pockets.

However, one morning, accident took Micah to the bolted gate just as the children came trooping home in the early autumn sunset; for in those days they kept students of any age at work as many hours of the day as possible. A little fay, with curls as sunny as the tendrils of the grape, caught sight of him first. Her hat was wreathed with scarlet maple leaves;

her dress was as ruddy as the cheeks of the apples. She seemed the sprite of autumn. She ran toward him, with arms outstretched, crying:

"Oh, Master Rood! Do come and play. Where hast thou been so long? We have wanted some apples, and the plaguy old gate was locked."

For the first time for months the pall of remembrance that hung over Micah's dead happiness was lifted, and the spirit of that time came back to him. He caught the little one in his brawny arms and threw her high, while she shrieked with terror and delight. After this the children gave no quarter. The breach begun, they sallied in and stormed the fortress. Like a dream of water to a man who is perishing of thirst, who knows while he yet dreams that he must wake and find his bliss an agony, this hour of innocence was to Micah. He ran, and leaped, and frolicked with the children in the shade of the trees till the orchard rang with their shouts, while the sky changed from daffodil to crimson, from crimson to gray, and sank into a deep autumn twilight. Micah stuffed their little pockets with fruit, and bade them run home. But they lingered dissatisfied.

"I wish he would give us of the golden apples," they whispered among themselves. At last one plucked up courage.

"Good Master Rood, give us of the gold apples, if thou please."

Micah shook his head sternly. They entreated him with eyes and tongues. They saw a chance for a frolic. They clung to him, climbed his back, and danced about him, shouting:

"The gold apples! The gold apples!"

A sudden change came over him; he marched to the tree with a look men wear when they go to battle.

"There is blood in them!" he cried hoarsely. "They are accursed accursed!"

The children shrieked with delight at what they thought a jest.

"Blood in the apples! Ha! ha! ha!" and they rolled over one another on the grass, fighting for the windfalls.

"I tell ye 'tis so!" Micah continued. He took one of the apples and broke it into halves.

"Look," he cried, and in his eyes there came a look in which the light of reason was waning. The children pressed about him, peeping over each other at the apple. On the broken side of both halves, from the rind to the core, was a blood-red streak the width of a child's little finger. An amazed silence fell on the little group.

"Home with ye now!" he cried huskily. "Home with ye, and tell what ye have seen! Run, ye brats."

"Then let us take some of the apples with us," they persisted.

"Ha!" he cried, "ye tale-bearers! I know the trick ye'd play! Here then—"

He shook the tree like a giant. The apples rolled to the ground so fast that they looked like strands of amber beads. The children, laughing and shouting, gathered them as they fell. They began to compare the red spots. In some the drop of blood was found just under the skin, and a thin streak of carmine that penetrated to the core and colored the silvery pulp; in others it was an isolated clot, the size of a whortleberry, and on a few a narrow crescent of crimson reached half-way around the outside of the shining rind.

Suddenly a noise, not loud but agonizing, startled the little ones. They looked up at their friend. He had become horrible. His face was contorted until it was unrecognizable; his eyes were fixed on the ground as if he beheld a specter there. Shrieking, they ran from the orchard, nor cast one fearful glance behind.

The next day the smith, filled with curiosity by the tales of the children, found an odd hour in which to visit Micah Rood's house. He invited the tailor, a man thin with hunger for gossip, to go with him. The gate of the orchard stood open, flapping on its hinges as the children had left it. The visitors sauntered through, thinking to find Micah in the house, for it was the noon hour. They tasted of this fruit and that, tried a pear, now an apricot, now a pippin.

"The tree of the gold apples is right in the center," said the smith.

He pointed. The tailor looked; then his legs doubled under him as naturally as they ever did on the bench. The smith looked; his arm dropped by his side. After a time the two men went on, clinging to each other like children in the dark.

Micah Rood, with his sunny hair tangled in the branches, his tongue black and protruding, his face purple, and his clinched hands stained with dirt, hung from the tree of the golden apples. Beneath him, in a trench, from which the ground had been clawed by human hands, lay a shapeless, discolored bundle of clothes. A skull lay at one end of the trench, and beneath it a moldy pack was found with precious stones amid the decaying contents.

2

The Devil and Tom Walker

By Washington Irving

A FEW MILES FROM BOSTON, IN MASSACHUSETTS, THERE IS A DEEP inlet winding several miles into the interior of the country from Charles Bay, and terminating in a thickly wooded swamp, or morass.

On one side of this inlet is a beautiful dark grove; on the opposite side the land rises abruptly from the water's edge, into a high ridge on which grow a few scattered oaks of great age and immense size. Under one of these gigantic trees, according to old stories, there was a great amount of treasure buried by Kidd the pirate.

The inlet allowed a facility to bring the money in a boat secretly and at night to the very foot of the hill. The elevation of the place permitted a good look out to be kept that no one was at hand, while the remarkable trees formed good landmarks by which the place might easily be found again. The old stories add, moreover, that the devil presided at the hiding of the money, and took it under his guardianship; but this, it is well known, he always does with buried treasure, particularly when it has been ill gotten. Be that as it may, Kidd never returned to recover his wealth; being shortly after seized at Boston, sent out to England, and there hanged for a pirate.

About the year 1727, just at the time when earthquakes were prevalent in New England, and shook many tall sinners down upon their knees, there lived near this place a meagre miserly fellow of the name of Tom Walker.

He had a wife as miserly as himself; they were so miserly that they even conspired to cheat each other. Whatever the woman could lay hands on she hid away: a hen could not cackle but she was on the alert to secure the new-laid egg. Her husband was continually prying about to detect her secret hoards, and many and fierce were the conflicts that took place about what ought to have been common property.

They lived in a forlorn-looking house that stood alone and had an air of starvation. A few straggling savin trees, emblems of sterility, grew near it; no smoke ever curled from its chimney; no traveller stopped at its door. A miserable horse, whose ribs were as articulate as the bars of a gridiron, stalked about a field where a thin carpet of moss, scarcely covering the ragged beds of pudding stone, tantalized and balked his hunger; and sometimes he would lean his head over the fence, look piteously at the passer by, and seem to petition deliverance from this land of famine. The house and its inmates had altogether a bad name. Tom's wife was a tall termagant, fierce of temper, loud of tongue, and strong of arm. Her voice was often heard in wordy warfare with her husband; and his face sometimes showed signs that their conflicts were not confined to words. No one ventured, however, to interfere between them; the lonely wayfarer shrunk within himself at the horrid clamour and clapper clawing; eyed the den of discord askance, and hurried on his way, rejoicing, if a bachelor, in his celibacy.

One day that Tom Walker had been to a distant part of the neighbourhood, he took what he considered a short cut homewards through the swamp. Like most short cuts, it was an ill chosen route. The swamp was thickly grown with great gloomy pines and hemlocks, some of them ninety feet high; which made it dark at noonday, and a retreat for all the owls of the neighbourhood. It was full of pits and quagmires, partly covered with weeds and mosses; where the green surface often betrayed the traveller into a gulf of black smothering mud; there were also dark and stagnant pools, the abodes of the tadpole, the bull-frog, and the water snake, and where trunks of pines and hemlocks lay half drowned, half rotting, looking like alligators, sleeping in the mire.

Tom had long been picking his way cautiously through this treacherous forest; stepping from tuft to tuft of rushes and roots which afforded precarious footholds among deep sloughs; or pacing carefully, like a cat, along the prostrate trunks of trees; startled now and then by the sudden screaming of the bittern, or the quacking of a wild duck, rising on the wing from some solitary pool. At length he arrived at a piece of firm ground, which ran out like a peninsula into the deep bosom of the swamp. It had been one of the strong holds of the Indians during their wars with the first colonists. Here they had thrown up a kind of fort which they had looked upon as almost impregnable, and had used as a place of refuge for their squaws and children. Nothing remained of the Indian fort but a few embankments gradually sinking to the level of the surrounding earth, and already overgrown in part by oaks and other forest trees, the foliage of which formed a contrast to the dark pines and hemlocks of the swamp.

It was late in the dusk of evening that Tom Walker reached the old fort, and he paused there for a while to rest himself. Any one but he would have felt unwilling to linger in this lonely melancholy place, for the common people had a bad opinion of it from the stories handed down from the time of the Indian wars; when it was asserted that the savages held incantations here and made sacrifices to the evil spirit. Tom Walker, however, was not a man to be troubled with any fears of the kind.

He reposed himself for some time on the trunk of a fallen hemlock, listening to the boding cry of the tree toad, and delving with his walking staff into a mound of black mould at his feet. As he turned up the soil unconsciously, his staff struck against something hard. He raked it out of the vegetable mould, and lo! a cloven skull with an Indian tomahawk buried deep in it, lay before him. The rust on the weapon showed the time that had elapsed since this death blow had been given. It was a dreary memento of the fierce struggle that had taken place in this last foothold of the Indian warriors.

"Humph!" said Tom Walker, as he gave the skull a kick to shake the dirt from it.

"Let that skull alone!" said a gruff voice.

Tom lifted up his eyes and beheld a great black man, seated directly opposite him on the stump of a tree. He was exceedingly surprised, having neither seen nor heard any one approach, and he was still more perplexed on observing, as well as the gathering gloom would permit, that the stranger was neither negro nor Indian. It is true, he was dressed in a rude, half Indian garb, and had a red belt or sash swathed round his body, but his face was neither black nor copper colour, but swarthy and dingy and begrimed with soot, as if he had been accustomed to toil among fires and forges. He had a shock of coarse black hair, that stood out from his head in all directions; and bore an axe on his shoulder.

He scowled for a moment at Tom with a pair of great red eyes.

"What are you doing in my grounds?" said the black man, with a hoarse growling voice.

"Your grounds?" said Tom, with a sneer; "no more your grounds than mine: they belong to Deacon Peabody."

"Deacon Peabody be d—d," said the stranger, "as I flatter myself he will be, if he does not look more to his own sins and less to his neighbour's. Look yonder, and see how Deacon Peabody is faring."

Tom looked in the direction that the stranger pointed, and beheld one of the great trees, fair and flourishing without, but rotten at the core, and saw that it had been nearly hewn through, so that the first high wind was likely to blow it down. On the bark of the tree was scored the name of Deacon Peabody. He now looked round and found most of the tall trees marked with the name of some great men of the colony, and all more or less scored by the axe. The one on which he had been seated, and which had evidently just been hewn down, bore the name of Crowninshield; and he recollected a mighty rich man of that name, who made a vulgar display of wealth, which it was whispered he had acquired by buccaneering.

"He's just ready for burning!" said the black man, with a growl of triumph. "You see I am likely to have a good stock of firewood for winter."

"But what right have you," said Tom, "to cut down Deacon Peabody's timber?"

"The right of prior claim," said the other. "This woodland belonged to me long before one of your white faced race put foot upon the soil."

"And pray, who are you, if I may be so bold?" said Tom.

"Oh, I go by various names. I am the Wild Huntsman in some countries; the Black Miner in others. In this neighbourhood I am known by the name of the Black Woodsman. I am he to whom the red men devoted this spot, and now and then roasted a white man by way of sweet smelling sacrifice. Since the red men have been exterminated by you white savages, I amuse myself by presiding at the persecutions of quakers and anabaptists; I am the great patron and prompter of slave dealers, and the grand master of the Salem witches."

"The upshot of all which is, that, if I mistake not," said Tom, sturdily, "you are he commonly called Old Scratch."

"The same at your service!" replied the black man, with a half civil nod.

Such was the opening of this interview, according to the old story, though it has almost too familiar an air to be credited. One would think that to meet with such a singular personage in this wild lonely place, would have shaken any man's nerves: but Tom was a hard-minded fellow, not easily daunted, and he had lived so long with a termagant wife, that he did not even fear the devil.

It is said that after this commencement, they had a long and earnest conversation together, as Tom returned homewards. The black man told him of great sums of money which had been buried by Kidd the pirate, under the oak trees on the high ridge not far from the morass. All these were under his command and protected by his power, so that none could find them but such as propitiated his favour. These he offered to place within Tom Walker's reach, having conceived an especial kindness for him: but they were to be had only on certain conditions. What these conditions were, may easily be surmised, though Tom never disclosed them publicly. They must have been very hard, for he required time to think of them, and he was not a man to stick at trifles where money was in view. When they had reached the edge of the swamp the stranger paused.

"What proof have I that all you have been telling me is true?" said Tom.

"There is my signature," said the black man, pressing his finger on Tom's forehead. So saying, he turned off among the thickets of the swamp, and seemed, as Tom said, to go down, down, down, into the earth, until nothing but his head and shoulders could be seen, and so on until he totally disappeared.

When Tom reached home he found the black print of a finger burnt, as it were, into his forehead, which nothing could obliterate.

The first news his wife had to tell him was the sudden death of Absalom Crowninshield the rich buccaneer. It was announced in the papers with the usual flourish, that "a great man had fallen in Israel."

Tom recollected the tree which his black friend had just hewn down, and which was ready for burning. "Let the freebooter roast," said Tom, "who cares!" He now felt convinced that all he had heard and seen was no illusion.

He was not prone to let his wife into his confidence; but as this was an uneasy secret, he willingly shared it with her. All her avarice was awakened at the mention of hidden gold, and she urged her husband to comply with the black man's terms and secure what would make them wealthy for life. However Tom might have felt disposed to sell himself to the devil, he was determined not to do so to oblige his wife; so he flatly refused out of the mere spirit of contradiction. Many and bitter were the quarrels they had on the subject, but the more she talked the more resolute was Tom not to be damned to please her. At length she determined to drive the bargain on her own account, and if she succeeded, to keep all the gain to herself.

Being of the same fearless temper as her husband, she set off for the old Indian fort towards the close of a summer's day. She was many hours absent. When she came back she was reserved and sullen in her replies. She spoke something of a black man whom she had met about twilight, hewing at the root of a tall tree. He was sulky, however, and would not come to terms; she was to go again with a propitiatory offering, but what it was she forebore to say.

The next evening she set off again for the swamp, with her apron heavily laden. Tom waited and waited for her, but in vain: midnight came, but she did not make her appearance; morning, noon, night returned, but still she did not come. Tom now grew uneasy for her safety; especially as he found she had carried off in her apron the silver teapot and spoons and every portable article of value. Another night elapsed, another morning came; but no wife. In a word, she was never heard of more.

What was her real fate nobody knows, in consequence of so many pretending to know. It is one of those facts that have become confounded by a variety of historians. Some asserted that she lost her way among the tangled mazes of the swamp and sunk into some pit or slough; others, more uncharitable, hinted that she had eloped with the household booty, and made off to some other province; while others assert that the tempter had decoyed her into a dismal quagmire on top of which her hat was found lying. In confirmation of this, it was said a great black man with an axe on his shoulder was seen late that very evening coming out of the swamp, carrying a bundle tied in a check apron, with an air of surly triumph.

The most current and probable story, however, observes that Tom Walker grew so anxious about the fate of his wife and his property that he set out at length to seek them both at the Indian fort. During a long summer's afternoon he searched about the gloomy place, but no wife was to be seen. He called her name repeatedly, but she was nowhere to be heard. The bittern alone responded to his voice, as he flew screaming by; or the bull-frog croaked dolefully from a neighbouring pool. At length, it is said, just in the brown hour of twilight, when the owls began to hoot and the bats to flit about, his attention was attracted by the clamour of carrion crows that were hovering about a cypress tree. He looked and beheld a bundle tied in a check apron and hanging in the branches of the tree; with a great vulture perched hard by, as if keeping watch upon it. He leaped with joy, for he recognized his wife's apron, and supposed it to contain the household valuables.

"Let us get hold of the property," said he, consolingly to himself, "and we will endeavour to do without the woman."

As he scrambled up the tree the vulture spread its wide wings, and sailed off screaming into the deep shadows of the forest. Tom seized the check apron, but, woful sight! found nothing but a heart and liver tied up in it.

Such, according to the most authentic old story, was all that was to be found of Tom's wife. She had probably attempted to deal with the black man as she had been accustomed to deal with her husband; but though a female scold is generally considered a match for the devil, yet in this instance she appears to have had the worst of it. She must have died game however; for it is said Tom noticed many prints of cloven feet deeply stamped about the tree, and several handsful of hair, that looked as if they had been plucked from the coarse black shock of the woodsman. Tom knew his wife's prowess by experience. He shrugged his shoulders as he looked at the signs of a fierce clapper clawing. "Egad," said he to himself, "Old Scratch must have had a tough time of it!"

Tom consoled himself for the loss of his property with the loss of his wife; for he was a man of fortitude. He even felt something like gratitude towards the black woodsman, who he considered had done him a kindness. He sought, therefore, to cultivate a farther acquaintance with him, but for some time without success; the old black legs played shy, for whatever people may think, he is not always to be had for calling for; he knows how to play his cards when pretty sure of his game.

At length, it is said, when delay had whetted Tom's eagerness to the quick, and prepared him to agree to any thing rather than not gain the promised treasure, he met the black man one evening in his usual woodsman dress, with his axe on his shoulder, sauntering along the edge of the swamp, and humming a tune. He affected to receive Tom's advance with great indifference, made brief replies, and went on humming his tune.

By degrees, however, Tom brought him to business, and they began to haggle about the terms on which the former was to have the pirate's treasure. There was one condition which need not be mentioned, being generally understood in all cases where the devil grants favours; but there were others about which, though of less importance, he was inflexibly obstinate. He insisted that the money found through his means should be employed in his service. He proposed, therefore, that Tom should employ it in the black traffick; that is to say, that he should fit out a slave ship. This, however, Tom resolutely refused; he was bad enough in all conscience; but the devil himself could not tempt him to turn slave dealer.

Finding Tom so squeamish on this point, he did not insist upon it, but proposed instead that he should turn usurer; the devil being extremely anxious for the increase of usurers, looking upon them as his peculiar people.

To this no objections were made, for it was just to Tom's taste.

"You shall open a broker's shop in Boston next month," said the black man.

"I'll do it to-morrow, if you wish," said Tom Walker.

"You shall lend money at two per cent. a month."

"Egad, I'll charge four!" replied Tom Walker.

"You shall extort bonds, foreclose mortgages, drive the merchant to bankruptcy—"

"I'll drive him to the d—l," cried Tom Walker, eagerly.

"You are the usurer for my money!" said the black legs, with delight. "When will you want the rhino?"

"This very night."

"Done!" said the devil.

"Done!" said Tom Walker. So they shook hands, and struck a bargain.

A few days' time saw Tom Walker seated behind his desk in a counting house in Boston. His reputation for a ready moneyed man, who would lend money out for a good consideration, soon spread abroad. Every body remembers the days of Governor Belcher, when money was particularly scarce. It was a time of paper credit. The country had been deluged with government bills; the famous Land Bank had been established; there had been a rage for speculating; the people had run mad with schemes for new settlements; for building cities in the wilderness; land jobbers went about with maps of grants, and townships, and Eldorados, lying nobody knew where, but which every body was ready to purchase. In a word, the great speculating fever which breaks out every now and then in the country, had raged to an alarming degree, and every body was dreaming of making sudden fortunes from nothing. As usual the fever had subsided; the dream had gone off, and the imaginary fortunes with it; the patients were left in doleful plight, and the whole country resounded with the consequent cry of "hard times."

At this propitious time of public distress did Tom Walker set up as a usurer in Boston. His door was soon thronged by customers. The needy and the adventurous; the gambling speculator; the dreaming land jobber; the thriftless tradesman; the merchant with cracked credit; in short, every one driven to raise money by desperate means and desperate sacrifices, hurried to Tom Walker.

Thus Tom was the universal friend of the needy, and he acted like a "friend in need"; that is to say, he always exacted good pay and good security. In proportion to the distress of the applicant was the hardness of his terms. He accumulated bonds and mortgages; gradually squeezed his customers closer and closer; and sent them at length, dry as a sponge, from his door.

In this way he made money hand over hand; became a rich and mighty man, and exalted his cocked hat upon change. He built himself, as usual, a vast house, out of ostentation; but left the greater part of it unfinished and unfurnished out of parsimony. He even set up a carriage in the fullness of his vain glory, though he nearly starved the horses which drew it; and as the ungreased wheels groaned and screeched on the axle trees, you would have thought you heard the souls of the poor debtors he was squeezing.

As Tom waxed old, however, he grew thoughtful. Having secured the good things of this world, he began to feel anxious about those of the next. He thought with regret on the bargain he had made with his black friend, and set his wits to work to cheat him out of the conditions. He became, therefore, all of a sudden, a violent church goer. He prayed loudly and strenuously as if heaven were to be taken by force of lungs. Indeed, one might always tell when he had sinned most during the week, by the clamour of his Sunday devotion. The quiet christians who had been modestly and steadfastly travelling Zionward, were struck with self reproach at seeing themselves so suddenly outstripped in their career by this new-made convert. Tom was as rigid in religious, as in money matters; he was a stern supervisor and censurer of his neighbours, and seemed to think every sin entered up to their account became a credit on his own side of the page. He even talked of the expediency of reviving the persecution of quakers and anabaptists. In a word, Tom's zeal became as notorious as his riches.

Still, in spite of all this strenuous attention to forms, Tom had a lurking dread that the devil, after all, would have his due. That he might not be taken unawares, therefore, it is said he always carried a small Bible in his coat pocket. He had also a great folio Bible on his counting house desk, and would frequently be found reading it when people called on business; on such occasions he would lay his green spectacles on the book, to mark the place, while he turned round to drive some usurious bargain.

Some say that Tom grew a little crack brained in his old days, and that fancying his end approaching, he had his horse new shod, saddled and bridled, and buried with his feet uppermost; because he supposed that at the last day the world would be turned upside down; in which case he should find his horse standing ready for mounting, and he was determined at the worst to give his old friend a run for it. This, however, is probably a mere old wives fable. If he really did take such a precaution it was totally superfluous; at least so says the authentic old legend which closes his story in the following manner.

On one hot afternoon in the dog days, just as a terrible black thundergust was coming up, Tom sat in his counting house in his white linen cap and India silk morning gown. He was on the point of foreclosing a mortgage, by which he would complete the ruin of an unlucky land speculator for whom he had professed the greatest friendship. The poor land jobber begged him to grant a few months indulgence. Tom had grown testy and irritated and refused another day.

"My family will be ruined and brought upon the parish," said the land jobber.

"Charity begins at home," replied Tom, "I must take care of myself in these hard times."

"You have made so much money out of me," said the speculator.

Tom lost his patience and his piety. "The devil take me," said he, "if I have made a farthing!"

Just then there were three loud knocks at the street door. He stepped out to see who was there. A black man was holding a black horse which neighed and stamped with impatience.

"Tom, you're come for!" said the black fellow, gruffly. Tom shrunk back, but too late. He had left his little Bible at the bottom of his coat pocket, and his big Bible on the desk buried under the mortgage he was about to foreclose: never was sinner taken more unawares. The black man whisked him like a child astride the horse and away he galloped in the midst of a thunder storm. The clerks stuck their pens behind their ears and stared after him from the windows. Away went Tom Walker, dashing down the streets; his white cap bobbing up and down; his morning gown fluttering in the wind, and his steed striking fire out of the pavement at every bound. When the clerks turned to look for the black man he had disappeared.

Tom Walker never returned to foreclose the mortgage. A countryman who lived on the borders of the swamp, reported that in the height of the thunder gust he had heard a great clattering of hoofs and a howling along the road, and that when he ran to the window he just caught sight of a figure, such as I have described, on a horse that galloped like mad across the fields, over the hills and down into the black hemlock swamp towards the old Indian fort; and that shortly after a thunderbolt fell in that direction which seemed to set the whole forest in a blaze.

The good people of Boston shook their heads and shrugged their shoulders, but had been so much accustomed to witches and goblins and tricks of the devil in all kinds of shapes from the first settlement of the colony, that they were not so much horror struck as might have been expected. Trustees were appointed to take charge of Tom's effects. There was nothing, however, to administer upon. On searching his coffers all his bonds and mortgages were found reduced to cinders. In place of gold and silver his iron chest was filled with chips and shavings; two skeletons lay in his stable instead of his half starved horses, and the very next day his great house took fire and was burnt to the ground.

Such was the end of Tom Walker and his ill gotten wealth. Let all griping money brokers lay this story to heart. The truth of it is not to be doubted. The very hole under the oak trees, from whence he dug Kidd's money is to be seen to this day; and the neighbouring swamp and old Indian fort is often haunted on stormy nights by a figure on horseback, in a morning gown and white cap, which is doubtless the troubled spirit of the usurer. In fact, the story has resolved itself into a proverb, and is the origin of that popular saying, prevalent throughout New England, of "The Devil and Tom Walker."

3

An Occurrence at Owl Creek Bridge

By Ambrose Bierce

A MAN STOOD UPON A RAILROAD BRIDGE IN NORTHERN ALABAMA, looking down into the swift water twenty feet below. The man's hands were behind his back, the wrists bound with a cord. A rope closely encircled his neck. It was attached to a stout cross-timber above his head and the slack fell to the level of his knees. Some loose boards laid upon the sleepers supporting the metals of the railway supplied a footing for him and his executioners—two private soldiers of the Federal army, directed by a sergeant who in civil life may have been a deputy sheriff. At a short remove upon the same temporary platform was an officer in the uniform of his rank, armed. He was a captain. A sentinel at each end of the bridge stood with his rifle in the position known as "support," that is to say, vertical in front of the left shoulder, the hammer resting on the forearm thrown straight across the chest—a formal and unnatural position, enforcing an erect carriage of the body. It did not appear to be the duty of these two men to know what was occurring at the center of the bridge; they merely blockaded the two ends of the foot planking that traversed it.

Beyond one of the sentinels nobody was in sight; the railroad ran straight away into a forest for a hundred yards, then, curving, was lost to view. Doubtless there was an outpost farther along. The other bank of the stream was open ground—a gentle acclivity topped with a stockade of vertical tree trunks, loopholed for rifles, with a single embrasure through which protruded the muzzle of a brass cannon commanding the bridge. Midway of the slope between the bridge and fort were the spectators—a single company of infantry in line, at "parade rest," the butts of the rifles on the ground, the barrels inclining slightly backward against the right shoulder, the hands crossed upon the stock. A lieutenant stood at the right of the line, the point of his sword upon the ground, his left hand resting upon his right. Excepting the group of four at the center of the bridge, not a man moved. The company faced the bridge, staring stonily, motionless. The sentinels, facing the banks of the stream, might have been statues to adorn the bridge. The captain stood with folded arms, silent, observing the work of his subordinates, but making no sign. Death is a dignitary who when he comes announced is to be received with formal manifestations of respect, even by those most familiar with him. In the code of military etiquette silence and fixity are forms of deference.

The man who was engaged in being hanged was apparently about thirty-five years of age. He was a civilian, if one might judge from his habit, which was that of a planter. His features were good—a straight nose, firm mouth, broad forehead, from which his long, dark hair was combed straight back, falling behind his ears to the collar of his well-fitting frock coat. He wore a mustache and pointed beard, but no whiskers; his eyes were large and dark gray, and had a kindly expression which one would hardly have expected in one whose neck was in the hemp. Evidently this was no vulgar assassin. The liberal military code makes provision for hanging many kinds of persons, and gentlemen are not excluded.

The preparations being complete, the two private soldiers stepped aside and each drew away the plank upon which he had been standing. The sergeant turned to the captain, saluted and placed himself immediately behind that officer, who in turn moved apart one pace. These movements left the condemned man and the sergeant standing on the two ends of the same plank, which spanned three of the cross-ties of the bridge. The end upon which the civilian stood almost, but not quite, reached a fourth. This plank had been held in place by the weight of the captain; it was now held by that of the sergeant. At a signal from the former the latter would step aside, the plank would tilt and the condemned man go down between two ties. The arrangement commended itself to his judgment as simple and effective. His face had not been covered nor his eyes bandaged. He looked a moment at his "unsteadfast footing," then let his gaze wander to the swirling water of the stream racing madly beneath his feet. A piece of dancing driftwood caught his attention and his eyes followed it down the current. How slowly it appeared to move, what a sluggish stream!

He closed his eyes in order to fix his last thoughts upon his wife and children. The water, touched to gold by the early sun, the brooding mists under the banks at some distance down the stream, the fort, the soldiers, the piece of drift—all had distracted him. And now he became conscious of a new disturbance. Striking through the thought of his dear ones was a sound which he could neither ignore nor understand, a sharp, distinct, metallic percussion like the stroke of a blacksmith's hammer upon the anvil; it had the same ringing quality. He wondered what it was, and whether immeasurably distant or near by—it seemed both. Its recurrence was regular, but as slow as the tolling of a death knell. He awaited each stroke with impatience and—he knew not why—apprehension. The intervals of silence grew progressively longer, the delays became maddening. With their greater infrequency the sounds increased in strength and sharpness. They hurt his ear like the thrust of a knife; he feared he would shriek. What he heard was the ticking of his watch.

He unclosed his eyes and saw again the water below him. "If I could free my hands," he thought, "I might throw off the noose and spring into the stream. By diving I could evade the bullets and, swimming vigorously, reach the bank, take to the woods and get away home. My home, thank God, is as yet outside their lines; my wife and little ones are still beyond the invader's farthest advance."

As these thoughts, which have here to be set down in words, were flashed into the doomed man's brain rather than evolved from it the captain nodded to the sergeant. The sergeant stepped aside.

Peyton Farquhar was a well-to-do planter, of an old and highly respected Alabama family. Being a slave owner and like other slave owners a politician he was naturally an original secessionist and ardently devoted to the Southern cause. Circumstances of an imperious nature, which it is unnecessary to relate here, had prevented him from taking service with the gallant army that had fought the disastrous campaigns ending with the fall of Corinth, and he chafed under the inglorious restraint, longing for the release of his energies, the larger life of the soldier, the opportunity for distinction. That opportunity, he felt, would come, as it comes to all in war time. Meanwhile he did what he could. No service was too humble for him to perform in aid of the South, no adventure too perilous for him to undertake if consistent with the character of a civilian who was at heart a soldier, and who in good faith and without too much qualification assented to at least a part of the frankly villainous dictum that all is fair in love and war.

One evening while Farquhar and his wife were sitting on a rustic bench near the entrance to his grounds, a gray-clad soldier rode up to the gate and asked for a drink of water. Mrs. Farquhar was only too happy to serve him with her own white hands. While she was fetching the water her husband approached the dusty horseman and inquired eagerly for news from the front.

"The Yanks are repairing the railroads," said the man, "and are getting ready for another advance. They have reached the Owl Creek bridge, put it in order and built a stockade on the north bank. The commandant has issued an order, which is posted everywhere, declaring that any civilian caught interfering with the railroad, its bridges, tunnels or trains will be summarily hanged. I saw the order."

"How far is it to the Owl Creek bridge?" Farquhar asked.

"About thirty miles."

"Is there no force on this side the creek?"

"Only a picket post half a mile out, on the railroad, and a single sentinel at this end of the bridge."

"Suppose a man—a civilian and student of hanging—should elude the picket post and perhaps get the better of the sentinel," said Farquhar, smiling, "what could he accomplish?"

The soldier reflected. "I was there a month ago," he replied. "I observed that the flood of last winter had lodged a great quantity of driftwood against the wooden pier at this end of the bridge. It is now dry and would burn like tow."

The lady had now brought the water, which the soldier drank. He thanked her ceremoniously, bowed to her husband and rode away. An hour later, after nightfall, he repassed the plantation, going northward in the direction from which he had come. He was a Federal scout.

As Peyton Farquhar fell straight downward through the bridge he lost consciousness and was as one already dead. From this state he was awakened—ages later, it seemed to him—by the pain of a sharp pressure upon his throat, followed by a sense of suffocation. Keen, poignant agonies seemed to shoot from his neck downward through every fiber of his body and limbs. These pains appeared to flash along well-defined lines of ramification and to beat with an inconceivably rapid periodicity. They seemed like streams of pulsating fire heating him to an intolerable temperature. As to his head, he was conscious of nothing but a feeling of fullness—of congestion. These sensations were unaccompanied by thought. The intellectual part of his nature was already effaced; he had power only to feel, and feeling was torment. He was conscious of motion.

Encompassed in a luminous cloud, of which he was now merely the fiery heart, without material substance, he swung through unthinkable arcs of oscillation, like a vast pendulum. Then all at once, with terrible suddenness, the light about him shot upward with the noise of a loud splash; a frightful roaring was in his ears, and all was cold and dark. The power of thought was restored; he knew that the rope had broken and he had fallen into the stream. There was no additional strangulation; the noose about his neck was already suffocating him and kept the water from his lungs. To die of hanging at the bottom of a river!—the idea seemed to him ludicrous. He opened his eyes in the darkness and saw above him a gleam of light, but how distant, how inaccessible! He was still sinking, for the light became fainter and fainter until it was a mere glimmer. Then it began to grow and brighten, and he knew that he was rising toward the surface—knew it with reluctance, for he was now very comfortable. "To be hanged and drowned," he thought, "that is not so bad; but I do not wish to be shot. No; I will not be shot; that is not fair."

He was not conscious of an effort, but a sharp pain in his wrist apprised him that he was trying to free his hands. He gave the struggle his attention, as an idler might observe the feat of a juggler, without interest in the outcome. What splendid effort!—what magnificent, what superhuman strength! Ah, that was a fine endeavor! Bravo! The cord fell away; his arms parted and floated upward, the hands dimly seen on each side in the growing light. He watched them with a new interest as first one and then the other pounced upon the noose at his neck. They tore it away and thrust it fiercely aside, its undulations resembling those of a water snake. "Put it back, put it back!" He thought he shouted these words to his hands, for the undoing of the noose had been succeeded by the direst pang that he had yet experienced. His neck ached horribly; his brain was on fire; his heart, which had been fluttering faintly, gave a great leap, trying to force itself out at his mouth. His whole body was racked and wrenched with an insupportable anguish! But his disobedient hands gave no heed to the command. They beat the water vigorously with quick, downward strokes, forcing him to the surface. He felt his head emerge; his eyes were blinded by the sunlight; his chest expanded convulsively, and with a supreme and crowning agony his lungs engulfed a great draught of air, which instantly he expelled in a shriek!

He was now in full possession of his physical senses. They were, indeed, preternaturally keen and alert. Something in the awful disturbance of his organic system had so exalted and refined them that they made record of things never before perceived. He felt the ripples upon his face and heard their separate sounds as they struck. He looked at the forest on the bank of the stream, saw the individual trees, the leaves and the veining of each leaf—saw the very insects upon them: the locusts, the brilliant-bodied flies, the gray spiders stretching their webs from twig to twig. He noted the prismatic colors in all the dewdrops upon a million blades of grass. The humming of the gnats that danced above the eddies of the stream, the beating of the dragon flies' wings, the strokes of the water-spiders' legs, like oars which had lifted their boat—all these made audible music. A fish slid along beneath his eyes and he heard the rush of its body parting the water.

He had come to the surface facing down the stream; in a moment the visible world seemed to wheel slowly round, himself the pivotal point, and he saw the bridge, the fort, the soldiers upon the bridge, the captain, the sergeant, the two privates, his executioners. They were in silhouette against the blue sky. They shouted and gesticulated, pointing at him. The captain had drawn his pistol, but did not fire; the others were unarmed. Their movements were grotesque and horrible, their forms gigantic.

Suddenly he heard a sharp report and something struck the water smartly within a few inches of his head, spattering his face with spray. He heard a second report, and saw one of the sentinels with his rifle at his shoulder, a light cloud of blue smoke rising from the muzzle. The man in the water saw the eye of the man on the bridge gazing into his own through the sights of the rifle. He observed that it was a gray eye and remembered having read that gray eyes were keenest, and that all famous marksmen had them. Nevertheless, this one had missed.

A counter-swirl had caught Farquhar and turned him half round; he was again looking into the forest on the bank opposite the fort. The sound of a clear, high voice in a monotonous singsong now rang out behind him and came across the water with a distinctness that pierced and subdued all other sounds, even the beating of the ripples in his ears. Although no soldier, he had frequented camps enough to know the dread significance of that deliberate, drawling, aspirated chant; the lieutenant on shore was taking a part in the morning's work. How coldly and pitilessly—with what an even, calm intonation, presaging, and enforcing tranquillity in the men—with what accurately measured intervals fell those cruel words:

"Attention, company! . . . Shoulder arms! . . . Ready! . . . Aim! . . . Fire!"

Farquhar dived—dived as deeply as he could. The water roared in his ears like the voice of Niagara, yet he heard the dulled thunder of the volley and, rising again toward the surface, met shining bits of metal, singularly flattened, oscillating slowly downward. Some of them touched him on the face and hands, then fell away, continuing their descent. One lodged between his collar and neck; it was uncomfortably warm and he snatched it out.

As he rose to the surface, gasping for breath, he saw that he had been a long time under water; he was perceptibly farther down stream nearer to safety. The soldiers had almost finished reloading; the metal ramrods flashed all at once in the sunshine as they were drawn from the barrels, turned in the air, and thrust into their sockets. The two sentinels fired again, independently and ineffectually.

The hunted man saw all this over his shoulder; he was now swimming vigorously with the current. His brain was as energetic as his arms and legs; he thought with the rapidity of lightning.

"The officer," he reasoned, "will not make that martinet's error a second time. It is as easy to dodge a volley as a single shot. He has probably already given the command to fire at will. God help me, I cannot dodge them all!"

An appalling plash within two yards of him was followed by a loud, rushing sound, *diminuendo*, which seemed to travel back through the air to the fort and died in an explosion which stirred the very river to its deeps!

A rising sheet of water curved over him, fell down upon him, blinded him, strangled him! The cannon had taken a hand in the game. As he shook his head free from the commotion of the smitten water he heard the deflected shot humming through the air ahead, and in an instant it was cracking and smashing the branches in the forest beyond.

"They will not do that again," he thought; "the next time they will use a charge of grape. I must keep my eye upon the gun; the smoke will apprise me—the report arrives too late; it lags behind the missile. That is a good gun."

Suddenly he felt himself whirled round and round—spinning like a top. The water, the banks, the forests, the now distant bridge, fort and men—all were commingled and blurred. Objects were represented by their colors only; circular horizontal streaks of color—that was all he saw. He had been caught in a vortex and was being whirled on with a velocity of advance and gyration that made him giddy and sick. In a few moments he was flung upon the gravel at the foot of the left bank of the stream—the southern bank—and behind a projecting point which concealed him from his enemies. The sudden arrest of his motion, the abrasion of one of his hands on the gravel, restored him, and he wept with delight. He dug his fingers into the sand, threw it over himself in handfuls and audibly blessed it. It looked like diamonds, rubies, emeralds; he could think of nothing beautiful which it did not resemble. The trees upon the bank were giant garden plants; he noted a definite order in their arrangement, inhaled the fragrance of their blooms. A strange, roseate light shone through the spaces among their trunks and the wind made in their branches the music of Æolian harps. He had no wish to perfect his escape—was content to remain in that enchanting spot until retaken.

A whiz and rattle of grapeshot among the branches high above his head roused him from his dream. The baffled cannoneer had fired him a random farewell. He sprang to his feet, rushed up the sloping bank, and plunged into the forest.

All that day he traveled, laying his course by the rounding sun. The forest seemed interminable; nowhere did he discover a break in it, not even a woodman's road. He had not known that he lived in so wild a region. There was something uncanny in the revelation.

By nightfall he was fatigued, footsore, famishing. The thought of his wife and children urged him on. At last he found a road which led him in what he knew to be the right direction. It was as wide and straight as a city street, yet it seemed untraveled. No fields bordered it, no dwelling anywhere. Not so much as the barking of a dog suggested human habitation. The black bodies of the trees formed a straight wall on both sides, terminating on the horizon in a point, like a diagram in a lesson in perspective. Overhead, as he looked up through this rift in the wood, shone great garden stars looking unfamiliar and grouped in strange constellations. He was sure they were arranged in some order which had a secret and malign significance. The wood on either side was full of singular noises, among which—once, twice, and again—he distinctly heard whispers in an unknown tongue.

His neck was in pain and lifting his hand to it found it horribly swollen. He knew that it had a circle of black where the rope had bruised it. His eyes felt congested; he could no longer close them. His tongue was swollen with thirst; he relieved its fever by thrusting it forward from between his teeth into the cold air. How softly the turf had carpeted the untraveled avenue—he could no longer feel the roadway beneath his feet!

Doubtless, despite his suffering, he had fallen asleep while walking, for now he sees another scene—perhaps he has merely recovered from a delirium. He stands at the gate of his own home. All is as he left it, and all bright and beautiful in the morning sunshine. He must have traveled the entire night. As he pushes open the gate and passes up the wide white walk, he sees a flutter of female garments; his wife, looking fresh and cool and sweet, steps down from the veranda to meet him. At the bottom of the steps she stands waiting, with a smile of ineffable joy, an attitude of

35

matchless grace and dignity. Ah, how beautiful she is! He springs forward with extended arms. As he is about to clasp her he feels a stunning blow upon the back of the neck; a blinding white light blazes all about him with a sound like the shock of a cannon—then all is darkness and silence!

Peyton Farquhar was dead; his body, with a broken neck, swung gently from side to side beneath the timbers of the Owl Creek bridge.

4

The Snow-Image: A Childish Miracle

By Nathaniel Hawthorne

ONE AFTERNOON OF A COLD WINTER'S DAY, WHEN THE SUN SHONE FORTH with chilly brightness, after a long storm, two children asked leave of their mother to run out and play in the new-fallen snow. The elder child was a little girl, whom, because she was of a tender and modest disposition, and was thought to be very beautiful, her parents, and other people who were familiar with her, used to call Violet. But her brother was known by the style and title of Peony, on account of the ruddiness of his broad and round little phiz, which made everybody think of sunshine and great scarlet flowers. The father of these two children, a certain Mr. Lindsey, it is important to say, was an excellent but exceedingly matter of fact sort of man, a dealer in hardware, and was sturdily accustomed to take what is called the common-sense view of all matters that came under his consideration. With a heart about as tender as other people's, he had a head as hard and impenetrable, and therefore, perhaps, as empty, as one of the iron pots which it was a part of his business to sell. The mother's character, on the other hand, had a strain of poetry in it, a trait of unworldly beauty,—a delicate and dewy flower, as it were, that had survived out of her imaginative youth, and still kept itself alive amid the dusty realities of matrimony and motherhood.

So, Violet and Peony, as I began with saying, besought their mother to let them run out and play in the new snow; for, though it had looked so dreary and dismal, drifting downward out of the gray sky, it had a very cheerful aspect, now that the sun was shining on it. The children dwelt in a city, and had no wider play-place than a little garden before the house, divided by a white fence from the street, and with a pear-tree and two or three plum-trees overshadowing it, and some rosebushes just in front of the parlor windows. The trees and shrubs, however, were now leafless, and their twigs were enveloped in the light snow, which thus made a kind of wintry foliage, with here and there a pendent icicle for the fruit.

"Yes, Violet,—yes, my little Peony," said their kind mother, "you may go out and play in the new snow."

Accordingly, the good lady bundled up her darlings in woollen jackets and wadded sacks, and put comforters round their necks, and a pair of striped gaiters on each little pair of legs, and worsted mittens on their hands, and gave them a kiss apiece, by way of a spell to keep away Jack Frost. Forth sallied the two children, with a hop-skip-and-jump, that carried them at once into the very heart of a huge snowdrift, whence Violet emerged like a snow-bunting, while little Peony floundered out with his round face in full bloom. Then what a merry time had they! To look at them, frolicking in the wintry garden, you would have thought that the dark and pitiless storm had been sent for no other purpose but to provide a new plaything for Violet and Peony; and that they themselves had been created, as the snowbirds were, to take delight only in the tempest, and in the white mantle which is spread over the earth.

At last, when they had frosted one another all over with handfuls of snow, Violet, after laughing heartily at little Peony's figure, was struck with a new idea.

"You look exactly like a snow-image, Peony," said she, "if your cheeks were not so red. And that puts me in mind! Let us make an image out of snow,—an image of a little girl,—and it shall be our sister, and shall run about and play with us all winter long. Won't it be nice?"

"O, yes!" cried Peony, as plainly as he could speak, for he was but a little boy. "That will be nice! And mamma shall see it!"

"Yes," answered Violet; "mamma shall see the new little girl. But she must not make her come into the warm parlor; for, you know, our little snow-sister will not love the warmth."

And forthwith the children began this great business of making a snow-image that should run about; while their mother, who was sitting at the window and overheard some of their talk, could not help smiling at the gravity with which they set about it. They really seemed to imagine that there would be no difficulty whatever in creating a live little girl out of the snow. And, to say the truth, if miracles are ever to be wrought, it will be by putting our hands to the work in precisely such a simple and undoubting frame of mind as that in which Violet and Peony now undertook to perform one, without so much as knowing that it was a miracle. So thought the mother; and thought, likewise, that the new snow, just fallen from heaven, would be excellent material to make new beings of, if it were not so very cold. She gazed at the children a moment longer, delighting to watch their little figures,—the girl, tall for her age, graceful and agile, and so delicately colored that she looked like a cheerful thought more than a physical reality; while Peony expanded in breadth rather than height, and rolled along on his short and sturdy legs as substantial as an elephant, though not quite so big. Then the mother resumed her work. What it was I forget; but she was either trimming a silken bonnet for Violet, or darning a pair of stockings for little Peony's short legs. Again, however, and again, and yet other agains, she could not help turning her head to the window to see how the children got on with their snow-image.

Indeed, it was an exceedingly pleasant sight, those bright little souls at their task! Moreover, it was really wonderful to observe how knowingly and skilfully they managed the matter. Violet assumed the chief direction, and told Peony what to do, while, with her own delicate fingers, she shaped out all the nicer parts of the snow-figure. It seemed, in fact, not so much to be made by the children, as to grow up under their hands, while they were playing and prattling about it. Their mother was quite surprised at this; and the longer she looked, the more and more surprised she grew.

"What remarkable children mine are!" thought she, smiling with a mother's pride; and, smiling at herself, too, for being so proud of them. "What other children could have made anything so like a little girl's figure out of snow at the first trial? Well; but now I must finish Peony's new frock, for his grandfather is coming to-morrow, and I want the little fellow to look handsome."

So she took up the frock, and was soon as busily at work again with her needle as the two children with their snow-image. But still, as the needle travelled hither and thither through the seams of the dress, the mother made her toil light and happy by listening to the airy voices of Violet and Peony. They kept talking to one another all the time, their tongues being quite as active as their feet and hands. Except at intervals, she could not distinctly hear what was said, but had merely a sweet impression that they were in a most loving mood, and were enjoying themselves highly, and that the business of making the snow-image went prosperously on. Now and then, however, when Violet and Peony happened to raise their voices, the words were as audible as if they had been spoken in the very parlor where the mother sat. O, how delightfully those words echoed in her heart, even though they meant nothing so very wise or wonderful, after all!

But you must know a mother listens with her heart much more than with her ears; and thus she is often delighted with the trills of celestial music, when other people can hear nothing of the kind.

"Peony, Peony!" cried Violet to her brother, who had gone to another part of the garden, "bring me some of that fresh snow, Peony, from the very farthest corner, where we have not been trampling. I want it to shape our little snow-sister's bosom with. You know that part must be quite pure, just as it came out of the sky!"

"Here it is, Violet!" answered Peony, in his bluff tone,—but a very sweet tone, too,—as he came floundering through the half-trodden drifts. "Here is the snow for her little bosom. O Violet, how beau-ti-ful she begins to look!"

"Yes," said Violet thoughtfully and quietly; our snow-sister does look very lovely. I did not quite know, Peony, that we could make such a sweet little girl as this."

The mother, as she listened, thought how fit and delightful an incident it would be, if fairies, or still better, if angel-children were to come from paradise, and play invisibly with her own darlings, and help them to make their snow-image, giving it the features of celestial babyhood! Violet and Peony would not be aware of their immortal playmates,—only they would see that the image grew very beautiful while they worked at it, and would think that they themselves had done it all.

"My little girl and boy deserve such playmates, if mortal children ever did!" said the mother to herself; and then she smiled again at her own motherly pride.

Nevertheless, the idea seized upon her imagination; and, ever and anon, she took a glimpse out of the window, half dreaming that she might see the golden-haired children of paradise sporting with her own golden-haired Violet and bright-cheeked Peony.

Now, for a few moments, there was a busy and earnest but indistinct hum of the two children's voices, as Violet and Peony wrought together with one happy consent. Violet still seemed to be the guiding spirit, while Peony acted rather as a laborer, and brought her the snow from far and near. And yet the little urchin evidently had a proper understanding of the matter, too!

"Peony, Peony!" cried Violet; for her brother was again at the other side of the garden. "Bring me those light wreaths of snow that have rested on the lower branches of the pear-tree. You can clamber on the snowdrift, Peony, and reach them easily. I must have them to make some ringlets for our snow-sister's head!"

"Here they are, Violet!" answered the little boy. "Take care you do not break them. Well done! Well done! How pretty!"

"Does she not look sweetly?" said Violet, with a very satisfied tone; "and now we must have some little shining bits of ice, to make the brightness of her eyes. She is not finished yet. Mamma will see how very beautiful she is; but papa will say, 'Tush! nonsense!—come in out of the cold!'"

"Let us call mamma to look out," said Peony; and then he shouted lustily, "Mamma! mamma!! mamma!!! Look out, and see what a nice 'ittle girl we are making!"

The mother put down her work for an instant, and looked out of the window. But it so happened that the sun—for this was one of the shortest days of the whole year—had sunken so nearly to the edge of the world that his setting shine came obliquely into the lady's eyes. So she was dazzled, you must understand, and could not very distinctly observe what was in the garden. Still, however, through all that bright, blinding dazzle of the sun and the new snow, she beheld a small white figure in the garden, that seemed to have a wonderful deal of human likeness about it. And she saw Violet and Peony,—indeed, she looked more at them than at the image,—she saw the two children still at work; Peony bringing fresh snow, and Violet applying it to the figure as scientifically as a sculptor adds clay to his model. Indistinctly as she discerned the snow-child, the mother thought to herself that never before was there a snow-figure so cunningly made, nor ever such a dear little girl and boy to make it.

"They do everything better than other children," said she very complacently. "No wonder they make better snow-images!"

She sat down again to her work, and made as much haste with it as possible; because twilight would soon come, and Peony's frock was not yet finished, and grandfather was expected, by railroad, pretty early in the morning. Faster and faster, therefore, went her flying fingers. The children, likewise, kept busily at work in the garden, and still the mother listened, whenever she could catch a word. She was amused to observe how their little imaginations had got mixed up with what they were doing, and carried away by it. They seemed positively to think that the snow-child would run about and play with them.

"What a nice playmate she will be for us, all winter long!" said Violet. "I hope papa will not be afraid of her giving us a cold! Sha'n't you love her dearly, Peony?"

"O, yes!" cried Peony. "And I will hug her, and she shall sit down close by me, and drink some of my warm milk!"

"O, no, Peony!" answered Violet, with grave wisdom. "That will not do at all. Warm milk will not be wholesome for our little snow-sister. Little snow-people, like her, eat nothing but icicles. No, no, Peony we must not give her anything warm to drink!"

There was a minute or two of silence; for Peony, whose short legs were never weary, had gone on a pilgrimage again to the other side of the garden. All of a sudden, Violet cried out, loudly and joyfully,—

"Look here, Peony! Come quickly! A light has been shining on her cheek out of that rose-colored cloud! And the color does not go away! Is not that beautiful!"

"Yes; it is beau-ti-ful," answered Peony, pronouncing the three syllables with deliberate accuracy. "O Violet, only look at her hair! It is all like gold!

"O, certainly," said Violet with tranquillity, as if it were very much a matter of course. "That color, you know, comes from the golden clouds that we see up there in the sky. She is almost finished now. But her lips must be made very red,—redder than her cheeks. Perhaps, Peony, it will make them red if we both kiss them!"

Accordingly, the mother heard two smart little smacks, as if both her children were kissing the snow-image on its frozen mouth. But, as this did not seem to make the lips quite red enough, Violet next proposed that the snow-child should be invited to kiss Peony's scarlet cheek.

"Come, 'ittle snow-sister, kiss me!" cried Peony.

"There! she has kissed you," added Violet, and now her lips are very red. And she blushed a little, too!"

"O, what a cold kiss!" cried Peony.

Just then, there came a breeze of the pure west wind, sweeping through the garden and rattling the parlor windows. It sounded so wintry cold, that the mother was about to tap on the window-pane with her thimbled finger, to summon the two children in, when they both cried out to her with one voice. The tone was not a tone of surprise, although they were evidently a good deal excited; it appeared rather as if they were very much rejoiced at some event that had now happened, but which they had been looking for, and had reckoned upon all along.

"Mamma! mamma! We have finished our little snow-sister, and she is running about the garden with us!"

"What imaginative little beings my children are!" thought the mother, putting the last few stitches into Peony's frock. "And it is strange, too, that they make me almost as much a child as they themselves are! I can hardly help believing, now, that the snow-image has really come to life!"

"Dear mamma!" cried Violet, "pray look out and see what a sweet playmate we have!"

The mother, being thus entreated, could no longer delay to look forth from the window. The sun was now gone out of the sky, leaving, however, a rich inheritance of his brightness among those purple and golden clouds which make the sunsets of winter so magnificent. But there was not the slightest gleam or dazzle, either on the window or on the snow; so that the good lady could look all over the garden, and see everything and everybody in it. And what do you think she saw there? Violet and Peony, of course, her own two darling children. Ah, but whom or what did she see besides? Why, if you will believe me, there was a small figure of a girl, dressed all in white, with rose-tinged cheeks and ringlets of golden hue, playing about the garden with the two children! A stranger though she was, the child seemed to be on as familiar terms with Violet and Peony, and they with her, as if all the three had been playmates during the whole of their little lives. The mother thought to herself that it must certainly be the daughter of one of the neighbors, and that, seeing Violet and Peony in the garden, the child had run across the street to play with them. So this kind lady went to the door, intending to invite the little runaway into her comfortable parlor; for, now that the sunshine was withdrawn, the atmosphere, out of doors, was already growing very cold.

But, after opening the house door, she stood an instant on the threshold, hesitating whether she ought to ask the child to come in, or whether she should even speak to her. Indeed, she almost doubted whether it were a real child after all, or only a light wreath of the new-fallen snow, blown hither and thither about the garden by the intensely cold west wind. There was certainly something very singular in the aspect of the little stranger. Among all the children of the neighborhood, the lady could remember no such face, with its pure white, and delicate rose color, and the golden ringlets tossing about the forehead and cheeks. And as for her dress, which was entirely of white, and fluttering in the breeze, it was such as no reasonable woman would put upon a little girl, when sending her out to play, in the depth of winter. It made this kind and careful mother shiver only to look at those small feet, with nothing in the world on them, except a very thin pair of white slippers. Nevertheless, airily as she was clad, the child seemed to feel not the slightest inconvenience from the cold, but danced so lightly over the snow that the tips of her toes left hardly a print in its surface; while Violet could but just keep pace with her, and Peony's short legs compelled him to lag behind.

Once, in the course of their play, the strange child placed herself between Violet and Peony, and, taking a hand of each, skipped merrily forward and they along with her. Almost immediately, however, Peony pulled away his little fist, and began to rub it as if the fingers were tingling with cold; while Violet also released herself, though with less abruptness, gravely remarking that it was better not to take hold of hands. The white-robed damsel said not a word, but danced about, just as merrily as before. If Violet and Peony did not choose to play with her, she could make just as good a playmate of the brisk and cold west wind, which kept blowing her all about the garden, and took such liberties with her, that they seemed to have been friends for a long time. All this while, the mother stood on the threshold, wondering how a little girl could look so much like a flying snowdrift, or how a snowdrift could look so very like a little girl. She called Violet, and whispered to her.

"Violet, my darling, what is this child's name?" asked she. "Does she live near us?"

"Why, dearest mamma," answered Violet, laughing to think that her mother did not comprehend so very plain an affair, "this is our little snow-sister whom we have just been making!"

"Yes, dear mamma," cried Peony, running to his mother, and looking up simply into her face. "This is our snow-image! Is it not a nice 'ittle child?"

At this instant a flock of snowbirds came flitting through the air. As was very natural, they avoided Violet and Peony. But—and this looked strange—they flew at once to the white-robed child, fluttered eagerly about her head, alighted on her shoulders, and seemed to claim her as an old acquaintance. She, on her part, was evidently as glad to see these little birds, old Winter's grandchildren, as they were to see her, and welcomed them by holding out both her hands. Hereupon, they each and all tried to alight on her two palms and ten small fingers and thumbs, crowding one another off, with an immense fluttering of their tiny wings. One dear little bird nestled tenderly in her bosom; another put its bill to her lips. They were as joyous, all the while, and seemed as much in their element, as you may have seen them when sporting with a snowstorm.

Violet and Peony stood laughing at this pretty sight; for they enjoyed the merry time which their new playmate was having with these small-winged visitants, almost as much as if they themselves took part in it.

"Violet," said her mother, greatly perplexed, "tell me the truth, without any jest. Who is this little girl?"

"My darling mamma," answered Violet, looking seriously into her mother's face, and apparently surprised that she should need any further explanation, "I have told you truly who she is. It is our little snow-image, which Peony and I have been making. Peony will tell you so, as well as I."

"Yes, mamma," asseverated Peony, with much gravity in his crimson little phiz; "this is 'ittle snow-child. Is not she a nice one? But, mamma, her hand is, O, so very cold!"

While mamma still hesitated what to think and what to do, the street gate was thrown open, and the father of Violet and Peony appeared, wrapped in a pilot-cloth sack, with a fur cap drawn down over his ears, and the thickest of gloves upon his hands. Mr. Lindsey was a middle-aged man, with a weary and yet a happy look in his wind-flushed and frost-pinched face, as if he had been busy all the day long, and was glad to get back to his quiet home. His eyes brightened at the sight of his wife and children, although he could not help uttering a word or two of surprise, at finding the whole family in the open air, on so bleak a day, and after sunset too. He soon perceived the little white stranger sporting to and fro in the garden, like a dancing snow-wreath, and the flock of snowbirds fluttering about her head.

"Pray, what little girl may that be?" inquired this very sensible man. "Surely her mother must be crazy to let her go out in such bitter weather as it has been to-day, with only that flimsy white gown and those thin slippers!"

"My dear husband," said his wife, "I know no more about the little thing than you do. Some neighbor's child, I suppose. Our Violet and Peony," she added, laughing at herself for repeating so absurd a story, "insist that she is nothing but a snow-image, which they have been busy about in the garden almost all the afternoon."

As she said this, the mother glanced her eyes toward the spot where the children's snow-image had been made. What was her surprise, on perceiving that there was not the slightest trace of so much labor!—no image at all!—no piled-up heap of snow!—nothing whatever, save the prints of little footsteps around a vacant space! "This is very strange!" said she.

"What is strange, dear mother?" asked Violet. "Dear father, do not you see how it is? This is our snow-image, which Peony and I have made, because we wanted another playmate. Did not we, Peony?"

"Yes, papa," said crimson Peony. "This be our 'ittle snow-sister. Is she not beautiful? But she gave me such a cold kiss!"

"Poh, nonsense, children!" cried their good, honest father, who, as we have already intimated had an exceedingly common-sensible way of looking at matters. "Do not tell me of making live figures out of snow. Come, wife; this little stranger must not stay out in the bleak air a moment longer. We will bring her into the parlor; and you shall give her a supper of warm bread and milk, and make her as comfortable as you can. Meanwhile, I will inquire among the neighbors; or, if necessary, send the city-crier about the streets, to give notice of a lost child."

So saying, this honest and very kind-hearted man was going toward the little white damsel, with the best intentions in the world. But Violet and Peony, each seizing their father by the hand, earnestly besought him not to make her come in.

"Dear father," cried Violet, putting herself before him, "it is true what I have been telling you! This is our little snow-girl, and she cannot live any longer than while she breathes the cold west wind. Do not make her come into the hot room!"

"Yes, father," shouted Peony, stamping his little foot, so mightily was he in earnest, "this be nothing but our 'ittle snow-child! She will not love the hot fire!"

"Nonsense, children, nonsense, nonsense!" cried the father, half vexed, half laughing at what he considered their foolish obstinacy.

"Run into the house this moment! It is too late to play any longer now. I must take care of this little girl immediately, or she will catch her death-a-cold!"

"Husband! dear husband!" said his wife, in a low voice,—for she had been looking narrowly at the snow-child, and was more perplexed than ever,—"there is something very singular in all this. You will think me foolish,—but—but—may it not be that some invisible angel has been attracted by the simplicity and good faith with which our children set about their undertaking? May he not have spent an hour of his immortality in playing with those dear little souls? and so the result is what we call a miracle. No, no! Do not laugh at me; I see what a foolish thought it is!"

"My dear wife," replied the husband, laughing heartily, "you are as much a child as Violet and Peony."

And in one sense so she was, for all through life she had kept her heart full of childlike simplicity and faith, which was as pure and clear as crystal; and, looking at all matters through this transparent medium, she sometimes saw truths so profound that other people laughed at them as nonsense and absurdity.

But now kind Mr. Lindsey had entered the garden, breaking away from his two children, who still sent their shrill voices after him, beseeching him to let the snow-child stay and enjoy herself in the cold west wind. As he approached, the snowbirds took to flight. The little white damsel, also, fled backward, shaking her head, as if to say, "Pray, do not touch me!" and roguishly, as it appeared, leading him through the deepest of the snow. Once, the good man stumbled, and floundered down upon his face, so that, gathering himself up again, with the snow sticking to his rough pilot-cloth sack, he looked as white and wintry as a snow-image of the largest size. Some of the neighbors, meanwhile, seeing him from their windows, wondered what could possess poor Mr. Lindsey to be running about his garden in pursuit of a snowdrift, which the west wind was driving hither and thither! At length, after a vast deal of trouble, he chased the little stranger into a corner, where she could not possibly escape him. His wife had been looking on, and, it being nearly twilight, was wonderstruck to observe how the snow-child gleamed and sparkled, and how she seemed to shed a glow all round about her; and when driven into the corner, she positively glistened like a star! It was a frosty kind of brightness, too, like that of an icicle in the moonlight. The wife thought it strange that good Mr. Lindsey should see nothing remarkable in the snow-child's appearance.

"Come, you odd little thing!" cried the honest man, seizing her by the hand, "I have caught you at last, and will make you comfortable in spite of yourself. We will put a nice warm pair of worsted stockings on your frozen little feet, and you shall have a good thick shawl to wrap yourself in. Your poor white nose, I am afraid, is actually frost-bitten. But we will make it all right. Come along in."

And so, with a most benevolent smile on his sagacious visage, all purple as it was with the cold, this very well-meaning gentleman took the snow-child by the hand and led her toward the house. She followed him, droopingly and reluctant; for all the glow and sparkle was gone out of her figure; and whereas just before she had resembled a bright, frosty, star-gemmed evening, with a crimson gleam on the cold horizon, she now looked as dull and languid as a thaw. As kind Mr. Lindsey led her up the steps of the door, Violet and Peony looked into his face,—their eyes full of tears, which froze before they could run down their cheeks,—and again entreated him not to bring their snow-image into the house.

"Not bring her in!" exclaimed the kindhearted man. "Why, you are crazy, my little Violet!—quite crazy, my small Peony! She is so cold, already, that her hand has almost frozen mine, in spite of my thick gloves. Would you have her freeze to death?"

His wife, as he came up the steps, had been taking another long, earnest, almost awe-stricken gaze at the little white stranger. She hardly knew whether it was a dream or no; but she could not help fancying that she saw the delicate print of Violet's fingers on the child's neck. It looked just as if, while Violet was shaping out the image, she had given it a gentle pat with her hand, and had neglected to smooth the impression quite away.

"After all, husband," said the mother, recurring to her idea that the angels would be as much delighted to play with Violet and Peony as she herself was,—"after all, she does look strangely like a snow-image! I do believe she is made of snow!"

A puff of the west wind blew against the snow-child, and again she sparkled like a star.

"Snow!" repeated good Mr. Lindsey, drawing the reluctant guest over his hospitable threshold. "No wonder she looks like snow. She is half frozen, poor little thing! But a good fire will put everything to rights!"

Without further talk, and always with the same best intentions, this highly benevolent and common-sensible individual led the little white damsel—drooping, drooping, drooping, more and more—out of the frosty air, and into his comfortable parlor. A Heidenberg stove, filled to the brim with intensely burning anthracite, was sending a bright gleam through the isinglass of its iron door, and causing the vase of water on its top to fume and bubble with excitement. A warm, sultry smell was diffused throughout the room. A thermometer on the wall farthest from the stove stood at eighty degrees. The parlor was hung with red curtains, and covered with a red carpet, and looked just as warm as it felt. The difference betwixt the atmosphere here and the cold, wintry twilight out of doors, was like stepping at once from Nova Zembla to the hottest part of India, or from the North Pole into an oven. O, this was a fine place for the little white stranger!

The common-sensible man placed the snow-child on the hearth-rug, right in front of the hissing and fuming stove.

"Now she will be comfortable!" cried Mr. Lindsey, rubbing his hands and looking about him, with the pleasantest smile you ever saw. Make yourself at home, my child."

Sad, sad and drooping, looked the little white maiden, as she stood on the hearth-rug, with the hot blast of the stove striking through her like a pestilence. Once, she threw a glance wistfully toward the windows, and caught a glimpse, through its red curtains, of the snow covered roofs, and the stars glimmering frostily, and all the delicious intensity of the cold night. The bleak wind rattled the window-panes, as if it were summoning her to come forth. But there stood the snow-child, drooping, before the hot stove!

But the common-sensible man saw nothing amiss.

"Come, wife," said he, "let her have a pair of thick stockings and a woollen shawl or blanket directly; and tell Dora to give her some warm supper as soon as the milk boils. You, Violet and Peony, amuse your little friend. She is out of spirits, you see, at finding herself in a strange place. For my part, I will go around among the neighbors, and find out where she belongs."

The mother, meanwhile, had gone in search of the shawl and stockings; for her own view of the matter, however subtle and delicate, had given way, as it always did, to the stubborn materialism of her husband.

Without heeding the remonstrances of his two children, who still kept murmuring that their little snow-sister did not love the warmth, good Mr. Lindsey took his departure, shutting the parlor door carefully behind him. Turning up the collar of his sack over his ears, he emerged from the house, and had barely reached the street gate, when he was recalled by the screams of Violet and Peony, and the rapping of a thimbled finger against the parlor window.

"Husband! husband!" cried his wife, showing her horror-stricken face through the window-panes. "There is no need of going for the child's parents!"

"We told you so, father!" screamed Violet and Peony, as he reentered the parlor. "You would bring her in; and now our poor—dear beautiful little snow-sister is thawed!"

And their own sweet little faces were already dissolved in tears; so that their father, seeing what strange things occasionally happen in this every-day world, felt not a little anxious lest his children might be going to thaw too! In the utmost perplexity, he demanded an explanation of his wife. She could only reply, that, being summoned to the parlor by the cries of Violet and Peony, she found no trace of the little white maiden, unless it were the remains of a heap of snow, which, while she was gazing at it, melted quite away upon the hearth-rug.

"And there you see all that is left of it!" added she, pointing to a pool of water in front of the stove.

"Yes, father," said Violet, looking reproachfully at him through her tears, "there is all that is left of our dear little snow-sister!"

"Naughty father!" cried Peony, stamping his foot, and—I shudder to say—shaking his little fist at the common-sensible man. "We told you how it would be! What for did you bring her in?"

And the Heidenberg stove, through the isinglass of its door, seemed to glare at good Mr. Lindsey, like a red-eyed demon, triumphing in the mischief which it had done!

This, you will observe, was one of those rare cases, which yet will occasionally happen, where common-sense finds itself at fault. The remarkable story of the snow-image, though to that sagacious class of people to whom good Mr. Lindsey belongs it may seem but a childish affair is, nevertheless, capable of being moralized in various methods, greatly for their edification. One of its lessons, for instance, might be, that it behooves men, and especially men of benevolence, to consider well what they are about, and, before acting on their philanthropic purposes, to be quite sure that they comprehend the nature and all the relations of the business in hand. What has been established as an element of good to one being may prove absolute mischief to another; even as the warmth of the parlor was proper enough for children of flesh and blood, like Violet and Peony,—though by no means very wholesome, even for them, but involved nothing short of annihilation to the unfortunate snow-image.

But, after all, there is no teaching anything to wise men of good Mr. Lindsey's stamp. They know everything,—O, to be sure!—everything that has been, and everything that is, and everything that, by any future possibility, can be. And, should some phenomenon of nature or Providence transcend their system, they will not recognize it, even if it come to pass under their very noses.

"Wife," said Mr. Lindsey, after a fit of silence, "see what a quantity of snow the children have brought in on their feet! It has made quite a puddle here before the stove. Pray tell Dora to bring some towels and sop it up!"

5

A Ghost of the Sierras

By Bret Harte

IT WAS A VAST SILENCE OF PINES, REDOLENT WITH BALSAMIC BREATH, and muffled with the dry dust of dead bark and matted mosses. Lying on our backs, we looked upward through a hundred feet of clear, unbroken interval to the first lateral branches that formed the flat canopy above us. Here and there the fierce sun, from whose active persecution we had just escaped, searched for us through the woods, but its keen blade was dulled and turned aside by intercostal boughs, and its brightness dissipated in nebulous mists throughout the roofing of the dim, brown aisles around us. We were in another atmosphere, under another sky; indeed, in another world than the dazzling one we had just quitted. The grave silence seemed so much a part of the grateful coolness, that we hesitated to speak, and for some moments lay quietly outstretched on the pine tassels where we had first thrown ourselves. Finally, a voice broke the silence:—

"Ask the old Major; he knows all about it!"

The person here alluded to under that military title was myself. I hardly need explain to any Californian that it by no means followed that I was a "Major," or that I was "old," or that I knew anything about "it," or indeed what "it" referred to. The whole remark was merely one of the usual conventional feelers to conversation,—a kind of social preamble, quite common to our slangy camp intercourse. Nevertheless, as I was always known as the Major, perhaps for no better reason than that the speaker, an old journalist, was always called Doctor, I recognized the fact so far as to kick aside an intervening saddle, so that I could see the speaker's face on a level with my own, and said nothing.

"About ghosts!" said the Doctor, after a pause, which nobody broke or was expected to break. "Ghosts, sir! That's what we want to know. What are we doing here in this blanked old mausoleum of Calaveras County, if it isn't to find out something about 'em, eh?"

Nobody replied.

"Thar's that haunted house at Cave City. Can't be more than a mile or two away, anyhow. Used to be just off the trail."

A dead silence.

The Doctor (addressing space generally), "Yes, sir; it *was* a mighty queer story."

Still the same reposeful indifference. We all knew the Doctor's skill as a *raconteur*, we all knew that a story was coming, and we all knew that any interruption would be fatal. Time and time again, in our prospecting experience, had a word of polite encouragement, a rash expression of interest, even a too eager attitude of silent expectancy, brought the Doctor to a sudden change of subject. Time and time again have we seen the unwary stranger stand amazed and bewildered between our own indifference and the sudden termination of a promising anecdote, through his own unlucky interference. So we said nothing. "The Judge"—another instance of arbitrary nomenclature—pretended to sleep. Jack began to twist a *cigarrito*. Thornton bit off the ends of pine needles reflectively.

"Yes, sir," continued the Doctor, coolly resting the back of his head on the palms of his hands, "it *was* rather curious. All except the murder. *That's* what gets me, for the murder had no new points, no fancy touches, no sentiment, no mystery. Was just one of the old style, 'sub-head' paragraphs. Old-fashioned miner scrubs along on hardtack and beans, and saves up a little money to go home and see relations. Old-fashioned assassin sharpens up knife, old style; loads old flint-lock, brass-mounted pistol; walks in on old-fashioned miner one dark night, sends him home to his relations away back to several generations, and walks off with the swag. No mystery *there*; nothing to clear up; subsequent revelations only impertinence. Nothing for any ghost to do—who meant business. More than that, over forty murders, same old kind, committed every year in Calaveras, and no spiritual post obits coming due every anniversary; no assessments made on the peace and quiet of the surviving community. I

54

tell you what, boys, I've always been inclined to throw off on the Cave City ghost for that alone. It's a bad precedent, sir. If that kind o' thing is going to obtain in the foot-hills, we'll have the trails full of chaps formerly knocked over by Mexicans and road agents; every little camp and grocery will have stock enough on hand to go into business, and where's there any security for surviving life and property, eh? What's your opinion, Judge, as a fair-minded legislator?"

Of course there was no response. Yet it was part of the Doctor's system of aggravation to become discursive at these moments, in the hope of interruption, and he continued for some moments to dwell on the terrible possibility of a state of affairs in which a gentleman could no longer settle a dispute with an enemy without being subjected to succeeding spiritual embarrassment. But all this digression fell upon apparently inattentive ears.

"Well, sir, after the murder, the cabin stood for a long time deserted and tenantless. Popular opinion was against it. One day a ragged prospector, savage with hard labor and harder luck, came to the camp, looking for a place to live and a chance to prospect. After the boys had taken his measure, they concluded that he'd already tackled so much in the way of difficulties that a ghost more or less wouldn't be of much account. So they sent him to the haunted cabin. He had a big yellow dog with him, about as ugly and as savage as himself; and the boys sort o' congratulated themselves, from a practical view-point, that while they were giving the old ruffian a shelter, they were helping in the cause of Christianity against ghosts and goblins. They had little faith in the old man, but went their whole pile on that dog. That's where they were mistaken.

"The house stood almost three hundred feet from the nearest cave, and on dark nights, being in a hollow, was as lonely as if it had been on the top of Shasta. If you ever saw the spot when there was just moon enough to bring out the little surrounding clumps of chaparral until they looked like crouching figures, and make the bits of broken quartz glisten like skulls, you'd begin to understand how big a contract that man and that yellow dog undertook.

"They went into possession that afternoon, and old Hard Times set out to cook his supper. When it was over he sat down by the embers and lit his pipe, the yellow dog lying at his feet. Suddenly 'Rap! rap!' comes from the door. 'Come in,' says the man, gruffly. 'Rap!' again. 'Come in and be d—d to you,' says the man, who has no idea of getting up to open the door. But no one responded, and the next moment smash goes the only sound pane in the only window. Seeing this, old Hard Times gets up, with the devil in his eye, and a revolver in his hand, followed by the yellow dog, with every tooth showing, and swings open the door. No one there! But as the man opened the door, that yellow dog, that had been so chipper before, suddenly begins to crouch and step backward, step by step, trembling and shivering, and at last crouches down in the chimney, without even so much as looking at his master. The man slams the door shut again, but there comes another smash.

"This time it seems to come from inside the cabin, and it isn't until the man looks around and sees everything quiet that he gets up, without speaking, and makes a dash for the door, and tears round outside the cabin like mad, but finds nothing but silence and darkness. Then he comes back swearing and calls the dog. But that great yellow dog that the boys would have staked all their money on is crouching under the bunk, and has to be dragged out like a coon from a hollow tree, and lies there, his eyes starting from their sockets; every limb and muscle quivering with fear, and his very hair drawn up in bristling ridges. The man calls him to the door. He drags himself a few steps, stops, sniffs, and refuses to go further. The man calls him again, with an oath and a threat. Then, what does that yellow dog do? He crawls edgewise towards the door, crouching himself against the bunk till he's flatter than a knife blade; then, half way, he stops. Then that d—d yellow dog begins to walk gingerly—lifting each foot up in the air, one after the other, still trembling in every limb. Then he stops again. Then he crouches. Then he gives one little shuddering leap—not straight forward, but up—clearing the floor about six inches, as if—"

"Over something," interrupted the Judge, hastily, lifting himself on his elbow.

The Doctor stopped instantly. "Juan," he said coolly, to one of the Mexican packers, "quit foolin' with that *riata*. You'll have that stake out and that mule loose in another minute. Come over this way!"

The Mexican turned a scared, white face to the Doctor, muttering something, and let go the deer-skin hide. We all up-raised our voices with one accord, the Judge most penitently and apologetically, and implored the Doctor to go on. "I'll shoot the first man who interrupts you again," added Thornton, persuasively.

But the Doctor, with his hands languidly under his head, had lost his interest. "Well, the dog ran off to the hills, and neither the threats nor cajoleries of his master could ever make him enter the cabin again. The next day the man left the camp. What time is it? Getting on to sundown, ain't it? Keep off my leg, will you, you d—d Greaser, and stop stumbling round there! Lie down."

But we knew that the Doctor had not completely finished his story, and we waited patiently for the conclusion. Meanwhile the old, gray silence of the woods again asserted itself, but shadows were now beginning to gather in the heavy beams of the roof above, and the dim aisles seemed to be narrowing and closing in around us. Presently the Doctor recommenced lazily, as if no interruption had occurred.

"As I said before, I never put much faith in that story, and shouldn't have told it, but for a rather curious experience of my own. It was in the spring of '62, and I was one of a party of four, coming up from O'Neill's, when we had been snowed up. It was awful weather; the snow had changed to sleet and rain after we crossed the divide, and the water was out everywhere; every ditch was a creek, every creek a river. We had lost two horses on the North Fork, we were dead beat, off the trail, and sloshing round, with night coming on, and the level hail like shot in our faces. Things were looking bleak and scary when, riding a little ahead of the party, I saw a light twinkling in a hollow beyond. My horse was still fresh, and calling out to the boys to follow me and bear for the light, I struck out for it. In another moment I was before a little cabin that half burrowed in the black chaparral; I dismounted and rapped at the door. There was no response. I then tried to force the door, but it was fastened securely from within. I was all the more surprised when one of the boys, who had overtaken me, told me that he had just seen through a window a man reading by the fire. Indignant at this inhospitality, we both made a resolute onset against the door, at the same time raising our angry voices to a yell. Suddenly there was a quick response, the hurried withdrawing of a bolt, and the door opened.

"The occupant was a short, thick-set man, with a pale, careworn face, whose prevailing expression was one of gentle good humor and patient suffering. When we entered, he asked us hastily why we had not 'sung out' before.

"'But we *knocked*!' I said, impatiently, 'and almost drove your door in.'

"'That's nothing,' he said, patiently. 'I'm used to *that*.'

"I looked again at the man's patient, fateful face, and then around the cabin. In an instant the whole situation flashed before me. 'Are we not near Cave City?' I asked.

"'Yes,' he replied, 'it's just below. You must have passed it in the storm.'

"'I see.' I again looked around the cabin. 'Isn't this what they call the haunted house?'

"He looked at me curiously. 'It is,' he said, simply.

"You can imagine my delight! Here was an opportunity to test the whole story, to work down to the bed rock, and see how it would pan out! We were too many and too well armed to fear tricks or dangers from outsiders. If—as one theory had been held—the disturbance was kept up by a band of concealed marauders or road agents, whose purpose was to preserve their haunts from intrusion, we were quite able to pay them back in kind for any assault. I need not say that the boys were delighted with this prospect when the fact was revealed to them. The only one doubtful or apathetic spirit there was our host, who quietly resumed his seat and his book, with his old expression of patient martyrdom. It would have been easy for me to have drawn him out, but I felt that I did not want to corroborate anybody else's experience; only to record my own. And I thought it better to keep the boys from any predisposing terrors.

"We ate our supper, and then sat, patiently and expectant, around the fire. An hour slipped away, but no disturbance; another hour passed as monotonously. Our host read his book; only the dash of hail against the roof broke the silence. But—"

The Doctor stopped. Since the last interruption, I noticed he had changed the easy slangy style of his story to a more perfect, artistic, and even studied manner. He dropped now suddenly into his old colloquial speech, and quietly said: "If you don't quit stumbling over those *riatas*, Juan, I'll hobble *you*. Come here, there; lie down, will you?"

We all turned fiercely on the cause of this second dangerous interruption, but a sight of the poor fellow's pale and frightened face withheld our vindictive tongues. And the Doctor, happily, of his own accord, went on:—

"But I had forgotten that it was no easy matter to keep these high-spirited boys, bent on a row, in decent subjection; and after the third hour passed without a supernatural exhibition, I observed, from certain winks and whispers, that they were determined to get up indications of their own. In a few moments violent rappings were heard from all parts of the cabin; large stones (adroitly thrown up the chimney) fell with a heavy thud on the roof. Strange groans and ominous yells seemed to come from the outside (where the interstices between the logs were wide enough). Yet, through all this uproar, our host sat still and patient, with no sign of indignation or reproach upon his good-humored but haggard features. Before long it became evident that this exhibition was exclusively for *his* benefit. Under the thin disguise of asking him to assist them in discovering the disturbers *outside* the cabin, those inside took advantage of his absence to turn the cabin topsy-turvy.

"'You see what the spirits have done, old man,' said the arch leader of this mischief. 'They've upset that there flour barrel while we wasn't looking, and then kicked over the water jug and spilled all the water!'

"The patient man lifted his head and looked at the flour-strewn walls. Then he glanced down at the floor, but drew back with a slight tremor.

"'It ain't water!' he said, quietly.

"'What is it, then?'

"'It's *blood*! Look!'"

The nearest man gave a sudden start and sank back white as a sheet.

"For there, gentlemen, on the floor, just before the door, where the old man had seen the dog hesitate and lift his feet, there!

there!—gentlemen—upon my honor, slowly widened and broadened a dark red pool of human blood! Stop him! Quick! Stop him, I say!"

There was a blinding flash that lit up the dark woods, and a sharp report! When we reached the Doctor's side he was holding the smoking pistol, just discharged, in one hand, while with the other he was pointing to the rapidly disappearing figure of Juan, our Mexican *vaquero*!

"Missed him! by G-d!" said the Doctor. "But did you hear him? Did you see his livid face as he rose up at the name of blood? Did you see his guilty conscience in his face. Eh? Why don't you speak? What are you staring at?"

"Was it the murdered man's ghost, Doctor?" we all panted in one quick breath.

"Ghost be d—d! No! But in that Mexican *vaquero*—that cursed Juan Ramirez!—I saw and shot at his murderer!"

6

The Lady's Maid's Bell

By Edith Wharton

I

IT WAS THE AUTUMN AFTER I HAD THE TYPHOID. I'D BEEN THREE
months in hospital, and when I came out I looked so weak and tottery
that the two or three ladies I applied to were afraid to engage me. Most of
my money was gone, and after I'd boarded for two months, hanging about
the employment agencies, and answering any advertisement that looked
any way respectable, I pretty nearly lost heart, for fretting hadn't made me
fatter, and I didn't see why my luck should ever turn. It did though—or
I thought so at the time. A Mrs. Railton, a friend of the lady that first
brought me out to the States, met me one day and stopped to speak to me:
she was one that had always a friendly way with her. She asked me what
ailed me to look so white, and when I told her, "Why, Hartley," says she,
"I believe I've got the very place for you. Come in to-morrow and we'll
talk about it."

The next day, when I called, she told me the lady she'd in mind was
a niece of hers, a Mrs. Brympton, a youngish lady, but something of an
invalid, who lived all the year round at her country-place on the Hudson,
owing to not being able to stand the fatigue of town life.

"Now, Hartley," Mrs. Railton said, in that cheery way that always
made me feel things must be going to take a turn for the better—"now
understand me; it's not a cheerful place I'm sending you to. The house is
big and gloomy; my niece is nervous, vaporish; her husband—well, he's
generally away; and the two children are dead. A year ago I would as soon

have thought of shutting a rosy active girl like you into a vault; but you're not particularly brisk yourself just now, are you? and a quiet place, with country air and wholesome food and early hours, ought to be the very thing for you. Don't mistake me," she added, for I suppose I looked a trifle downcast; "you may find it dull but you won't be unhappy. My niece is an angel. Her former maid, who died last spring, had been with her twenty years and worshiped the ground she walked on. She's a kind mistress to all, and where the mistress is kind, as you know, the servants are generally good-humored, so you'll probably get on well enough with the rest of the household. And you're the very woman I want for my niece: quiet, well-mannered, and educated above your station. You read aloud well, I think? That's a good thing; my niece likes to be read to. She wants a maid that can be something of a companion: her last was, and I can't say how she misses her. It's a lonely life . . .well, have you decided?"

"Why, ma'am," I said, "I'm not afraid of solitude."

"Well, then, go; my niece will take you on my recommendation. I'll telegraph her at once and you can take the afternoon train. She has no one to wait on her at present, and I don't want you to lose any time."

I was ready enough to start, yet something in me hung back; and to gain time I asked, "And the gentleman, ma'am?"

"The gentleman's almost always away, I tell you," said Mrs. Railton, quick-like—"and when he's there," says she suddenly, "you've only to keep out of his way."

I took the afternoon train and got out at D—— station at about four o'clock. A groom in a dog-cart was waiting, and we drove off at a smart pace. It was a dull October day, with rain hanging close overhead, and by the time we turned into Brympton Place woods the daylight was almost gone. The drive wound through the woods for a mile or two, and came out on a gravel court shut in with thickets of tall black-looking shrubs. There were no lights in the windows, and the house *did* look a bit gloomy.

I had asked no questions of the groom, for I never was one to get my notion of new masters from their other servants: I prefer to wait and see for myself. But I could tell by the look of everything that I had got into the right kind of house, and that things were done handsomely. A pleasant-faced cook met me at the back door and called the house-maid to show me up to my room. "You'll see madam later," she said. "Mrs. Brympton has a visitor."

I hadn't fancied Mrs. Brympton was a lady to have many visitors, and somehow the words cheered me. I followed the house-maid upstairs, and saw, through a door on the upper landing, that the main part of the house seemed well-furnished, with dark paneling and a number of old portraits. Another flight of stairs led us up to the servants' wing. It was almost dark now, and the house-maid excused herself for not having brought a light. "But there's matches in your room," she said, "and if you go careful you'll be all right. Mind the step at the end of the passage. Your room is just beyond."

I looked ahead as she spoke, and half-way down the passage I saw a woman standing. She drew back into a doorway as we passed and the house-maid didn't appear to notice her. She was a thin woman with a white face, and a darkish stuff gown and apron. I took her for the house-keeper and thought it odd that she didn't speak, but just gave me a long look as she went by. My room opened into a square hall at the end of the passage. Facing my door was another which stood open: the house-maid exclaimed when she saw it:

"There—Mrs. Blinder's left that door open again!" said she, closing it.

"Is Mrs. Blinder the housekeeper?"

"There's no housekeeper: Mrs. Blinder's the cook."

"And is that her room?"

"Laws, no," said the house-maid, cross-like. "That's nobody's room. It's empty, I mean, and the door hadn't ought to be open. Mrs. Brympton wants it kept locked."

She opened my door and led me into a neat room, nicely furnished, with a picture or two on the walls; and having lit a candle she took leave, telling me that the servants'-hall tea was at six, and that Mrs. Brympton would see me afterward.

I found them a pleasant-spoken set in the servants' hall, and by what they let fall I gathered that, as Mrs. Railton had said, Mrs. Brympton was the kindest of ladies; but I didn't take much notice of their talk, for I was watching to see the pale woman in the dark gown come in. She didn't show herself, however, and I wondered if she ate apart; but if she wasn't the housekeeper, why should she? Suddenly it struck me that she might be a trained nurse, and in that case her meals would of course be served in her room. If Mrs. Brympton was an invalid it was likely enough she had a nurse. The idea annoyed me, I own, for they're not always the easiest to get on with, and if I'd known I shouldn't have taken the place. But there I was and there was no use pulling a long face over it; and not being one to ask questions I waited to see what would turn up.

When tea was over the house-maid said to the footman: "Has Mr. Ranford gone?" and when he said yes, she told me to come up with her to Mrs. Brympton.

Mrs. Brympton was lying down in her bedroom. Her lounge stood near the fire and beside it was a shaded lamp. She was a delicate-looking lady, but when she smiled I felt there was nothing I wouldn't do for her. She spoke very pleasantly, in a low voice, asking me my name and age and so on, and if I had everything I wanted, and if I wasn't afraid of feeling lonely in the country.

"Not with you I wouldn't be, madam," I said, and the words surprised me when I'd spoken them, for I'm not an impulsive person; but it was just as if I'd thought aloud.

She seemed pleased at that, and said she hoped I'd continue in the same mind; then she gave me a few directions about her toilet, and said Agnes the house-maid would show me next morning where things were kept.

"I am tired to-night, and shall dine upstairs," she said. "Agnes will bring me my tray, that you may have time to unpack and settle yourself; and later you may come and undress me."

"Very well, ma'am," I said. "You'll ring, I suppose?"

I thought she looked odd.

"No—Agnes will fetch you," says she quickly, and took up her book again.

Well—that was certainly strange: a lady's maid having to be fetched by the house-maid whenever her lady wanted her! I wondered if there were no bells in the house; but the next day I satisfied myself that there was one in every room, and a special one ringing from my mistress's room to mine; and after that it did strike me as queer that, whenever Mrs. Brympton wanted anything, she rang for Agnes, who had to walk the whole length of the servants' wing to call me.

But that wasn't the only queer thing in the house. The very next day I found out that Mrs. Brympton had no nurse; and then I asked Agnes about the woman I had seen in the passage the afternoon before. Agnes said she had seen no one, and I saw that she thought I was dreaming. To be sure, it was dusk when we went down the passage, and she had excused herself for not bringing a light; but I had seen the woman plain enough to know her again if we should meet. I decided that she must have been a friend of the cook's, or of one of the other women servants: perhaps she had come down from town for a night's visit, and the servants wanted it kept secret. Some ladies are very stiff about having their servants' friends in the house overnight. At any rate, I made up my mind to ask no more questions.

In a day or two another odd thing happened. I was chatting one afternoon with Mrs. Blinder, who was a friendly disposed woman, and had been longer in the house than the other servants, and she asked me if I was quite comfortable and had everything I needed. I said I had no fault to find with my place or with my mistress, but I thought it odd that in so large a house there was no sewing-room for the lady's maid.

"Why," says she, "there *is* one: the room you're in is the old sewing-room."

"Oh," said I; "and where did the other lady's maid sleep?"

At that she grew confused, and said hurriedly that the servants' rooms had all been changed about last year, and she didn't rightly remember.

That struck me as peculiar, but I went on as if I hadn't noticed: "Well, there's a vacant room opposite mine, and I mean to ask Mrs. Brympton if I mayn't use that as a sewing-room."

To my astonishment, Mrs. Blinder went white, and gave my hand a kind of squeeze. "Don't do that, my dear," said she, trembling-like. "To tell you the truth, that was Emma Saxon's room, and my mistress has kept it closed ever since her death."

"And who was Emma Saxon?"

"Mrs. Brympton's former maid."

"The one that was with her so many years?" said I, remembering what Mrs. Railton had told me.

Mrs. Blinder nodded.

"What sort of woman was she?"

"No better walked the earth," said Mrs. Blinder. "My mistress loved her like a sister."

"But I mean—what did she look like?"

Mrs. Blinder got up and gave me a kind of angry stare. "I'm no great hand at describing," she said; "and I believe my pastry's rising." And she walked off into the kitchen and shut the door after her.

II

I had been near a week at Brympton before I saw my master. Word came that he was arriving one afternoon, and a change passed over the whole household. It was plain that nobody loved him below stairs. Mrs. Blinder took uncommon care with the dinner that night, but she snapped at the kitchen-maid in a way quite unusual with her; and Mr. Wace, the butler, a serious, slow-spoken man, went about his duties as if he'd been getting ready for a funeral. He was a great Bible-reader, Mr. Wace was, and had a beautiful assortment of texts at his command; but that day he used such dreadful language, that I was about to leave the table, when he assured me it was all out of Isaiah; and I noticed that whenever the master came Mr. Wace took to the prophets.

About seven, Agnes called me to my mistress's room; and there I found Mr. Brympton. He was standing on the hearth; a big fair bull-necked man, with a red face and little bad-tempered blue eyes: the kind of man a young simpleton might have thought handsome, and would have been like to pay dear for thinking it.

He swung about when I came in, and looked me over in a trice. I knew what the look meant, from having experienced it once or twice in my former places. Then he turned his back on me, and went on talking to his wife; and I knew what *that* meant, too. I was not the kind of morsel he was after. The typhoid had served me well enough in one way: it kept that kind of gentleman at arm's length.

"This is my new maid, Hartley," says Mrs. Brympton in her kind voice; and he nodded and went on with what he was saying.

In a minute or two he went off, and left my mistress to dress for dinner, and I noticed as I waited on her that she was white, and chill to the touch.

Mr. Brympton took himself off the next morning, and the whole house drew a long breath when he drove away. As for my mistress, she put on her hat and furs (for it was a fine winter morning) and went out for a walk in the gardens, coming back quite fresh and rosy, so that for a minute, before her color faded, I could guess what a pretty young lady she must have been, and not so long ago, either.

She had met Mr. Ranford in the grounds, and the two came back together, I remember, smiling and talking as they walked along the terrace under my window. That was the first time I saw Mr. Ranford, though I had often heard his name mentioned in the hall. He was a neighbor, it appeared, living a mile or two beyond Brympton, at the end of the village; and as he was in the habit of spending his winters in the country he was almost the only company my mistress had at that season. He was a slight tall gentleman of about thirty, and I thought him rather melancholy-looking till I saw his smile, which had a kind of surprise in it, like the first warm day in spring. He was a great reader, I heard, like my mistress, and the two were forever borrowing books of one another, and sometimes (Mr. Wace told me) he would read aloud to Mrs. Brympton by the hour, in the big dark library where she sat in the winter afternoons. The servants all liked him, and perhaps that's more of a compliment than the masters suspect. He had a friendly word for every one of us, and we were all glad to think that Mrs. Brympton had a pleasant companionable gentleman like that to keep her company when the master was away. Mr. Ranford seemed on excellent terms with Mr. Brympton too; though I couldn't but wonder that two gentlemen so unlike each other should be so friendly. But then I knew how the real quality can keep their feelings to themselves.

As for Mr. Brympton, he came and went, never staying more than a day or two, cursing the dullness and the solitude, grumbling at everything, and (as I soon found out) drinking a deal more than was good for him.

After Mrs. Brympton left the table he would sit half the night over the old Brympton port and madeira, and once, as I was leaving my mistress's room rather later than usual, I met him coming up the stairs in such a state that I turned sick to think of what some ladies have to endure and hold their tongues about.

The servants said very little about their master; but from what they let drop I could see it had been an unhappy match from the beginning. Mr. Brympton was coarse, loud, and pleasure-loving; my mistress quiet, retiring, and perhaps a trifle cold. Not that she was not always pleasant-spoken to him: I thought her wonderfully forbearing; but to a gentleman as free as Mr. Brympton I dare say she seemed a little offish.

Well, things went on quietly for several weeks. My mistress was kind, my duties were light, and I got on well with the other servants. In short, I had nothing to complain of; yet there was always a weight on me. I can't say why it was so, but I know it was not the loneliness that I felt. I soon got used to that; and being still languid from the fever, I was thankful for the quiet and the good country air. Nevertheless, I was never quite easy in my mind. My mistress, knowing I had been ill, insisted that I should take my walk regularly, and often invented errands for me:—a yard of ribbon to be fetched from the village, a letter posted, or a book returned to Mr. Ranford. As soon as I was out of doors my spirits rose, and I looked forward to my walks through the bare moist-smelling woods; but the moment I caught sight of the house again my heart dropped down like a stone in a well. It was not a gloomy house exactly, yet I never entered it but a feeling of gloom came over me.

Mrs. Brympton seldom went out in winter; only on the finest days did she walk an hour at noon on the south terrace. Excepting Mr. Ranford, we had no visitors but the doctor, who drove over from D—— about once a week. He sent for me once or twice to give me some trifling direction about my mistress, and though he never told me what her illness was, I thought, from a waxy look she had now and then of a morning, that it might be the heart that ailed her. The season was soft and unwholesome, and in January we had a long spell of rain. That was a sore trial to me, I own, for I couldn't go out, and sitting over my sewing all day, listening to the drip, drip of the eaves, I grew so nervous that the least sound made me jump. Somehow, the thought of that locked room across the passage began to weigh on me. Once or twice, in the long rainy nights, I fancied I heard noises there; but that was nonsense, of course, and the daylight drove such notions out of my head. Well, one morning Mrs. Brympton gave me quite a start of pleasure by telling me she wished me to go to town for some shopping. I hadn't known till then how low my spirits had fallen. I set off in high glee, and my first sight of the crowded streets and the cheerful-looking shops quite took me out of myself. Toward afternoon, however, the noise and confusion began to tire me, and I was actually looking forward to the quiet of Brympton, and thinking how I should enjoy the drive home through the dark woods, when I ran across an old acquaintance, a maid I had once been in service with. We had lost sight of each other for a number of years, and I had to stop and tell her what had happened to me in the interval. When I mentioned where I was living she rolled up her eyes and pulled a long face.

"What! The Mrs. Brympton that lives all the year at her place on the Hudson? My dear, you won't stay there three months."

"Oh, but I don't mind the country," says I, offended somehow at her tone. "Since the fever I'm glad to be quiet."

She shook her head. "It's not the country I'm thinking of. All I know is she's had four maids in the last six months, and the last one, who was friend of mine, told me nobody could stay in the house."

"Did she say why?" I asked.

"No—she wouldn't give me her reason. But she says to me, *Mrs. Ansey,* she says, *if ever a young woman as you know of thinks of going there, you tell her it's not worth while to unpack her boxes.*"

"Is she young and handsome?" said I, thinking of Mr. Brympton.

"Not her! She's the kind that mothers engage when they've gay young gentlemen at college."

Well, though I knew the woman was an idle gossip, the words stuck in my head, and my heart sank lower than ever as I drove up to Brympton in the dusk. There *was* something about the house—I was sure of it now . . .

When I went in to tea I heard that Mr. Brympton had arrived, and I saw at a glance that there had been a disturbance of some kind. Mrs.

Blinder's hand shook so that she could hardly pour the tea, and Mr. Wace quoted the most dreadful texts full of brimstone. Nobody said a word to me then, but when I went up to my room Mrs. Blinder followed me.

"Oh, my dear," says she, taking my hand, "I'm so glad and thankful you've come back to us!"

That struck me, as you may imagine. "Why," said I, "did you think I was leaving for good?"

"No, no, to be sure," said she, a little confused, "but I can't a-bear to have madam left alone for a day even." She pressed my hand hard, and, "Oh, Miss Hartley," says she, "be good to your mistress, as you're a Christian woman." And with that she hurried away, and left me staring.

A moment later Agnes called me to Mrs. Brympton. Hearing Mr. Brympton's voice in her room, I went round by the dressing-room, thinking I would lay out her dinner-gown before going in. The dressing-room is a large room with a window over the portico that looks toward the gardens. Mr. Brympton's apartments are beyond. When I went in, the door into the bedroom was ajar, and I heard Mr. Brympton saying angrily:— "One would suppose he was the only person fit for you to talk to."

"I don't have many visitors in winter," Mrs. Brympton answered quietly.

"You have *me!*" he flung at her, sneeringly.

"You are here so seldom," said she.

"Well—whose fault is that? You make the place about as lively as the family vault—"

With that I rattled the toilet things, to give my mistress warning, and she rose and called me in.

The two dined alone, as usual, and I knew by Mr. Wace's manner at supper that things must be going badly. He quoted the prophets something terrible, and worked on the kitchen-maid so that she declared she wouldn't go down alone to put the cold meat in the icebox. I felt nervous myself, and after I had put my mistress to bed I was half tempted to go down again and persuade Mrs. Blinder to sit up awhile over a game of cards. But I heard her door closing for the night and so I went on to my own room. The rain had begun again, and the drip, drip, drip seemed to be dropping into my brain. I lay awake listening to it, and turning over what my friend in town had said. What puzzled me was that it was always the maids who left . . .

After a while I slept; but suddenly a loud noise wakened me. My bell had rung. I sat up, terrified by the unusual sound, which seemed to go on jangling through the darkness. My hands shook so that I couldn't find the matches. At length I struck a light and jumped out of bed. I began to think I must have been dreaming; but I looked at the bell against the wall, and there was the little hammer still quivering.

I was just beginning to huddle on my clothes when I heard another sound. This time it was the door of the locked room opposite mine softly opening and closing. I heard the sound distinctly, and it frightened me so that I stood stock still. Then I heard a footstep hurrying down the passage toward the main house. The floor being carpeted, the sound was very faint, but I was quite sure it was a woman's step. I turned cold with the thought of it, and for a minute or two I dursn't breathe or move. Then I came to my senses.

"Alice Hartley," says I to myself, "someone left that room just now and ran down the passage ahead of you. The idea isn't pleasant, but you may as well face it. Your mistress has rung for you, and to answer her bell you've got to go the way that other woman has gone."

Well—I did it. I never walked faster in my life, yet I thought I should never get to the end of the passage or reach Mrs. Brympton's room. On the way I heard nothing and saw nothing: all was dark and quiet as the grave. When I reached my mistress's door the silence was so deep that I began to think I must be dreaming, and was half minded to turn back. Then a panic seized me, and I knocked.

There was no answer, and I knocked again, loudly. To my astonishment the door was opened by Mr. Brympton. He started back when he saw me, and in the light of my candle his face looked red and savage.

"*You?*" he said, in a queer voice. "*How many of you are there, in God's name?*"

At that I felt the ground give under me; but I said to myself that he had been drinking, and answered as steadily as I could: "May I go in, sir? Mrs. Brympton has rung for me."

"You may all go in, for what I care," says he, and, pushing by me, walked down the hall to his own bedroom. I looked after him as he went, and to my surprise I saw that he walked as straight as a sober man.

I found my mistress lying very weak and still, but she forced a smile when she saw me, and signed to me to pour out some drops for her. After that she lay without speaking, her breath coming quick, and her eyes closed. Suddenly she groped out with her hand, and "*Emma*," says she, faintly.

"It's Hartley, madam," I said. "Do you want anything?"

She opened her eyes wide and gave me a startled look.

"I was dreaming," she said. "You may go, now, Hartley, and thank you kindly. I'm quite well again, you see." And she turned her face away from me.

III

There was no more sleep for me that night, and I was thankful when daylight came.

Soon afterward, Agnes called me to Mrs. Brympton. I was afraid she was ill again, for she seldom sent for me before nine, but I found her sitting up in bed, pale and drawn-looking, but quite herself.

"Hartley," says she quickly, "will you put on your things at once and go down to the village for me? I want this prescription made up—" here she hesitated a minute and blushed—"and I should like you to be back again before Mr. Brympton is up."

"Certainly, madam," I said.

"And—stay a moment—" she called me back as if an idea had just struck her—"while you're waiting for the mixture, you'll have time to go on to Mr. Ranford's with this note."

It was a two-mile walk to the village, and on my way I had time to turn things over in my mind. It struck me as peculiar that my mistress should wish the prescription made up without Mr. Brympton's knowledge; and, putting this together with the scene of the night before, and with much else that I had noticed and suspected, I began to wonder if the poor lady was weary of her life, and had come to the mad resolve of ending it. The idea took such hold on me that I reached the village on a run, and dropped breathless into a chair before the chemist's counter. The good man, who was just taking down his shutters, stared at me so hard that it brought me to myself.

"Mr. Limmel," I says, trying to speak indifferently, "will you run your eye over this, and tell me if it's quite right?"

He put on his spectacles and studied the prescription.

"Why, it's one of Dr. Walton's," says he. "What should be wrong with it?"

"Well—is it dangerous to take?"

"Dangerous—how do you mean?"

I could have shaken the man for his stupidity.

"I mean—if a person was to take too much of it—by mistake of course—" says I, my heart in my throat.

"Lord bless you, no. It's only lime-water. You might feed it to a baby by the bottleful."

I gave a great sigh of relief and hurried on to Mr. Ranford's. But on the way another thought struck me. If there was nothing to conceal about my visit to the chemist's, was it my other errand that Mrs. Brympton wished me to keep private? Somehow, that thought frightened me worse than the other. Yet the two gentlemen seemed fast friends, and I would have staked my head on my mistress's goodness. I felt ashamed of my suspicions, and concluded that I was still disturbed by the strange events of the night. I left the note at Mr. Ranford's, and hurrying back to Brympton, slipped in by a side door without being seen, as I thought.

An hour later, however, as I was carrying in my mistress's breakfast, I was stopped in the hall by Mr. Brympton.

"What were you doing out so early?" he says, looking hard at me.

"Early—me, sir?" I said, in a tremble.

"Come, come," he says, an angry red spot coming out on his forehead, "didn't I see you scuttling home through the shrubbery an hour or more ago?"

I'm a truthful woman by nature, but at that a lie popped out ready-made. "No, sir, you didn't," said I and looked straight back at him.

He shrugged his shoulders and gave a sullen laugh. "I suppose you think I was drunk last night?" he asked suddenly.

"No, sir, I don't," I answered, this time truthfully enough.

He turned away with another shrug. "A pretty notion my servants have of me!" I heard him mutter as he walked off.

Not till I had settled down to my afternoon's sewing did I realize how the events of the night had shaken me. I couldn't pass that locked door without a shiver. I knew I had heard someone come out of it, and walk down the passage ahead of me. I thought of speaking to Mrs. Blinder or to Mr. Wace, the only two in the house who appeared to have an inkling of what was going on, but I had a feeling that if I questioned them they would deny everything, and that I might learn more by holding my tongue and keeping my eyes open. The idea of spending another night opposite the locked room sickened me, and once I was seized with the notion of packing my trunk and taking the first train to town; but it wasn't in me to throw over a kind mistress in that manner, and I tried to go on with my sewing as if nothing had happened.

I hadn't worked ten minutes before the sewing machine broke down. It was one I had found in the house, a good machine but a trifle out of order: Mrs. Blinder said it had never been used since Emma Saxon's death. I stopped to see what was wrong, and as I was working at the machine a drawer which I had never been able to open slid forward and a photograph fell out. I picked it up and sat looking at it in a maze. It was a woman's likeness, and I knew I had seen the face somewhere—the eyes had an asking look that I had felt on me before. And suddenly I remembered the pale woman in the passage.

I stood up, cold all over, and ran out of the room. My heart seemed to be thumping in the top of my head, and I felt as if I should never get away from the look in those eyes. I went straight to Mrs. Blinder. She was taking her afternoon nap, and sat up with a jump when I came in.

"Mrs. Blinder," said I, "who is that?" And I held out the photograph.

She rubbed her eyes and stared.

"Why, Emma Saxon," says she. "Where did you find it?"

I looked hard at her for a minute. "Mrs. Blinder," I said, "I've seen that face before."

Mrs. Blinder got up and walked over to the looking-glass. "Dear me! I must have been asleep," she says. "My front is all over one ear. And now do run along, Miss Hartley, dear, for I hear the clock striking four, and I must go down this very minute and put on the Virginia ham for Mr. Brympton's dinner."

IV

To all appearances, things went on as usual for a week or two. The only difference was that Mr. Brympton stayed on, instead of going off as he usually did, and that Mr. Ranford never showed himself. I heard Mr. Brympton remark on this one afternoon when he was sitting in my mistress's room before dinner:

"Where's Ranford?" says he. "He hasn't been near the house for a week. Does he keep away because I'm here?"

Mrs. Brympton spoke so low that I couldn't catch her answer.

"Well," he went on, "two's company and three's trumpery; I'm sorry to be in Ranford's way, and I suppose I shall have to take myself off again in a day or two and give him a show." And he laughed at his own joke.

The very next day, as it happened, Mr. Ranford called. The footman said the three were very merry over their tea in the library, and Mr. Brympton strolled down to the gate with Mr. Ranford when he left.

I have said that things went on as usual; and so they did with the rest of the household; but as for myself, I had never been the same since the night my bell had rung. Night after night I used to lie awake, listening for it to ring again, and for the door of the locked room to open stealthily. But the bell never rang, and I heard no sound across the passage. At last the silence began to be more dreadful to me than the most mysterious sounds. I felt that *someone* was cowering there, behind the locked door, watching and listening as I watched and listened, and I could almost have cried out, "Whoever you are, come out and let me see you face to face, but don't lurk there and spy on me in the darkness!"

Feeling as I did, you may wonder I didn't give warning. Once I very nearly did so; but at the last moment something held me back. Whether it was compassion for my mistress, who had grown more and more dependent on me, or unwillingness to try a new place, or some other feeling that I couldn't put a name to, I lingered on as if spell-bound, though every night was dreadful to me, and the days but little better.

For one thing, I didn't like Mrs. Brympton's looks. She had never been the same since that night, no more than I had. I thought she would brighten up after Mr. Brympton left, but though she seemed easier in her mind, her spirits didn't revive, nor her strength either. She had grown attached to me, and seemed to like to have me about; and Agnes told me one day that, since Emma Saxon's death, I was the only maid her mistress had taken to. This gave me a warm feeling for the poor lady, though after all there was little I could do to help her.

After Mr. Brympton's departure, Mr. Ranford took to coming again, though less often than formerly. I met him once or twice in the grounds, or in the village, and I couldn't but think there was a change in him too; but I set it down to my disordered fancy.

The weeks passed, and Mr. Brympton had now been a month absent. We heard he was cruising with a friend in the West Indies, and Mr. Wace said that was a long way off, but though you had the wings of a dove and went to the uttermost parts of the earth, you couldn't get away from the Almighty. Agnes said that as long as he stayed away from Brympton the Almighty might have him and welcome; and this raised a laugh, though Mrs. Blinder tried to look shocked, and Mr. Wace said the bears would eat us.

We were all glad to hear that the West Indies were a long way off, and I remember that, in spite of Mr. Wace's solemn looks, we had a very merry dinner that day in the hall. I don't know if it was because of my being in better spirits, but I fancied Mrs. Brympton looked better too, and seemed more cheerful in her manner. She had been for a walk in the morning, and after luncheon she lay down in her room, and I read aloud to her. When she dismissed me I went to my own room feeling quite bright and happy, and for the first time in weeks walked past the locked door without thinking of it. As I sat down to my work I looked out and saw a few snow-flakes falling. The sight was pleasanter than the eternal rain, and I pictured to myself how pretty the bare gardens would look in their white mantle. It seemed to me as if the snow would cover up all the dreariness, indoors as well as out.

The fancy had hardly crossed my mind when I heard a step at my side. I looked up, thinking it was Agnes.

"Well, Agnes—," said I, and the words froze on my tongue; for there, in the door, stood Emma Saxon.

I don't know how long she stood there. I only know I couldn't stir or take my eyes from her. Afterward I was terribly frightened, but at the time it wasn't fear I felt, but something deeper and quieter. She looked at me long and hard, and her face was just one dumb prayer to me—but how in the world was I to help her? Suddenly she turned, and I heard her walk down the passage. This time I wasn't afraid to follow—I felt that I must know what she wanted. I sprang up and ran out. She was at the other end of the passage, and I expected her to take the turn toward my mistress's room; but instead of that she pushed open the door that led to the backstairs. I followed her down the stairs, and across the passageway to the back door. The kitchen and hall were empty at that hour, the servants being off duty, except for the footman, who was in the pantry. At the door she stood still a moment, with another look at me; then she turned the handle, and stepped out. For a minute I hesitated. Where was she leading me to? The door had closed softly after her, and I opened it and looked out, half-expecting to find that she had disappeared. But I saw her a few yards off hurrying across the courtyard to the path through the woods. Her figure looked black and lonely in the snow, and for a second my heart failed me and I thought of turning back. But all the while she was drawing me after her; and catching up an old shawl of Mrs. Blinder's I ran out into the open.

Emma Saxon was in the wood path now. She walked on steadily, and I followed at the same pace, till we passed out of the gates and reached the high-road. Then she struck across the open fields to the village. By this time the ground was white, and as she climbed the slope of a bare hill ahead of me I noticed that she left no footprints behind her. At sight of that my heart shriveled up within me, and my knees were water. Somehow, it was worse here than indoors. She made the whole countryside seem lonely as the grave, with none but us two in it, and no help in the wide world.

Once I tried to go back; but she turned and looked at me, and it was as if she had dragged me with ropes. After that I followed her like a dog. We came to the village and she led me through it, past the church and the blacksmith's shop, and down the lane to Mr. Ranford's. Mr. Ranford's house stands close to the road: a plain old-fashioned building, with a flagged path leading to the door between box-borders. The lane was deserted, and as I turned into it I saw Emma Saxon pause under the old elm by the gate. And now another fear came over me. I saw that we had reached the end of our journey, and that it was my turn to act. All the way from Brympton I had been asking myself what she wanted of me, but I had followed in a trance, as it were, and not till I saw her stop at Mr. Ranford's gate did my brain begin to clear itself. I stood a little way off in the snow, my heart beating fit to strangle me, and my feet frozen to the ground; and she stood under the elm and watched me.

I knew well enough that she hadn't led me there for nothing. I felt there was something I ought to say or do—but how was I to guess what it was? I had never thought harm of my mistress and Mr. Ranford, but I was sure now that, from one cause or another, some dreadful thing hung over them. *She* knew what it was; she would tell me if she could; perhaps she would answer if I questioned her.

It turned me faint to think of speaking to her; but I plucked up heart and dragged myself across the few yards between us. As I did so, I heard the house door open and saw Mr. Ranford approaching. He looked handsome and cheerful, as my mistress had looked that morning, and at sight of him the blood began to flow again in my veins.

"Why, Hartley," said he, "what's the matter? I saw you coming down the lane just now, and came out to see if you had taken root in the snow." He stopped and stared at me. "What are you looking at?" he says.

I turned toward the elm as he spoke, and his eyes followed me; but there was no one there. The lane was empty as far as the eye could reach.

A sense of helplessness came over me. She was gone, and I had not been able to guess what she wanted. Her last look had pierced me to the marrow; and yet it had not told me! All at once, I felt more desolate than when she had stood there watching me. It seemed as if she had left me all alone to carry the weight of the secret I couldn't guess. The snow went round me in great circles, and the ground fell away from me . . .

A drop of brandy and the warmth of Mr. Ranford's fire soon brought me to, and I insisted on being driven back at once to Brympton. It was nearly dark, and I was afraid my mistress might be wanting me. I explained to Mr. Ranford that I had been out for a walk and had been taken with a fit of giddiness as I passed his gate. This was true enough; yet I never felt more like a liar than when I said it.

When I dressed Mrs. Brympton for dinner she remarked on my pale looks and asked what ailed me. I told her I had a headache, and she said she would not require me again that evening, and advised me to go to bed.

It was a fact that I could scarcely keep on my feet; yet I had no fancy to spend a solitary evening in my room. I sat downstairs in the hall as long as I could hold my head up; but by nine I crept upstairs, too weary to care what happened if I could but get my head on a pillow. The rest of the household went to bed soon afterward; they kept early hours when the master was away, and before ten I heard Mrs. Blinder's door close, and Mr. Wace's soon after.

It was a very still night, earth and air all muffled in snow. Once in bed I felt easier, and lay quiet, listening to the strange noises that come out in a house after dark. Once I thought I heard a door open and close again below: it might have been the glass door that led to the gardens. I got up and peered out of the window; but it was in the dark of the moon, and nothing visible outside but the streaking of snow against the panes.

I went back to bed and must have dozed, for I jumped awake to the furious ringing of my bell. Before my head was clear I had sprung out of bed, and was dragging on my clothes. *It is going to happen now*, I heard myself saying; but what I meant I had no notion. My hands seemed to be covered with glue—I thought I should never get into my clothes. At last I opened my door and peered down the passage. As far as my candle flame carried, I could see nothing unusual ahead of me. I hurried on, breathless; but as I pushed open the baize door leading to the main hall my heart stood still, for there at the head of the stairs was Emma Saxon, peering dreadfully down into the darkness.

For a second I couldn't stir; but my hand slipped from the door, and as it swung shut the figure vanished. At the same instant there came another sound from below stairs—a stealthy mysterious sound, as of a latchkey turning in the house door. I ran to Mrs. Brympton's room and knocked.

There was no answer, and I knocked again. This time I heard someone moving in the room; the bolt slipped back and my mistress stood before me. To my surprise I saw that she had not undressed for the night. She gave me a startled look.

"What is this, Hartley?" she says in a whisper. "Are you ill? What are you doing here at this hour?"

"I am not ill, madam; but my bell rang."

At that she turned pale, and seemed about to fall.

"You are mistaken," she said harshly; "I didn't ring. You must have been dreaming." I had never heard her speak in such a tone. "Go back to bed," she said, closing the door on me.

But as she spoke I heard sounds again in the hall below: a man's step this time; and the truth leaped out on me.

"Madam," I said, pushing past her, "there is someone in the house—"

"Someone—?"

"Mr. Brympton, I think—I hear his step below—"

A dreadful look came over her, and without a word, she dropped flat at my feet. I fell on my knees and tried to lift her: by the way she breathed I saw it was no common faint. But as I raised her head there came quick steps on the stairs and across the hall: the door was flung open, and there stood Mr. Brympton, in his traveling clothes, the snow dripping from him. He drew back with a start as he saw me kneeling by my mistress.

"What the devil is this?" he shouted. He was less high-colored than usual, and the red spot came out on his forehead.

"Mrs. Brympton has fainted, sir," said I.

He laughed unsteadily and pushed by me. "It's a pity she didn't choose a more convenient moment. I'm sorry to disturb her, but—"

I raised myself up aghast at the man's action.

"Sir," said I, "are you mad? What are you doing?"

"Going to meet a friend," said he, and seemed to make for the dressing-room.

At that my heart turned over. I don't know what I thought or feared; but I sprang up and caught him by the sleeve.

"Sir, sir," said I, "for pity's sake look at your wife!"

He shook me off furiously.

"It seems that's done for me," says he, and caught hold of the dressing-room door.

At that moment I heard a slight noise inside. Slight as it was, he heard it too, and tore the door open; but as he did so he dropped back. On the threshold stood Emma Saxon. All was dark behind her, but I saw her plainly, and so did he. He threw up his hands as if to hide his face from her; and when I looked again she was gone.

He stood motionless, as if the strength had run out of him; and in the stillness my mistress suddenly raised herself, and opening her eyes fixed a look on him. Then she fell back, and I saw the death-flutter pass over her . . .

We buried her on the third day, in a driving snow-storm. There were few people in the church, for it was bad weather to come from town, and I've a notion my mistress was one that hadn't many near friends. Mr. Ranford was among the last to come, just before they carried her up the aisle. He was in black, of course, being such a friend of the family, and I never saw a gentleman so pale. As he passed me, I noticed that he leaned a trifle on a stick he carried; and I fancy Mr. Brympton noticed it too, for the red spot came out sharp on his forehead, and all through the service he kept staring across the church at Mr. Ranford, instead of following the prayers as a mourner should.

When it was over and we went out to the graveyard, Mr. Ranford had disappeared, and as soon as my poor mistress's body was underground, Mr. Brympton jumped into the carriage nearest the gate and drove off without a word to any of us. I heard him call out, "To the station," and we servants went back alone to the house.

7

A Ghost Story

By Mark Twain

I took a large room, far up Broadway, in a huge old building whose upper stories had been wholly unoccupied for years until I came. The place had long been given up to dust and cobwebs, to solitude and silence. I seemed groping among the tombs and invading the privacy of the dead, that first night I climbed up to my quarters. For the first time in my life a superstitious dread came over me; and as I turned a dark angle of the stairway and an invisible cobweb swung its hazy woof in my face and clung there, I shuddered as one who had encountered a phantom.

I was glad enough when I reached my room and locked out the mold and the darkness. A cheery fire was burning in the grate, and I sat down before it with a comforting sense of relief. For two hours I sat there, thinking of bygone times; recalling old scenes, and summoning half-forgotten faces out of the mists of the past; listening, in fancy, to voices that long ago grew silent for all time, and to once familiar songs that nobody sings now. And as my reverie softened down to a sadder and sadder pathos, the shrieking of the winds outside softened to a wail, the angry beating of the rain against the panes diminished to a tranquil patter, and one by one the noises in the street subsided, until the hurrying footsteps of the last belated straggler died away in the distance and left no sound behind.

The fire had burned low. A sense of loneliness crept over me. I arose and undressed, moving on tiptoe about the room, doing stealthily what I had to do, as if I were environed by sleeping enemies whose slumbers it would be fatal to break. I covered up in bed, and lay listening to the rain and wind and the faint creaking of distant shutters, till they lulled me to sleep.

I slept profoundly, but how long I do not know. All at once I found myself awake, and filled with a shuddering expectancy. All was still. All but my own heart—I could hear it beat. Presently the bedclothes began to slip away slowly toward the foot of the bed, as if some one were pulling them! I could not stir; I could not speak. Still the blankets slipped deliberately away, till my breast was uncovered. Then with a great effort I seized them and drew them over my head. I waited, listened, waited. Once more that steady pull began, and once more I lay torpid a century of dragging seconds till my breast was naked again. At last I roused my energies and snatched the covers back to their place and held them with a strong grip. I waited. By and by I felt a faint tug, and took a fresh grip. The tug strengthened to a steady strain—it grew stronger and stronger. My hold parted, and for the third time the blankets slid away. I groaned. An answering groan came from the foot of the bed! Beaded drops of sweat stood upon my forehead. I was more dead than alive. Presently I heard a heavy footstep in my room—the step of an elephant, it seemed to me—it was not like anything human. But it was moving from me—there was relief in that. I heard it approach the door—pass out without moving bolt or lock—and wander away among the dismal corridors, straining the floors and joists till they creaked again as it passed—and then silence reigned once more.

When my excitement had calmed, I said to myself, "This is a dream—simply a hideous dream." And so I lay thinking it over until I convinced myself that it was a dream, and then a comforting laugh relaxed my lips and I was happy again. I got up and struck a light; and when I found that the locks and bolts were just as I had left them, another soothing laugh welled in my heart and rippled from my lips. I took my pipe and lit it, and was just sitting down before the fire, when—down went the pipe out of my nerveless fingers, the blood forsook my cheeks, and my placid breathing was cut short with a gasp! In the ashes on the hearth, side by side with my own bare footprint, was another, so vast that in comparison mine was but an infant's! Then I had had a visitor, and the elephant tread was explained.

I put out the light and returned to bed, palsied with fear. I lay a long time, peering into the darkness, and listening.—Then I heard a grating noise overhead, like the dragging of a heavy body across the floor; then the throwing down of the body, and the shaking of my windows in response to the concussion. In distant parts of the building I heard the muffled slamming of doors. I heard, at intervals, stealthy footsteps creeping in and out among the corridors, and up and down the stairs. Sometimes these noises approached my door, hesitated, and went away again. I heard the clanking of chains faintly, in remote passages, and listened while the clanking grew nearer—while it wearily climbed the stairways, marking each move by the loose surplus of chain that fell with an accented rattle upon each succeeding step as the goblin that bore it advanced. I heard muttered sentences; half uttered screams that seemed smothered violently; and the swish of invisible garments, the rush of invisible wings. Then I became conscious that my chamber was invaded—that I was not alone. I heard sighs and breathings about my bed, and mysterious whisperings. Three little spheres of soft phosphorescent light appeared on the ceiling directly over my head, clung and glowed there a moment, and then dropped—two of them upon my face and one upon the pillow. They spattered, liquidly, and felt warm. Intuition told me they had turned to gouts of blood as they fell—I needed no light to satisfy myself of that. Then I saw pallid faces, dimly luminous, and white uplifted hands, floating bodiless in the air—floating a moment and then disappearing. The whispering ceased, and the voices and the sounds, and a solemn stillness followed. I waited and listened. I felt that I must have light or die. I was weak with fear. I slowly raised myself toward a sitting posture, and my face came in contact with a clammy hand! All strength went from me apparently, and I fell back like a stricken invalid. Then I heard the rustle of a garment—it seemed to pass to the door and go out.

When everything was still once more, I crept out of bed, sick and feeble, and lit the gas with a hand that trembled as if it were aged with a hundred years. The light brought some little cheer to my spirits. I sat down and fell into a dreamy contemplation of that great footprint in the ashes. By and by its outlines began to waver and grow dim. I glanced up and the broad gas flame was slowly wilting away. In the same moment I heard that elephantine tread again. I noted its approach, nearer and nearer, along the musty halls, and dimmer and dimmer the light waned. The tread reached my very door and paused—the light had dwindled to a sickly blue, and all things about me lay in a spectral twilight. The door did not open, and yet I felt a faint gust of air fan my cheek, and presently was conscious of a huge, cloudy presence before me. I watched it with fascinated eyes. A pale glow stole over the Thing; gradually its cloudy folds took shape—an arm appeared, then legs, then a body, and last a great sad face looked out of the vapor. Stripped of its filmy housings, naked, muscular and comely, the majestic Cardiff Giant loomed above me!

All my misery vanished—for a child might know that no harm could come with that benignant countenance. My cheerful spirits returned at once, and in sympathy with them the gas flamed up brightly again. Never a lonely outcast was so glad to welcome company as I was to greet the friendly giant. I said:

"Why, is it nobody but you? Do you know, I have been scared to death for the last two or three hours? I am most honestly glad to see you. I wish I had a chair—Here, here, don't try to sit down in that thing—"

But it was too late. He was in it before I could stop him and down he went—I never saw a chair shivered so in my life.

"Stop, stop, you'll ruin ev—"

Too late again. There was another crash, and another chair was resolved into its original elements.

"Confound it, haven't you got any judgment at all? Do you want to ruin all the furniture in the place? Here, here, you petrified fool—"

But it was no use. Before I could arrest him he had sat down on the bed, and it was a melancholy ruin.

"Now what sort of a way is that to do? First you come lumbering about the place bringing a legion of vagabond goblins along with you to worry me to death, and then when I overlook an indelicacy of costume which would not be tolerated anywhere by cultivated people except in a respectable theater, and not even there if the nudity were of your sex, you repay me by wrecking all the furniture you can find to sit down on. And why will you? You damage yourself as much as you do me. You have broken off the end of your spinal column, and littered up the floor with chips of your hams till the place looks like a marble yard. You ought to be ashamed of yourself—you are big enough to know better."

"Well, I will not break any more furniture. But what am I to do? I have not had a chance to sit down for a century." And the tears came into his eyes.

"Poor devil," I said, "I should not have been so harsh with you. And you are an orphan, too, no doubt. But sit down on the floor here—nothing else can stand your weight—and besides, we cannot be sociable with you away up there above me; I want you down where I can perch on this high countinghouse stool and gossip with you face to face." So he sat down on the floor, and lit a pipe which I gave him, threw one of my red blankets over his shoulders, inverted my sitzbath on his head, helmet fashion, and made himself picturesque and comfortable. Then he crossed his ankles, while I renewed the fire, and exposed the flat, honeycombed bottoms of his prodigious feet to the grateful warmth.

"What is the matter with the bottom of your feet and the back of your legs, that they are gouged up so?"

"Infernal chilblains—I caught them clear up to the back of my head, roosting out there under Newell's farm. But I love the place; I love it as one loves his old home. There is no peace for me like the peace I feel when I am there."

We talked along for half an hour, and then I noticed that he looked tired, and spoke of it.

"Tired?" he said. "Well, I should think so. And now I will tell you all about it, since you have treated me so well. I am the spirit of the Petrified Man that lies across the street there in the museum. I am the ghost of the Cardiff Giant. I can have no rest, no peace, till they have given that poor body burial again. Now what was the most natural thing for me to do, to make men satisfy this wish? Terrify them into it! Haunt the place where the body lay! So I haunted the museum night after night. I even got other spirits to help me. But it did no good, for nobody ever came to the museum at midnight. Then it occurred to me to come over the way and haunt this place a little. I felt that if I ever got a hearing I must succeed, for I had the most efficient company that perdition could furnish. Night after night we have shivered around through these mildewed halls, dragging chains, groaning, whispering, tramping up and down stairs, till, to tell you the truth, I am almost worn out. But when I saw a light in your room tonight I roused my energies again and went at it with a deal of the old freshness. But I am tired out—entirely fagged out. Give me, I beseech you, give me some hope!"

I lit off my perch in a burst of excitement, and exclaimed:

"This transcends everything! Everything that ever did occur! Why you poor blundering old fossil, you have had all your trouble for nothing—you have been haunting a plaster cast of yourself—the real Cardiff Giant is in Albany!

"Confound it, don't you know your own remains?"

I never saw such an eloquent look of shame, of pitiable humiliation, overspread a countenance before.

The Petrified Man rose slowly to his feet, and said:

"Honestly, is that true?"

"As true as I am sitting here."

He took the pipe from his mouth and laid it on the mantel, then stood irresolute a moment (unconsciously, from old habit, thrusting his hands where his pantaloons pockets should have been, and meditatively dropping his chin on his breast); and finally said:

"Well—I never felt so absurd before. The Petrified Man has sold everybody else, and now the mean fraud has ended by selling its own ghost! My son, if there is any charity left in your heart for a poor friendless phantom like me, don't let this get out. Think how you would feel if you had made such an ass of yourself."

I heard his stately tramp die away, step by step down the stairs and out into the deserted street, and felt sorry that he was gone, poor fellow—and sorrier still that he had carried off my red blanket and my bathtub.

8

The Night Call

By Henry van Dyke

I

THE FIRST CAPRICE OF NOVEMBER SNOW HAD SKETCHED THE WORLD IN white for an hour in the morning. After mid-day, the sun came out, the wind turned warm, and the whiteness vanished from the landscape. By evening, the low ridges and the long plain of New Jersey were rich and sad again, in russet and dull crimson and old gold; for the foliage still clung to the oaks and elms and birches, and the dying monarchy of autumn retreated slowly before winter's cold republic.

In the old town of Calvinton, stretched along the highroad, the lamps were lit early as the saffron sunset faded into humid night. A mist rose from the long, wet street and the sodden lawns, muffling the houses and the trees and the college towers with a double veil, under which a pallid aureole encircled every light, while the moon above, languid and tear-ful, waded slowly through the mounting fog. It was a night of delay and expectation, a night of remembrance and mystery, lonely and dim and full of strange, dull sounds.

In one of the smaller houses on the main street the light in the win-dow burned late. Leroy Carmichael was alone in his office reading Bal-zac's story of "The Country Doctor." He was not a gloomy or despondent person, but the spirit of the night had entered into him. He had yielded himself, as young men of ardent temperament often do, to the subduing magic of the fall. In his mind, as in the air, there was a soft, clinging mist, and blurred lights of thought, and a still foreboding of change. A sense of the vast tranquil movement of Nature, of her sympathy and of her indifference, sank deeply into his heart. For a time he realised that all things, and he, too, some day, must grow old; and he felt the universal pathos of it more sensitively, perhaps, than he would ever feel it again.

If you had told Carmichael that this was what he was thinking about as he sat in his bachelor quarters on that November night, he would have stared at you and then laughed.

"Nonsense," he would have answered, cheerfully. "I'm no sentimentalist: only a bit tired by a hard afternoon's work and a rough ride home. Then, Balzac always depresses me a little. The next time I'll take some quinine and Dumas: he is a tonic."

But, in fact, no one came in to interrupt his musings and rouse him to that air of cheerfulness with which he always faced the world, and to which, indeed (though he did not know it), he owed some measure of his delay in winning the confidence of Calvinton.

He had come there some five years ago with a particularly good outfit to practice medicine in that quaint and alluring old burgh, full of antique hand-made furniture and traditions. He had not only been well trained for his profession in the best medical school and hospital of New York, but he was also a graduate of Calvinton College (in which his father had been a professor for a time), and his granduncle was a Grubb, a name high in the Golden Book of Calvintonian aristocracy and inscribed upon tombstones in every village within a radius of fifteen miles. Consequently the young doctor arrived well accredited, and was received in his first year with many tokens of hospitality in the shape of tea-parties and suppers.

But the final and esoteric approval of Calvinton was a thing apart from these mere fashionable courtesies and worldly amenities—a thing not to be bestowed without due consideration and satisfactory reasons. Leroy Carmichael failed, somehow or other, to come up to the requirements for a leading physician in such a conservative community. In the judgment of Calvinton he was a clever young man; but he lacked poise and gravity. He walked too lightly along the streets, swinging his stick, and greeting his acquaintances blithely, as if he were rather glad to be alive. Now this is a sentiment, if you analyse it, near akin to vanity, and, therefore, to be discountenanced in your neighbour and concealed in yourself. How can a man be glad that he is alive, and frankly show it, without a touch of conceit and a reprehensible forgetfulness of the presence of original sin even in the best families? The manners of a professional man, above all, should at once express and impose humility.

Young Dr. Carmichael, Calvinton said, had been spoiled by his life in New York. It had made him too gay, light-hearted, almost frivolous. It was possible that he might know a good deal about medicine, though doubtless that had been exaggerated; but it was certain that his temperament needed chastening before he could win the kind of confidence that Calvinton had given to the venerable Dr. Coffin, whose face was like a monument, and whose practice rested upon the two pillars of podophyllin and predestination.

So Carmichael still felt, after his five years' work, that he was an outsider; felt it rather more indeed than when he had first come. He had enough practice to keep him in good health and spirits. But his patients were along the side streets and in the smaller houses and out in the country. He was not called, except in a chance emergency, to the big houses with the white pillars. The inner circle had not yet taken him in.

He wondered how long he would have to work and wait for that. He knew that things in Calvinton moved slowly; but he knew also that its silent and subconscious judgments sometimes crystallised with incredible rapidity and hardness. Was it possible that he was already classified in the group that came near but did not enter, an inhabitant but not a real burgher, a half-way citizen and a lifelong new-comer? That would be rough; he would not like growing old in that way.

But perhaps there was no such invisible barrier hemming in his path. Perhaps it was only the naturally slow movement of things that hindered him. Some day the gate would open. He would be called in behind those white pillars into the world of which his father had often told him stories and traditions. There he would prove his skill and his worth. He would make himself useful and trusted by his work. Then he could marry the girl he loved, and win a firm place and a real home in the old town whose strange charm held him so strongly even in the vague sadness of this autumnal night.

He turned again from these musings to his Balzac, and read the wonderful pages in which Benassis tells the story of his consecration to his profession and Captain Genestas confides the little Adrien to his care, and then the beautiful letter in which the boy describes the country doctor's death and burial. The simple pathos of it went home to Carmichael's heart.

"It is a fine life, after all," said he to himself, as he shut the book at midnight and laid down his pipe. "No man has a better chance than a doctor to come close to the real thing. Human nature is his patient, and each case is a symptom. It's worth while to work for the sake of getting nearer to the reality and doing some definite good by the way. I'm glad that this isn't one of those mystical towns where Christian Science and Buddhism and all sorts of vagaries flourish. Calvinton may be difficult, but it's not obscure. And some day I'll feel its pulse and get at the heart of it."

The silence of the little office was snapped by the nervous clamour of the electric bell, shrilling with a night call.

II

Dr. Carmichael turned on the light in the hall, and opened the front door. A tall, dark man of military aspect loomed out of the mist, and, behind him, at the curbstone, the outline of a big motorcar was dimly visible. He held out a visiting-card inscribed "Baron de Mortemer," and spoke slowly and courteously, but with a strong nasal accent and a tone of insistent domination.

"You are the Dr. Carmichael, yes? You speak French—no? It is a pity. There is need of you at once—a patient—it is very pressing. You will come with me, yes?"

"But I do not know you, sir," said the doctor; "you are—"

"The Baron de Mortemer," broke in the stranger, pointing to the card as if it answered all questions. "It is the Baroness who is very suffering—I pray you to come without delay."

"But what is it?" asked the doctor. "What shall I bring with me? My instrument-case?"

The Baron smiled with his lips and frowned with his eyes. "Not at all," he said, "Madame expects not an arrival—it is not so bad as that—but she has had a sudden access of anguish—she has demanded you. I pray you to come at the instant. Bring what pleases you, what you think best, but come!"

The man's manner was not agitated, but it was strangely urgent, overpowering, constraining; his voice was like a pushing hand. Carmichael threw on his coat and hat, hastily picked up his medicine-satchel and a portable electric battery, and followed the Baron to the motor.

The great car started easily and rolled softly purring down the deserted street. The houses were all asleep, and the college buildings dark as empty fortresses. The moon-threaded mist clung closely to the town like a shroud of gauze, not concealing the form beneath, but making its immobility more mysterious. The trees drooped and dripped with moisture, and the leaves seemed ready, almost longing, to fall at a touch. It was one of those nights when the solid things of the world, the houses and the hills and the woods and the very earth itself, grow unreal to the point of vanishing; while the impalpable things, the presences of life and death which travel on the unseen air, the influences of the far-off starry lights, the silent messages and presentiments of darkness, the ebb and flow of vast currents of secret existence all around us, seem so close and vivid that they absorb and overwhelm us with their intense reality.

Through this realm of indistinguishable verity and illusion, strangely imposed upon the familiar, homely street of Calvinton, the machine ran smoothly, faintly humming, as the Frenchman drove it with masterskill—itself a dream of embodied power and speed. Gliding by the last cottages of Town's End where the street became the highroad, the car ran swiftly through the open country for a mile until it came to a broad entrance. The gate was broken from the leaning posts and thrown to one side. Here the machine turned in and laboured up a rough, grass-grown carriage-drive.

Carmichael knew that they were at Castle Gordon, one of the "old places" of Calvinton, which he often passed on his country drives. The house stood well back from the road, on a slight elevation, looking down over the oval field that was once a lawn, and the scattered elms and pines and Norway firs that did their best to preserve the memory of a noble plantation. The building was colonial; heavy stone walls covered with yellow stucco; tall white wooden pillars ranged along a narrow portico; a style which seemed to assert that a Greek temple was good enough for the residence of an American gentleman. But the clean buff and white of the house had long since faded. The stucco had cracked, and, here and there, had fallen from the stones. The paint on the pillars was dingy, peeling in round blisters and narrow strips from the grey wood underneath. The trees were ragged and untended, the grass uncut, the driveway overgrown with weeds and gullied by rains—the whole place looked forsaken. Carmichael had always supposed that it was vacant. But he had not passed that way for nearly a month, and, meantime, it might have been reopened and tenanted.

The Baron drove the car around to the back of the house and stopped there.

"Pardon," said he, "that I bring you not to the door of entrance; but this is the more convenient."

He knocked hurriedly and spoke a few words in French. The key grated in the lock and the door creaked open. A withered, wiry little man, dressed in dark grey, stood holding a lighted candle, which flickered in the draught. His head was nearly bald; his sallow, hairless face might have been of any age from twenty to a hundred years; his eyes between their narrow red lids were glittering and inscrutable as those of a snake. As he bowed and grinned, showing his yellow, broken teeth, Carmichael thought that he had never seen a more evil face or one more clearly marked with the sign of the drug-fiend.

"My chauffeur, Gaspard," said the Baron, "also my valet, my cook, my chambermaid, my man to do all, what you call factotum, is it not? But he speaks not English, so pardon me once more."

He spoke a few words to the man, who shrugged his shoulders and smiled with the same deferential grimace while his unchanging eyes gleamed through their slits. Carmichael caught only the word "Madame" while he was slipping off his overcoat, and understood that they were talking of his patient.

"Come," said the Baron, "he says that it goes better, at least not worse—that is always something. Let us mount at the instant."

The hall was bare, except for a table on which a kitchen lamp was burning, and two chairs with heavy automobile coats and rugs and veils thrown upon them. The stairway was uncarpeted, and the dust lay thick under the banisters. At the door of the back room on the second floor the Baron paused and knocked softly. A low voice answered, and he went in, beckoning the doctor to follow.

III

If Carmichael lived to be a hundred he could never forget that first impression. The room was but partly furnished, yet it gave at once the idea that it was inhabited; it was even, in some strange way, rich and splendid. Candles on the mantelpiece and a silver travelling-lamp on the dressing-table threw a soft light on little articles of luxury, and photographs in jewelled frames, and a couple of well-bound books, and a gilt clock marking the half-hour after midnight. A wood fire burned in the wide chimney-place, and before it a rug was spread. At one side there was a huge mahogany four-post bedstead, and there, propped up by the pillows, lay the noblest-looking woman that Carmichael had ever seen.

She was dressed in some clinging stuff of soft black, with a diamond at her breast, and a deep-red cloak thrown over her feet. She must have been past middle age, for her thick, brown hair was already touched with silver, and one lock of snow-white lay above her forehead. But her face was one of those which time enriches; fearless and tender and high-spirited, a speaking face in which the dark-lashed grey eyes were like words of wonder and the sensitive mouth like a clear song. She looked at the young doctor and held out her hand to him.

"I am glad to see you," she said, in her low, pure voice, "very glad! You are Roger Carmichael's son. Oh, I am glad to see you indeed."

"You are very kind," he answered, "and I am glad also to be of any service to you, though I do not yet know who you are."

The Baron was bending over the fire rearranging the logs on the andirons. He looked up sharply and spoke in his strong nasal tone.

"Pardon! Madame la Baronne de Mortemer, j'ai l'honneur de vous pre-senter Monsieur le Docteur Carmichael."

The accent on the "doctor" was marked. A slight shadow came upon the lady's face. She answered, quietly:

"Yes, I know. The doctor has come to see me because I was ill. We will talk of that in a moment. But first I want to tell him who I am—and by another name. Dr. Carmichael, did your father ever speak to you of Jean Gordon?"

"Why, yes," he said, after an instant of thought, "it comes back to me now quite clearly. She was the young girl to whom he taught Latin when he first came here as a college instructor. He was very fond of her. There was one of her books in his library—I have it now—a little volume of Horace, with a few translations in verse written on the fly-leaves, and her name on the title-page—Jean Gordon. My father wrote under that, 'My best pupil, who left her lessons unfinished.' He was very fond of the book, and so I kept it when he died."

The lady's eyes grew moist, but the tears did not fall. They trembled in her voice.

"I was that Jean Gordon—a girl of fifteen—your father was the best man I ever knew. You look like him, but he was handsomer than you. Ah, no, I was not his best pupil, but his most wilful and ungrateful one. Did he never tell you of my running away—of the unjust suspicions that fell on him—of his voyage to Europe?"

"Never," answered Carmichael. "He only spoke, as I remember, of your beauty and your brightness, and of the good times that you all had when this old house was in its prime."

"Yes, yes," she said, quickly and with strong feeling, "they were good times, and he was a man of honour. He never took an unfair advantage, never boasted of a woman's favour, never tried to spare himself. He was an American man. I hope you are like him."

The Baron, who had been leaning on the mantel, crossed the room impatiently and stood beside the bed. He spoke in French again, dragging the words in his insistent, masterful voice, as if they were something heavy which he laid upon his wife.

Her grey eyes grew darker, almost black, with enlarging pupils. She raised herself on the pillows as if about to get up. Then she sank back again and said, with an evident effort:

"Rene, I must beg you not to speak in French again. The doctor does not understand it. We must be more courteous. And now I will tell him about my sudden illness to-night. It was the first time—like a flash of lightning—an ice-cold hand of pain—"

Even as she spoke a swift and dreadful change passed over her face. Her colour vanished in a morbid pallor; a cold sweat lay like death-dew on her forehead; her eyes were fixed on some impending horror; her lips, blue and rigid, were strained with an unspeakable, intolerable anguish. Her left arm stiffened as if it were gripped in a vise of pain. Her right hand fluttered over her heart, plucking at an unseen weight. It seemed as if an invisible, silent death-wind were quenching the flame of her life. It flickered in an agony of strangulation.

"Be quick," cried the doctor; "lay her head lower on the pillows, loosen her dress, warm her hands."

He had caught up his satchel, and was looking for a little vial. He found it almost empty. But there were four or five drops of the yellowish, oily liquid. He poured them on his handkerchief and held it close to the lady's mouth. She was still breathing regularly though slowly, and as she inhaled the pungent, fruity smell, like the odour of a jargonelle pear, a look of relief flowed over her face, her breathing deepened, her arm and her lips relaxed, the terror faded from her eyes.

He went to his satchel again and took out a bottle of white tablets marked "Nitroglycerin." He gave her one of them, and when he saw her look of peace grow steadier, after a minute, he prepared the electric battery. Softly he passed the sponges charged with their mysterious current over her temples and her neck and down her slender arms and blue-veined wrists, holding them for a while in the palms of her hands, which grew rosy.

In all this the Baron had helped as he could, and watched closely, but without a word. He was certainly not indifferent; neither was he distressed; the expression of his black eyes and heavy, passionless face was that of presence of mind, self-control covering an intense curiosity. Carmichael conceived a vague sentiment of dislike for the man.

When the patient rested easily they stepped outside the room together for a moment.

"It is the *angina*, I suppose," droned the Baron, "*hein*? That is of great inconvenience. But I think it is the false one, that is much less grave—not truly dangerous, *hein*?"

"My dear sir," answered Carmichael, "who can tell the difference between a false and a true *angina pectoris*, except by a post-mortem? The symptoms are much alike, the result is sometimes identical, if the paroxysm is severe enough. But in this case I hope that you may be right. Your wife's illness is severe, dangerous, but not necessarily fatal. This attack has passed and may not recur for months or even years."

The lip-smile came back under the Baron's sullen eyes.

"Those are the good news, my dear doctor," said he, slowly. "Then we shall be able to travel soon, perhaps to-morrow or the next day. It is of an extreme importance. This place is insufferable to me. We have engagements in Washington—a gay season."

Carmichael looked at him steadily and spoke with deliberation.

"Baron, you must understand me clearly. This is a serious case. If I had not come in time your wife might be dead now. She cannot possibly be moved for a week, perhaps it may take a month fully to restore her strength. After that she must have a winter of absolute quiet and repose."

The Frenchman's face hardened; his brows drew together in a black line, and he lifted his hand quickly with a gesture of irritation. Then he bowed.

"As you will, doctor! And for the present moment, what is it that I may have the honour to do for your patient?"

"Just now," said the doctor, "she needs a stimulant—a glass of sherry or of brandy, if you have it—and a hot-water bag—you have none? Well, then, a couple of bottles filled with hot water and wrapped in a cloth to put at her feet. Can you get them?"

The Baron bowed again, and went down the stairs. As Carmichael returned to the bedroom he heard the droning, insistent voice below calling "Gaspard, Gaspard!"

The great grey eyes were open as he entered the room, and there was a sense of release from pain and fear in them that was like the deepest kind of pleasure.

"Yes, I am much better," said she; "the attack has passed. Will it come again? No? Not soon, you mean. Well, that is good. You need not tell me what it is—time enough for that to-morrow. But come and sit by me. I want to talk to you. Your first name is—"

"Leroy," he answered. "But you are weak; you must not talk much."

"Only a little," she replied, smiling; "it does me good. Leroy was your mother's name—yes? It is not a Calvinton name. I wonder where your father met her. Perhaps in France when he came to look for me. But he did not find me—no, indeed—I was well hidden then—but he found your mother. You are young enough to be my son. Will you be a friend to me for your father's sake?"

She spoke gently, in a tone of infinite kindness and tender grace, with pauses in which a hundred unspoken recollections and appeals were suggested. The young man was deeply moved. He took her hand in his firm clasp.

"Gladly," he said, "and for your sake too. But now I want you to rest."

"Oh," she answered, "I am resting now. But let me talk a little more. It will not harm me. I have been through so much! Twice married—a great fortune to spend—all that the big world can give. But now I am very tired of the whirl. There is only one thing I want—to stay here in Calvinton. I rebelled against it once; but it draws me back. There is a strange magic in the place. Haven't you felt it? How do you explain it?"

"Yes," he said, "I have felt it surely, but I can't explain it, unless it is a kind of ancient peace that makes you wish to be at home here even while you rebel."

She nodded her head and smiled softly.

"That is it," she said, hesitating for a moment. "But my husband—you see he is a very strong man, and he loves the world, the whirling life—he took a dislike to this place at once. No wonder, with the house in such a state! But I have plenty of money—it will be easy to restore the house. Only, sometimes I think he cares more for the money than—but no matter what I think. He wishes to go on at once—to-morrow, if we can. I hate the thought of it. Is it possible for me to stay? Can you help me?"

"Dear lady," he answered, lifting her hand to his lips, "set your mind at rest. I have already told him that it is impossible for you to go for many days. You can arrange to move to the inn to-morrow, and stay there while you direct the putting of your house in order."

A sound in the hallway announced the return of the Baron and Gaspard with the hot-water bottles and the cognac. The doctor made his patient as comfortable as possible for the night, prepared a sleeping-draught, and gave directions for the use of the tablets in an emergency.

"Good night," he said, bending over her. "I will see you in the morning. You may count upon me."

"I do," she said, with her eyes resting on his; "thank you for all. I shall expect you—*au revoir*."

As they went down the stairs he said to the Baron, "Remember, absolute repose is necessary. With that you are safe enough for to-night. But you may possibly need more of the nitrite of amyl. My vial is empty. I will write the prescription, if you will allow me."

"In the dining-room," said the Baron, taking up the lamp and throwing open the door of the back room on the right. The floor had been hastily swept and the rubbish shoved into the fireplace. The heavy chairs stood along the wall. But two of them were drawn up at the head of the long mahogany table, and dishes and table utensils from a travelling-basket were lying there, as if a late supper had been served.

"You see," said the Baron, drawling, "our banquet-hall! Madame and I have dined in this splendour to-night. Is it possible that you write here?"

His secret irritation, his insolence, his contempt spoke clearly enough in his tone. The remark was almost like an intentional insult. For a second Carmichael hesitated. "No," he thought, "why should I quarrel with him? He is only sullen. He can do no harm."

He pulled a chair to the foot of the table, took out his tablet and his fountain-pen, and wrote the prescription. Tearing off the leaf, he folded it crosswise and left it on the table.

In the hall, as he put on his coat he remembered the paper.

"My prescription," he said, "I must take it to the druggist to-night."

"Permit me," said the Baron, "the room is dark. I will take the paper, and procure the drug as I return from escorting the doctor to his residence."

He went into the dark room, groped about for a moment, and returned, closing the door behind him.

"Come, Monsieur," he said, "your work at the Chateau Gordon is finished for this night. I shall leave you with yourself—at home, as you say—in a few moments. Gaspard—Gaspard, *fermez la porte a clé*!"

The strong nasal voice echoed through the house, and the servant ran lightly down the stairs. His master muttered a few sentences to him, holding up his right hand as he did so, with the five fingers extended, as if to impress something on the man's mind.

"*Pardon*," he said, turning to Carmichael, "that I speak always French, after the rebuke. But this time it is of necessity. I repeat the instruction for the *pilules*. One at each hour until eight o'clock—five, not more—it is correct? Come, then, our equipage is always harnessed, always ready, how convenient!"

The two men did not speak as the car rolled through the brumous night. A rising wind was sifting the fog. The moon had set. The loosened leaves came whirling, fluttering, sinking through the darkness like a flight of huge dying moths. Now and then they brushed the faces of the travellers with limp, moist wings.

The red night-lamp in the drug-store was still burning. Carmichael called the other's attention to it.

"You have the prescription?"

"Without doubt!" he answered. "After I have escorted you, I shall procure the drug."

The doctor's front door was lit up as he had left it. The light streamed out rather brightly and illumined the Baron's sullen black eyes and smiling lips as he leaned from the car, lifting his cap.

"A thousand thanks, my dear doctor, you have been excessively kind; yes, truly of an excessive goodness for us. It is a great pleasure—how do you tell it in English?—it is a great pleasure to have met you. *Adieu*."

"Till to-morrow morning!" said Carmichael, cheerfully, waving his hand.

The Baron stared at him curiously, and lifted his cap again.

"*Adieu!*" droned the insistent voice, and the great car slid into the dark.

IV

The next morning was of crystal. It was after nine when Carmichael drove his electric-phaeton down the leaf-littered street, where the country wagons and the decrepit hacks were already meandering placidly, and out along the highroad, between the still green fields. It seemed to him as if the experience of the past night were "such stuff as dreams are made of." Yet the impression of what he had seen and heard in that firelit chamber—of the eyes, the voice, the hand of that strangely lovely lady—of her vision of sudden death, her essentially lonely struggle with it, her touching words to him when she came back to life—all this was so vivid and unforgettable that he drove straight to Castle Gordon.

The great house was shut up like a tomb: every door and window was closed, except where half of one of the shutters had broken loose and hung by a single hinge. He drove around to the back. It was the same there. A cobweb was spun across the lower corner of the door and tiny drops of moisture jewelled it. Perhaps it had been made in the early morning. If so, no one had come out of the door since night.

Carmichael knocked, and knocked again. No answer. He called. No reply. Then he drove around to the portico with the tall white pillars and tried the front door. It was locked. He peered through the half-open window into the drawing-room. The glass was crusted with dirt and the room was dark. He was trying to make out the outlines of the huddled furniture when he heard a step behind him. It was the old farmer from the nearest cottage on the road.

"Mornin', doctor! I seen ye comin' in, and tho't ye might want to see the house."

"Good morning, Scudder! I do, if you'll let me in. But first tell me about these automobile tracks in the drive."

The old man gazed at him with a kind of dull surprise as if the question were foolish.

"Why, ye made 'em yerself, comin' up, didn't ye?"

"I mean those larger tracks—they were made by a much heavier car than mine."

"Oh," said the old man, nodding, "them was made by a big machine that come in here las' week. You see this house's bin shet up 'bout ten years, ever sence ol' Jedge Gordon died. B'longs to Miss Jean—her that run off with the Eye-talyin. She kinder wants to sell it, and kinder not—ye see—"

"Yes," interrupted Carmichael, "but about that big machine—when did you say it was here?"

"P'raps four or five days ago; I think it was a We'nsday. Two fellers from Philadelfy—said they wanted to look at the house, tho't of buyin' it. So I bro't 'em in, but when they seen the outside of it they said they didn't want to look at it no more—too big and too crumbly!"

"And since then no one has been here?"

"Not a soul—leastways nobody that I seen. I don't s'pose you think o' buyin' the house, doc'! It's too lonely for an office, ain't it?"

"You're right, Scudder, much too lonely. But I'd like to look through the old place, if you will take me in."

The hall, with the two chairs and the table, on which a kitchen lamp with a half-inch of oil in it was standing, gave no sign of recent habitation. Carmichael glanced around him and hurried up the stairway to the bedroom. A tall four-poster stood in one corner, with a coverlet apparently hiding a mattress and some pillows. A dressing-table stood against the wall, and in the middle of the floor there were a few chairs. A half-open closet door showed a pile of yellow linen. The daylight sifted dimly into the room through the cracks of the shutters.

"Scudder," said Carmichael, "I want you to look around carefully and tell me whether you see any signs of any one having been here lately."

The old man stared, and turned his eyes slowly about the room. Then he shook his head.

"Can't say as I do. Looks pretty much as it did when me and my wife breshed it up in October. Ye see it's kinder clean fer an old house—not much dust from the road here. That linen and that bed's bin here sence I c'n remember. Them burnt logs mus' be left over from old Jedge Gordon's time. He died in here. But what's the matter, doc'? Ye think tramps or burglers—"

"No," said Carmichael, "but what would you say if I told you that I was called here last night to see a patient, and that the patient was the Miss Jean Gordon of whom you have just told me?"

"What d'ye mean?" said the old man, gaping. Then he gazed at the doctor pityingly, and shook his head. "I know ye ain't a drinkin' man, doc', so I wouldn't say nothin'. But I guess ye bin dreamin'. Why, las' time Miss Jean writ to me—her name's Mortimer now, and her husband's a kinder Barrin or some sorter furrin noble,—she was in Paris, not mor'n two weeks ago! Said she was dyin' to come back to the ol' place agin, but she wa'n't none too well, and didn't guess she c'd manage it. Ef ye said ye seen her here las' night—why—well, I'd jest think ye'd bin dreamin'. P'raps ye're a little under the weather—bin workin' too hard?"

"I never was better, Scudder, but sometimes curious notions come to me. I wanted to see how you would take this one. Now we'll go downstairs again."

The old man laughed, but doubtfully, as if he was still puzzled by the talk, and they descended the creaking, dusty stairs. Carmichael turned at once into the dining-room.

The rubbish was still in the fireplace, the chairs ranged along the wall. There were no dishes on the long table; but at the head of it two chairs; and at the foot, one; and in front of that, lying on the table, a folded bit of paper. Carmichael picked it up and opened it.

It was his prescription for the nitrite of amyl.

He hesitated a moment; then refolded the paper and put it in his vest-pocket.

Seated in his car, with his hand on the lever, he turned to Scudder, who was watching him with curious eyes.

"I'm very much obliged to you, Scudder, for taking me through the house. And I'll be more obliged to you if you'll just keep it to yourself— what I said to you about last night."

"Sure," said the old man, nodding gravely. "I like ye, doc', and that kinder talk might do ye harm here in Calvinton. We don't hold much to dreams and visions down this way. But, say, 'twas a mighty interestin' dream, wa'n't it? I guess Miss Jean hones for them white pillars, many a day—they sorter stand for old times. They draw ye, don't they?"

"Yes, my friend," said Carmichael as he moved the lever, "they speak of the past. There is a magic in those white pillars. They draw you."

9

Tom Toothacre's Ghost Story

By Harriet Beecher Stowe

WHAT IS IT ABOUT THAT OLD HOUSE IN SHERBOURNE?" SAID AUNT Nabby to Sam Lawson, as he sat drooping over the coals of a great fire one October evening.

Aunt Lois was gone to Boston on a visit; and, the smart spice of her scepticism being absent, we felt the more freedom to start our story-teller on one of his legends.

Aunt Nabby sat trotting her knitting-needles on a blue-mixed yarn stocking. Grandmamma was knitting in unison at the other side of the fire. Grandfather sat studying "The Boston Courier." The wind outside was sighing in fitful wails, creaking the pantry-doors, occasionally puffing in a vicious gust down the broad throat of the chimney. It was a drizzly, sleety evening; and the wet lilac bushes now and then rattled and splashed against the window as the wind moaned and whispered through them.

We boys had made preparation for a comfortable evening. We had enticed Sam to the chimney corner, and drawn him a mug of cider. We had set down a row of apples to roast on the hearth, which even now were giving faint sighs and sputters as their plump sides burst in the genial heat. The big oak back-log simmered and bubbled, and distilled large drops down amid the ashes; and the great hickory forestick had just burned out into solid bright coals, faintly skimmed over with white ashes. The whole area of the big chimney was full of a sleepy warmth and brightness just calculated to call forth fancies and visions. It only wanted somebody now to set Sam off; and Aunt Nabby broached the ever-interesting subject of haunted houses.

"Wal, now, Miss Badger," said Sam, "I ben over there, and walked round that are house consid'able; and I talked with Granny Hokum and Aunt Polly, and they've putty much come to the conclusion that they'll hev to move out on't. Ye see these 'ere noises, they keep 'em awake nights; and Aunt Polly, she gets 'stericky; and Hannah Jane, she says, ef they stay in the house, *she* can't live with 'em no longer. And what can them lone women do without Hannah Jane? Why, Hannah Jane, she says these two months past she's seen a woman, regular, walking up and down the front hall between twelve and one o'clock at night; and it's jist the image and body of old Ma'am Tillotson, Parson Hokum's mother, that everybody know'd was a thunderin' kind o' woman, that kep' every thing in a muss while she was alive. What the old crittur's up to now there ain't no knowin'. Some folks seems to think it's a sign Granny Hokum's time's comin'. But Lordy massy I says she to me, says she, 'Why, Sam, I don't know nothin' what I've done, that Ma'am Tillotson should be set loose on me.' Anyway they've all got so narvy, that Jed Hokum has ben up from Needham, and is goin' to cart 'em all over to live with him. Jed, he's for hushin' on't up, 'cause he says it brings a bad name on the property. Wal, I talked with Jed about it; and says I to Jed, says I, 'now, ef you'll take my advice, jist you give that are old house a regular overhaulin, and paint it over with tew coats o' paint, and that are'll clear 'em out, if any thing will. Ghosts is like bedbugs,—they can't stan fresh paint,' says I. 'They allers clear out. I've seen it tried on a ship that got haunted.'"

"Why, Sam, do ships get haunted?"

"To be sure they do!—haunted the wust kind. Why, I could tell ye a story'd make your har rise on e'end, only I'm 'fraid of frightening boys when they're jist going to bed."

"Oh! you can't frighten Horace," said my grandmother. "He will go and sit out there in the graveyard till nine o'clock nights, spite of all I tell him."

"Do tell, Sam!" we urged. "What was it about the ship?" Sam lifted his mug of cider, deliberately turned it round and round in his hands, eyed it affectionately, took a long drink, and set it down in front of him on the hearth, and began:—

"Ye 'member I telled you how I went to sea down East, when I was a boy, 'long with Tom Toothacre. Wal, Tom, he reeled off a yarn one night that was 'bout the toughest I ever hed the pullin' on. And it come all straight, too, from Tom. 'Twa'n't none o' yer hearsay: 'twas what he seen with his own eyes. Now, there wa'n't no nonsense 'bout Tom, not a bit on't; and he wa'n't afeard o' the divil himself; and he ginally saw through things about as straight as things could be seen through. This 'ere happened when Tom was mate o' 'The Albatross,' and they was a-runnin' up to the Banks for a fare o' fish. 'The Albatross' was as handsome a craft as ever ye see; and Cap'n Sim Witherspoon, he was skipper—a rail nice likely man he was. I heard Tom tell this 'ere one night to the boys on 'The Brilliant,' when they was all a-settin' round the stove in the cabin one foggy night that we was to anchor in Frenchman's Bay, and all kind o' layin' off loose.

"Tom, he said they was having a famous run up to the Banks. There was a spankin' southerly, that blew 'em along like all natur'; and they was hevin' the best kind of a time, when this 'ere southerly brought a pesky fog down on 'em, and it grew thicker than hasty-puddin'. Ye see, that are's the pester o' these 'ere southerlies: they's the biggest fog-breeders there is goin'. And so, putty soon, you couldn't see half ship's length afore you.

"Wal, they all was down to supper, except Dan Sawyer at the wheel, when there come sich a crash as if heaven and earth was a-splittin', and then a scrapin' and thump bumpin' under the ship, and gin 'em sich a h'ist that the pot o' beans went rollin', and brought up jam ag'in the bulkhead; and the fellers was keeled over,—men and pork and beans kinder permiscus.

"'The divil!' says Tom Toothacre, 'we've run down somebody. Look out, up there!'

"Dan, he shoved the helm hard down, and put her up to the wind, and sung out, 'Lordy massy! we've struck her right amidships!'

"'Struck what?' they all yelled, and tumbled up on deck.

"'Why, a little schooner,' says Dan. 'Didn't see her till we was right on her. She's gone down tack and sheet. Look! there's part o' the wreck a-floating off: don't ye see?'

"Wal, they didn't see, 'cause it was so thick you couldn't hardly see your hand afore your face. But they put about, and sent out a boat, and kind o' sarched round; but, Lordy massy ye might as well looked for a drop of water in the Atlantic Ocean. Whoever they was, it was all done gone and over with 'em for this life, poor critturs!

"Tom says they felt confoundedly about it; but what could they do? Lordy massy! what can any on us do? There's places where folks jest lets go 'cause they hes to. Things ain't as they want 'em, and they can't alter 'em. Sailors ain't so rough as they look: they'z feelin' critturs, come to put things right to 'em. And there wasn't one on 'em who wouldn't 'a' worked all night for a chance o' saving some o' them poor fellows. But there 'twas, and 'twa'n't no use trying.

"Wal, so they sailed on; and by 'm by the wind kind o' chopped round no'theast, and then come round east, and sot in for one of them regular east blows and drizzles that takes the starch out o' fellers more'n a regular storm. So they concluded they might as well put into a little bay there, and come to anchor.

"So they sot an anchor-watch, and all turned in.

"Wal, now comes the particular curus part o' Tom's story; and it was more curus 'cause Tom was one that wouldn't 'a' believed no other man that had told it. Tom was one o' your sort of philosophers. He was fer lookin' into things, and wa'n't in no hurry 'bout believin'; so that this 'un was more 'markable on account of it's bein' Tom that seen it than ef it had ben others.

"Tom says that night he hed a pesky toothache that sort o' kep' grumblin' and jumpin' so he couldn't go to sleep; and he lay in his bunk, a-turnin' this way and that, till long past twelve o'clock.

"Tom had a 'thwart-ship bunk where he could see into every bunk on board, except Bob Coffin's; and Bob was on the anchor-watch. Wal, he lay there, tryin' to go to sleep, hearin' the men snorin' like bull-frogs in a swamp, and watchin' the lantern a-swingin' back and forward; and the sou'westers and pea-jackets were kinder throwin' their long shadders up and down as the vessel sort o' rolled and pitched,—for there was a heavy swell on,—and then he'd hear Bob Coffin tramp, tramp, trampin' overhead,—for Bob had a pretty heavy foot of his own,—and all sort o' mixed up together with Tom's toothache, so he couldn't get to sleep. Finally,

Tom, he bit off a great chaw o' 'baccy, and got it well sot in his cheek, and kind o' turned over to lie on't, and ease the pain. Wal, he says he laid a spell, and dropped off in a sort o' doze, when he woke in such a chill his teeth chattered, and the pain come on like a knife, and he bounced over, thinking the fire had gone out in the stove.

"Wal, sure enough, he see a man a-crouchin' over the stove, with his back to him, a-stretchin' out his hands to warm 'em. He had on a sou'wester and a pea-jacket, with a red tippet round his neck; and his clothes was drippin' as if he'd just come in from a rain.

"'What the divil!' says Tom. And he riz right up, and rubbed his eyes. 'Bill Bridges,' says he, 'what shine be you up to now?' For Bill was a master oneasy crittur, and allers a-gettin' up and walkin' nights; and Tom, he thought it was Bill. But in a minute he looked over, and there, sure enough, was Bill, fast asleep in his bunk, mouth wide open, snoring like a Jericho ram's-horn. Tom looked round, and counted every man in his bunk, and then says he, 'Who the devil is this? for there's Bob Coffin on deck, and the rest is all here.'

"Wal, Tom wa'n't a man to be put under too easy. He hed his thoughts about him allers; and the fust he thought in every pinch was what to do. So he sot considerin' a minute, sort o' winkin' his eyes to be sure he saw straight, when, sure enough, there come another man backin' down the companion-way.

"'Wal, there's Bob Coffin, anyhow,' says Tom to himself. But no, the other man, he turned: Tom see his face; and, sure as you live, it was the face of a dead corpse. Its eyes was sot, and it jest came as still across the cabin, and sot down by the stove, and kind o' shivered, and put out its hands as if it was gettin' warm.

"Tom said that there was a cold air round in the cabin, as if an iceberg was comin' near, and he felt cold chills running down his back; but he jumped out of his bunk, and took a step forward. 'Speak!' says he. 'Who be you? and what do you want?'

"They never spoke, nor looked up, but kept kind o' shivering and crouching over the stove.

"'Wal,' says Tom, 'I'll see who you be, anyhow.' And he walked right up to the last man that come in, and reached out to catch hold of his coat-collar; but his hand jest went through him like moonshine, and in a minute he all faded away; and when he turned round the other one was gone too. Tom stood there, looking this way and that; but there warn't nothing but the old stove, and the lantern swingin', and the men all snorin' round in their bunks. Tom, he sung out to Bob Coffin. 'Hullo, up there!' says he. But Bob never answered, and Tom, he went up, and found Bob down on his knees, his teeth a-chatterin' like a bag o' nails, trying to say his prayers; and all he could think of was, 'Now I lay me,' and he kep going that over and over. Ye see, boys, Bob was a drefful wicked, swearin' crittur, and hadn't said no prayers since he was tew years old, and it didn't come natural to him. Tom give a grip on his collar, and shook him. 'Hold yer yawp,' said he. 'What you howlin' about? What's up?'

"'Oh, Lordy massy!' says Bob, 'we're sent for,—all on us,—there's been two on 'em: both on 'em went right by me!'

"Wal, Tom, he hed his own thoughts; but he was bound to get to the bottom of things, anyway. Ef 'twas the devil, well and good—he wanted to know it. Tom jest wanted to hev the matter settled one way or t'other: so he got Bob sort o' stroked down, and made him tell what he saw.

"Bob, he stood to it that he was a-standin' right for'ard, a-leanin' on the windlass, and kind o' hummin' a tune, when he looked down, and see a sort o' queer light in the fog; and he went and took a look over the bows, when up came a man's head in a sort of sou'wester, and then a pair of hands, and catched at the bob-stay; and then the hull figger of a man riz right out o' the water, and clim up on the martingale till he could reach the jib-stay with his hands, and then he swung himself right up onto the bowsprit, and stepped aboard, and went past Bob, right aft, and down into the cabin. And he hadn't more'n got down, afore he turned round, and there was another comin' in over the bowsprit, and he went by him, and down below: so there was two on 'em, jest as Tom had seen in the cabin.

"Tom he studied on it a spell, and finally says he, 'Bob, let you and me keep this 'ere to ourselves, and see ef it'll come again. Ef it don't, well and good: ef it does—why, we'll see about it.'

"But Tom he told Cap'n Witherspoon, and the Cap'n he agreed to keep an eye out the next night. But there warn't nothing said to the rest o' the men.

"Wal, the next night they put Bill Bridges on the watch. The fog had lifted, and they had a fair wind, and was going on steady. The men all turned in, and went fast asleep, except Cap'n Witherspoon, Tom and Bob Coffin. Wal, sure enough, 'twixt twelve and one o'clock, the same thing came over, only there war four men 'stead o' two. They come in jes' so over the bowsprit, and they looked neither to right nor left, but clim down stairs, and sot down, and crouched and shivered over the stove jist like the others. Wal, Bill Bridges, he came tearin' down like a wild-cat, frightened half out o' his wits, screechin', 'Lord, have mercy! we're all goin' to the devil!' And then they all vanished.

"'Now, Cap'n, what's to be done?' says Tom. 'Ef these 'ere fellows is to take passage, we can't do nothin' with the boys: that's clear.'

"Wal, so it turned out; for, come next night, there was six on 'em come in, and the story got round, and the boys was all on eend. There wa'n't no doin' nothin' with 'em. Ye see, it's allers jest so. Not but what dead folks is jest as 'spectable as they was afore they's dead. These might 'a' been as good fellers as any aboard; but it's human natur'. The minute a feller's dead, why, you sort o' don't know 'bout him; and it's kind o' skeery hevin' on him round, and so 'twan't no wonder the boys didn't feel as if they could go on with the vy'ge, ef these 'ere fellers was all to take passage. Come to look, too, there war consid'able of a leak stove in the vessel; and the boys, they all stood to it, ef they went farther, that they'd all go to the bottom. For, ye see, once the story got a-goin', every one on 'em saw a new thing every night. One on 'em saw the baitmill a-grindin', without no hands to grind it; and another saw fellers up aloft, workin' in the sails. Wal, the fact war, they jest had to put about,—run back to Castine.

"Wal, the owners, they hushed up things the best they could; and they put the vessel on the stocks, and worked her over, and put a new coat o' paint on her, and called her 'The Betsey Ann'; and she went a good vy'ge to the Banks, and brought home the biggest fare o' fish that had been for a long time; and she's made good vy'ges ever since; and that jest proves what I've been a-saying,—that there's nothin' to drive out ghosts like fresh paint."

10

A Strange Story from the Coast

By Rebecca Harding Davis

THE INCIDENT OF WHICH YOU HAVE ASKED ME TO GIVE YOU AN ACCOUNT occurred six years ago, but the details are still fresh in my memory. The matter impressed me at the time with peculiar force. I am quite sure that I cannot convey any of this impression to you. I can only give you the facts, and very probably your shrewd common sense will readily find a rational explanation of them. I confess honestly, however, that I have never been able to account for them to myself on any ordinary basis of reasoning.

In February of 1873 her physician ordered C—— to the seashore. Our medical men were then just beginning to find out that the tonic of a bath of salt air for lungs and body, even in winter, was a surer restorer of exhausted vitality than the usual prescriptions of interminable quinine and beef-tea.

We went down together to an old farmhouse on the New Jersey coast in which we had spent a summer years before. The farmer, who was also, according to a common custom there, captain of a coast-schooner, was trading in the South that winter, and had taken his wife with him. We rented the house, opened it, built up fires and began housekeeping in a couple of hours. The older part of the house, built long before the Revolution, consisted of log huts joined one to another, through whose vacant rooms and fireless chimneys the wind from the sea whistled drearily, but the living-room and chamber which we occupied, with their double doors, red rag-carpets and hearths heaped with blazing logs from the wrecks which strewed the beach, were snug and comfortable enough. Outside, the solitude and silence, even at noonday, were so profound that it was incredible to us that we were but a day's journey from New York. This was surely some forgotten outskirt of the world which we had first discovered. The windows on one side of the living-room opened on the vast sweep of water, swelling and sinking that day gray and sullen under the low wintry sky; and on the other upon a plane of sand as interminable, broken at intervals by swamps overgrown with black bare laurel-bushes, by pine woods and by a few lonely fishermen's houses, the surf-boats set up on end against them, rows of crab-cars and seine-reels fronting the leafless orchards.

When C—— and I had visited this coast before it had borrowed a certain gayety and lightness from the summer. The marshes were rich in color; artists were camping under their yellow umbrellas here and there, catching brilliant effects of sky or water; sportsmen from New York in irreproachable shooting-rig were popping at the snipe among the reeds; the sea and bay were full of white scudding sails. But in winter it lapsed back to its primitive condition: the land seemed to answer the sea out of depths of immeasurable age and silence. The only sign of life was the trail of smoke upward to the clouds from some distant cabin, or a ghostly sail flitting along the far horizon. The sand heaped itself day by day in fantastic unbroken ridges along the beach. The very fences and houses had grown hoary with lichen and gray moss that shivered unwholesomely in the wind. Some of these old log houses had been built two centuries ago by Quaker refugees from England under the Proprietary Barclay. They built the houses and settled down in them, so far barred out of the world on this lonely coast that they did not know when their old persecutor Charles was dead. We were almost persuaded that they had forgotten to die themselves when we saw the old gray-coated, slow-moving folk going in and out of these houses, with the same names as those of the men who built them, the same features and inexorable habits of hard work and prosy gossip, the same formal tricks of speech and strange superstitions. Indeed, these people usually live to an old age so extreme that it seems as if Death himself forgot this out-of-the-way corner of the world on his rounds. In many of the houses there had been but two generations since the days of the Stuarts, son and father living far beyond the ninetieth year.

A wiry, withered youth of seventy-six, Captain Jeremiah Holdcomb (who is still living, by the way), whom we met one day on the beach, constituted himself our guide and protector: he took us from farmhouse to farmhouse by day to make friends with the "old people," always coming in at night to tell us the histories of them and of their houses, and to chuckle boyishly over the "onaccountable notions of them as was gettin' on in years," and to sip a glass of toddy, unctuously smacking his withered lips and wagging his white poll.

One day, as a storm was rising, C—— and I led the old man across the garden at an earlier hour than usual to set him safely on his way homeward. A raw nor'easter blew heavily off sea that evening; the sun had not been seen for two days; the fog was banked up to landward in solid wet masses; the landscape was walled in by it until nothing was left in view but our house and the rotted leaves of the garden-beds, half buried now in drifted sand.

"You have never told us the history of this house, captain?" said C——, looking back at the dilapidated log building behind us.

Holdcomb, as I thought, evaded the question at first. The house, he said when C—— urged it, had been built by a family named Whynne, and still belonged to them, the young man from whom we rented it being himself only a tenant. The Whynnes were of the oldest Quaker stock; the men had always followed the water; they "took to brandy," Holdcomb said, "as a lamb to its dam's milk. Men and women was oneasy, wanderin' folk." But they all came home to this house at the last, which was the reason, he supposed, they were so longlived. He referred here to a belief which we had found current among these people, that a man's hold upon life was stronger in the house in which he was born than in any other.

"Because thar," explained the captain, "is where the yerth first got a grip on him, and thar's the last place it'll be loosened. Now, the Whynnes all lived in this house to an oncommon old age. Thar was a kind of backbone of obstinacy in them all. I reckon Death himself had to have a tough fight with them before he got them under. Old Abner Whynne lived to be a hunderd and four. He died—let me see—he died just sixty year ago, come January. Priscilla was his youngest da'ater. She's livin' yet: she's got no notion of dyin'. She's the only Whynne, though, that is livin'."

On further inquiry it appeared that this said Priscilla had married a Perot, and, being now a childless widow, occupied the Perot house, another decayed old habitation on the other side of the marshes, to the north.

"She was ninety-two last June," said Holdcomb. "It's thirty years since she has been able to hear thunder. But she keeps a-watchin' and a-watchin' out of them black eyes of hern. God knows what fur. But whenever I see her I says to myself, 'It'll come to you some day, Priscilla,' says I, whatever it be. She's got an awful holt on livin', that ther woman. All the Whynnes had, as I told you. She's a mere shackle of bones, and as deaf as that dead sherk yander, but she's got a kind of life in her yet, sech as these pink-an'-white mishy young gells never knowed. I'll take you to see her to-morrow. If she gets a sight of anybody that's come from out of the towns and the crowd, it kind of gives her a fresh start. Yes, we'll go and see her to-morrow," climbing over the bars. "Well, I'll be goin' now. That's all ther is to tell about this house."

"No, no," said C——. "One moment, captain. Those queer squares of brick at the end of the garden, what are they?"

The old man shuffled uneasily: "I don't see no brick. I don't know nothin about 'em."

"Surely, you can see them—close to the house, almost covered with the sand. They look like the entrance to a vault—or they might be graves."

By this time Holdcomb had succeeded in ridding his startled face of every glimmer of meaning, "Oh, them?" staring at them with unconcern. "They were ther long before I was born. I wouldn't worry myself about them if I was you. They've somethin' to do, 's likely, with them old Whynnes that's dead an' gone. I'd let 'em rest. Never dig deep into a rotten ma'ash, 's we say hereabouts."

With that old Jeremiah hobbled quickly away, and C—— and I returned to the house, pausing to look curiously at the sunken squares of brick over which the sand had drifted deep. I remember that C—— remarked irritably that it was evident that the old man knew for what purpose they had been built there, and chose to conceal it from us.

"There is something evil about them," she added, declaring that whenever she passed them she was conscious of some sudden unpleasant physical influence, as though she had breathed miasma. Her illness had made her peculiarly susceptible to outside influences, real or imaginary. I thought nothing more at the time, therefore, of her assertion, though later circumstances reminded me of it.

The next day we crossed the marshes under Jeremiah's guidance, and found Priscilla in the old Perot house. This woman differed from any other human being I had ever seen in some indescribable way. The peculiar effect of it upon me returns whenever I remember her: I would rather see a ghost than think of that nightmare of a woman.

Age had ravaged and gnawed her away mercilessly: nothing was left of her in the world but a little quick-moving shadow. The delicate features, the restless, birdlike hands, the shrunken outline of shape, made but a silhouette of the actual woman that she once had been. The brown flannel gown and crossed white handkerchief which she wore after the Quaker fashion seemed to me like a load hung upon a ghost. For the rest, she was vivacious, keen, hard; she talked incessantly in a shrill, vehement pipe; our answers necessarily were written or by signs. She welcomed us with a kind of fierce eagerness, examined the cut and material of our clothes, and questioned us about the city and the news of the day with the delight of a prisoner to whose dungeon had come a glimmer of light from the world outside. She chattered in return the gossip of the neighborhood—gossip which from her lips obscurely hinted at malignant and foul meanings—occasionally rebutting old Holdcomb with savage contempt.

"But she's not such a bad un," he said, turning deprecatingly to us. "Naterally, she's a kind, decent soul, Priscilla is. But, you see, it's excitement to her to talk that way: all them Whynnes must have excitement of one sort or another. The men took to liquor, and the women—Now, Priscilla—" suddenly checking himself: "it's like bein' shut up in jail, what with livin' here alone and that dreadful deafness."

The old creature had gone, moving with a quick, nervous step, to a corner cupboard, from which she brought out a plate of seed-cakes. She stood holding them out to me, poising herself on tiptoe, her dark luminous eyes fixed on me from underneath the shaggy white brows.

"No, C——," I said, "this is not a bad woman: she is not immodest nor malignant." Yet I drew back from her. Now I was conscious wherein she differed from other aged people. It was a young woman who looked out of those strange eyes at me. Old Priscilla Perot, in the isolation of her thirty years of deafness, had grown vulgar and bitter in her speech, but back of that was another creature, who was not vulgar, who never spoke. I fancied that it looked out with all the unsatisfied passion and longing of youth through these eyes before me. They seemed perpetually challenging the world to give back something that was lost with a silent, sad entreaty strangely at variance with the shrill, mean talk that came from the woman's lips. I wondered idly when this creature in her had ever lived, and what had killed it, and whether it would ever, in all the ages to come, waken and live again. How many possible human beings, after all, die in each of us and are forgotten before the body gives up too and has to be hidden out of sight!

Old Priscilla went out into the kitchen and bustled aimlessly about. Our coming had made her restless; she laughed without cause; frequent nervous shudders passed over her lean body.

"It's always the way when any one from the city comes near her," said Jeremiah. "She was main fond of the crowd and of town."

"So I should have guessed," said C——. "Do you notice the dainty dress and the high shoes and jaunty bit of ribbon in her cap? Yet she impresses me strangely, as though she might have had once a much finer, more delicate, nature than she shows to us.—She has not always lived here? What is her history?" turning to Holdcomb.

The old fellow gave a scared look at the wan little figure skipping in and out of the dark kitchen: "Lord! how should I know? She belongs to them as was dead and gone before my time." To stop short all further inquiry he began talking to her by signs. She perched herself upon the high wooden chair at one side of the fireplace, looking at C——, her head a little on one side.

"She wants to know what changes I remember in this place?" for so Holdcomb had interpreted C——'s question. "Not many—not many: my time has been so short. Now, my father could remember when a good part of Ocean and Monmouth counties was under the sea. But *he* lived to a good age. Under this house where you are there's been dug up sherks' teeth and the backbones of whales. My grandfather, 's likely, could remember when they swam over this field," pursing up her thin lips thoughtfully. "Thee wasn't here in the war of 1812?" turning sharply on C——.

"No."

"I was here: I had come home for the first time from New York then. I watched the English vessels come up the inlet: it was a gusty afternoon like this. They had come up to plunder the farms. The men that weren't Friends took their guns and went down to fire on them from the shore."

"And those that were Friends?" asked C——.

"Took their guns and went along," with a shrill laugh and nod. "Oh, the young people in the house were terribly frightened. It was all I could do to keep their courage up, silly children."

"Were you not afraid?"

"No. I wasn't young, and I had nothing to lose." She had turned her head, with her back to us, and was talking into the darkness. She hurled out the last words with a kind of defiance. "I had nothing to lose."

"True enough!" said Jeremiah, with many wags of the head and senile blinks of sympathy; but, catching our inquiring looks, he recovered himself with a sudden deprecatory cough and leaned his chin on his cane, silent and attentive.

"I set the children to barring up the windows," continued Priscilla after a moment's pause, "and then I took a ladder and climbed on to the roof. I put my back against the chimney and my feet on the top rung, and there I saw the fight. Our men hid among the salt grass of the ma'ash and picked 'em off one by one. They was main good shots. I saw Ben Stover aim at a man up on the foremast, and then there was a whiff of smoke and down he went in a lump into the water. They said his dyin' yell was terrible to hear," she added with a chuckle.

"What became of Stover after that?" asked Jeremiah.

"He died when he was a young man—only sixty or thereabout. He used to go up and down the beach lookin' for Kidd's treasure, muttering to himself. They said he went mad because there was blood on his hands, him bein' a Quaker. But I knew different from that: it was the money drove him mad—Kidd's money—he was so sure of finding it."

She fell back in her chair, breathless with her vehemence. But in a few minutes she sat upright again and thrust her bloodless, peaked face into mine. "Where did thee say thee came from?"

"New York, mother," signed Jeremiah.

"New York—a-ah!" drawing in her breath. "I lived nigh New York— in a country-place three mile from town, but now they tell me it's in the heart of the city, built over with huckster-shops. Does thee know it?"

I shook my head.

"No, nobody would remember it." she said gently. "I would know it: nothing they could build on it would hide it from me." Her eyes deepened in their sad quiet, the shrill tones softened. For the moment it was the voice of a young woman that we heard.

C—— was about to question her, but Jeremiah interposed: "Take care! Don't ask her what she means. Never before sin' I've known her has she spoken of the time she was in New York. God knows what's drove them words out of her now!"

To change the current of her thoughts he leaned forward and told her by signs the story of our coming to the Whynne house. I was quite willing that she should be turned from any dangerous subjects: I had the uncomfortable feeling when with her that we were dealing with Death himself, or with some forgotten part of a past age more alien and incomprehensible than Death.

"Thee is living in my house?" turning sharply on us. "Yes, it's mine: it will never belong to any but a Whynne. I know every board in it."

Her head dropped on her breast and her eyes were fixed on vacancy. After waiting a few moments, finding that she had apparently forgotten us, we rose to leave her. As C—— came up to bid her good-bye she said, "You will come to your house while we are there?"

"I?" She started up, standing erect without her staff: her voice was feebler than a whisper, her hands were clasped over her head. But it was the voice and gesture of a young, passionate woman. "Into that house? I'll never cross the threshold while I'm living. It's just a step across the ma'ash, thee knows," appealing to Jeremiah, "but it's nigh sixty year since I put my foot in it. I've never forgot that I was Josiah Perot's wife. There's them waitin' for me there as Josiah never could abide. But when I'm dead—"

She threw out her arms with a sudden indescribable gesture of freedom. "I'll have done with Josiah Perot when I'm dead."

C—— drew me away, and we hurried homeward. Glancing back, we could see the woman standing in the doorway: her back was turned toward us, looking out to Sea.

It was a gusty, chilly afternoon. Spectral whitish drifts of fog were blown inland across the marshes. The sun went down in an angry yellow glare which foreboded ill; and then the night fell suddenly, unusually dark, full of shrill whispers of the wind through the swamps and the threatening roar of the sea.

We had, however, I remember, a comfortable hot supper soon ready, and we closed the curtains and heaped up the fire in the living-room to shut out the darkness and strange noises without.

When supper was over and Captain Holdcomb was seated with his pipe in the chimney-corner, we urged him to tell us the history of Priscilla without reserve.

"There's not much to tell," he said. "She was born in this house, and she married Josiah Perot well on in life; and if Josiah was a bit stupid he was a steady, God-fearin' fellow; and that's more than could be said of any Whynne that ever lived."

"But before she married Perot?"

"Well, nothin' happened remarkable—onless," he added reluctantly, "that curious occurrence at Abner Whynne's death. I kin tell you about that," dropping into the singsong of an oft-told tale. "Abner Whynne was this woman's father. He lived to be a hunderd and four. He lived with his wife down to Sherk River, for the old people had give up this house to their da'ater Peggy, who married Sam Volk."

"Where was Priscilla?"

"Well, I might as well tell the whole on't. It was like this. She wa'n't like the rest on 'em. She wa'n't ez handsome as Peggy, but she was of a different sort, I've heard say—finer an' harder to please. She went up to New York, and ther she fell in with a Captain John Salterre, commanding a brig that run to the Mediterranean. He war a handsome fellow, 'cordin' to accounts, and of a high family—very different from the Whynnes. Word came back that she war married to him, and next (that al'ays was the queer part of it to me) that he had sent her to school. Oh, I've heard my father say when she came back in 1812 she could speak one of them foreign tongues quite fluent. Her father al'ays set great store by Priscilla, though she never come anigh him. Peggy grew to be a humble, hard-workin' woman in middle age, and war a faithful da'ater. But, Lord! he cared not a copper cent for her. It was all 'My da'ater Priscilla,' because she had made the grand marriage in New York. When her mother died down to Sherk River, Peggy war ther. She said, 'now, daddy, thee must come along home to me.'—'I will not, Margaret, he says.—'But thee must,' says she: 'thee cannot live here alone.' For he was then ninety-eight.—'I hev my lines to watch,' says he. For he was a fisherman, thee knows. 'Very well, daddy,' says Peggy, 'thee can set thee lines in the inlet jest as well as Sherk River.' Then she ups and packs his clock and his wooden chair (it's this one I'm sittin' on, only it had a sheep-skin cover on then) and his tea-kettle and his fire-dogs, so's he might feel at home, and she fixed them all up in this hyar room back of me." Jeremiah, with his staff, pushed open the door into the half-ruined chamber behind him. The log walls had fallen to decay half a century ago, but there was the fireplace with rusted irons on the hearth—the very fire-dogs he had mentioned, perhaps.

"That was his room, and he could do as he pleased in it. He used to set by the door yander, his old deaf yaller dog Turk lyin' atween his knees, both on 'em a-lookin' out at the sea hour in an' hour out. He lived on here with Peggy for six year. In that time no word came from Priscilla. He used to talk about her and her grandeur to the men a-fishin', but we all knowed it was jest his notions, for she never sent him a letter or made a sign. I was a peart young lad then, rising sixteen. It's jest sixty year ago, last October, when one mornin' Peggy went in to get the old man's coffee for him. She al'ays made his bite of breakfast ready afore anything else. 'I'll have no coffee, Peggy,' says he.—'Is thee sick, daddy?' says she. For it was the first time he had ever refused his breakfast. As for sickness, he had never been sick an hour since any living man could remember, though as to his boyhood nobody was left on this yerth that remembered that. So Peggy was sort of stunned. 'Is thee sick?' says she.—'No: I never was better,' he says; 'but I'll eat naught, I tell thee.' So he fell asleep, and Peggy went out. But she could not 'tend to her work, she was that dazed. She told me she was mendin' Sam's nets that mornin' (Sam was her husband), and presently out comes daddy dressed and leanin' on his staff as usual. He sat down in this chair by the fire yander, and she brought him his breakfast, and he ate it. About an hour after Joshua Van Dorn came in, and he and Peggy talked of the blue mackerel, for there was a school of them in, and Sam hed made a good haul that mornin'. Joshua was but a boy about twenty, but a strong, rugged fellow. Abner said nothin' to him until he was on his feet to go: then he says, 'Joshua, Sam'll be out eel-fishin' to-night, and I want thee to come an' watch with me. I'll die to-night when the tide goes out.' Joshua thought it was jest his notions. 'All right, daddy' says he, winkin' at Peggy. 'I'll come and watch with thee, and eat breakfast with thee too in the mornin'. Who'll I bring with me? Jeremiah Holdcomb?'—'Jeremiah'll do as well as another: it's the same to me. It'll not take a strong man to streak me,' says the old man; and he laughed, looking down at himself. For he was lean like Priscilla. The Whynnes wear away with age. Peggy said he sot 'most all day by the door yander, lookin' out to sea. Ther's some think that old sea-farin' men hes a warnin' from the water when their time's come. I dunno how that may be. But old Abner he sot lookin' out all day. When Sam come in he talked about the blue-mackerel haul. Sam watched him keerful, but he couldn't see as there was aught the matter with him."

"Was no clergyman sent for ?" demanded C——. "Did nobody remind him of the God that he was going to meet?"

Jeremiah looked up startled, chuckled and grew suddenly grave: "Nobody'd go to a Whynne with that sort of talk. I doubt ef old Abner in all his hunderd year had ever thought of a God, any more than his dog Turk hed. Him and Priscilla war jest alike. They belonged to this yerth. But as to their turnin' up agen in any other—I dunno: I reckon they won't," shaking his head decisively.

"Go on with the story," said C——.

"Well, come evenin', Sam started out eel-fishin'. Daddy nodded to him. 'Good-bye, Sam Volk, says he: 'I'll be gone afore thee gets back. Sam humored him. 'Good-bye, daddy,' he says. 'Is there aught I ken do for thee afore I go?'—'No,' he says, 'no.' But he took Sam's hand and kept looking up at him. 'Onless,' he says, 'thee could fetch Priscilla hyar. I'd like to hev seen the girl afore I go. I hev it on my mind ther's somethin' she wants to say to me.'—'I can't do that, thee knows, daddy,' says Sam. For we all thought she was in foreign parts. But she'd been livin' in New York for four year, and that very night, as it turned out, she was on her way home in John Van Dorn's schooner.

"Well, Joshua and I come in to watch. We sent Peggy to bed at the usual time, eight o'clock, for neither she nor we thought aught ra'aly ailed the old man. He took no notice of her when she went, nor of the children: he never could abide children. 'I'll make you some toddy, boys, to keep you awake,' he says; and we war willin'. Ther was not a man on the Jarsey coast could brew toddy like old Abner. It was prime toddy, that's a fact. He drank a bit, and then he went to bed (he wouldn't hev any help in ondressin'), and when he was stretched out he whistled for old Turk, and the brute lay down across his feet. 'Good fellow! good fellow!' he says, and he put his hand on the dog's head and straightened himself, and so went to sleep. About ten o'clock Joshua called to me: he was standin' by the bed. 'Jerry,' says he, 'ther's a queer settlin' in the old man's face, and his pulse is mighty low. Shouldn't wonder ef he'd been in the right of it about himself, after all.'—'Shell I call Peggy?' I says— 'no,' says he: 'wait a bit.' But in a hour he says, 'Jerry, go and call Peggy.' So I called her. But what could we do? He was goin' out with the tide. He didn't move or speak, and his eyes were shet: he didn't hear Peggy or the children when they was cryin' about him. His breath got slowly thinner and thinner, and his flesh colder. When Peggy called to him he took no notice, but the dog raised himself after a while on his fore legs and looked in his face and gave a howl. I declar' it skeert me, it was so like a human bein'. The old man stirred at that, and sort of smiled, and his lips moved as if to say 'Good fellow!' But he was too far gone to speak. Then it was all quiet. I opened the window yander" (pointing to the square opening in the ruined wall of the room outside), "and I stood by it watchin' the tide go down, jest as you might be doin' now. And he lay on the bed hyar jest by the door. It was a clear night, and I could see the line of white surf sinkin' lower and lower. I knowed by Peggy's face, leanin' over him, that he was goin' with it fast. At last the sea fell out of sight into the darkness. Then I shut the window: I knowed it was all over. When I come up to the bed he was dead: Joshua was closin' his eyes. We folded his hands and straightened him. It seemed to me but a few minutes till he was stark and stiff and dreadful cold. I remember Joshua said it was onusual, and was because there was so little blood in his body, but how that might be I dunno. We sot with him till mornin'. Now, here's the cur'ous part of the story. You'll likely not believe it, but I'll tell you word for word, jest as it happened. An hour after Abner Whynne died his da'ater Priscilla come to the house. She had landed at the inlet, where the men war a-fishin', and Sam brought her over. She war not a very young woman, but she was like a lady—very fine appearing. She was greatly excited when she found her father dead, though she skercely spoke a word. 'You come too late,' says Peggy. 'You might have given him a deal of comfort. But you're too late.' I didn't know before that Peggy war so bitter agen her.—'I must speak to him,' she said; and she tore off the sheet and put her hand to his heart. I could see her start when she felt the cold. 'Daddy!' she cried, 'daddy!'—'Let the dead rest, Priscilla,' says Peggy.—'Go out, all of you,' she says, motionin' to the door. 'Let me have him to myself.'

"I went out, an' took Peggy. Priscilla kept a-cryin' in a low voice, 'Daddy! daddy!' I went outside—I was that cur'ous—and looked in the window. Fur God! I tell you the truth. The dead man opened his eyes and sat up. 'Why did you bring me back?' he said. 'Why did you not let me alone, Priscilla? I was at rest.' She leaned over him, sobbin'. Presently he says, 'Is your husband here?' Then she whispered something. God knows what. But I reckon the whole truth was wrenched out of her. You can't lie to the dead. He sat up in the bed, and I saw him point with one hand to the door. 'Begone!' says he: 'you are no da'ater of mine.' She stood a minute, and then came out, and ran a-past me, cryin', into the dark."

"Of course you only fancied that you saw the man alive through the window?" said C——.

"I dunno," said Holdcomb doggedly. "I do know as she has never crossed the doorway from that night, and that's sixty year gone. And," lowering his voice, "when we come back into the room the old man was dead and stark as we had left him. *But he was sitting bolt upright in the bed.*"

"What do you suppose she had told him?"

"Oh, that soon come out. She never had been John Salterre's wife. A sort of shame had seized her at last, and she had left him and come home. She's lived hyar ever since. Four year later she married Josiah Perot, who was a heap better husband than she deserved. She married him for a home: she never could abide to work. But nobody ever thought she cared aught for him. The Whynnes never forget, and I believe she thinks of John Salterre at this minute, and keers for him jest the same as she did when she war a young girl."

"What became of him? Did he ever find her?" I asked.

Jeremiah hesitated: "I didn't mean to tell thee that. A year after her father died Salterre found out whar she was, and put off straight from New York on a schooner for this inlet. The schooner—the *Petrel* it was— struck the bar out yander, and the crew was lost, Salterre and all. They war buried in the sand on the beach, jest where they come ashore, 's the custom was."

The old man rose and began to put on his coat. We were not sorry to have him go. His ghastly story made us quite willing to close the door on the dilapidated apartment outside and to turn our thoughts to cheerfuller matters.

For a week afterward the threatened nor'-east storm kept us in-doors. The captain did not come to pay his daily visit, and we heard from a neighbor that he "was attendin' on Priscilla Perot, who was waitin' her call."

"Jerry's a main good doctor," she added. "But I doubt he'll not keep old Priscilla. She's bein' took off afore her time: the Whynnes live to a great old age. But they say she's been restlesslike ever since she talked to thee about her young days in this house."

The storm continued to rage so heavily that it shut us in to an absolute solitude. Even the hardiest fishermen did not venture out upon the beach. On the second night it abated. C—— and I were sitting by the fire reading between ten and eleven o'clock, when, finding that the beating of the rain upon the roof had ceased, I opened the door into the ruined room of which Holdcomb had told the story, and looked out. The wind had changed: the storm-clouds were driving to the east, and were banked on that horizon in a solid rampart; the moon shone out whitely on the surging sea and on the drenched marshes webbed with the swollen black lines of the creeks. The tide-water had risen to an unprecedented height, and was within three feet of our door.

I called C—— to look. "If the storm had lasted a few hours longer," I said, "the Whynne house would have gone at last."

We both stood in the doorway between the living-room, in which we had been sitting, and Abner Whynne's old chamber. The latter was clearly lighted by the moon and by the fire and lamplight in the room behind us. As I looked down through the broken wall to the marsh, C—— touched my arm, whispering, "Who is this?"

I turned. A small dark figure was crossing the beach, coming up toward the house. It came with such rapidity that before I had time to speak it stood in the outer doorway, and was in the room beside us.

"Priscilla!" cried C——.

The woman had reached the spot where, as Jeremiah told us, her father had died. She halted there a moment. I saw her face as distinctly as that of C——, being about the same distance from both. It was Priscilla, and yet not Priscilla. The weight of age had dropped away. *This* was the creature which I had fancied still lived in the woman, young, passionate, it might be wicked, but in no sense Perot's vulgar, malignant widow.

She hesitated but a moment, and then passed through the back door into the garden, where the sand lay heaped by the storm in deep wet drifts. C—— and I hurried after her, each with the same thought, that the dying woman had become deranged and had escaped from her attendants with the wild fancy of reaching her old home. She suddenly flung out her arms with a vehement gesture of triumph, and passed around a projection of the wall. We reached the spot in an instant. It was the place where the mysterious heaps of brick were erected, one of which rose slightly above the sand. She was not there: sea and marsh and beach were utterly vacant.

We went into the house, and, I am bound to confess, we slept little that night.

Captain Holdcomb came early the next morning.

"The widow Perot is dead at last," was his first greeting.

"What time did she die?" asked C——.

"Last night at half-past ten o'clock." C—— rose, and going out beckoned the old man to follow her. "These are graves," she said, pointing to the heap of bricks. "Who were buried here?"

"I didn't keer to tell thee: I was afraid it might make thee oncomfortable. But—as thee knows so much the crew of the *Petrel* was buried onder them. That one which is part oncovered by the wind is whar Captain John Salterre is laid."

The old man never knew our reason for asking. There is my ghost-story, the only one for which I have never heard a rational explanation.

11

The Woman at Seven Brothers

By Wilbur Daniel Steele

I TELL YOU SIR, I WAS INNOCENT. I DIDN'T KNOW ANY MORE ABOUT THE world at twenty-two than some do at twelve. My uncle and aunt in Duxbury brought me up strict; I studied hard in high school, I worked hard after hours, and I went to church twice on Sundays, and I can't see it's right to put me in a place like this, with crazy people. Oh yes, I know they're crazy—you can't tell *me*. As for what they said in court about finding her with her husband, that's the Inspector's lie, sir, because he's down on me, and wants to make it look like my fault.

No, sir, I can't say as I thought she was handsome—not at first. For one thing, her lips were too thin and white, and her color was bad. I'll tell you a fact, sir; that first day I came off to the Light I was sitting on my cot in the store-room (that's where the assistant keeper sleeps at the Seven Brothers), as lonesome as I could be, away from home for the first time, and the water all around me, and, even though it was a calm day, pounding enough on the ledge to send a kind of a *woom-woom-woom* whining up through all that solid rock of the tower. And when old Fedderson poked his head down from the living-room with the sunshine above making a kind of bright frame around his hair and whiskers, to give me a cheery, "Make yourself to home, son!" I remember I said to myself: "*He's* all right. I'll get along with *him*. But his wife's enough to sour milk." That was queer, because she was so much under him in age—'long about twenty-eight or so, and him nearer fifty. But that's what I said, sir.

Of course that feeling wore off, same as any feeling will wear off sooner or later in a place like the Seven Brothers. Cooped up in a place like that you come to know folks so well that you forget what they *do* look like. There was a long time I never noticed her, any more than you'd notice the cat. We used to sit of an evening around the table, as if you were Fedderson there, and me here, and her somewhere back there, in the rocker, knitting. Fedderson would be working on his Jacob's-ladder, and I'd be reading. He'd been working on that Jacob's-ladder a year, I guess, and every time the Inspector came off with the tender he was so astonished to see how good that ladder was that the old man would go to work and make it better. That's all he lived for.

If I was reading, as I say, I daren't take my eyes off the book, or Fedderson had me. And then he'd begin—what the Inspector said about him. How surprised the member of the board had been, that time, to see everything so clean about the light. What the Inspector had said about Fedderson's being stuck here in a second-class light—best keeper on the coast. And so on and so on, till either he or I had to go aloft and have a look at the wicks.

He'd been there twenty-three years, all told, and he'd got used to the feeling that he was kept down unfair—so used to it, I guess, that he fed on it, and told himself how folks ashore would talk when he was dead and gone—best keeper on the coast—kept down unfair. Not that he said that to me. No, he was far too loyal and humble and respectful, doing his duty without complaint, as anybody could see.

And all that time, night after night, hardly ever a word out of the woman. As I remember it, she seemed more like a piece of furniture than anything else—not even a very good cook, nor over and above tidy. One day, when he and I were trimming the lamp, he passed the remark that his *first* wife used to dust the lens and take a pride in it. Not that he said a word against Anna, though. He never said a word against any living mortal; he was too upright.

I don't know how it came about; or, rather, I *do* know, but it was so sudden, and so far away from my thoughts, that it shocked me, like the world turned over. It was at prayers. That night I remember Fedderson was uncommon long-winded. We'd had a batch of newspapers out by the tender, and at such times the old man always made a long watch of it, getting the world straightened out. For one thing, the United States minister to Turkey was dead. Well, from him and his soul, Fedderson got on to Turkey and the Presbyterian college there, and from that to heathen in general. He rambled on and on, like the surf on the ledge, *woom-woom-woom*, never coming to an end.

You know how you'll be at prayers sometimes. My mind strayed. I counted the canes in the chair-seat where I was kneeling; I plaited a corner of the table-cloth between my fingers for a spell, and by and by my eyes went wandering up the back of the chair.

The woman, sir, was looking at me. Her chair was back to mine, close, and both our heads were down in the shadow under the edge of the table, with Fedderson clear over on the other side by the stove. And there were her two eyes hunting mine between the spindles in the shadow. You won't believe me, sir, but I tell you I felt like jumping to my feet and running out of the room—it was so queer.

I don't know what her husband was praying about after that. His voice didn't mean anything, no more than the seas on the ledge away down there. I went to work to count the canes in the seat again, but all my eyes were in the top of my head. It got so I couldn't stand it. We were at the Lord's prayer, saying it singsong together, when I had to look up again. And there her two eyes were, between the spindles, hunting mine. Just then all of us were saying, "Forgive us our trespasses—" I thought of it afterward.

When we got up she was turned the other way, but I couldn't help seeing her cheeks were red. It was terrible. I wondered if Fedderson would notice, though I might have known he wouldn't—not him. He was in too much of a hurry to get at his Jacob's-ladder, and then he had to tell me for the tenth time what the Inspector'd said that day about getting him another light—Kingdom Come, maybe, he said.

I made some excuse or other and got away. Once in the store-room, I sat down on my cot and stayed there a long time, feeling queerer than anything. I read a chapter in the Bible, I don't know why. After I'd got my boots off I sat with them in my hands for as much as an hour, I guess, staring at the oil-tank and its lopsided shadow on the wall. I tell you, sir, I was shocked. I was only twenty-two remember, and I was shocked and horrified.

And when I did turn in, finally, I didn't sleep at all well. Two or three times I came to, sitting straight up in bed. Once I got up and opened the outer door to have a look. The water was like glass, dim, without a breath of wind, and the moon just going down. Over on the black shore I made out two lights in a village, like a pair of eyes watching. Lonely? My, yes! Lonely and nervous. I had a horror of her, sir. The dinghy-boat hung on its davits just there in front of the door, and for a minute I had an awful hankering to climb into it, lower away, and row off, no matter where. It sounds foolish.

Well, it seemed foolish next morning, with the sun shining and everything as usual—Fedderson sucking his pen and wagging his head over his eternal "log," and his wife down in the rocker with her head in the newspaper, and her breakfast work still waiting. I guess that jarred it out of me more than anything else—sight of her slouched down there, with her stringy, yellow hair and her dusty apron and the pale back of her neck, reading the Society Notes. *Society Notes*! Think of it! For the first time since I came to Seven Brothers I wanted to laugh.

I guess I did laugh when I went aloft to clean the lamp and found everything so free and breezy, gulls flying high and little whitecaps making under a westerly. It was like feeling a big load dropped off your shoulders. Fedderson came up with his dust-rag and cocked his head at me.

"What's the matter, Ray?" said he.

"Nothing," said I. And then I couldn't help it. "Seems kind of out of place for Society Notes," said I, "out here at Seven Brothers."

He was the other side of the lens, and when he looked at me he had a thousand eyes, all sober. For a minute I thought he was going on dusting, but then he came out and sat down on a sill.

"Sometimes," said he, "I get to thinking it may be a mite dull for her out here. She's pretty young, Ray. Not much more'n a girl, hardly."

"Not much more'n a *girl*!" It gave me a turn, sir, as though I'd seen my aunt in short dresses.

"It's a good home for her, though," he went on slow. "I've seen a lot worse ashore, Ray. Of course if I could get a shore light—"

"Kingdom Come's a shore light."

He looked at me out of his deep-set eyes, and then he turned them around the light-room, where he'd been so long.

"No," said he, wagging his head. "It ain't for such as me."

I never saw so humble a man.

"But look here," he went on, more cheerful. "As I was telling her just now, a month from yesterday's our fourth anniversary, and I'm going to take her ashore for the day and give her a holiday—new hat and everything. A girl wants a mite of excitement now and then, Ray."

There it was again, that "girl." It gave me the fidgets, sir. I had to do something about it. It's close quarters for last names in a light, and I'd taken to calling him Uncle Matt soon after I came. Now, when I was at table that noon I spoke over to where she was standing by the stove, getting him another help of chowder.

"I guess I'll have some, too, *Aunt* Anna," said I, matter of fact.

She never said a word nor gave a sign—just stood there kind of round-shouldered, dipping the chowder. And that night at prayers I hitched my chair around the table, with its back the other way.

You get awful lazy in a lighthouse, some ways. No matter how much tinkering you've got, there's still a lot of time and there's such a thing as too much reading. The changes in weather get monotonous, too, by and by; the light burns the same on a thick night as it does on a fair one. Of course there's the ships, north-bound, south-bound—wind-jammers, freighters, passenger-boats full of people. In the watches at night you can see their lights go by, and wonder what they are, how they're laden, where they'll fetch up, and all. I used to do that almost every evening when it was my first watch, sitting out on the walk-around up there with my legs hanging over the edge and my chin propped on the railing—lazy. The Boston boat was the prettiest to see, with her three tiers of port-holes lit, like a string of pearls wrapped round and round a woman's neck—well away, too, for the ledge must have made a couple of hundred fathoms off the Light, like a white dog-tooth of a breaker, even on the darkest night.

Well, I was lolling there one night, as I say, watching the Boston boat go by, not thinking of anything special, when I heard the door on the other side of the tower open and footsteps coming around to me.

By and by I nodded toward the boat and passed the remark that she was fetching in uncommon close to-night. No answer. I made nothing of that, for oftentimes Fedderson wouldn't answer, and after I'd watched the lights crawling on through the dark a spell, just to make conversation I said I guessed there'd be a bit of weather before long.

"I've noticed," said I, "when there's weather coming on, and the wind in the northeast, you can hear the orchestra playing aboard of her just over there. I make it out now. Do you?"

"Yes. Oh—yes—! *I hear it all right!*"

You can imagine I started. It wasn't him, but *her*. And there was something in the way she said that speech, sir—something—well—unnatural. Like a hungry animal snapping at a person's hand.

I turned and looked at her sidewise. She was standing by the railing, leaning a little outward, the top of her from the waist picked out bright by the lens behind her. I didn't know what in the world to say, and yet I had a feeling I ought not to sit there mum.

"I wonder," said I, "what that captain's thinking of, fetching in so handy to-night. It's no way. I tell you, if 'twasn't for this light, she'd go to work and pile up on the ledge some thick night—" She turned at that and stared straight into the lens. I didn't like the look of her face. Somehow, with its edges cut hard all around and its two eyes closed down to slits, like a cat's, it made a kind of mask.

"And then," I went on, uneasy enough—"and then where'd all their music be of a sudden, and their goings-on and their singing—"

"And dancing!" She clipped me off so quick it took my breath.

"D-d-dancing?" said I.

"That's dance-music," said she. She was looking at the boat again.

"How do you know?" I felt I had to keep on talking.

Well, sir—she laughed. I looked at her. She had on a shawl of some stuff or other that shined in the light; she had it pulled tight around her with her two hands in front at her breast, and I saw her shoulders swaying in tune.

"How do I *know*?" she cried. Then she laughed again, the same kind of a laugh. It was queer, sir, to see her, and to hear her. She turned, as quick as that, and leaned toward me. "Don't you know how to dance, Ray?" said she.

"N-no," I managed, and I was going to say "*Aunt Anna*," but the thing choked in my throat.

I tell you she was looking square at me all the time with her two eyes and moving with the music as if she didn't know it. By heavens, sir, it came over me of a sudden that she wasn't so bad-looking, after all. I guess I must have sounded like a fool.

"You—you see," said I, "she's cleared the rip there now, and the music's gone. You—you hear?"

"Yes," said she, turning back slow. "That's where it stops every night—night after night—it stops just there—at the rip."

When she spoke again her voice was different. I never heard the like of it, thin and taut as a thread. It made me shiver, sir.

"I hate 'em!" That's what she said. "I hate 'em all. I'd like to see 'em dead. I'd love to see 'em torn apart on the rocks, night after night. I could bathe my hands in their blood, night after night."

And do you know, sir, I saw it with my own eyes, her hands moving in each other above the rail. But it was her voice, though. I didn't know what to do, or what to say, so I poked my head through the railing and looked down at the water. I don't think I'm a coward, sir, but it was like a cold—ice-cold—hand, taking hold of my beating heart.

When I looked up finally, she was gone. By and by I went in and had a look at the lamp, hardly knowing what I was about. Then, seeing by my watch it was time for the old man to come on duty, I started to go below. In the Seven Brothers, you understand, the stair goes down in a spiral through a well against the south wall and first there's the door to the keeper's room and then you come to another, and that's the living-room, and then down to the store-room. And at night, if you don't carry a lantern, it's as black as the pit.

Well, down I went, sliding my hand along the rail, and as usual I stopped to give a rap on the keeper's door, in case he was taking a nap after supper. Sometimes he did.

I stood there, blind as a bat, with my mind still up on the walk around. There was no answer to my knock. I hadn't expected any. Just from habit, and with my right foot already hanging down for the next step, I reached out to give the door one more tap for luck.

Do you know, sir, my hand didn't fetch up on anything. The door had been there a second before, and now the door wasn't there. My hand just went on going through the dark, on and on, and I didn't seem to have sense or power enough to stop it. There didn't seem any air in the well to breathe, and my ears were drumming to the surf—that's how scared I was. And then my hand touched the flesh of a face, and something in the dark said, "Oh!" no louder than a sigh.

Next thing I knew, sir, I was down in the living-room, warm and yellow-lit, with Fedderson cocking his head at me across the table, where he was at that eternal Jacob's-ladder of his.

"What's the matter, Ray?" said he. "Lord's sake, Ray!"

"Nothing," said I. Then I think I told him I was sick. That night I wrote a letter to A.L. Peters, the grain-dealer in Duxbury, asking for a job—even though it wouldn't go ashore for a couple of weeks, just the writing of it made me feel better.

It's hard to tell you how those two weeks went by. I don't know why, but I felt like hiding in a corner all the time. I had to come to meals, but I didn't look at her, though, not once, unless it was by accident. Fedderson thought I was still ailing and nagged me to death with advice and so on. One thing I took care not to do, I can tell you, and that was to knock on his door till I'd made certain he wasn't below in the living-room—though I was tempted to.

Yes, sir; that's a queer thing, and I wouldn't tell you if I hadn't set out to give you the truth. Night after night, stopping there on the landing in that black pit, the air gone out of my lungs and the surf drumming in my ears and sweat standing cold on my neck—and one hand lifting up in the air—God forgive me, sir! Maybe I did wrong not to look at her more, drooping about her work in her gingham apron, with her hair stringing.

When the Inspector came off with the tender, that time, I told him I was through. That's when he took the dislike to me, I guess, for he looked at me kind of sneering and said, soft as I was, I'd have to put up with it till next relief. And then, said he, there'd be a whole house-cleaning at Seven Brothers, because he'd gotten Fedderson the berth at Kingdom Come. And with that he slapped the old man on the back.

I wish you could have seen Fedderson, sir. He sat down on my cot as if his knees had given 'way. Happy? You'd think he'd be happy, with all his dreams come true. Yes, he was happy, beaming all over—for a minute. Then, sir, he began to shrivel up. It was like seeing a man cut down in his prime before your eyes. He began to wag his head.

"No," said he. "No, no; it's not for such as me. I'm good enough for Seven Brothers, and that's all, Mr. Bayliss. That's all."

And for all the Inspector could say, that's what he stuck to. He'd figured himself a martyr so many years, nursed that injustice like a mother with her first-born, sir; and now in his old age, so to speak, they weren't to rob him of it. Fedderson was going to wear out his life in a second-class light, and folks would talk—that was his idea. I heard him hailing down as the tender was casting off:

"See you to-morrow, Mr. Bayliss. Yep. Coming ashore with the wife for a spree. Anniversary. Yep."

But he didn't sound much like a spree. They *had* robbed him, partly, after all. I wondered what *she* thought about it. I didn't know till night. She didn't show up to supper, which Fedderson and I got ourselves—had a headache, he said. It was my early watch. I went and lit up and came back to read a spell. He was finishing off the Jacob's-ladder, and thoughtful, like a man that's lost a treasure. Once or twice I caught him looking about the room on the sly. It was pathetic, sir.

Going up the second time, I stepped out on the walk-around to have a look at things. She was there on the seaward side, wrapped in that silky thing. A fair sea was running across the ledge and it was coming on a little thick—not too thick. Off to the right the Boston boat was blowing, *whroom-whroom!* Creeping up on us, quarter-speed. There was another fellow behind her, and a fisherman's conch farther offshore.

I don't know why, but I stopped beside her and leaned on the rail. She didn't appear to notice me, one way or another. We stood and we stood, listening to the whistles, and the longer we stood the more it got on my nerves, her not noticing me. I suppose she'd been too much on my mind lately. I began to be put out. I scraped my feet. I coughed. By and by I said out loud:

"Look here, I guess I better get out the fog-horn and give those fellows a toot."

"Why?" said she, without moving her head—calm as that.

"*Why?*" It gave me a turn, sir. For a minute I stared at her. "Why? Because if she don't pick up this light before very many minutes she'll be too close in to wear—tide'll have her on the rocks—that's why!"

I couldn't see her face, but I could see one of her silk shoulders lift a little, like a shrug. And there I kept on staring at her, a dumb one, sure enough. I know what brought me to was hearing the Boston boat's three sharp toots as she picked up the light—mad as anything—and swung her helm a-port. I turned away from her, sweat stringing down my face, and walked around to the door. It was just as well, too, for the feed-pipe was plugged in the lamp and the wicks were popping. She'd have been out in another five minutes, sir.

When I'd finished, I saw that woman standing in the doorway. Her eyes were bright. I had a horror of her, sir, a living horror.

"If only the light had been out," said she, low and sweet.

"God forgive you," said I. "You don't know what you're saying." She went down the stair into the well, winding out of sight, and as long as I could see her, her eyes were watching mine. When I went, myself, after a few minutes, she was waiting for me on that first landing, standing still in the dark. She took hold of my hand, though I tried to get it away.

"Good-by," said she in my ear.

"Good-by?" said I. I didn't understand.

"You heard what he said to-day—about Kingdom Come? Be it so— on his own head. I'll never come back here. Once I set foot ashore—I've got friends in Brightonboro, Ray."

I got away from her and started on down. But I stopped. "Brightonboro?" I whispered back. "Why do you tell *me?*" My throat was raw to the words, like a sore.

"So you'd know," said she.

Well, sir, I saw them off next morning, down that new Jacob's-ladder into the dinghy-boat, her in a dress of blue velvet and him in his best cutaway and derby—rowing away, smaller and smaller, the two of them. And then I went back and sat on my cot, leaving the door open and the ladder still hanging down the wall, along with the boat-falls.

I don't know whether it was relief, or what. I suppose I must have been worked up even more than I'd thought those past weeks, for now it was all over I was like a rag. I got down on my knees, sir, and prayed to God for the salvation of my soul, and when I got up and climbed to the living-room it was half past twelve by the clock. There was rain on the windows and the sea was running blue-black under the sun. I'd sat there all that time not knowing there was a squall.

It was funny; the glass stood high, but those black squalls kept coming and going all afternoon, while I was at work up in the light-room. And I worked hard, to keep myself busy. First thing I knew it was five, and no sign of the boat yet. It began to get dim and kind of purplish-gray over the land. The sun was down. I lit up, made everything snug, and got out the night-glasses to have another look for that boat. He'd said he intended to get back before five. No sign. And then, standing there, it came over me that of course he wouldn't be coming off—he'd be hunting *her*, poor old fool. It looked like I had to stand two men's watches that night.

Never mind. I felt like myself again, even if I hadn't had any dinner or supper. Pride came to me that night on the walk-around, watching the boats go by—little boats, big boats, the Boston boat with all her pearls and her dance-music. They couldn't see me; they didn't know who I was; but to the last of them, they depended on *me*. They say a man must be born again. Well, I was born again. I breathed deep in the wind.

Dawn broke hard and red as a dying coal. I put out the light and started to go below. Born again; yes, sir. I felt so good I whistled in the well, and when I came to the first door on the stair I reached out in the dark to give it a rap for luck. And then, sir, the hair prickled all over my scalp, when I found my hand just going on and on through the air, the same as it had gone once before, and all of a sudden I wanted to yell, because I thought I was going to touch flesh. It's funny what their just forgetting to close their door did to me, isn't it?

Well, I reached for the latch and pulled it to with a bang and ran down as if a ghost was after me. I got up some coffee and bread and bacon for breakfast. I drank the coffee. But somehow I couldn't eat, all along of that open door. The light in the room was blood. I got to thinking. I thought how she'd talked about those men, women, and children on the rocks, and how she'd made to bathe her hands over the rail. I almost jumped out of my chair then; it seemed for a wink she was there beside the stove watching me with that queer half-smile—really, I seemed to see her for a flash across the red table-cloth in the red light of dawn.

"Look here!" said I to myself, sharp enough; and then I gave myself a good laugh and went below. There I took a look out of the door, which was still open, with the ladder hanging down. I made sure to see the poor old fool come pulling around the point before very long now.

My boots were hurting a little, and, taking them off, I lay down on the cot to rest, and somehow I went to sleep. I had horrible dreams. I saw her again standing in that blood-red kitchen, and she seemed to be washing her hands, and the surf on the ledge was whining up the tower, louder and louder all the time, and what it whined was, "Night after night—night after night." What woke me was cold water in my face.

The store-room was in gloom. That scared me at first; I thought night had come, and remembered the light. But then I saw the gloom was of a storm. The floor was shining wet, and the water in my face was spray, flung up through the open door. When I ran to close it, it almost made me dizzy to see the gray-and-white breakers marching past. The land was gone; the sky shut down heavy overhead; there was a piece of wreckage on the back of a swell, and the Jacob's-ladder was carried clean away. How that sea had picked up so quick I can't think. I looked at my watch and it wasn't four in the afternoon yet.

When I closed the door, sir, it was almost dark in the store-room. I'd never been in the Light before in a gale of wind. I wondered why I was shivering so, till I found it was the floor below me shivering, and the walls and stair. Horrible crunchings and grindings ran away up the tower, and now and then there was a great thud somewhere, like a cannon-shot in a cave. I tell you, sir, I was alone, and I was in a mortal fright for a minute or so. And yet I had to get myself together. There was the light up there not tended to, and an early dark coming on and a heavy night and all, and I had to go. And I had to pass that door.

You'll say it's foolish, sir, and maybe it *was* foolish. Maybe it was because I hadn't eaten. But I began thinking of that door up there the minute I set foot on the stair, and all the way up through that howling dark well I dreaded to pass it. I told myself I wouldn't stop. I didn't stop. I felt the landing underfoot and I went on, four steps, five—and then I couldn't. I turned and went back. I put out my hand and it went on into nothing. That door, sir, was open again.

I left it be; I went on up to the light-room and set to work. It was Bedlam there, sir, screeching Bedlam, but I took no notice. I kept my eyes down. I trimmed those seven wicks, sir, as neat as ever they were trimmed; I polished the brass till it shone, and I dusted the lens. It wasn't till that was done that I let myself look back to see who it was standing there, half out of sight in the well. It was her, sir.

"Where'd you come from?" I asked. I remember my voice was sharp.

"Up Jacob's-ladder," said she, and hers was like the syrup of flowers.

I shook my head. I was savage, sir. "The ladder's carried away."

"I cast it off," said she, with a smile.

"Then," said I, "you must have come while I was asleep." Another thought came on me heavy as a ton of lead. "And where's *he*?" said I. "Where's the boat?"

"He's drowned," said she, as easy as that. "And I let the boat go adrift. You wouldn't hear me when I called."

"But look here," said I. "If you came through the store-room, why didn't you wake me up? Tell me that!" It sounds foolish enough, me standing like a lawyer in court, trying to prove she *couldn't* be there.

She didn't answer for a moment. I guess she sighed, though I couldn't hear for the gale, and her eyes grew soft, sir, so soft.

"I couldn't," said she. "You looked so peaceful—dear one."

My cheeks and neck went hot, sir, as if a warm iron was laid on them. I didn't know what to say. I began to stammer, "What do you mean—" but she was going back down the stair, out of sight. My God sir, and I used not to think she was good-looking!

I started to follow her. I wanted to know what she meant. Then I said to myself, "If I don't go—if I wait here—she'll come back." And I went to the weather side and stood looking out of the window. Not that there was much to see. It was growing dark, and the Seven Brothers looked like the mane of a running horse, a great, vast, white horse running into the wind. The air was a-welter with it. I caught one peep of a fisherman, lying down flat trying to weather the ledge, and I said, "God help them all to-night," and then I went hot at the sound of that "God."

I was right about her, though. She was back again. I wanted her to speak first, before I turned, but she wouldn't. I didn't hear her go out; I didn't know what she was up to till I saw her coming outside on the walk-around, drenched wet already. I pounded on the glass for her to come in and not be a fool; if she heard she gave no sign of it.

There she stood, and there I stood watching her. Lord, sir—was it just that I'd never had eyes to see? Or are there women who bloom? Her clothes were shining on her, like a carving, and her hair was let down like a golden curtain tossing and streaming in the gale, and there she stood with her lips half open, drinking, and her eyes half closed, gazing straight away over the Seven Brothers, and her shoulders swaying, as if in tune with the wind and water and all the ruin. And when I looked at her hands over the rail, sir, they were moving in each other as if they bathed, and then I remembered, sir.

A cold horror took me. I knew now why she had come back again. She wasn't a woman—she was a devil. I turned my back on her. I said to myself: "It's time to light up. You've got to light up"—like that, over and over, out loud. My hand was shivering so I could hardly find a match; and when I scratched it, it only flared a second and then went out in the back draught from the open door. She was standing in the doorway, looking at me. It's queer, sir, but I felt like a child caught in mischief.

"I—I—was going to light up," I managed to say, finally.

"Why?" said she. No, I can't say it as she did.

"*Why?*" said I. "*My God!*"

She came nearer, laughing, as if with pity, low, you know. "Your God? And who is your God? What is God? What is anything on a night like this?"

I drew back from her. All I could say anything about was the light.

"Why not the dark?" said she. "Dark is softer than light—tenderer—dearer than light. From the dark up here, away up here in the wind and storm, we can watch the ships go by, you and I. And you love me so. You've loved me so long, Ray."

"I never have!" I struck out at her. "I don't! I don't!"

Her voice was lower than ever, but there was the same laughing pity in it. "Oh yes, you have." And she was near me again.

"I have?" I yelled. "I'll show you! I'll show you if I have!"

I got another match, sir, and scratched it on the brass. I gave it to the first wick, the little wick that's inside all the others. It bloomed like a yellow flower. "I *have?*" I yelled, and gave it to the next.

Then there was a shadow, and I saw she was leaning beside me, her two elbows on the brass, her two arms stretched out above the wicks, her bare forearms and wrists and hands. I gave a gasp:

"Take care! You'll burn them! For God's sake—"

She didn't move or speak. The match burned my fingers and went out, and all I could do was stare at those arms of hers, helpless. I'd never noticed her arms before. They were rounded and graceful and covered with a soft down, like a breath of gold. Then I heard her speaking close to my ear.

"Pretty arms," she said. "Pretty arms!"

I turned. Her eyes were fixed on mine. They seemed heavy, as if with sleep, and yet between their lids they were two wells, deep and deep, and as if they held all the things I'd ever thought or dreamed in them. I looked away from them, at her lips. Her lips were red as poppies, heavy with redness. They moved, and I heard them speaking:

"Poor boy, you love me so, and you want to kiss me—don't you?"

"No," said I. But I couldn't turn around. I looked at her hair. I'd always thought it was stringy hair. Some hair curls naturally with damp, they say, and perhaps that was it, for there were pearls of wet on it, and it was thick and shimmering around her face, making soft shadows by the temples. There was green in it, queer strands of green like braids.

"What is it?" said I.

"Nothing but weed," said she, with that slow, sleepy smile.

Somehow or other I felt calmer than I had any time. "Look here," said I. "I'm going to light this lamp." I took out a match, scratched it, and touched the third wick. The flame ran around, bigger than the other two together. But still her arms hung there. I bit my lip. "By God, I will!" said I to myself, and I lit the fourth.

It was fierce, sir, fierce! And yet those arms never trembled. I had to look around at her. Her eyes were still looking into mine, so deep and deep, and her red lips were still smiling with that queer, sleepy droop; the only thing was that tears were raining down her cheeks—big, glowing round, jewel tears. It wasn't human, sir. It was like a dream.

"Pretty arms," she sighed, and then, as if those words had broken something in her heart, there came a great sob bursting from her lips. To hear it drove me mad. I reached to drag her away, but she was too quick, sir; she cringed from me and slipped out from between my hands. It was like she faded away, sir, and went down in a bundle, nursing her poor arms and mourning over them with those terrible, broken sobs.

The sound of them took the manhood out of me—you'd have been the same, sir. I knelt down beside her on the floor and covered my face.

"Please!" I moaned. "Please! Please!" That's all I could say. I wanted her to forgive me. I reached out a hand, blind, for forgiveness, and I couldn't find her anywhere. I had hurt her so, and she was afraid of me, of *me*, sir, who loved her so deep it drove me crazy.

I could see her down the stair, though it was dim and my eyes were filled with tears. I stumbled after her, crying, "Please! Please!" The little wicks I'd lit were blowing in the wind from the door and smoking the glass beside them black. One went out. I pleaded with them, the same as I would plead with a human being. I said I'd be back in a second. I promised. And I went on down the stair, crying like a baby because I'd hurt her, and she was afraid of me—of *me*, sir.

She had gone into her room. The door was closed against me and I could hear her sobbing beyond it, broken-hearted. My heart was broken too. I beat on the door with my palms. I begged her to forgive me. I told her I loved her. And all the answer was that sobbing in the dark.

And then I lifted the latch and went in, groping, pleading. "Dearest—please! Because I love you!"

I heard her speak down near the floor. There wasn't any anger in her voice; nothing but sadness and despair.

"No," said she. "You don't love me, Ray. You never have."

"I do! I have!"

"No, no," said she, as if she was tired out.

"Where are you?" I was groping for her. I thought, and lit a match. She had got to the door and was standing there as if ready to fly. I went toward her, and she made me stop. She took my breath away. "I hurt your arms," said I, in a dream.

"No," said she, hardly moving her lips. She held them out to the match's light for me to look and there was never a scar on them—not even that soft, golden down was singed, sir. "You can't hurt my body," said she, sad as anything. "Only my heart, Ray; my poor heart."

I tell you again, she took my breath away. I lit another match. "How can you be so beautiful?" I wondered.

She answered in riddles—but oh, the sadness of her, sir. "Because," said she, "I've always so wanted to be."

"How come your eyes so heavy?" said I.

"Because I've seen so many things I never dreamed of," said she.

"How come your hair so thick?"

"It's the seaweed makes it thick," said she smiling queer, queer.

"How come seaweed there?"

"Out of the bottom of the sea."

She talked in riddles, but it was like poetry to hear her, or a song.

"How come your lips so red?" said I.

"Because they've wanted so long to be kissed."

Fire was on me, sir. I reached out to catch her, but she was gone, out of the door and down the stair. I followed, stumbling. I must have tripped on the turn, for I remember going through the air and fetching up with a crash, and I didn't know anything for a spell—how long I can't say. When I came to, she was there, somewhere, bending over me, crooning, "My love—my love—" under her breath like, a song.

But then when I got up, she was not where my arms went; she was down the stair again, just ahead of me. I followed her. I was tottering and dizzy and full of pain. I tried to catch up with her in the dark of the store-room, but she was too quick for me, sir, always a little too quick for me. Oh, she was cruel to me, sir. I kept bumping against things, hurting myself still worse, and it was cold and wet and a horrible noise all the while, sir; and then, sir, I found the door was open, and a sea had parted the hinges.

I don't know how it all went, sir. I'd tell you if I could, but it's all so blurred—sometimes it seems more like a dream. I couldn't find her any more; I couldn't hear her; I went all over, everywhere. Once, I remember, I found myself hanging out of that door between the davits, looking down into those big black seas and crying like a baby. It's all riddles and blur. I can't seem to tell you much, sir. It was all—all—I don't know.

I was talking to somebody else—not her. It was the Inspector. I hardly knew it was the Inspector. His face was as gray as a blanket, and his eyes were bloodshot, and his lips were twisted. His left wrist hung down, awkward. It was broken coming aboard the Light in that sea. Yes, we were in the living-room. Yes, sir, it was daylight—gray daylight. I tell you, sir, the man looked crazy to me. He was waving his good arm toward the weather windows, and what he was saying, over and over, was this:

"*Look what you done, damn you! Look what you done!*"

And what I was saying was this:

"*I've lost her!*"

I didn't pay any attention to him, nor him to me. By and by he did, though. He stopped his talking all of a sudden, and his eyes looked like the devil's eyes. He put them up close to mine. He grabbed my arm with his good hand, and I cried, I was so weak.

"Johnson," said he, "is that it? By the living God—if you got a woman out here, Johnson!"

"No," said I. "I've lost her."

"What do you mean—lost her?"

"It was dark," said I—and it's funny how my head was clearing up— "and the door was open—the store-room door—and I was after her—and I guess she stumbled, maybe—and I lost her."

"Johnson," said he, "what do you mean? You sound crazy—downright crazy. Who?"

"Her," said I. "Fedderson's wife."

"*Who?*"

"Her," said I. And with that he gave my arm another jerk.

"Listen," said he, like a tiger. "Don't try that on me. It won't do any good—that kind of lies—not where *you're* going to. Fedderson and his wife, too—the both of 'em's drowned deader 'n a door-nail."

"I know," said I, nodding my head. I was so calm it made him wild.

"You're crazy! Crazy as a loon, Johnson!" And he was chewing his lip red. "I know, because it was me that found the old man laying on Back Water Flats yesterday morning—*me*! And she'd been with him in the boat, too, because he had a piece of her jacket tore off, tangled in his arm."

"I know," said I, nodding again, like that.

"You know *what*, you *crazy, murdering fool*?" Those were his words to me, sir.

"I know," said I, "what I know."

"And *I* know," said he, "what *I* know."

And there you are, sir. He's Inspector. I'm—nobody.

12

The Furnished Room

By O. Henry

RESTLESS, SHIFTING, FUGACIOUS AS TIME ITSELF IS A CERTAIN VAST BULK of the population of the red brick district of the lower West Side. Homeless, they have a hundred homes. They flit from furnished room to furnished room, transients forever—transients in abode, transients in heart and mind. They sing "Home, Sweet Home" in ragtime; they carry their lares et penates in a bandbox; their vine is entwined about a picture hat; a rubber plant is their fig tree.

Hence the houses of this district, having had a thousand dwellers, should have a thousand tales to tell, mostly dull ones, no doubt; but it would be strange if there could not be found a ghost or two in the wake of all these vagrant guests.

One evening after dark a young man prowled among these crumbling red mansions, ringing their bells. At the twelfth he rested his lean hand baggage upon the step and wiped the dust from his hatband and forehead. The bell sounded faint and far away in some remote, hollow depths.

To the door of this, the twelfth house whose bell he had rung, came a housekeeper who made him think of an unwholesome, surfeited worm that had eaten its nut to a hollow shell and now sought to fill the vacancy with edible lodgers.

He asked if there was a room to let.

"Come in," said the housekeeper. Her voice came from her throat; her throat seemed lined with fur. "I have the third-floor-back, vacant since a week back. Should you wish to look at it?"

The young man followed her up the stairs. A faint light from no particular source mitigated the shadows of the halls. They trod noiselessly upon a stair carpet that its own loom would have forsworn. It seemed to have become vegetable; to have degenerated in that rank, sunless air to lush lichen or spreading moss that grew in patches to the staircase and was viscid under the foot like organic matter. At each turn of the stairs were vacant niches in the wall. Perhaps plants had once been set within them. If so, they had died in that foul and tainted air. It may be that statues of the saints had stood there, but it was not difficult to conceive that imps and devils had dragged them forth in the darkness and down to the unholy depths of some furnished pit below.

"This is the room," said the housekeeper, from her furry throat. "It's a nice room. It ain't often vacant. I had some most elegant people in it last summer—no trouble at all, and paid in advance to the minute. The water's at the end of the hall. Sprowls and Mooney kept it three months. They done a vaudeville sketch. Miss B'retta Sprowls—you may have heard of her—oh, that was just the stage names—right there over the dresser is where the marriage certificate hung, framed. The gas is here, and you see there is plenty of closet room. It's a room everybody likes. It never stays idle long."

"Do you have many theatrical people rooming here?" asked the young man.

"They comes and goes. A good proportion of my lodgers is connected with the theaters. Yes, sir, this is the theatrical district. Actor people never stays long anywhere. I get my share. Yes, they comes and they goes."

He engaged the room, paying for a week in advance. He was tired, he said, and would take possession at once. He counted out the money. The room had been made ready, she said, even to towels and water. As the housekeeper moved away he put, for the thousandth time, the question that he carried at the end of his tongue.

"A young girl—Miss Vashner—Miss Eloise Vashner—do you remember such a one among your lodgers? She would be singing on the stage, most likely. A fair girl, of medium height and slender, with reddish gold hair and a dark mole near her left eyebrow."

"No, I don't remember the name. Them stage people has names they change as often as their rooms. No, I don't call that one to mind."

No. Always no. Five months of ceaseless interrogation and the inevitable negative. So much time spent by day in questioning managers, agents, schools and choruses; by night among the audiences of theaters from all-star casts down to music halls so low that he dreaded to find what he most hoped for. He who had loved her best had tried to find her. He was sure that since her disappearance from home this great, water-girt city held her somewhere, but it was like a monstrous quicksand, shifting its particles constantly, with no foundation, its upper granules of today buried tomorrow in ooze and slime.

The furnished room received its latest guest with a first glow of pseudo hospitality, a hectic, haggard, perfunctory welcome like the specious smile of a demirep. The sophistical comfort came in reflected gleams from the decayed furniture, the ragged brocade upholstery of a couch and two chairs, a foot-wide cheap pier glass between the two windows, from one or two gilt picture frames and a brass bedstead in a corner.

The guest reclined, inert, upon a chair, while the room, confused in speech as though it were an apartment in Babel, tried to discourse to him of its divers tenantry.

A polychromatic rug like some brilliant-flowered, rectangular, tropical islet lay surrounded by a billowy sea of soiled matting. Upon the gay-papered wall were those pictures that pursue the homeless one from house to house—The Huguenot Lovers, The First Quarrel, The Wedding Breakfast, Psyche at the Fountain. The mantel's chastely severe outline was ingloriously veiled behind some pert drapery drawn rakishly askew like the sashes of the Amazonian ballet. Upon it was some desolate flotsam cast aside by the room's marooned when a lucky sail had borne them to a fresh port— a trifling vase or two, pictures of actresses, a medicine bottle, some stray cards out of a deck. One by one, as the characters of a cryptograph became explicit, the little signs left by the furnished room's procession of guests developed a significance. The threadbare space in the rug in front of the dresser told that lovely women had marched in the throng. The tiny fingerprints on the wall spoke of little prisoners trying to feel their way to sun and air. A splattered stain, raying like the shadow of a bursting bomb, witnessed where a hurled glass or bottle had splintered with its contents against the wall. Across the pier glass had been scrawled with a diamond in staggering letters the name Marie. It seemed that the succession of dwellers in the furnished room had turned in fury—perhaps tempted beyond forbearance by its garish coldness—and wreaked upon it their passions. The furniture was chipped and bruised; the couch, distorted by bursting springs, seemed a horrible monster that had been slain during the stress of some grotesque convulsion. Some more potent upheaval had cloven a great slice from the marble mantel. Each plank in the floor owned its particular cant and shriek as from a separate and individual agony. It seemed incredible that all this malice and injury had been wrought upon the room by those who had called it for a time their home; and yet it may have been the cheated home instinct surviving blindly, the resentful rage at false household gods that had kindled their wrath. A hut that is our own we can sweep and adorn and cherish.

The young tenant in the chair allowed these thoughts to file, softshod, through his mind, while there drifted into the room furnished sounds and furnished scents. He heard in one room a tittering and incontinent, slack laughter; in others the monologue of a scold, the rattling of dice, a lullaby, and one crying dully; above him a banjo tinkled with spirit. Doors banged somewhere; the elevated trains roared intermittently; a cat yowled miserably upon a back fence. And he breathed the breath of the house—a dank savor rather than a smell—a cold, musty effluvium as from underground vaults mingled with the reeking exhalations of linoleum and mildewed and rotten woodwork.

Then suddenly, as he rested there, the room was filled with the strong, sweet odor of mignonette. It came as upon a single buffet of wind with such sureness and fragrance and emphasis that it almost seemed a living visitant. And the man cried aloud, "What, dear?" as if he had been called, and sprang up and faced about. The rich odor clung to him and wrapped him around. He reached out his arms for it, all his senses for the time confused and commingled. How could one be peremptorily called by an odor? Surely it must have been a sound. But was it not the sound that had touched, that had caressed him?

"She has been in this room," he cried, and he sprang to wrest from it a token, for he knew he would recognize the smallest thing that had belonged to her or that she had touched. This enveloping scent of mignonette, the odor that she had loved and made her own—whence came it?

The room had been but carelessly set in order. Scattered upon the flimsy dresser scarf were half a dozen hairpins—those discreet, indistinguishable friends of womankind, feminine of gender, infinite of mood and uncommunicative of tense. These he ignored, conscious of their triumphant lack of identity. Ransacking the drawers of the dresser he came upon a discarded, tiny, ragged handkerchief. He pressed it to his face. It was racy and insolent with heliotrope; he hurled it to the floor. In another drawer he found odd buttons, a theater program, a pawnbroker's card, two lost marshmallows, a book on the divination of dreams. In the last was a woman's black satin hair bow, which halted him, poised between ice and fire. But the black satin hair bow also is femininity's demure, impersonal common ornament and tells no tales.

And then he traversed the room like a hound on the scent, skimming the walls, considering the corners of the bulging matting on his hands and knees, rummaging mantel and tables, the curtains and hangings, the drunken cabinet in the corner, for a visible sign, unable to perceive that she was there beside, around, against, within, above him, clinging to him, wooing him, calling him so poignantly through the finer senses that even his grosser ones became cognizant of the call. Once again he answered loudly, "Yes, dear!" and turned, wild-eyed, to gaze on vacancy, for he could not yet discern form and color and love and outstretched arms in the odor of mignonette. Oh, God! Whence that odor, and since when have odors had a voice to call! Thus he groped.

He burrowed in crevices and corners, and found corks and cigarettes. These he passed in passive contempt. But once he found in a fold of the matting a half-smoked cigar, and this he ground beneath his heel with a green and trenchant oath. He sifted the room, from end to end. He found dreary and ignoble small records of many a peripatetic tenant; but of her whom he sought, and who may have lodged there, and whose spirit seemed to hover there, he found no trace.

And then he thought of the housekeeper.

He ran from the haunted room downstairs and to a door that showed a crack of light. She came out to his knock. He smothered his excitement as best he could.

"Will you tell me, madam," he besought her, "who occupied the room I have before I came?"

"Yes, sir. I can tell you again. Twas Sprowls and Mooney, as I said. Miss B'retta Sprowls it was in the theaters, but Missis Mooney she was. My house is well known for respectability. The marriage certificate hung, framed, on a nail over—"

"What kind of a lady was Miss Sprowls—in looks, I mean?"

"Why, black-haired, sir, short, and stout, with a comical face. They left a week ago Tuesday."

"And before they occupied it?"

"Why, there was a single gentleman connected with the draying business. He left owing me a week. Before him was Missis Crowder and her two children, that stayed four months; and back of them was old Mr. Doyle, whose sons paid for him. He kept the room six months. That goes back a year, sir, and further I do not remember."

He thanked her and crept back to his room. The room was dead. The essence that had vivified it was gone. The perfume of mignonette had departed. In its place was the old, stale odor of moldy house furniture, of atmosphere in storage.

The ebbing of his hope drained his faith. He sat staring at the yellow, singing gaslight. Soon he walked to the bed and began to tear the sheets into strips. With the blade of his knife he drove them tightly into every crevice around windows and door. When all was snug and taut he turned out the light, turned the gas full on again and laid himself gratefully upon the bed.

It was Mrs. McCool's night to go with the can for beer. So she fetched it and sat with Mrs. Purdy in one of those subterranean retreats where housekeepers forgather and the worm dieth seldom.

"I rented out my third-floor-back this evening," said Mrs. Purdy, across a fine circle of foam. "A young man took it. He went up to bed two hours ago."

"Now, did ye, Mrs. Purdy, ma'am?" said Mrs. McCool, with intense admiration. "You do be a wonder for rentin' rooms of that kind. And did ye tell him, then?" she concluded in a husky whisper laden with mystery.

"Rooms," said Mrs. Purdy, in her furriest tones, "are furnished for to rent. I did not tell him, Mrs. McCool."

"'Tis right ye are, ma'am; 'tis by renting rooms we kape alive. Ye have the rale sense for business, ma'am. There be many people will rayjict the rentin' of a room if they be tould a suicide has been after dyin' in the bed of it."

"As you say, we has our living to be making," remarked Mrs. Purdy.

"Yis, ma'am; 'tis true. 'Tis just one wake ago this day I helped ye lay out the third-floor-back. A pretty slip of a colleen she was to be killin' herself wid the gas—a swate little face she had, Mrs. Purdy, ma'am."

"She'd a-been called handsome, as you say," said Mrs. Purdy, assenting but critical, "but for that mole she had a-growin' by her left eyebrow. Do fill up your glass again, Mrs. McCool."

13

The Cross-Roads

By Amy Lowell

A BULLET THROUGH HIS HEART AT DAWN. ON THE TABLE A LETTER signed with a woman's name. A wind that goes howling round the house, and weeping as in shame. Cold November dawn peeping through the windows, cold dawn creeping over the floor, creeping up his cold legs, creeping over his cold body, creeping across his cold face. A glaze of thin yellow sunlight on the staring eyes. Wind howling through bent branches. A wind which never dies down. Howling, wailing. The gazing eyes glitter in the sunlight. The lids are frozen open and the eyes glitter.

The thudding of a pick on hard earth. A spade grinding and crunching. Overhead, branches writhing, winding, interlacing, unwinding, scattering; tortured twinings, tossings, creakings. Wind flinging branches apart, drawing them together, whispering and whining among them. A waning, lobsided moon cutting through black clouds. A stream of pebbles and earth and the empty spade gleams clear in the moonlight, then is rammed again into the black earth. Tramping of feet. Men and horses. Squeaking of wheels.

"Whoa! Ready, Jim?"

"All ready."

Something falls, settles, is still. Suicides have no coffin.

"Give us the stake, Jim. Now."

Pound! Pound!

"He'll never walk. Nailed to the ground."

An ash stick pierces his heart, if it buds the roots will hold him. He is a part of the earth now, clay to clay. Overhead the branches sway, and writhe, and twist in the wind. He'll never walk with a bullet in his heart, and an ash stick nailing him to the cold, black ground.

Six months he lay still. Six months. And the water welled up in his body, and soft blue spots chequered it. He lay still, for the ash stick held him in place. Six months! Then her face came out of a mist of green. Pink and white and frail like Dresden china, lilies-of-the-valley at her breast, puce-coloured silk sheening about her. Under the young green leaves, the horse at a foot-pace, the high yellow wheels of the chaise scarcely turning, her face, rippling like grain a-blowing, under her puce-coloured bonnet; and burning beside her, flaming within his correct blue coat and brass buttons, is someone. What has dimmed the sun? The horse steps on a rolling stone; a wind in the branches makes a moan. The little leaves tremble and shake, turn and quake, over and over, tearing their stems. There is a shower of young leaves, and a sudden-sprung gale wails in the trees.

The yellow-wheeled chaise is rocking—rocking, and all the branches are knocking—knocking. The sun in the sky is a flat, red plate, the branches creak and grate. She screams and cowers, for the green foliage is a lowering wave surging to smother her. But she sees nothing. The stake holds firm. The body writhes, the body squirms. The blue spots widen, the flesh tears, but the stake wears well in the deep, black ground. It holds the body in the still, black ground.

Two years! The body has been in the ground two years. It is worn away; it is clay to clay. Where the heart moulders, a greenish dust, the stake is thrust. Late August it is, and night; a night flauntingly jewelled with stars, a night of shooting stars and loud insect noises. Down the road to Tilbury, silence—and the slow flapping of large leaves. Down the road to Sutton, silence—and the darkness of heavy-foliaged trees. Down the road to Wayfleet, silence—and the whirring scrape of insects in the branches. Down the road to Edgarstown, silence—and stars like stepping-stones in a pathway overhead. It is very quiet at the cross-roads, and the sign-board points the way down the four roads, endlessly points the way where nobody wishes to go.

A horse is galloping, galloping up from Sutton. Shaking the wide, still leaves as he goes under them. Striking sparks with his iron shoes; silencing the katydids. Dr. Morgan riding to a child-birth over Tilbury way; riding to deliver a woman of her first-born son. One o'clock from Wayfleet bell tower, what a shower of shooting stars! And a breeze all of a sudden, jarring the big leaves and making them jerk up and down. Dr. Morgan's hat is blown from his head, the horse swerves, and curves away from the sign-post. An oath—spurs—a blurring of grey mist. A quick left twist, and the gelding is snorting and racing down the Tilbury road with the wind dropping away behind him.

The stake has wrenched, the stake has started, the body, flesh from flesh, has parted. But the bones hold tight, socket and ball, and clamping them down in the hard, black ground is the stake, wedged through ribs and spine. The bones may twist, and heave, and twine, but the stake holds them still in line. The breeze goes down, and the round stars shine, for the stake holds the fleshless bones in line.

Twenty years now! Twenty long years! The body has powdered itself away; it is clay to clay. It is brown earth mingled with brown earth. Only flaky bones remain, lain together so long they fit, although not one bone is knit to another. The stake is there too, rotted through, but upright still, and still piercing down between ribs and spine in a straight line.

Yellow stillness is on the cross-roads, yellow stillness is on the trees. The leaves hang drooping, wan. The four roads point four yellow ways, saffron and gamboge ribbons to the gaze. A little swirl of dust blows up Tilbury road, the wind which fans it has not strength to do more; it ceases, and the dust settles down. A little whirl of wind comes up Tilbury road. It brings a sound of wheels and feet. The wind reels a moment and faints to nothing under the sign-post. Wind again, wheels and feet louder. Wind again—again—again. A drop of rain, flat into the dust. Drop!—Drop! Thick heavy raindrops, and a shricking wind bending the great trees and wrenching off their leaves.

Under the black sky, bowed and dripping with rain, up Tilbury road, comes the procession. A funeral procession, bound for the graveyard at Wayfleet. Feet and wheels—feet and wheels. And among them one who is carried.

The bones in the deep, still earth shiver and pull. There is a quiver through the rotted stake. Then stake and bones fall together in a little puffing of dust.

Like meshes of linked steel the rain shuts down behind the procession, now well along the Wayfleet road.

He wavers like smoke in the buffeting wind. His fingers blow out like smoke, his head ripples in the gale. Under the sign-post, in the pouring rain, he stands, and watches another quavering figure drifting down the Wayfleet road. Then swiftly he streams after it. It flickers among the trees. He licks out and winds about them. Over, under, blown, contorted. Spindrift after spindrift; smoke following smoke. There is a wailing through the trees, a wailing of fear, and after it laughter—laughter—laughter, skirling up to the black sky. Lightning jags over the funeral procession. A heavy clap of thunder. Then darkness and rain, and the sound of feet and wheels.

14

Jean-ah Poquelin

By George Washington Cable

IN THE FIRST DECADE OF THE PRESENT CENTURY, WHEN THE NEWLY
established American Government was the most hateful thing in Louisiana—when the Creoles were still kicking at such vile innovations as
the trial by jury, American dances, anti-smuggling laws, and the printing
of the Governor's proclamation in English—when the Anglo-American
flood that was presently to burst in a crevasse of immigration upon the
delta had thus far been felt only as slippery seepage which made the Creole tremble for his footing—there stood, a short distance above what is
now Canal Street, and considerably back from the line of villas which
fringed the river-bank on Tchoupitoulas Road, an old colonial planta-
tion-house half in ruin.

It stood aloof from civilization, the tracts that had once been its
indigo fields given over to their first noxious wildness, and grown up into
one of the horridest marshes within a circuit of fifty miles.

The house was of heavy cypress, lifted up on pillars, grim, solid, and
spiritless, its massive build a strong reminder of days still earlier, when
every man had been his own peace officer and the insurrection of the blacks
a daily contingency. Its dark, weatherbeaten roof and sides were hoisted
up above the jungly plain in a distracted way, like a gigantic ammunition-
wagon stuck in the mud and abandoned by some retreating army. Around
it was a dense growth of low water willows, with half a hundred sorts of
thorny or fetid bushes, savage strangers alike to the "language of flowers" and to the botanist's Greek. They were hung with countless strands
of discolored and prickly smilax, and the impassable mud below bristled

with *chevaux de frise* of the dwarf palmetto. Two lone forest-trees, dead cypresses, stood in the centre of the marsh, dotted with roosting vultures. The shallow strips of water were hid by myriads of aquatic plants, under whose coarse and spiritless flowers, could one have seen it, was a harbor of reptiles, great and small, to make one shudder to the end of his days.

The house was on a slightly raised spot, the levee of a draining canal. The waters of this canal did not run; they crawled, and were full of big, ravening fish and alligators, that held it against all comers.

Such was the home of old Jean Marie Poquelin, once an opulent indigo planter, standing high in the esteem of his small, proud circle of exclusively male acquaintances in the old city; now a hermit, alike shunned by and shunning all who had ever known him. "The last of his line," said the gossips. His father lies under the floor of the St. Louis Cathedral, with the wife of his youth on one side, and the wife of his old age on the other. Old Jean visits the spot daily. His half-brother—alas! there was a mystery; no one knew what had become of the gentle, young half brother, more than thirty years his junior, whom once he seemed so fondly to love, but who, seven years ago, had disappeared suddenly, once for all, and left no clew of his fate.

They had seemed to live so happily in each other's love. No father, mother, wife to either, no kindred upon earth. The elder a bold, frank, impetuous, chivalric adventurer; the younger a gentle, studious, book-loving recluse; they lived upon the ancestral estate like mated birds, one always on the wing, the other always in the nest.

There was no trait in Jean Marie Poquelin, said the old gossips, for which he was so well known among his few friends as his apparent fondness for his "little brother."

"Jacques said this," and "Jacques said that;" he "would leave this or that, or any thing to Jacques," for "Jacques was a scholar," and "Jacques was good," or "wise," or "just," or "far-sighted," as the nature of the case required; and "he should ask Jacques as soon as he got home," since Jacques was never elsewhere to be seen.

It was between the roving character of the one brother, and the book-ishness of the other, that the estate fell into decay. Jean Marie, generous gentleman, gambled the slaves away one by one, until none was left, man or woman, but one old African mute.

The indigo-fields and vats of Louisiana had been generally abandoned as unremunerative. Certain enterprising men had substituted the culture of sugar; but while the recluse was too apathetic to take so active a course, the other saw larger, and, at times, equally respectable profits, first in smuggling, and later in the African slave-trade. What harm could he see in it? The whole people said it was vitally necessary, and to minister to a vital public necessity,—good enough, certainly, and so he laid up many a doubloon, that made him none the worse in the public regard.

One day old Jean Marie was about to start upon a voyage that was to be longer, much longer, than any that he had yet made. Jacques had begged him hard for many days not to go, but he laughed him off, and finally said, kissing him:

"*Adieu, 'tit frère.*"

"No," said Jacques, "I shall go with you."

They left the old hulk of a house in the sole care of the African mute, and went away to the Guinea coast together.

Two years after, old Poquelin came home without his vessel. He must have arrived at his house by night. No one saw him come. No one saw "his little brother;" rumor whispered that he, too, had returned, but he had never been seen again.

A dark suspicion fell upon the old slave-trader. No matter that the few kept the many reminded of the tenderness that had ever marked his bearing to the missing man. The many shook their heads. "You know he has a quick and fearful temper;" and "why does he cover his loss with mystery?" "Grief would out with the truth." "But," said the charitable few, "look in his face; see that expression of true humanity." The many did look in his face, and, as he looked in theirs, he read the silent question: "Where is thy brother Abel?" The few were silenced, his former friends died off, and the name of Jean Marie Poquelin became a symbol of witchery, devilish crime, and hideous nursery fictions.

The man and his house were alike shunned. The snipe and duck hunters forsook the marsh, and the wood-cutters abandoned the canal.

Sometimes the hardier boys who ventured out there snake-shooting heard a slow thumping of oar-locks on the canal. They would look at each other for a moment half in consternation, half in glee, then rush from their sport in wanton haste to assail with their gibes the unoffending, withered old man who, in rusty attire, sat in the stern of a skiff, rowed homeward by his white-headed African mute.

"O Jean-ah Poquelin! O Jean-ah! Jean-ah Poquelin!"

It was not necessary to utter more than that. No hint of wickedness, deformity, or any physical or moral demerit; merely the name and tone of mockery: "Oh, Jean-ah Poquelin!" and while they tumbled one over another in their needless haste to fly, he would rise carefully from his seat, while the aged mute, with downcast face, went on rowing, and rolling up his brown fist and extending it toward the urchins, would pour forth such an unholy broadside of French imprecation and invective as would all but craze them with delight.

Among both blacks and whites the house was the object of a thousand superstitions. Every midnight they affirmed, the *feu follet* came out of the marsh and ran in and out of the rooms, flashing from window to window. The story of some lads, whose words in ordinary statements were worthless, was generally credited, that the night they camped in the woods, rather than pass the place after dark, they saw, about sunset, every window blood-red, and on each of the four chimneys an owl sitting, which turned his head three times round, and moaned and laughed with a human voice. There was a bottomless well, everybody professed to know, beneath the sill of the big front door under the rotten veranda; whoever set his foot upon that threshold disappeared forever in the depth below.

What wonder the marsh grew as wild as Africa! Take all the Faubourg Ste. Marie, and half the ancient city, you would not find one graceless dare-devil reckless enough to pass within a hundred yards of the house after nightfall.

The alien races pouring into old New Orleans began to find the few streets named for the Bourbon princes too strait for them. The wheel of fortune, beginning to whirl, threw them off beyond the ancient corporation lines, and sowed civilization and even trade upon the lands of the Graviers and Girods. Fields became roads, roads streets. Everywhere the leveller was peering through his glass, rodsmen were whacking their way through willow-brakes and rose-hedges, and the sweating Irishmen tossed the blue clay up with their long-handled shovels.

"Ha! that is all very well," quoth the Jean-Baptistes, fueling the reproach of an enterprise that asked neither co-operation nor advice of them, "but wait till they come yonder to Jean Poquelin's marsh; ha! ha! ha!" The supposed predicament so delighted them, that they put on a mock terror and whirled about in an assumed stampede, then caught their clasped hands between their knees in excess of mirth, and laughed till the tears ran; for whether the street-makers mired in the marsh, or contrived to cut through old "Jean-ah's" property, either event would be joyful. Meantime a line of tiny rods, with bits of white paper in their split tops, gradually extended its way straight through the haunted ground, and across the canal diagonally.

"We shall fill that ditch," said the men in mud-boots, and brushed close along the chained and padlocked gate of the haunted mansion. Ah, Jean-ah Poquelin, those were not Creole boys, to be stampeded with a little hard swearing.

He went to the Governor. That official scanned the odd figure with no slight interest. Jean Poquelin was of short, broad frame, with a bronzed leonine face. His brow was ample and deeply furrowed. His eye, large and black, was bold and open like that of a war-horse, and his jaws shut together with the firmness of iron. He was dressed in a suit of Attakapas cottonade, and his shirt unbuttoned and thrown back from the throat and bosom, sailor-wise, showed a herculean breast; hard and grizzled. There was no fierceness or defiance in his look, no harsh ungentleness, no symptom of his unlawful life or violent temper; but rather a peaceful and peaceable fearlessness. Across the whole face, not marked in one or another feature, but as it were laid softly upon the countenance like an almost imperceptible veil, was the imprint of some great grief. A careless eye might easily overlook it, but, once seen, there it hung—faint, but unmistakable.

The Governor bowed.

"*Parlez-vous français?*" asked the figure.

"I would rather talk English, if you can do so," said the Governor.

"My name, Jean Poquelin."

"How can I serve you, Mr. Poquelin?"

"My 'ouse is yond'; *dans le marais là-bas.*"

The Governor bowed.

"Dat *marais* billong to me."

"Yes, sir."

"To me; Jean Poquelin; I hown 'im meself."

"Well, sir?"

"He don't billong to you; I get him from me father."

"That is perfectly true, Mr. Poquelin, as far as I am aware."

"You want to make strit pass yond'?"

"I do not know, sir; it is quite probable; but the city will indemnify you for any loss you may suffer—you will get paid, you understand."

"Strit can't pass dare."

"You will have to see the municipal authorities about that, Mr. Poquelin."

A bitter smile came upon the old man's face:

"*Pardon, Monsieur,* you is not *le Gouverneur?*"

"Yes."

"*Mais,* yes. You har *le Gouverneur*—yes. Veh-well. I come to you. I tell you, strit can't pass at me 'ouse."

"But you will have to see—"

"I come to you. You is *le Gouverneur.* I know not the new laws. I ham a Fr-r-rench-a-man! Fr-rench-a-man have something *aller au contraire*— he come at his *Gouverneur.* I come at you. If me not had been bought from me king like *bossals* in the hold time, ze king gof—France would-a-show *Monsieur le Gouverneur* to take care his men to make strit in right places. *Mais,* I know; we billong to *Monsieur le Président.* I want you do somesin for me, eh?"

"What is it?" asked the patient Governor.

"I want you tell *Monsieur le Président,* strit—can't—pass —at—me—'ouse."

"Have a chair, Mr. Poquelin;" but the old man did not stir. The Governor took a quill and wrote a line to a city official, introducing Mr.

Poquelin, and asking for him every possible courtesy. He handed it to him, instructing him where to present it.

"Mr. Poquelin," he said with a conciliatory smile, "tell me, is it your house that our Creole citizens tell such odd stories about?"

The old man glared sternly upon the speaker, and with immovable features said:

"You don't see me trade some Guinea nigga'?"

"Oh, no."

"You don't see me make some smuggling."

"No, sir; not at all."

"But, I am Jean Marie Poquelin. I mine me hown bizniss. Dat all right? Adieu."

He put his hat on and withdrew. By and by he stood, letter in hand, before the person to whom it was addressed. This person employed an interpreter.

"He says," said the interpreter to the officer, "he come to make you the fair warning how you muz not make the street pas' at his 'ouse."

The officer remarked that "such impudence was refreshing;" but the experienced interpreter translated freely.

"He says: 'Why you don't want?'" said the interpreter.

The old slave-trader answered at some length.

"He says," said the interpreter, again turning to the officer, "the marass is a too unhealth' for peopl' to live."

"But we expect to drain his old marsh; it's not going to be a marsh."

"*Il dit—*" The interpreter explained in French.

The old man answered tersely.

"He says the canal is a private," said the interpreter.

"Oh! *that* old ditch; that's to be filled up. Tell the old man we're going to fix him up nicely."

Translation being duly made, the man in power was amused to see a thunder-cloud gathering on the old man's face.

"Tell him," he added, "by the time we finish, there'll not be a ghost left in his shanty."

The interpreter began to translate, but—

"*J' comprends, J' comprends,*" said the old man, with an impatient gesture, and burst forth, pouring curses upon the United States, the President, the Territory of Orleans, Congress, the Governor and all his subordinates, striding out of the apartment as he cursed, while the object of his maledictions roared with merriment and rammed the floor with his foot.

"Why, it will make his old place worth ten dollars to one," said the official to the interpreter.

"'Tis not for de worse of de property," said the interpreter.

"I should guess not," said the other, whittling his chair,—"seems to me as if some of these old Creoles would liever live in a crawfish hole than to have a neighbor."

"You know what make old Jean Poquelin make like that? I will tell you. You know"—

The interpreter was rolling a cigarette, and paused to light his tinder; then, as the smoke poured in a thick double stream from his nostrils, he said, in a solemn whisper:

"He is a witch."

"Ho, ho, ho!" laughed the other.

"You don't believe it? What you want to bet?" cried the interpreter, jerking himself half up and thrusting out one arm while he bared it of its coat-sleeve with the hand of the other. "What you want to bet?"

"How do you know?" asked the official.

"Dass what I goin' to tell you. You know, one evening I was shooting some *grosbec*. I killed three, but I had trouble to fine them, it was becoming so dark. When I have them I start' to come home; then I got to pas' at Jean Poquelin's house."

"Ho, ho, ho!" laughed the other, throwing his leg over the arm of his chair.

"Wait," said the interpreter. "I come along slow, not making some noises; still, still—"

"And scared," said the smiling one.

"*Mais*, wait. I get all pas' the 'ouse. 'Ah!' I say; 'all right!' Then I see two thing' before! Hah! I get as cold and humide, and shake like a leaf. You think it was nothing? There I see, so plain as can be (though it was making nearly dark), I see Jean—Marie—Po-que-lin walkin' right in front, and right there beside of him was something like a man—but not a man—white like paint!—I dropp' on the grass from scared—they pass'; so sure as I live 'twas the ghos' of Jacques Poquelin, his brother!"

"Pooh!" said the listener.

"I'll put my han' in the fire," said the interpreter.

"But did you never think," asked the other, "that that might be Jack Poquelin, as you call him, alive and well, and for some cause hid away by his brother?"

"But there har' no cause!" said the other, and the entrance of third parties changed the subject.

Some months passed and the street was opened. A canal was first dug through the marsh, the small one which passed so close to Jean Poquelin's house was filled, and the street, or rather a sunny road, just touched a corner of the old mansion's dooryard. The morass ran dry. Its venomous denizens slipped away through the bulrushes; the cattle roaming freely upon its hardened surface trampled the superabundant undergrowth. The bellowing frogs croaked to westward. Lilies and the flower-de-luce sprang up in the place of reeds; smilax and poison-oak gave way to the purple-plumed iron-weed and pink spiderwort; the bindweeds ran every-where blooming as they ran, and on one of the dead cypresses a giant creeper hung its green burden of foliage and lifted its scarlet trumpets. Sparrows and red-birds flitted through the bushes, and dewberries grew ripe beneath. Over all these came a sweet, dry smell of salubrity which the place had not known since the sediments of the Mississippi first lifted it from the sea.

But its owner did not build. Over the willow-brakes, and down the vista of the open street, bright new houses, some singly, some by ranks, were prying in upon the old man's privacy. They even settled down toward his southern side. First a wood-cutter's hut or two, then a market gar-dener's shanty, then a painted cottage, and all at once the faubourg had flanked and half surrounded him and his dried-up marsh.

Ah! then the common people began to hate him. "The old tyrant!"

"You don't mean an old *tyrant*?"

"Well, then, why don't he build when the public need demands it? What does he live in that unneighborly way for?"

"The old pirate!"

"The old kidnapper!" How easily even the most ultra Louisianians put on the imported virtues of the North when they could be brought to bear against the hermit. "There he goes, with the boys after him! Ah! ha! ha! Jean-ah Poquelin! Ah! Jean-ah! Aha! aha! Jean-ah Marie! Jean-ah Poquelin! The old villain!" How merrily the swarming Américains echo the spirit of persecution! "The old fraud," they say—"pretends to live in a haunted house, does he? We'll tar and feather him some day. Guess we can fix him."

He cannot be rowed home along the old canal now; he walks. He has broken sadly of late, and the street urchins are ever at his heels. It is like the days when they cried: "Go up, thou bald-head," and the old man now and then turns and delivers ineffectual curses.

To the Creoles—to the incoming lower class of superstitious Germans, Irish, Sicilians, and others—he became an omen and embodiment of public and private ill-fortune. Upon him all the vagaries of their superstitions gathered and grew. If a house caught fire, it was imputed to his machinations. Did a woman go off in a fit, he had bewitched her. Did a child stray off for an hour, the mother shivered with the apprehension that Jean Poquelin had offered him to strange gods. The house was the subject of every bad boy's invention who loved to contrive ghostly lies. "As long as that house stands we shall have bad luck. Do you not see our peas and beans dying, our cabbages and lettuce going to seed and our gardens turning to dust, while every day you can see it raining in the woods? The rain will never pass old Poquelin's house. He keeps a fetich. He has conjured the whole Faubourg St. Marie. And why, the old wretch? Simply because our playful and innocent children call after him as he passes."

A "Building and Improvement Company," which had not yet got its charter, "but was going to," and which had not, indeed, any tangible capital yet, but "was going to have some," joined the "Jean-ah Poquelin" war. The haunted property would be such a capital site for a market-house! They sent a deputation to the old mansion to ask its occupant to sell. The deputation never got beyond the chained gate and a very barren interview with the African mute. The President of the Board was then empowered (for he had studied French in Pennsylvania and was considered qualified) to call and persuade M. Poquelin to subscribe to the company's stock; but—

"Fact is, gentlemen," he said at the next meeting, "it would take us at least twelve months to make Mr. Pokaleen understand the rather original features of our system, and he wouldn't subscribe when we'd done; besides, the only way to see him is to stop him on the street."

There was a great laugh from the Board; they couldn't help it. "Better meet a bear robbed of her whelps," said one.

"You're mistaken as to that," said the President. "I did meet him, and stopped him, and found him quite polite. But I could get no satisfaction from him; the fellow wouldn't talk in French, and when I spoke in English he hoisted his old shoulders up, and gave the same answer to every thing I said."

"And that was—?" asked one or two, impatient of the pause.

"That it 'don't worse w'ile?'"

One of the Board said: "Mr. President, this market-house project, as I take it, is not altogether a selfish one; the community is to be benefited by it. We may feel that we are working in the public interest [the Board smiled knowingly], if we employ all possible means to oust this old nuisance from among us. You may know that at the time the street was cut through, this old Poquelann did all he could to prevent it. It was owing to a certain connection which I had with that affair that I heard a ghost story [smiles, followed by a sudden dignified check]—ghost story, which, of course, I am not going to relate; but I *may* say that my profound conviction, arising from a prolonged study of that story, is, that this old villain, John Poquelann, has his brother locked up in that old house. Now, if this is so, and we can fix it on him, I merely *suggest* that we can make the matter highly useful. I don't know," he added, beginning to sit down, "but that it is an action we owe to the community—hem!"

"How do you propose to handle the subject?" asked the President.

"I was thinking," said the speaker, "that, as a Board of Directors, it would be unadvisable for us to authorize any action involving trespass; but if you, for instance, Mr. President, should, as it were, for mere curiosity, *request* some one, as, for instance, our excellent Secretary, simply as a personal favor, to look into the matter—this is merely a suggestion."

The Secretary smiled sufficiently to be understood that, while he certainly did not consider such preposterous service a part of his duties as secretary, he might, notwithstanding, accede to the President's request; and the Board adjourned.

Little White, as the Secretary was called, was a mild, kind-hearted little man, who, nevertheless, had no fear of any thing, unless it was the fear of being unkind.

"I tell you frankly," he privately said to the President, "I go into this purely for reasons of my own."

The next day, a little after nightfall, one might have descried this little man slipping along the rear fence of the Poquelin place, preparatory to vaulting over into the rank, grass-grown yard, and bearing himself altogether more after the manner of a collector of rare chickens than according to the usage of secretaries.

The picture presented to his eye was not calculated to enliven his mind. The old mansion stood out against the western sky, black and silent. One long, lurid pencil-stroke along a sky of slate was all that was left of daylight. No sign of life was apparent; no light at any window, unless it might have been on the side of the house hidden from view. No owls were on the chimneys, no dogs were in the yard.

He entered the place, and ventured up behind a small cabin which stood apart from the house. Through one of its many crannies he easily detected the African mute crouched before a flickering pine-knot, his head on his knees, fast asleep.

He concluded to enter the mansion, and, with that view, stood and scanned it. The broad rear steps of the veranda would not serve him; he might meet some one midway. He was measuring, with his eye, the proportions of one of the pillars which supported it, and estimating the practicability of climbing it, when he heard a footstep. Some one dragged a chair out toward the railing, then seemed to change his mind and began to pace the veranda, his footfalls resounding on the dry boards with singular loudness. Little White drew a step backward, got the figure between himself and the sky, and at once recognized the short, broad-shouldered form of old Jean Poquelin.

He sat down upon a billet of wood, and, to escape the stings of a whining cloud of mosquitoes, shrouded his face and neck in his handkerchief, leaving his eyes uncovered.

He had sat there but a moment when he noticed a strange, sickening odor, faint, as if coming from a distance, but loathsome and horrid.

Whence could it come? Not from the cabin; not from the marsh, for it was as dry as powder. It was not in the air; it seemed to come from the ground.

Rising up, he noticed, for the first time, a few steps before him a narrow footpath leading toward the house. He glanced down it—ha! right there was some one coming—ghostly white!

Quick as thought, and as noiselessly, he lay down at full length against the cabin. It was bold strategy, and yet, there was no denying it, little White felt that he was frightened. "It is not a ghost," he said to himself. "I *know* it cannot be a ghost;" but the perspiration burst out at every pore, and the air seemed to thicken with heat. "It is a living man," he said in his thoughts. "I hear his footstep, and I hear old Poquelin's footsteps, too, separately, over on the veranda. I am not discovered; the thing has passed; there is that odor again; what a smell of death! Is it coming back? Yes. It stops at the door of the cabin. Is it peering in at the sleeping mute? It moves away. It is in the path again. Now it is gone." He shuddered. "Now, if I dare venture, the mystery is solved." He rose cautiously, close against the cabin, and peered along the path.

The figure of a man, a presence if not a body—but whether clad in some white stuff or naked the darkness would not allow him to determine—had turned, and now, with a seeming painful gait, moved slowly from him. "Great Heaven! can it be that the dead do walk?" He withdrew again the hands which had gone to his eyes. The dreadful object passed between two pillars and under the house. He listened. There was a faint sound as of feet upon a staircase; then all was still except the measured tread of Jean Poquelin walking on the veranda, and the heavy respirations of the mute slumbering in the cabin.

The little Secretary was about to retreat; but as he looked once more toward the haunted house a dim light appeared in the crack of a closed window, and presently old Jean Poquelin came, dragging his chair, and sat down close against the shining cranny. He spoke in a low, tender tone in the French tongue, making some inquiry. An answer came from within. Was it the voice of a human? So unnatural was it—so hollow, so discordant, so unearthly—that the stealthy listener shuddered again from head to foot, and when something stirred in some bushes near by—though it may have been nothing more than a rat—and came scuttling through the grass, the little Secretary actually turned and fled. As he left the enclosure he moved with bolder leisure through the bushes; yet now and then he spoke aloud: "Oh, oh! I see, I understand!" and shut his eyes in his hands.

How strange that henceforth little White was the champion of Jean Poquelin! In season and out of season—wherever a word was uttered against him—the Secretary, with a quiet, aggressive force that instantly arrested gossip, demanded upon what authority the statement or conjecture was made; but as he did not condescend to explain his own remarkable attitude, it was not long before the disrelish and suspicion which had followed Jean Poquelin so many years fell also upon him.

It was only the next evening but one after his adventure that he made himself a source of sullen amazement to one hundred and fifty boys, by ordering them to desist from their wanton hallooing. Old Jean Poquelin, standing and shaking his cane, rolling out his long-drawn maledictions, paused and stared, then gave the Secretary a courteous bow and started on. The boys, save one, from pure astonishment, ceased but a ruffianly little Irish lad, more daring than any had yet been, threw a big hurtling clod, that struck old Poquelin between the shoulders and burst like a shell. The enraged old man wheeled with uplifted staff to give chase to the scampering vagabond; and—he may have tripped, or he may not, but he fell full length. Little White hastened to help him up, but he waved him off with a fierce imprecation and staggering to his feet resumed his way homeward. His lips were reddened with blood.

Little White was on his way to the meeting of the Board. He would have given all he dared spend to have staid away, for he felt both too fierce and too tremulous to brook the criticisms that were likely to be made.

"I can't help it, gentlemen; I can't help you to make a case against the old man, and I'm not going to."

"We did not expect this disappointment, Mr. White."

"I can't help that, sir. No, sir; you had better not appoint any more investigations. Somebody'll investigate himself into trouble. No, sir; it isn't a threat, it is only my advice, but I warn you that whoever takes the task in hand will rue it to his dying day—which may be hastened, too."

The President expressed himself "surprised."

"I don't care a rush," answered little White, wildly and foolishly. "I don't care a rush if you are, sir. No, my nerves are not disordered; my head's as clear as a bell. No, I'm *not* excited." A Director remarked that the Secretary looked as though he had waked from a nightmare.

"Well, sir, if you want to know the fact, I have; and if you choose to cultivate old Poquelin's society you can have one, too."

"White," called a facetious member, but White did not notice. "White," he called again.

"What?" demanded White, with a scowl.

"Did you see the ghost?"

"Yes, sir; I did," cried White, hitting the table, and handing the President a paper which brought the Board to other business.

The story got among the gossips that somebody (they were afraid to say little White) had been to the Poquelin mansion by night and beheld something appalling. The rumor was but a shadow of the truth, magnified and distorted as is the manner of shadows. He had seen skeletons walking, and had barely escaped the clutches of one by making the sign of the cross.

Some madcap boys with an appetite for the horrible plucked up courage to venture through the dried marsh by the cattle-path, and come before the house at a spectral hour when the air was full of bats. Something which they but half saw—half a sight was enough—sent them tearing back through the willow-brakes and acacia bushes to their homes, where they fairly dropped down, and cried:

"Was it White?"

"No—yes—nearly so—we can't tell—but we saw it." And one could hardly doubt, to look at their ashen faces, that they had, whatever it was.

"If that old rascal lived in the country we come from," said certain Américains, "he'd have been tarred and feathered before now, wouldn't he, Sanders?"

"Well, now he just would."

"And we'd have rid him on a rail, wouldn't we?"

"That's what I allow."

"Tell you what you *could* do." They were talking to some rollicking Creoles who had assumed an absolute necessity for doing *something*. "What is it you call this thing where an old man marries a young girl, and you come out with horns and"—

"*Charivari?*" asked the Creoles.

"Yes, that's it. Why don't you shivaree him?" Felicitous suggestion.

Little White, with his wife beside him, was sitting on their doorsteps on the sidewalk, as Creole custom had taught them, looking toward the sunset. They had moved into the lately-opened street. The view was not attractive on the score of beauty. The houses were small and scattered, and across the flat commons, spite of the lofty tangle of weeds and bushes, and spite of the thickets of acacia, they needs must see the dismal old Poquelin mansion, tilted awry and shutting out the declining sun. The moon, white and slender, was hanging the tip of its horn over one of the chimneys.

"And you say," said the Secretary, "the old black man has been going by here alone? Patty, suppose old Poquelin should be concocting some mischief; he don't lack provocation; the way that clod hit him the other day was enough to have killed him. Why, Patty, he dropped as quick as *that*! No wonder you haven't seen him. I wonder if they haven't heard something about him up at the drug-store. Suppose I go and see."

"Do," said his wife.

She sat alone for half an hour, watching that sudden going out of the day peculiar to the latitude.

"That moon is ghost enough for one house," she said, as her husband returned. "It has gone right down the chimney."

"Patty," said little White, "the drug-clerk says the boys are going to shivaree old Poquelin to-night. I'm going to try to stop it."

"Why, White," said his wife, "you'd better not. You'll get hurt."

"No, I'll not."

"Yes, you will."

"I'm going to sit out here until they come along. They're compelled to pass right by here."

"Why, White, it may be midnight before they start; you're not going to sit out here till then."

"Yes, I am."

"Well, you're very foolish," said Mrs. White in an undertone, looking anxious, and tapping one of the steps with her foot.

They sat a very long time talking over little family matters.

"What's that?" at last said Mrs. White.

"That's the nine-o'clock gun," said White, and they relapsed into a long-sustained, drowsy silence.

"Patty, you'd better go in and go to bed," said he at last.

"I'm not sleepy."

"Well, you're very foolish," quietly remarked little White, and again silence fell upon them.

"Patty, suppose I walk out to the old house and see if I can find out any thing."

"Suppose," said she, "you don't do any such—listen!"

Down the street arose a great hubbub. Dogs and boys were howling and barking; men were laughing, shouting, groaning, and blowing horns, whooping, and clanking cow-bells, whinnying, and howling, and rattling pots and pans.

"They are coming this way," said little White. "You had better go into the house, Patty."

"So had you."

"No. I'm going to see if I can't stop them."

"Why, White!"

"I'll be back in a minute," said White, and went toward the noise.

In a few moments the little Secretary met the mob. The pen hesitates on the word, for there is a respectable difference, measurable only on the scale of the half century, between a mob and a *charivari*. Little White lifted his ineffectual voice. He faced the head of the disorderly column, and cast himself about as if he were made of wood and moved by the jerk of a string. He rushed to one who seemed, from the size and clatter of his tin pan, to be a leader. "*Stop these fellows, Bienvenu, stop them just a minute, till I tell them something.*" Bienvenu turned and brandished his instruments of discord in an imploring way to the crowd. They slackened their pace, two or three hushed their horns and joined the prayer of little White and Bienvenu for silence. The throng halted. The hush was delicious.

"Bienvenu," said little White, "don't shivaree old Poquelin to-night; he's—"

"My fwang," said the swaying Bienvenu, "who tail you I goin' to chahivahi somebody, eh? Yon sink bickause I make a little playfool wiz zis tin pan zat I am *dhonk*?"

"Oh, no, Bienvenu, old fellow, you're all right. I was afraid you might not know that old Poquelin was sick, you know, but you're not going there, are you?"

"My fwang, I vay soy to tail you zat you ah dhonk as de dev'. I am *shem* of you. I ham ze servan' of ze *publique*. Zese *citoyens* goin' to wickwest Jean Poquelin to give to the Ursuline' two hondred fifty dolla'—"

"*Hé quoi!*" cried a listener, "*Cinq cent piastres, oui!*"

"*Oui!*" said Bienvenu, "and if he wiffuse we make him some lit' *musique*; ta-ra ta!" He hoisted a merry hand and foot, then frowning, added: "Old Poquelin got no bizniz dhink s'much w'isky."

"But, gentlemen," said little White, around whom a circle had gathered, "the old man is very sick."

"My faith!" cried a tiny Creole, "we did not make him to be sick. W'en we have say we going make *le charivari*, do you want that we hall tell a lie? My faith! 'sfools!"

"But you can shivaree somebody else," said desperate little White.

"*Oui!*" cried Bienvenu, "*et chahivahi* Jean-ah Poquelin tomo'w!"

"Let us go to Madame Schneider!" cried two or three, and amid huzzas and confused cries, among which was heard a stentorian Celtic call for drinks, the crowd again began to move.

"*Cent piastres pour l'hôpital de charité!*"

"Hurrah!"

"One hongred dolla' for Charity Hospital!"

"Hurrah!"

"Whang!" went a tin pan, the crowd yelled, and Pandemonium gaped again.

They were off at a right angle.

Nodding, Mrs. White looked at the mantle-clock.

"Well, if it isn't away after midnight."

The hideous noise down street was passing beyond earshot. She raised a sash and listened. For a moment there was silence. Some one came to the door.

"Is that you, White?"

"Yes." He entered. "I succeeded, Patty."

"Did you?" said Patty, joyfully.

"Yes. They've gone down to shivaree the old Dutchwoman who married her step-daughter's sweetheart. They say she has got to pay a hundred dollars to the hospital before they stop."

The couple retired, and Mrs. White slumbered. She was awakened by her husband snapping the lid of his watch.

"What time?" she asked.

"Half-past three. Patty, I haven't slept a wink. Those fellows are out yet. Don't you hear them?"

"Why, White, they're coming this way!"

"I know they are," said White, sliding out of bed and drawing on his clothes, "and they're coming fast. You'd better go away from that window, Patty. My! what a clatter!"

"Here they are," said Mrs. White, but her husband was gone. Two or three hundred men and boys pass the place at a rapid walk straight down the broad, new street, toward the hated house of ghosts. The din was terrific. She saw little White at the head of the rabble brandishing his arms and trying in vain to make himself heard; but they only shook their heads laughing and hooting the louder, and so passed, bearing him on before them.

Swiftly they pass out from among the houses, away from the dim oil lamps of the street, out into the broad starlit commons, and enter the willowy jungles of the haunted ground. Some hearts fail and their owners lag behind and turn back, suddenly remembering how near morning it is. But the most part push on, tearing the air with their clamor.

Down ahead of them in the long, thicket-darkened way there is— singularly enough—a faint, dancing light. It must be very near the old house; it is. It has stopped now. It is a lantern, and is under a well-known sapling which has grown up on the wayside since the canal was filled.

Now it swings mysteriously to and fro. A goodly number of the more ghost-fearing give up the sport; but a full hundred move forward at a run, doubling their devilish howling and banging.

Yes; it is a lantern, and there are two persons under the tree. The crowd draws near—drops into a walk; one of the two is the old African mute; he lifts the lantern up so that it shines on the other; the crowd recoils; there is a hush of all clangor, and all at once, with a cry of mingled fright and horror from every throat, the whole throng rushes back, dropping every thing, sweeping past little White and hurrying on, never stopping until the jungle is left behind, and then to find that not one in ten has seen the cause of the stampede, and not one of the tenth is certain what it was.

There is one huge fellow among them who looks capable of any villany. He finds something to mount on, and, in the Creole *patois*, calls a general halt. Bienvenu sinks down, and, vainly trying to recline gracefully, resigns the leadership. The herd gather round the speaker; he assures them that they have been outraged. Their right peaceably to traverse the public streets has been trampled upon. Shall such encroachments be endured? It is now daybreak. Let them go now by the open light of day and force a free passage of the public highway!

A scattering consent was the response, and the crowd, thinned now and drowsy, straggled quietly down toward the old house. Some drifted ahead, others sauntered behind, but every one, as he again neared the tree, came to a stand-still. Little White sat upon a bank of turf on the opposite side of the way looking very stern and sad. To each new-comer he put the same question:

"Did you come here to go to old Poquelin's?"

"Yes."

"He's dead." And if the shocked hearer started away he would say: "Don't go away."

"Why not?"

"I want you to go to the funeral presently."

If some Louisianian, too loyal to dear France or Spain to understand English, looked bewildered, some one would interpret for him; and presently they went. Little White led the van, the crowd trooping after him down the middle of the way. The gate, that had never been seen before unchained, was open. Stern little White stopped a short distance from it; the rabble stopped behind him. Something was moving out from under the veranda. The many whisperers stretched upward to see. The African mute came very slowly toward the gate, leading by a cord in the nose a small brown bull, which was harnessed to a rude cart. On the flat body of the cart, under a black cloth, were seen the outlines of a long box.

"Hats off, gentlemen," said little White, as the box came in view, and the crowd silently uncovered.

"Gentlemen," said little White, "here come the last remains of Jean Marie Poquelin, a better man, I'm afraid, with all his sins,—yes a better— a kinder man to his blood—a man of more self-forgetful goodness—than all of you put together will ever dare to be."

There was a profound hush as the vehicle came creaking through the gate; but when it turned away from them toward the forest, those in front started suddenly. There was a backward rush, then all stood still again staring one way; for there, behind the bier, with eyes cast down and labored step, walked the living remains—all that was left—of little Jacques Poquelin, the long-hidden brother—a leper, as white as snow.

Dumb with horror, the cringing crowd gazed upon the walking death. They watched, in silent awe, the slow *cortège* creep down the long, straight road and lessen on the view, until by and by it stopped where a wild, unfrequented path branched off into the undergrowth toward the rear of the ancient city.

"They are going to the *Terre aux Lépreux*," said one in the crowd. The rest watched them in silence.

The little bull was set free; the mute, with the strength of an ape, lifted the long box to his shoulder. For a moment more the mute and the leper stood in sight, while the former adjusted his heavy burden; then, without one backward glance upon the unkind human world, turning their faces toward the ridge in the depths of the swamp known as the Leper's Land, they stepped into the jungle, disappeared, and were never seen again.

15

Mistress Marian's Light

By Gertrude Morton

FAR DOWN THE MAINE COAST, IN ONE OF THE MANY HARBORS OF THAT good old State, is a picturesque little island inhabited by simple fisher folk. Generation after generation has been born, lived, and died in this same island village, yet all the people seem to retain the customs and quaint ways of fifty years ago; from the old, weather-worn sailor, to the youngest child among them, they seem, to an unusual degree, guileless and simple and kindly, while to the stranger within their gates their goodness is unlimited. It is like a reminiscence of bygone days to partake of their generous hospitality.

At a late hour one soft, sweet night in early summer, while sojourning for a time among these people, I noticed, far down on a point of land, that rocky and waveworn, makes out into the sea, a strange light, that seemed to be suspended a few feet from the earth. Soft and wavering it was, sometimes dim; but so unmistakably a light, that I was somewhat perplexed, and the next morning I asked my hostess the cause of the strange phenomenon.

The woman's countenance changed in an instant, and she assumed a sympathetic, pitying look as she replied, with a wise, uncanny shake of her head, "Why, that is Mistress Marian's light." And so she went on and told me this story.

Away down on the point, where the brown soil of the interior of the island begins to mingle with the white sand along the sea, there was, many years ago, a small cottage, built by a seafaring man, who, with his family, occupied it for a short time. They then removed to a neighboring shore, and the house remained untenanted many months.

In the course of time two strangers came to the island,—an old man and his little daughter. Venerable indeed was the father, and with his snow-white hair and beard, and his dignified, scholarly bearing, he might have been a king among men. No one seemed to know just when or how they came; they appeared suddenly and unexpectedly, and seemed to find relief in the quietness of the place. As a wandering meteor, travelling through limitless space, finds rest somewhere in God's great universe, so did these two strangers find a dwelling-place in this secluded spot.

To the little uninhabited cottage on the point they went, and the simple life of the islanders became their life. They became a part, and still not a part, of the fisher folk. The dignified old man was so unlike any one whom they had ever seen before that they were shy of him; and long though he lived among them, quietly assisting the needy, and lending a helping hand to all, they were never quite at ease with him, though they worshipped him from afar. It was as though he breathed a rarer atmosphere than they, and dwelt above them; and they were content to accept his kindness and to marvel at his greatness.

Not so the child, with her soft brown eyes and her gentle, winning manner. "A lady born and bred, she is," the good dames said, one to another, many times. But she was a child, strangely alone, so the motherly arms were opened to her, and the children made this little Marian their playmate.

They seemed to be people of means,—this father and daughter. The cottage was furnished comfortably, even luxuriously, and many books, some of them in quaint and curious bindings, were about. On the low walls hung several pictures, the like of which the islanders had never seen before; rich rugs covered the bare floors; a piece of rare Eastern embroidery was flung over a low couch; upon an oddly carved shelf were some bits of china, delicate and fragile, as though fashioned from rose leaves; while everywhere in the tiny house were evidences of refinement. From what faraway land the strangers came, or why they sought refuge on the little island, they themselves never said, nor were they ever questioned. The people, with their simple faith and childlike credulity, accepted the fact of their coming as they did all the good things that befell them,—thankful, asking naught.

So these two lived on in an alien land, their lives replete with the satisfaction that comes from helping others, their desire to do good satisfied by the appreciation with which their efforts were met. Thus the little girl, the dainty Marian, grew to maidenhood, learning much from her father and his books, but more from Nature: of the sea with its wonderful treasures; of the rocks that she loved, gaunt and gray though they were; of flowers and fishes and birds. She learned, too, much of human nature—the kindly side—from the people about her; and their interests she made hers. Every mother on the island felt a deep affection for her, and her young mates were proud to be called her friends. She was a constant surprise to them. The dainty gowns that she fashioned for herself, out of strange fabrics, were marvels; even her language seemed somehow different from theirs; and when a stranger chanced to visit the little building where they gathered on Sundays for worship, "our young lady," brown-eyed "Mistress Marian," was always pointed out with secret pride. So she grew to pure and noble womanhood, winning respect and admiration from all.

The lads of the village were filled with unspeakable delight when she spoke to them in her sweet, low voice. Not one of them but that would have risked his limbs, almost his life, for anything that she wanted,—a wild-flower, a stone, or a bright bit of seaweed. Yet for none of them had she more than a word or a smile, except for tall, manly Phil Anderson. From her childhood she had seemed to set him apart from all others as a hero; and when he came to her out on the rocks one sweet summer night, when the moon was softly shining and the sea was bright with the phosphorescent gleam, and told her of his love for her, she accepted it quietly and trustfully.

It was a happy summer for the two, passing all too quickly. When autumn came, Phil was to sail with his father on one more voyage—to make his fortune, he said; then he was coming back to marry Marian and to take her away into the great world of which they were never tired of talking.

So the weeks slipped by. October came. The trees donned their gayest colors; each bush took its own particular, matchless tint, and the breakers dashed high in the cool breeze, as though to speed the parting, which was even then at hand. One bright, cool morning Phil went down to the little house to say good-by. Tremblingly the old man bade the brave young sailor farewell, then sent him out to the rocks—the place of their betrothal—where Marian was waiting. Silently he took her in his strong arms, kissed her soft hair, her forehead and her sweet red lips, then turned and strode quickly away, as though he could not trust his courage longer.

A year passed, bringing two letters to Marian from her lover, telling her of such success as even his fondest hopes had failed to picture. At the end of the third year, just after another letter had come, telling her that the *Watersprite* was homeward bound, and happiness seemed in store for her, her father died. For months the old man had been slowly failing, living only in his daughter's happiness. Now that she did not need him longer, he seemed to lose all power of holding on to his life, and one evening passed quietly away with the setting of the sun.

The grief of the young girl was well-nigh unbearable. The only bright thing that life seemed to hold for her was the fact that her lover was on his way to her. So she waited anxiously, longingly, expecting tidings every day. But after the third letter no news came.

As the days lengthened to weeks, and the weeks to months, the islanders were filled with apprehension and forebodings. A gloom settled over the people, which even the lingering Indian summer failed to brighten; and when, one bleak November day, beneath a darkening sky, a strange vessel came into the harbor with tidings that the gallant *Watersprite* had sunk and every soul on board had perished, it was almost a relief to the anxious watchers. Certainty, though hard to bear, was better than hope deferred.

Gently did sympathetic friends tell the mournful news to the lonely girl at the point; but dazed and bewildered, she did not seem to comprehend their meaning. For days she lay in a kind of stupor, unheeding everything, even the presence of the kind old dame who watched by her side night and day with tear-dimmed eyes. Only when the waves dashed loudest would the girl stir uneasily, raising her head as though listening for some one's coming.

At last she awoke from her long sleep, coming back once more to life and to her senses; but the beautiful hair was as white as the foam that dashed against the rocks she used to love, and the dark eyes looked large and mournful beneath the snowy wealth. As strength slowly came back to her, so also came the firm conviction that her lover was not dead, but would one day return to her. So firm was her faith that she grew cheerful, almost happy. Once more she assumed her duties,—clothing little children, ministering to the sick and aged, helping weary housewives. There was not a person on the island who had not at one time or another felt her kindly influence or her strong, stimulating presence.

Every night at dusk, after her day's work was done, she would place a large bright light in the window of the little sitting-room that looked toward the harbor, leaving the curtain drawn aside, so that should he for whom she watched come at night, he would find her still waiting for him. Not a night did she fail in this most important of all her duties. Her light was a bright beacon. Sailors soon learned to know it and look for it, and they never looked in vain; it was always there, steady, clear, unwavering.

Thus passed several years, when suddenly, mysteriously, without a shadow of warning, Mistress Marian disappeared. As silently as years ago she had entered the life of the fisher folk, so now did she leave it; and as they knew not then whence she came, neither did they know now whither she went.

There were many conjectures as to her strange disappearance. One old sailor affirmed that one night when he was out fishing he saw a little boat come from the point, bearing a solitary passenger with snow-white hair, who rowed out toward a large ship that could be dimly seen, as through a fog, and was taken on board; then the huge ship quickly vanished. But as this old man was well known to take his black bottle with him on his fishing expeditions, and as no other person could be found who saw the wonderful ship, his story did not gain the credence that its ingenuity deserved. The most of the people inclined to the belief that she had gone back to her father's relatives; but how, when, or where, not even the old woman who lived with her could tell.

A decade or two passed, and the old house in its exposed locality grew more and more weatherworn and dilapidated; and finally, one winter, doubtless feeling that its time of usefulness had passed, it succumbed to fate and, during a heavy gale, fell to the ground. Some of the timbers were washed away, others were used for fire-wood by campers and fishermen; so that after a time nothing remained to mark the spot where the cottage had been, save a few damp, moss-covered logs.

But still in this same place on quiet summer nights during the hot sultry time of July and August,—the time when the *Watersprite* was said to have perished,—this weird, white, uncertain, trembling light, a few feet from the ground, is at times plainly seen. Not all the scientific explanations of wiser heads can convince the simple villagers that this strange light is any other than Marian's beacon for her sailor lover, or shake their faith in the plausibility of a story handed down from successive generations.

The merriest sailing party, rounding the point of a sweet summer night, will become subdued at the sight of the light, while the timid maiden will nestle closer to the skipper at the helm, as she says in awe-struck tones, "See! Mistress Marian's light is still burning."

16

Consequences

By Willa Cather

HENRY EASTMAN, A LAWYER, AGED FORTY, WAS STANDING BESIDE THE Flatiron building in a driving November rainstorm, signaling frantically for a taxi. It was six-thirty, and everything on wheels was engaged. The streets were in confusion about him, the sky was in turmoil above him, and the Flatiron building, which seemed about to blow down, threw water like a mill-shoot. Suddenly, out of the brutal struggle of men and cars and machines and people tilting at each other with umbrellas, a quiet, well-mannered limousine paused before him, at the curb, and an agreeable, ruddy countenance confronted him through the open window of the car.

"Don't you want me to pick you up, Mr. Eastman? I'm running directly home now."

Eastman recognized Kier Cavenaugh, a young man of pleasure, who lived in the house on Central Park South, where he himself had an apartment.

"Don't I?" he exclaimed, bolting into the car. "I'll risk getting your cushions wet without compunction. I came up in a taxi, but I didn't hold it. Bad economy. I thought I saw your car down on Fourteenth Street about half an hour ago."

The owner of the car smiled. He had a pleasant, round face and round eyes, and a fringe of smooth, yellow hair showed under the rim of his soft felt hat. "With a lot of little broilers fluttering into it? You did. I know some girls who work in the cheap shops down there. I happened to be down-town and I stopped and took a load of them home. I do sometimes. Saves their poor little clothes, you know. Their shoes are never any good."

Eastman looked at his rescuer. "Aren't they notoriously afraid of cars and smooth young men?" he inquired.

Cavenaugh shook his head. "They know which cars are safe and which are chancy. They put each other wise. You have to take a bunch at a time, of course. The Italian girls can never come along; their men shoot. The girls understand, all right; but their fathers don't. One gets to see queer places, sometimes, taking them home."

Eastman laughed drily. "Every time I touch the circle of your acquaintance, Cavenaugh, it's a little wider. You must know New York pretty well by this time."

"Yes, but I'm on my good behavior below Twenty-third Street," the young man replied with simplicity. "My little friends down there would give me a good character. They're wise little girls. They have grand ways with each other, a romantic code of loyalty. You can find a good many of the lost virtues among them."

The car was standing still in a traffic block at Fortieth Street, when Cavenaugh suddenly drew his face away from the window and touched Eastman's arm. "Look, please. You see that hansom with the bony gray horse—driver has a broken hat and red flannel around his throat. Can you see who is inside?"

Eastman peered out. The hansom was just cutting across the line, and the driver was making a great fuss about it, bobbing his head and waving his whip. He jerked his dripping old horse into Fortieth Street and clattered off past the Public Library grounds toward Sixth Avenue. "No, I couldn't see the passenger. Someone you know?"

"Could you see whether there was a passenger?" Cavenaugh asked.

"Why, yes. A man, I think. I saw his elbow on the apron. No driver ever behaves like that unless he has a passenger."

"Yes, I may have been mistaken," Cavenaugh murmured absentmindedly. Ten minutes or so later, after Cavenaugh's car had turned off Fifth Avenue into Fifty-eighth Street, Eastman exclaimed, "There's your same cabby, and his cart's empty. He's headed for a drink now, I suppose." The driver in the broken hat and the red flannel neck cloth was still brandishing the whip over his old gray. He was coming from the west now, and turned down Sixth Avenue, under the elevated.

Cavenaugh's car stopped at the bachelor apartment house between Sixth and Seventh Avenues where he and Eastman lived, and they went up in the elevator together. They were still talking when the lift stopped at Cavenaugh's floor, and Eastman stepped out with him and walked down the hall, finishing his sentence while Cavenaugh found his latch-key. When he opened the door, a wave of fresh cigarette smoke greeted them. Cavenaugh stopped short and stared into his hallway. "Now how in the devil—!" he exclaimed angrily.

"Someone waiting for you? Oh, no, thanks. I wasn't coming in. I have to work to-night. Thank you, but I couldn't." Eastman nodded and went up the two flights to his own rooms.

Though Eastman did not customarily keep a servant he had this winter a man who had been lent to him by a friend who was abroad. Rollins met him at the door and took his coat and hat.

"Put out my dinner clothes, Rollins, and then get out of here until ten o'clock. I've promised to go to a supper to-night. I shan't be dining. I've had a late tea and I'm going to work until ten. You may put out some kumiss and biscuit for me."

Rollins took himself off, and Eastman settled down at the big table in his sitting-room. He had to read a lot of letters submitted as evidence in a breach of contract case, and before he got very far he found that long paragraphs in some of the letters were written in German. He had a German dictionary at his office, but none here. Rollins had gone, and anyhow, the bookstores would be closed. He remembered having seen a row of dictionaries on the lower shelf of one of Cavenaugh's bookcases. Cavenaugh had a lot of books, though he never read anything but new stuff. Eastman prudently turned down his student's lamp very low—the thing had an evil habit of smoking—and went down two flights to Cavenaugh's door.

The young man himself answered Eastman's ring. He was freshly dressed for the evening, except for a brown smoking jacket, and his yellow hair had been brushed until it shone. He hesitated as he confronted his caller, still holding the door knob, and his round eyes and smooth forehead made their best imitation of a frown. When Eastman began to apologize, Cavenaugh's manner suddenly changed. He caught his arm and jerked him into the narrow hall. "Come in, come in. Right along!" he said excitedly. "Right along," he repeated as he pushed Eastman before him into his sitting-room. "Well I'll—" he stopped short at the door and looked about his own room with an air of complete mystification. The back window was wide open and a strong wind was blowing in. Cavenaugh walked over to the window and stuck out his head, looking up and down the fire escape. When he pulled his head in, he drew down the sash.

"I had a visitor I wanted you to see," he explained with a nervous smile. "At least I thought I had. He must have gone out that way," nodding toward the window.

"Call him back. I only came to borrow a German dictionary, if you have one. Can't stay. Call him back."

Cavenaugh shook his head despondently. "No use. He's beat it. Nowhere in sight."

"He must be active. Has he left something?" Eastman pointed to a very dirty white glove that lay on the floor under the window.

"Yes, that's his." Cavenaugh reached for his tongs, picked up the glove, and tossed it into the grate, where it quickly shriveled on the coals. Eastman felt that he had happened in upon something disagreeable, possibly something shady, and he wanted to get away at once. Cavenaugh stood staring at the fire and seemed stupid and dazed; so he repeated his request rather sternly, "I think I've seen a German dictionary down there among your books. May I have it?"

Cavenaugh blinked at him. "A German dictionary? Oh, possibly! Those were my father's. I scarcely know what there is." He put down the tongs and began to wipe his hands nervously with his handkerchief.

Eastman went over to the bookcase behind the Chesterfield, opened the door, swooped upon the book he wanted and stuck it under his arm. He felt perfectly certain now that something shady had been going on in Cavenaugh's rooms, and he saw no reason why he should come in for any hang-over. "Thanks. I'll send it back to-morrow," he said curtly as he made for the door.

Cavenaugh followed him. "Wait a moment. I wanted you to see him. You did see his glove," glancing at the grate.

Eastman laughed disagreeably. "I saw a glove. That's not evidence. Do your friends often use that means of exit? Somewhat inconvenient."

Cavenaugh gave him a startled glance. "Wouldn't you think so? For an old man, a very rickety old party? The ladders are steep, you know, and rusty." He approached the window again and put it up softly. In a moment he drew his head back with a jerk. He caught Eastman's arm and shoved him toward the window. "Hurry, please. Look! Down there." He pointed to the little patch of paved court four flights down.

The square of pavement was so small and the walls about it were so high, that it was a good deal like looking down a well. Four tall buildings backed upon the same court and made a kind of shaft, with flagstones at the bottom, and at the top a square of dark blue with some stars in it. At the bottom of the shaft Eastman saw a black figure, a man in a caped coat and a tall hat stealing cautiously around, not across the square of pavement, keeping close to the dark wall and avoiding the streak of light that fell on the flagstones from a window in the opposite house. Seen from that height he was of course fore-shortened and probably looked more shambling and decrepit than he was. He picked his way along with exaggerated care and looked like a silly old cat crossing a wet street. When he reached the gate that led into an alley way between two buildings, he felt about for the latch, opened the door a mere crack, and then shot out under the feeble lamp that burned in the brick arch over the gateway. The door closed after him.

"He'll get run in," Eastman remarked curtly, turning away from the window. "That door shouldn't be left unlocked. Any crook could come in. I'll speak to the janitor about it, if you don't mind," he added sarcastically.

"Wish you would." Cavenaugh stood brushing down the front of his jacket, first with his right hand and then with his left. "You saw him, didn't you?"

"Enough of him. Seems eccentric. I have to see a lot of buggy people. They don't take me in any more. But I'm keeping you and I'm in a hurry myself. Good night."

Cavenaugh put out his hand detainingly and started to say something; but Eastman rudely turned his back and went down the hall and out of the door. He had never felt anything shady about Cavenaugh before, and he was sorry he had gone down for the dictionary. In five minutes he was deep in his papers; but in the half hour when he was loafing before he dressed to go out, the young man's curious behavior came into his mind again.

Eastman had merely a neighborly acquaintance with Cavenaugh. He had been to a supper at the young man's rooms once, but he didn't particularly like Cavenaugh's friends; so the next time he was asked, he had another engagement. He liked Cavenaugh himself, if for nothing else than because he was so cheerful and trim and ruddy. A good complexion is always at a premium in New York, especially when it shines reassuringly on a man who does everything in the world to lose it. It encourages fellow mortals as to the inherent vigor of the human organism and the amount of bad treatment it will stand for. "Footprints that perhaps another," etc.

Cavenaugh, he knew, had plenty of money. He was the son of a Pennsylvania preacher, who died soon after he discovered that his ancestral acres were full of petroleum, and Kier had come to New York to burn some of the oil. He was thirty-two and was still at it; spent his life, literally, among the breakers. His motor hit the Park every morning as if it were the first time ever. He took people out to supper every night. He went from restaurant to restaurant, sometimes to half-a-dozen in an evening. The head waiters were his hosts and their cordiality made him happy. They made a life-line for him up Broadway and down Fifth Avenue. Cavenaugh was still fresh and smooth, round and plump, with a lustre to his hair and white teeth and a clear look in his round eyes. He seemed absolutely unwearied and unimpaired; never bored and never carried away.

Eastman always smiled when he met Cavenaugh in the entrance hall, serenely going forth to or returning from gladiatorial combats with joy, or when he saw him rolling smoothly up to the door in his car in the morning after a restful night in one of the remarkable new roadhouses he was always finding. Eastman had seen a good many young men disappear on Cavenaugh's route, and he admired this young man's endurance.

To-night, for the first time, he had got a whiff of something unwhole-some about the fellow—bad nerves, bad company, something on hand that he was ashamed of, a visitor old and vicious, who must have had a key to Cavenaugh's apartment, for he was evidently there when Cavenaugh returned at seven o'clock. Probably it was the same man Cavenaugh had seen in the hansom. He must have been able to let himself in, for Cav-enaugh kept no man but his chauffeur; or perhaps the janitor had been instructed to let him in. In either case, and whoever he was, it was clear enough that Cavenaugh was ashamed of him and was mixing up in ques-tionable business of some kind.

Eastman sent Cavenaugh's book back by Rollins, and for the next few weeks he had no word with him beyond a casual greeting when they happened to meet in the hall or the elevator. One Sunday morning Cav-enaugh telephoned up to him to ask if he could motor out to a roadhouse in Connecticut that afternoon and have supper; but when Eastman found there were to be other guests he declined.

On New Year's eve Eastman dined at the University Club at six o'clock and hurried home before the usual manifestations of insanity had begun in the streets. When Rollins brought his smoking coat, he asked him whether he wouldn't like to get off early.

"Yes, sir. But won't you be dressing, Mr. Eastman?" he inquired.

"Not to-night." Eastman handed him a bill. "Bring some change in the morning. There'll be fees."

Rollins lost no time in putting everything to rights for the night, and Eastman couldn't help wishing that he were in such a hurry to be off somewhere himself. When he heard the hall door close softly, he won-dered if there were any place, after all, that he wanted to go. From his window he looked down at the long lines of motors and taxis waiting for a signal to cross Broadway. He thought of some of their probable desti-nations and decided that none of those places pulled him very hard. The night was warm and wet, the air was drizzly. Vapor hung in clouds about the *Times* Building, half hid the top of it, and made a luminous haze along Broadway. While he was looking down at the army of wet, black carriage-tops and their reflected headlights and tail-lights, Eastman heard a ring at his door. He deliberated. If it were a caller, the hall porter would have telephoned up. It must be the janitor. When he opened the door, there stood a rosy young man in a tuxedo, without a coat or hat.

"Pardon. Should I have telephoned? I half thought you wouldn't be in."

Eastman laughed. "Come in, Cavenaugh. You weren't sure whether you wanted company or not, eh, and you were trying to let chance decide it? That was exactly my state of mind. Let's accept the verdict." When they emerged from the narrow hall into his sitting-room, he pointed out a seat by the fire to his guest. He brought a tray of decanters and soda bottles and placed it on his writing table.

Cavenaugh hesitated, standing by the fire. "Sure you weren't starting for somewhere?"

"Do I look it? No, I was just making up my mind to stick it out alone when you rang. Have one?" he picked up a tall tumbler.

"Yes, thank you. I always do."

Eastman chuckled. "Lucky boy! So will I. I had a very early dinner. New York is the most arid place on holidays," he continued as he rattled the ice in the glasses. "When one gets too old to hit the rapids down there, and tired of gobbling food to heathenish dance music, there is absolutely no place where you can get a chop and some milk toast in peace, unless you have strong ties of blood brotherhood on upper Fifth Avenue. But you, why aren't you starting for somewhere?"

The young man sipped his soda and shook his head as he replied:

"Oh, I couldn't get a chop, either. I know only flashy people, of course." He looked up at his host with such a grave and candid expression that Eastman decided there couldn't be anything very crooked about the fellow. His smooth cheeks were positively cherubic.

"Well, what's the matter with them? Aren't they flashing to-night?"

"Only the very new ones seem to flash on New Year's eve. The older ones fade away. Maybe they are hunting a chop, too."

"Well"—Eastman sat down—"holidays do dash one. I was just about to write a letter to a pair of maiden aunts in my old home town, up-state; old coasting hill, snow-covered pines, lights in the church windows. That's what you've saved me from."

Cavenaugh shook himself. "Oh, I'm sure that wouldn't have been good for you. Pardon me," he rose and took a photograph from the bookcase, a handsome man in shooting clothes. "Dudley, isn't it? Did you know him well?"

"Yes. An old friend. Terrible thing, wasn't it? I haven't got over the jolt yet."

"His suicide? Yes, terrible! Did you know his wife?"

"Slightly. Well enough to admire her very much. She must be terribly broken up. I wonder Dudley didn't think of that."

Cavenaugh replaced the photograph carefully, lit a cigarette, and standing before the fire began to smoke. "Would you mind telling me about him? I never met him, but of course I'd read a lot about him, and I can't help feeling interested. It was a queer thing."

Eastman took out his cigar case and leaned back in his deep chair. "In the days when I knew him best he hadn't any story, like the happy nations. Everything was properly arranged for him before he was born. He came into the world happy, healthy, clever, straight, with the right sort of connections and the right kind of fortune, neither too large nor too small. He helped to make the world an agreeable place to live in until he was twenty-six. Then he married as he should have married. His wife was a Californian, educated abroad. Beautiful. You have seen her picture?"

Cavenaugh nodded. "Oh, many of them."

"She was interesting, too. Though she was distinctly a person of the world, she had retained something, just enough of the large Western manner. She had the habit of authority, of calling out a special train if she needed it, of using all our ingenious mechanical contrivances lightly and easily, without over-rating them. She and Dudley knew how to live better than most people. Their house was the most charming one I have ever known in New York. You felt freedom there, and a zest of life, and safety—absolute sanctuary—from everything sordid or petty. A whole society like that would justify the creation of man and would make our planet shine with a soft, peculiar radiance among the constellations. You think I'm putting it on thick?"

The young man sighed gently. "Oh, no! One has always felt there must be people like that. I've never known any."

"They had two children, beautiful ones. After they had been married for eight years, Rosina met this Spaniard. He must have amounted to something. She wasn't a flighty woman. She came home and told Dudley how matters stood. He persuaded her to stay at home for six months and try to pull up. They were both fair-minded people, and I'm as sure as if I were the Almighty, that she did try. But at the end of the time, Rosina went quietly off to Spain, and Dudley went to hunt in the Canadian Rockies. I met his party out there. I didn't know his wife had left him and talked about her a good deal. I noticed that he never drank anything, and his light used to shine through the log chinks of his room until all hours, even after a hard day's hunting. When I got back to New York, rumors were creeping about. Dudley did not come back. He bought a ranch in Wyoming, built a big log house and kept splendid dogs and horses. One of his sisters went out to keep house for him, and the children were there when they were not in school. He had a great many visitors, and everyone who came back talked about how well Dudley kept things going.

"He put in two years out there. Then, last month, he had to come back on business. A trust fund had to be settled up, and he was administrator. I saw him at the club; same light, quick step, same gracious handshake. He was getting gray, and there was something softer in his manner; but he had a fine red tan on his face and said he found it delightful to be here in the season when everything is going hard. The Madison Avenue house had been closed since Rosina left it. He went there to get some things his sister wanted. That, of course, was the mistake. He went alone, in the afternoon, and didn't go out for dinner—found some sherry and tins of biscuit in the sideboard. He shot himself sometime that night. There were pistols in his smoking-room. They found burnt out candles beside him in the morning. The gas and electricity were shut off. I suppose there, in his own house, among his own things, it was too much for him. He left no letters."

Cavenaugh blinked and brushed the lapel of his coat. "I suppose," he said slowly, "that every suicide is logical and reasonable, if one knew all the facts."

Eastman roused himself. "No, I don't think so. I've known too many fellows who went off like that—more than I deserve, I think—and some of them were absolutely inexplicable. I can understand Dudley; but I can't see why healthy bachelors, with money enough, like ourselves, need such a device. It reminds me of what Dr. Johnson said, that the most discouraging thing about life is the number of fads and hobbies and fake religions it takes to put people through a few years of it."

"Dr. Johnson? The specialist? Oh, the old fellow!" said Cavenaugh imperturbably. "Yes, that's interesting. Still, I fancy if one knew the facts— Did you know about Wyatt?"

"I don't think so."

"You wouldn't, probably. He was just a fellow about town who spent money. He wasn't one of the *forestieri*, though. Had connections here and owned a fine old place over on Staten Island. He went in for botany, and had been all over, hunting things; rusts, I believe. He had a yacht and used to take a gay crowd down about the South Seas, botanizing. He really did botanize, I believe. I never knew such a spender—only not flashy. He helped a lot of fellows and he was awfully good to girls, the kind who come down here to get a little fun, who don't like to work and still aren't really tough, the kind you see talking hard for their dinner. Nobody knows what becomes of them, or what they get out of it, and there are hundreds of new ones every year. He helped dozens of 'em; it was he who got me curious about the little shop girls. Well, one afternoon when his tea was brought, he took prussic acid instead. He didn't leave any letters, either; people of any taste don't. They wouldn't leave any material reminder if they could help it. His lawyers found that he had just $314.72 above his debts when he died. He had planned to spend all his money, and then take his tea; he had worked it out carefully."

Eastman reached for his pipe and pushed his chair away from the fire. "That looks like a considered case, but I don't think philosophical suicides like that are common. I think they usually come from stress of feeling and are really, as the newspapers call them, desperate acts; done without a motive. You remember when Anna Karenina was under the wheels, she kept saying, 'Why am I here?'"

Cavenaugh rubbed his upper lip with his pink finger and made an effort to wrinkle his brows. "May I, please?" reaching for the whiskey. "But have you," he asked, blinking as the soda flew at him, "have you ever known, yourself, cases that were really inexplicable?"

"A few too many. I was in Washington just before Captain Jack Purden was married and I saw a good deal of him. Popular army man, fine record in the Philippines, married a charming girl with lots of money; mutual devotion. It was the gayest wedding of the winter, and they started for Japan. They stopped in San Francisco for a week and missed their boat because, as the bride wrote back to Washington, they were too happy to move. They took the next boat, were both good sailors, had exceptional weather. After they had been out for two weeks, Jack got up from his deck chair one afternoon, yawned, put down his book, and stood before his wife. 'Stop reading for a moment and look at me.' She laughed and asked him why. 'Because you happen to be good to look at.' He nodded to her, went back to the stern and was never seen again. Must have gone down to the lower deck and slipped overboard, behind the machinery. It was the luncheon hour, not many people about; steamer cutting through a soft green sea. That's one of the most baffling cases I know. His friends raked up his past, and it was as trim as a cottage garden. If he'd so much as dropped an ink spot on his fatigue uniform, they'd have found it. He wasn't emotional or moody; wasn't, indeed, very interesting; simply a good soldier, fond of all the pompous little formalities that make up a military man's life. What do you make of that, my boy?"

Cavenaugh stroked his chin. "It's very puzzling, I admit. Still, if one knew everything—"

"But we do know everything. His friends wanted to find something to help them out, to help the girl out, to help the case of the human creature."

"Oh, I don't mean things that people could unearth," said Cavenaugh uneasily. "But possibly there were things that couldn't be found out."

Eastman shrugged his shoulders. "It's my experience that when there are 'things' as you call them, they're very apt to be found. There is no such thing as a secret. To make any move at all one has to employ human agencies, employ at least one human agent. Even when the pirates killed the men who buried their gold for them, the bones told the story."

Cavenaugh rubbed his hands together and smiled his sunny smile.

"I like that idea. It's reassuring. If we can have no secrets, it means that we can't, after all, go so far afield as we might," he hesitated, "yes, as we might."

Eastman looked at him sourly. "Cavenaugh, when you've practised law in New York for twelve years, you find that people can't go far in any direction, except—" He thrust his forefinger sharply at the floor. "Even in that direction, few people can do anything out of the ordinary. Our range is limited. Skip a few baths, and we become personally objectionable. The slightest carelessness can rot a man's integrity or give him ptomaine poisoning. We keep up only by incessant cleansing operations, of mind and body. What we call character, is held together by all sorts of tacks and strings and glue."

Cavenaugh looked startled. "Come now, it's not so bad as that, is it? I've always thought that a serious man, like you, must know a lot of Launcelots." When Eastman only laughed, the younger man squirmed about in his chair. He spoke again hastily, as if he were embarrassed. "Your military friend may have had personal experiences, however, that his friends couldn't possibly get a line on. He may accidentally have come to a place where he saw himself in too unpleasant a light. I believe people can be chilled by a draft from outside, somewhere."

"Outside?" Eastman echoed. "Ah, you mean the far outside! Ghosts, delusions, eh?"

Cavenaugh winced. "That's putting it strong. Why not say tips from the outside? Delusions belong to a diseased mind, don't they? There are some of us who have no minds to speak of, who yet have had experiences. I've had a little something in that line myself and I don't look it, do I?"

Eastman looked at the bland countenance turned toward him. "Not exactly. What's your delusion?"

"It's not a delusion. It's a haunt."

The lawyer chuckled. "Soul of a lost Casino girl?"

"No; an old gentleman. A most unattractive old gentleman, who follows me about."

"Does he want money?"

Cavenaugh sat up straight. "No. I wish to God he wanted anything—but the pleasure of my society! I'd let him clean me out to be rid of him. He's a real article. You saw him yourself that night when you came to my rooms to borrow a dictionary, and he went down the fire-escape. You saw him down in the court."

"Well, I saw somebody down in the court, but I'm too cautious to take it for granted that I saw what you saw. Why, anyhow, should I see your haunt? If it was your friend I saw, he impressed me disagreeably. How did you pick him up?"

Cavenaugh looked gloomy. "That was queer, too. Charley Burke and I had motored out to Long Beach, about a year ago, sometime in October, I think. We had supper and stayed until late. When we were coming home, my car broke down. We had a lot of girls along who had to get back for morning rehearsals and things; so I sent them all into town in Charley's car, and he was to send a man back to tow me home. I was driving myself, and didn't want to leave my machine. We had not taken a direct road back; so I was stuck in a lonesome, woody place, no houses about. I got chilly and made a fire, and was putting in the time comfortably enough, when this old party steps up. He was in shabby evening clothes and a top hat, and had on his usual white gloves. How he got there, at three o'clock in the morning, miles from any town or railway, I'll leave it to you to figure out. *He* surely had no car. When I saw him coming up to the fire, I disliked him. He had a silly, apologetic walk. His teeth were chattering, and I asked him to sit down. He got down like a clothes-horse folding up. I offered him a cigarette, and when he took off his gloves I couldn't help noticing how knotted and spotty his hands were. He was asthmatic, and took his breath with a wheeze. 'Haven't you got anything—refreshing in there?' he asked, nodding at the car. When I told him I hadn't, he sighed. 'Ah, you young fellows are greedy. You drink it all up. You drink it all up, all up—up!' he kept chewing it over."

Cavenaugh paused and looked embarrassed again. "The thing that was most unpleasant is difficult to explain. The old man sat there by the fire and leered at me with a silly sort of admiration that was—well, more than humiliating. 'Gay boy, gay dog!' he would mutter, and when he grinned he showed his teeth, worn and yellow—shells. I remembered that it was better to talk casually to insane people; so I remarked carelessly that I had been out with a party and got stuck.

"'Oh yes, I remember,' he said, 'Flora and Lottie and Maybelle and Marcelline, and poor Kate.'

"He had named them correctly; so I began to think I had been hitting the bright waters too hard.

"Things I drank never had seemed to make me woody; but you can never tell when trouble is going to hit you. I pulled my hat down and tried to look as uncommunicative as possible; but he kept croaking on from time to time, like this: 'Poor Kate! Splendid arms, but dope got her. She took up with Eastern religions after she had her hair dyed. Got to going to a Swami's joint, and smoking opium. Temple of the Lotus, it was called, and the police raided it.'

"This was nonsense, of course; the young woman was in the pink of condition. I let him rave, but I decided that if something didn't come out for me pretty soon, I'd foot it across Long Island. There wasn't room enough for the two of us. I got up and took another try at my car. He hopped right after me.

"'Good car,' he wheezed, 'better than the little Ford.'

"I'd had a Ford before, but so has everybody; that was a safe guess.

"'Still,' he went on, 'that run in from Huntington Bay in the rain wasn't bad. Arrested for speeding, he-he.'

"It was true I had made such a run, under rather unusual circumstances, and had been arrested. When at last I heard my life-boat snorting up the road, my visitor got up, sighed, and stepped back into the shadow of the trees. I didn't wait to see what became of him, you may believe. That was visitation number one. What do you think of it?"

Cavenaugh looked at his host defiantly. Eastman smiled.

"I think you'd better change your mode of life, Cavenaugh. Had many returns?" he inquired.

"Too many, by far." The young man took a turn about the room and came back to the fire. Standing by the mantel he lit another cigarette before going on with his story:

"The second visitation happened in the street, early in the evening, about eight o'clock. I was held up in a traffic block before the Plaza. My chauffeur was driving. Old Nibbs steps up out of the crowd, opens the door of my car, gets in and sits down beside me. He had on wilted evening clothes, same as before, and there was some sort of heavy scent about him. Such an unpleasant old party! A thorough-going rotter; you knew it at once. This time he wasn't talkative, as he had been when I first saw him.

He leaned back in the car as if he owned it, crossed his hands on his stick and looked out at the crowd—sort of hungrily.

"I own I really felt a loathing compassion for him. We got down the avenue slowly. I kept looking out at the mounted police. But what could I do? Have him pulled? I was afraid to. I was awfully afraid of getting him into the papers.

"'I'm going to the New Astor,' I said at last. 'Can I take you anywhere?'

"'No, thank you,' says he. 'I get out when you do. I'm due on West 44th. I'm dining to-night with Marcelline—all that is left of her!'

"He put his hand to his hat brim with a grewsome salute. Such a scandalous, foolish old face as he had! When we pulled up at the Astor, I stuck my hand in my pocket and asked him if he'd like a little loan.

"'No, thank you, but'—he leaned over and whispered, ugh!—'but save a little, save a little. Forty years from now—a little—comes in handy. Save a little.'

"His eyes fairly glittered as he made his remark. I jumped out. I'd have jumped into the North River. When he tripped off, I asked my chauffeur if he'd noticed the man who got into the car with me. He said he knew someone was with me, but he hadn't noticed just when he got in. Want to hear any more?"

Cavenaugh dropped into his chair again. His plump cheeks were a trifle more flushed than usual, but he was perfectly calm. Eastman felt that the young man believed what he was telling him.

"Of course I do. It's very interesting. I don't see quite where you are coming out though."

Cavenaugh sniffed. "No more do I. I really feel that I've been put upon. I haven't deserved it any more than any other fellow of my kind. Doesn't it impress you disagreeably?"

"Well, rather so. Has anyone else seen your friend?"

"You saw him."

"We won't count that. As I said, there's no certainty that you and I saw the same person in the court that night. Has anyone else had a look in?"

"People sense him rather than see him. He usually crops up when I'm alone or in a crowd on the street. He never approaches me when I'm with people I know, though I've seen him hanging about the doors of theatres when I come out with a party; loafing around the stage exit, under a wall; or across the street, in a doorway. To be frank, I'm not anxious to introduce him. The third time, it was I who came upon him. In November my driver, Harry, had a sudden attack of appendicitis. I took him to the Presbyterian Hospital in the car, early in the evening. When I came home, I found the old villain in my rooms. I offered him a drink, and he sat down. It was the first time I had seen him in a steady light, with his hat off.

"His face is lined like a railway map, and as to color—Lord, what a liver! His scalp grows tight to his skull, and his hair is dyed until it's perfectly dead, like a piece of black cloth."

Cavenaugh ran his fingers through his own neatly trimmed thatch, and seemed to forget where he was for a moment.

"I had a twin brother, Brian, who died when we were sixteen. I have a photograph of him on my wall, an enlargement from a kodak of him, doing a high jump, rather good thing, full of action. It seemed to annoy the old gentleman. He kept looking at it and lifting his eyebrows, and finally he got up, tip-toed across the room, and turned the picture to the wall.

"'Poor Brian! Fine fellow, but died young,' says he.

"Next morning, there was the picture, still reversed."

"Did he stay long?" Eastman asked interestedly.

"Half an hour, by the clock."

"Did he talk?"

"Well, he rambled."

"What about?"

Cavenaugh rubbed his pale eyebrows before answering.

"About things that an old man ought to want to forget. His conversation is highly objectionable. Of course he knows me like a book; everything I've ever done or thought. But when he recalls them, he throws a bad light on them, somehow. Things that weren't much off color, look rotten. He doesn't leave one a shred of self-respect, he really doesn't. That's the amount of it." The young man whipped out his handkerchief and wiped his face.

"You mean he really talks about things that none of your friends know?"

"Oh, dear, yes! Recalls things that happened in school. Anything disagreeable. Funny thing, he always turns Brian's picture to the wall."

"Does he come often?"

"Yes, oftener, now. Of course I don't know how he gets in down-stairs. The hall boys never see him. But he has a key to my door. I don't know how he got it, but I can hear him turn it in the lock."

"Why don't you keep your driver with you, or telephone for me to come down?"

"He'd only grin and go down the fire escape as he did before. He's often done it when Harry's come in suddenly. Everybody has to be alone sometimes, you know. Besides, I don't want anybody to see him. He has me there."

"But why not? Why do you feel responsible for him?"

Cavenaugh smiled wearily. "That's rather the point, isn't it? Why do I? But I absolutely do. That identifies him, more than his knowing all about my life and my affairs."

Eastman looked at Cavenaugh thoughtfully. "Well, I should advise you to go in for something altogether different and new, and go in for it hard; business, engineering, metallurgy, something this old fellow wouldn't be interested in. See if you can make him remember logarithms."

Cavenaugh sighed. "No, he has me there, too. People never really change; they go on being themselves. But I would never make much trouble. Why can't they let me alone, damn it! I'd never hurt anybody, except, perhaps—"

"Except your old gentleman, eh?" Eastman laughed. "Seriously, Cavenaugh, if you want to shake him, I think a year on a ranch would do it. He would never be coaxed far from his favorite haunts. He would dread Montana."

Cavenaugh pursed up his lips. "So do I!"

"Oh, you think you do. Try it, and you'll find out. A gun and a horse beats all this sort of thing. Besides losing your haunt, you'd be putting ten years in the bank for yourself. I know a good ranch where they take people, if you want to try it."

"Thank you. I'll consider. Do you think I'm batty?"

"No, but I think you've been doing one sort of thing too long. You need big horizons. Get out of this."

Cavenaugh smiled meekly. He rose lazily and yawned behind his hand. "It's late, and I've taken your whole evening." He strolled over to the window and looked out. "Queer place, New York; rough on the little fellows. Don't you feel sorry for them, the girls especially? I do. What a fight they put up for a little fun! Why, even that old goat is sorry for them, the only decent thing he kept."

Eastman followed him to the door and stood in the hall, while Cavenaugh waited for the elevator. When the car came up Cavenaugh extended his pink, warm hand. "Good night."

The cage sank and his rosy countenance disappeared, his round-eyed smile being the last thing to go.

Weeks passed before Eastman saw Cavenaugh again. One morning, just as he was starting for Washington to argue a case before the Supreme Court, Cavenaugh telephoned him at his office to ask him about the Montana ranch he had recommended; said he meant to take his advice and go out there for the spring and summer.

When Eastman got back from Washington, he saw dusty trunks, just up from the trunk room, before Cavenaugh's door. Next morning, when he stopped to see what the young man was about, he found Cavenaugh in his shirt sleeves, packing.

"I'm really going; off to-morrow night. You didn't think it of me, did you?" he asked gaily.

"Oh, I've always had hopes of you!" Eastman declared. "But you are in a hurry, it seems to me."

"Yes, I am in a hurry." Cavenaugh shot a pair of leggings into one of the open trunks. "I telegraphed your ranch people, used your name, and they said it would be all right. By the way, some of my crowd are giving a little dinner for me at Rector's to-night. Couldn't you be persuaded, as it's a farewell occasion?" Cavenaugh looked at him hopefully.

Eastman laughed and shook his head. "Sorry, Cavenaugh, but that's too gay a world for me. I've got too much work lined up before me. I wish I had time to stop and look at your guns, though. You seem to know something about guns. You've more than you'll need, but nobody can have too many good ones." He put down one of the revolvers regretfully. "I'll drop in to see you in the morning, if you're up."

"I shall be up, all right. I've warned my crowd that I'll cut away before midnight."

"You won't, though," Eastman called back over his shoulder as he hurried down-stairs.

The next morning, while Eastman was dressing, Rollins came in greatly excited.

"I'm a little late, sir. I was stopped by Harry, Mr. Cavenaugh's driver. Mr. Cavenaugh shot himself last night, sir."

Eastman dropped his vest and sat down on his shoe-box. "You're drunk, Rollins," he shouted. "He's going away to-day!"

"Yes, sir. Harry found him this morning. Ah, he's quite dead, sir. Harry's telephoned for the coroner. Harry don't know what to do with the ticket."

Eastman pulled on his coat and ran down the stairway. Cavenaugh's trunks were strapped and piled before the door. Harry was walking up and down the hall with a long green railroad ticket in his hand and a look of complete stupidity on his face.

"What shall I do about this ticket, Mr. Eastman?" he whispered. "And what about his trunks? He had me tell the transfer people to come early. They may be here any minute. Yes, sir. I brought him home in the car last night, before twelve, as cheerful as could be."

"Be quiet, Harry. Where is he?"

"In his bed, sir."

Eastman went into Cavenaugh's sleeping-room. When he came back to the sitting-room, he looked over the writing table; railway folders, time-tables, receipted bills, nothing else. He looked up for the photograph of Cavenaugh's twin brother. There it was, turned to the wall. Eastman took it down and looked at it; a boy in track clothes, half lying in the air, going over the string shoulders first, above the heads of a crowd of lads who were running and cheering. The face was somewhat blurred by the motion and the bright sunlight. Eastman put the picture back, as he found it. Had Cavenaugh entertained his visitor last night, and had the old man been more convincing than usual? "Well, at any rate, he's seen to it that the old man can't establish identity. What a soft lot they are, fellows like poor Cavenaugh!" Eastman thought of his office as a delightful place.

17

The Tell-Tale Heart

By Edgar Allan Poe

Art is long, and Time is fleeting,
And our hearts, though stout and brave,
Still, like muffled drums, are beating
Funeral marches to the grave.

—Longfellow

TRUE!—NERVOUS—VERY, VERY DREADFULLY NERVOUS I HAD—BEEN and am; but why *will* you say that I am mad? The disease had sharpened my senses—not destroyed—not dulled them. Above all was the sense of hearing acute. I heard all things in the heaven and in the earth. I heard many things in hell. How, then, am I mad? Hearken! and observe how healthily—how calmly I can tell you the whole story.

It is impossible to say how first the idea entered my brain; but once conceived, it haunted me day and night. Object there was none. Passion there was none. I loved the old man. He had never wronged me. He had never given me insult. For his gold I had no desire. I think it was his eye! yes, it was this! He had the eye of a vulture—a pale blue eye, with a film over it. Whenever it fell upon me, my blood ran cold; and so by degrees—very gradually—I made up my mind to take the life of the old man, and thus rid myself of the eye forever.

Now this is the point. You fancy me mad. Madmen know nothing. But you should have seen me. You should have seen how wisely I proceeded—with what caution—with what foresight—with what dissimulation I went to work! I was never kinder to the old man than during the whole week before I killed him. And every night, about midnight, I turned the latch of his door and opened it—oh so gently! And then, when I had made an opening sufficient for my head, I put in a dark lantern, all closed, closed, so that no light shone out, and then I thrust in my head. Oh, you would have laughed to see how cunningly I thrust it in! I moved it slowly—very, very slowly, so that I might not disturb the old man's sleep. It took me an hour to place my whole head within the opening so far that I could see him as he lay upon his bed. Ha!—would a madman have been so wise as this? And then, when my head was well in the room, I undid the lantern cautiously—oh, so cautiously—cautiously (for the hinges creaked)—I undid it just so much that a single thin ray fell upon the vulture eye. And this I did for seven long nights—every night just at midnight—but I found the eye always closed; and so it was impossible to do the work; for it was not the old man who vexed me, but his Evil Eye. And every morning, when the day broke, I went boldly into the chamber, and spoke courageously to him, calling him by name in a hearty tone, and inquiring how he had passed the night. So you see he would have been a very profound old man, indeed, to suspect that every night, just at twelve, I looked in upon him while he slept. Upon the eighth night I was more than usually cautious in opening the door. A watch's minute hand moves more quickly than did mine. Never before that night had I *felt* the extent of my own powers—of my sagacity. I could scarcely contain my feelings of triumph. To think that there I was, opening the door, little by little, and he not even to dream of my secret deeds or thoughts. I fairly chuckled at the idea; and perhaps he heard me; for he moved on the bed suddenly, as if startled. Now you may think that I drew back—but no. His room was as black as pitch with the thick darkness, (for the shutters were close fastened, through fear of robbers,) and so I knew that he could not see the opening of the door, and I kept pushing it on steadily, steadily. I had my head in, and was about to open the lantern, when my thumb slipped upon the tin fastening, and the old man sprang up in bed, crying out—"Who's there?"

I kept quite still and said nothing. For a whole hour I did not move a muscle, and in the meantime I did not hear him lie down. He was still sitting up in the bed listening;—just as I have done, night after night, hearkening to the death watches in the wall.

Presently I heard a slight groan, and I knew it was the groan of mortal terror. It was not a groan of pain or of grief—oh, no!—it was the low stifled sound that arises from the bottom of the soul when overcharged with awe. I knew the sound well. Many a night, just at midnight, when all the world slept, it has welled up from my own bosom, deepening, with its dreadful echo, the terrors that distracted me. I say I knew it well. I knew what the old man felt, and pitied him, although I chuckled at heart. I knew that he had been lying awake ever since the first slight noise, when he had turned in the bed. His fears had been ever since growing upon him. He had been trying to fancy them causeless, but could not. He had been saying to himself—"It is nothing but the wind in the chimney—it is only a mouse crossing the floor," or "It is merely a cricket which has made a single chirp." Yes, he had been trying to comfort himself with these suppositions: but he had found all in vain. *All in vain*; because Death, in approaching him had stalked with his black shadow before him, and enveloped the victim. And it was the mournful influence of the unperceived shadow that caused him to feel—although he neither saw nor heard—to *feel* the presence of my head within the room.

When I had waited a long time, very patiently, without hearing him lie down, I resolved to open a little—a very, very little crevice in the lantern. So I opened it—you cannot imagine how stealthily, stealthily—until, at length a single dim ray, like the thread of the spider, shot from out the crevice and fell full upon the vulture eye.

It was open—wide, wide open—and I grew furious as I gazed upon it. I saw it with perfect distinctness—all a dull blue, with a hideous veil over it that chilled the very marrow in my bones; but I could see nothing else of the old man's face or person: for I had directed the ray as if by instinct, precisely upon the damned spot.

And have I not told you that what you mistake for madness is but over acuteness of the senses?—now, I say, there came to my ears a low, dull, quick sound, such as a watch makes when enveloped in cotton. I knew that sound well, too. It was the beating of the old man's heart. It increased my fury, as the beating of a drum stimulates the soldier into courage. But even yet I refrained and kept still. I scarcely breathed. I held the lantern motionless. I tried how steadily I could maintain the ray upon the eye. Meantime the hellish tattoo of the heart increased. It grew quicker and quicker, and louder and louder every instant. The old man's terror *must* have been extreme! It grew louder, I say, louder every moment!—do you mark me well? I have told you that I am nervous: so I am. And now at the dead hour of the night, amid the dreadful silence of that old house, so strange a noise as this excited me to uncontrollable terror. Yet, for some minutes longer I refrained and stood still. But the beating grew louder, louder! I thought the heart must burst. And now a new anxiety seized me—the sound would be heard by a neighbor! The old man's hour had come! With a loud yell, I threw open the lantern and leaped into the room. He shrieked once—once only. In an instant I dragged him to the floor, and pulled the heavy bed over him. I then smiled gaily, to find the deed so far done. But, for many minutes, the heart beat on with a muffled sound. This, however, did not vex me; it would not be heard through the wall. At length it ceased. The old man was dead. I removed the bed and examined the corpse. Yes, he was stone, stone dead. I placed my hand upon the heart and held it there many minutes. There was no pulsation. He was stone dead. His eye would trouble me no more.

If still you think me mad, you will think so no longer when I describe the wise precautions I took for the concealment of the body. The night waned, and I worked hastily, but in silence. First of all I dismembered the corpse. I cut off the head and the arms and the legs.

I then took up three planks from the flooring of the chamber, and deposited all between the scantlings. I then replaced the boards so cleverly, so cunningly, that no human eye—not even *his*—could have detected any thing wrong. There was nothing to wash out—no stain of any kind— no blood-spot whatever. I had been too wary for that. A tub had caught all—ha! ha!

When I had made an end of these labors, it was four o'clock—still dark as midnight. As the bell sounded the hour, there came a knocking at the street door. I went down to open it with a light heart,—for what had I now to fear? There entered three men, who introduced themselves, with perfect suavity, as officers of the police. A shriek had been heard by a neighbor during the night; suspicion of foul play had been aroused; information had been lodged at the police office, and they (the officers) had been deputed to search the premises.

I smiled,—for what had I to fear? I bade the gentlemen welcome. The shriek, I said, was my own in a dream. The old man, I mentioned, was absent in the country. I took my visitors all over the house. I bade them search—search well. I led them, at length, to his chamber. I showed them his treasures, secure, undisturbed. In the enthusiasm of my confidence, I brought chairs into the room, and desired them here to rest from their fatigues, while I myself, in the wild audacity of my perfect triumph, placed my own seat upon the very spot beneath which reposed the corpse of the victim.

The officers were satisfied. My manner had convinced them. I was singularly at ease. They sat, and while I answered cheerily, they chatted of familiar things. But, ere long, I felt myself getting pale and wished them gone. My head ached, and I fancied a ringing in my ears: but still they sat and still chatted. The ringing became more distinct:—it continued and became more distinct: I talked more freely to get rid of the feeling: but it continued and gained definiteness—until, at length, I found that the noise was not within my ears.

No doubt I now grew very pale;—but I talked more fluently, and with a heightened voice. Yet the sound increased—and what could I do? It was a low, dull, quick sound—much such a sound as a watch makes when enveloped in cotton. I gasped for breath—and yet the officers heard it not. I talked more quickly—more vehemently; but the noise steadily increased. I arose and argued about trifles, in a high key and with violent gesticulations; but the noise steadily increased. Why would they not be gone? I paced the floor to and fro with heavy strides, as if excited to fury by the observations of the men—but the noise steadily increased. Oh God! what could I do? I foamed—I raved—I swore! I swung the chair upon which I had been sitting, and grated it upon the boards, but the noise arose over all and continually increased. It grew louder—louder—louder! And still the men chatted pleasantly, and smiled. Was it possible they heard not? Almighty God!—no, no! They heard!—they suspected!—they *knew!*—they were making a mockery of my horror!—this I thought, and this I think. But anything was better than this agony! Anything was more tolerable than this derision! I could bear those hypocritical smiles no longer! I felt that I must scream or die!—and now—again!—hark! louder! louder! louder! *louder!*—

"Villains!" I shrieked, "dissemble no more! I admit the deed!—tear up the planks!—here, here!—it is the beating of his hideous heart!"

18

The Wind in the Rose-Bush

By Mary E. Wilkins Freeman

FORD VILLAGE HAS NO RAILROAD STATION, BEING ON THE OTHER SIDE OF the river from Porter's Falls, and accessible only by the ford which gives it its name, and a ferry line.

The ferry-boat was waiting when Rebecca Flint got off the train with her bag and lunch basket. When she and her small trunk were safely embarked she sat stiff and straight and calm in the ferry-boat as it shot swiftly and smoothly across stream. There was a horse attached to a light country wagon on board, and he pawed the deck uneasily. His owner stood near, with a wary eye upon him, although he was chewing, with as dully reflective an expression as a cow. Beside Rebecca sat a woman of about her own age, who kept looking at her with furtive curiosity; her husband, short and stout and saturnine, stood near her. Rebecca paid no attention to either of them. She was tall and spare and pale, the type of a spinster, yet with rudimentary lines and expressions of matronhood. She all unconsciously held her shawl, rolled up in a canvas bag, on her left hip, as if it had been a child. She wore a settled frown of dissent at life, but it was the frown of a mother who regarded life as a forward child, rather than as an overwhelming fate.

The other woman continued staring at her; she was mildly stupid, except for an over-developed curiosity which made her at times sharp beyond belief. Her eyes glittered, red spots came on her flaccid cheeks; she kept opening her mouth to speak, making little abortive motions. Finally she could endure it no longer; she nudged Rebecca boldly.

"A pleasant day," said she.

Rebecca looked at her and nodded coldly.

"Yes, very," she assented.

"Have you come far?"

"I have come from Michigan."

"Oh!" said the woman, with awe. "It's a long way," she remarked presently.

"Yes, it is," replied Rebecca, conclusively.

Still the other woman was not daunted; there was something which she determined to know, possibly roused thereto by a vague sense of incongruity in the other's appearance. "It's a long ways to come and leave a family," she remarked with painful slyness.

"I ain't got any family to leave," returned Rebecca shortly.

"Then you ain't—"

"No, I ain't."

"Oh!" said the woman.

Rebecca looked straight ahead at the race of the river.

It was a long ferry. Finally Rebecca herself waxed unexpectedly loquacious. She turned to the other woman and inquired if she knew John Dent's widow who lived in Ford Village. "Her husband died about three years ago," said she, by way of detail.

The woman started violently. She turned pale, then she flushed; she cast a strange glance at her husband, who was regarding both women with a sort of stolid keenness.

"Yes, I guess I do," faltered the woman finally.

"Well, his first wife was my sister," said Rebecca with the air of one imparting important intelligence.

"Was she?" responded the other woman feebly. She glanced at her husband with an expression of doubt and terror, and he shook his head forbiddingly.

"I'm going to see her, and take my niece Agnes home with me," said Rebecca.

Then the woman gave such a violent start that she noticed it.

"What is the matter?" she asked.

"Nothin', I guess," replied the woman, with eyes on her husband, who was slowly shaking his head, like a Chinese toy.

"Is my niece sick?" asked Rebecca with quick suspicion.

"No, she ain't sick," replied the woman with alacrity, then she caught her breath with a gasp.

"When did you see her?"

"Let me see; I ain't seen her for some little time," replied the woman. Then she caught her breath again.

"She ought to have grown up real pretty, if she takes after my sister. She was a real pretty woman," Rebecca said wistfully.

"Yes, I guess she did grow up pretty," replied the woman in a trembling voice.

"What kind of a woman is the second wife?"

The woman glanced at her husband's warning face. She continued to gaze at him while she replied in a choking voice to Rebecca:

"I—guess she's a nice woman," she replied. "I—don't know, I—guess so. I—don't see much of her."

"I felt kind of hurt that John married again so quick," said Rebecca; "but I suppose he wanted his house kept, and Agnes wanted care. I wasn't so situated that I could take her when her mother died. I had my own mother to care for, and I was school-teaching. Now mother has gone, and my uncle died six months ago and left me quite a little property, and I've given up my school, and I've come for Agnes. I guess she'll be glad to go with me, though I suppose her stepmother is a good woman, and has always done for her."

The man's warning shake at his wife was fairly portentous.

"I guess so," said she.

"John always wrote that she was a beautiful woman," said Rebecca.

Then the ferry-boat grated on the shore.

John Dent's widow had sent a horse and wagon to meet her sister-in-law. When the woman and her husband went down the road, on which Rebecca in the wagon with her trunk soon passed them, she said reproachfully:

"Seems as if I'd ought to have told her, Thomas."

"Let her find it out herself," replied the man. "Don't you go to burnin' your fingers in other folks' puddin', Maria."

"Do you s'pose she'll see anything?" asked the woman with a spasmodic shudder and a terrified roll of her eyes.

"See!" returned her husband with stolid scorn. "Better be sure there's anything to see."

"Oh, Thomas, they say—"

"Lord, ain't you found out that what they say is mostly lies?"

"But if it should be true, and she's a nervous woman, she might be scared enough to lose her wits," said his wife, staring uneasily after Rebecca's erect figure in the wagon disappearing over the crest of the hilly road.

"Wits that so easy upset ain't worth much," declared the man. "You keep out of it, Maria."

Rebecca in the meantime rode on in the wagon, beside a flaxen-headed boy, who looked, to her understanding, not very bright. She asked him a question, and he paid no attention. She repeated it, and he responded with a bewildered and incoherent grunt. Then she let him alone, after making sure that he knew how to drive straight.

They had traveled about half a mile, passed the village square, and gone a short distance beyond, when the boy drew up with a sudden Whoa! before a very prosperous-looking house. It had been one of the aboriginal cottages of the vicinity, small and white, with a roof extending on one side over a piazza, and a tiny "L" jutting out in the rear, on the right hand. Now the cottage was transformed by dormer windows, a bay window on the piazzaless side, a carved railing down the front steps, and a modern hard-wood door.

"Is this John Dent's house?" asked Rebecca.

The boy was as sparing of speech as a philosopher. His only response was in flinging the reins over the horse's back, stretching out one foot to the shaft, and leaping out of the wagon, then going around to the rear for the trunk. Rebecca got out and went toward the house. Its white paint had a new gloss; its blinds were an immaculate apple green; the lawn was trimmed as smooth as velvet, and it was dotted with scrupulous groups of hydrangeas and cannas.

"I always understood that John Dent was well-to-do," Rebecca reflected comfortably. "I guess Agnes will have considerable. I've got enough, but it will come in handy for her schooling. She can have advantages."

The boy dragged the trunk up the fine gravel-walk, but before he reached the steps leading up to the piazza, for the house stood on a terrace, the front door opened and a fair, frizzled head of a very large and handsome woman appeared. She held up her black silk skirt, disclosing voluminous ruffles of starched embroidery, and waited for Rebecca. She smiled placidly, her pink, double-chinned face widened and dimpled, but her blue eyes were wary and calculating. She extended her hand as Rebecca climbed the steps.

"This is Miss Flint, I suppose," said she.

"Yes, ma'am," replied Rebecca, noticing with bewilderment a curious expression compounded of fear and defiance on the other's face.

"Your letter only arrived this morning," said Mrs. Dent, in a steady voice. Her great face was a uniform pink, and her china-blue eyes were at once aggressive and veiled with secrecy.

"Yes, I hardly thought you'd get my letter," replied Rebecca. "I felt as if I could not wait to hear from you before I came. I supposed you would be so situated that you could have me a little while without putting you out too much, from what John used to write me about his circumstances, and when I had that money so unexpected I felt as if I must come for Agnes. I suppose you will be willing to give her up. You know she's my own blood, and of course she's no relation to you, though you must have got attached to her. I know from her picture what a sweet girl she must be, and John always said she looked like her own mother, and Grace was a beautiful woman, if she was my sister."

Rebecca stopped and stared at the other woman in amazement and alarm. The great handsome blonde creature stood speechless, livid, gasping, with her hand to her heart, her lips parted in a horrible caricature of a smile.

"Are you sick!" cried Rebecca, drawing near. "Don't you want me to get you some water!"

Then Mrs. Dent recovered herself with a great effort. "It is nothing," she said. "I am subject to—spells. I am over it now. Won't you come in, Miss Flint?"

As she spoke, the beautiful deep-rose colour suffused her face, her blue eyes met her visitor's with the opaqueness of turquoise—with a revelation of blue, but a concealment of all behind.

Rebecca followed her hostess in, and the boy, who had waited quiescently, climbed the steps with the trunk. But before they entered the door a strange thing happened. On the upper terrace close to the piazza-post, grew a great rose-bush, and on it, late in the season though it was, one small red, perfect rose.

Rebecca looked at it, and the other woman extended her hand with a quick gesture. "Don't you pick that rose!" she brusquely cried.

Rebecca drew herself up with stiff dignity.

"I ain't in the habit of picking other folks' roses without leave," said she.

As Rebecca spoke she started violently, and lost sight of her resentment, for something singular happened. Suddenly the rose-bush was agitated violently as if by a gust of wind, yet it was a remarkably still day. Not a leaf of the hydrangea standing on the terrace close to the rose trembled.

"What on earth—" began Rebecca, then she stopped with a gasp at the sight of the other woman's face. Although a face, it gave somehow the impression of a desperately clutched hand of secrecy.

"Come in!" said she in a harsh voice, which seemed to come forth from her chest with no intervention of the organs of speech. "Come into the house. I'm getting cold out here."

"What makes that rose-bush blow so when there isn't any wind?" asked Rebecca, trembling with vague horror, yet resolute.

"I don't see as it is blowing," returned the woman calmly. And as she spoke, indeed, the bush was quiet.

"It was blowing," declared Rebecca.

"It isn't now," said Mrs. Dent. "I can't try to account for everything that blows out-of-doors. I have too much to do."

She spoke scornfully and confidently, with defiant, unflinching eyes, first on the bush, then on Rebecca, and led the way into the house.

"It looked queer," persisted Rebecca, but she followed, and also the boy with the trunk.

Rebecca entered an interior, prosperous, even elegant, according to her simple ideas. There were Brussels carpets, lace curtains, and plenty of brilliant upholstery and polished wood.

"You're real nicely situated," remarked Rebecca, after she had become a little accustomed to her new surroundings and the two women were seated at the tea-table.

Mrs. Dent stared with a hard complacency from behind her silver-plated service. "Yes, I be," said she.

"You got all the things new?" said Rebecca hesitatingly, with a jealous memory of her dead sister's bridal furnishings.

"Yes," said Mrs. Dent; "I was never one to want dead folks' things, and I had money enough of my own, so I wasn't beholden to John. I had the old duds put up at auction. They didn't bring much."

"I suppose you saved some for Agnes. She'll want some of her poor mother's things when she is grown up," said Rebecca with some indignation.

The defiant stare of Mrs. Dent's blue eyes waxed more intense. "There's a few things up garret," said she.

"She'll be likely to value them," remarked Rebecca. As she spoke she glanced at the window. "Isn't it most time for her to be coming home?" she asked.

"Most time," answered Mrs. Dent carelessly; "but when she gets over to Addie Slocum's she never knows when to come home."

"Is Addie Slocum her intimate friend?"

"Intimate as any."

"Maybe we can have her come out to see Agnes when she's living with me," said Rebecca wistfully. "I suppose she'll be likely to be homesick at first."

"Most likely," answered Mrs. Dent.

"Does she call you mother?" Rebecca asked.

"No, she calls me Aunt Emeline," replied the other woman shortly. "When did you say you were going home?"

"In about a week, I thought, if she can be ready to go so soon," answered Rebecca with a surprised look.

She reflected that she would not remain a day longer than she could help after such an inhospitable look and question.

"Oh, as far as that goes," said Mrs. Dent, "it wouldn't make any difference about her being ready. You could go home whenever you felt that you must, and she could come afterward."

"Alone?"

"Why not? She's a big girl now, and you don't have to change cars."

"My niece will go home when I do, and not travel alone; and if I can't wait here for her, in the house that used to be her mother's and my sister's home, I'll go and board somewhere," returned Rebecca with warmth.

"Oh, you can stay here as long as you want to. You're welcome," said Mrs. Dent.

Then Rebecca started. "There she is!" she declared in a trembling, exultant voice. Nobody knew how she longed to see the girl.

"She isn't as late as I thought she'd be," said Mrs. Dent, and again that curious, subtle change passed over her face, and again it settled into that stony impassiveness.

Rebecca stared at the door, waiting for it to open. "Where is she?" she asked presently.

"I guess she's stopped to take off her hat in the entry," suggested Mrs. Dent.

Rebecca waited. "Why don't she come? It can't take her all this time to take off her hat."

For answer Mrs. Dent rose with a stiff jerk and threw open the door.

"Agnes!" she called. "Agnes!" Then she turned and eyed Rebecca. "She ain't there."

"I saw her pass the window," said Rebecca in bewilderment.

"You must have been mistaken."

"I know I did," persisted Rebecca.

"You couldn't have."

"I did. I saw first a shadow go over the ceiling, then I saw her in the glass there"—she pointed to a mirror over the sideboard opposite—"and then the shadow passed the window."

"How did she look in the glass?"

"Little and light-haired, with the light hair kind of tossing over her forehead."

"You couldn't have seen her."

"Was that like Agnes?"

"Like enough; but of course you didn't see her. You've been thinking so much about her that you thought you did."

"You thought *you* did."

"I thought I saw a shadow pass the window, but I must have been mistaken. She didn't come in, or we would have seen her before now. I knew it was too early for her to get home from Addie Slocum's, anyhow."

When Rebecca went to bed Agnes had not returned. Rebecca had resolved that she would not retire until the girl came, but she was very tired, and she reasoned with herself that she was foolish. Besides, Mrs. Dent suggested that Agnes might go to the church social with Addie Slocum. When Rebecca suggested that she be sent for and told that her aunt had come, Mrs. Dent laughed meaningly.

"I guess you'll find out that a young girl ain't so ready to leave a sociable, where there's boys, to see her aunt," said she.

"She's too young," said Rebecca incredulously and indignantly.

"She's sixteen," replied Mrs. Dent; "and she's always been great for the boys."

"She's going to school four years after I get her before she thinks of boys," declared Rebecca.

"We'll see," laughed the other woman.

After Rebecca went to bed, she lay awake a long time listening for the sound of girlish laughter and a boy's voice under her window; then she fell asleep.

The next morning she was down early. Mrs. Dent, who kept no servants, was busily preparing breakfast.

"Don't Agnes help you about breakfast?" asked Rebecca.

"No, I let her lay," replied Mrs. Dent shortly.

"What time did she get home last night?"

"She didn't get home."

"What?"

"She didn't get home. She stayed with Addie. She often does."

"Without sending you word?"

"Oh, she knew I wouldn't worry."

"When will she be home?"

"Oh, I guess she'll be along pretty soon."

Rebecca was uneasy, but she tried to conceal it, for she knew of no good reason for uneasiness. What was there to occasion alarm in the fact of one young girl staying overnight with another? She could not eat much breakfast. Afterward she went out on the little piazza, although her hostess strove furtively to stop her.

"Why don't you go out back of the house? It's real pretty—a view over the river," she said.

"I guess I'll go out here," replied Rebecca. She had a purpose: to watch for the absent girl.

Presently Rebecca came hustling into the house through the sitting-room, into the kitchen where Mrs. Dent was cooking.

"That rose-bush!" she gasped.

Mrs. Dent turned and faced her.

"What of it?"

"It's a-blowing."

"What of it?"

"There isn't a mite of wind this morning."

Mrs. Dent turned with an inimitable toss of her fair head. "If you think I can spend my time puzzling over such nonsense as—" she began, but Rebecca interrupted her with a cry and a rush to the door.

"There she is now!" she cried. She flung the door wide open, and curiously enough a breeze came in and her own gray hair tossed, and a paper blew off the table to the floor with a loud rustle, but there was nobody in sight.

"There's nobody here," Rebecca said.

She looked blankly at the other woman, who brought her rolling-pin down on a slab of pie-crust with a thud.

"I didn't hear anybody," she said calmly.

"*I saw somebody pass that window!*"

"You were mistaken again."

"I *know* I saw somebody."

"You couldn't have. Please shut that door."

Rebecca shut the door. She sat down beside the window and looked out on the autumnal yard, with its little curve of footpath to the kitchen door.

"What smells so strong of roses in this room?" she said presently. She sniffed hard.

"I don't smell anything but these nutmegs."

"It is not nutmeg."

"I don't smell anything else."

"Where do you suppose Agnes is?"

"Oh, perhaps she has gone over the ferry to Porter's Falls with Addie. She often does. Addie's got an aunt over there, and Addie's got a cousin, a real pretty boy."

"You suppose she's gone over there?"

"Mebbe. I shouldn't wonder."

"When should she be home?"

"Oh, not before afternoon."

Rebecca waited with all the patience she could muster. She kept reassuring herself, telling herself that it was all natural, that the other woman could not help it, but she made up her mind that if Agnes did not return that afternoon she should be sent for.

When it was four o'clock she started up with resolution. She had been furtively watching the onyx clock on the sitting-room mantel; she had timed herself. She had said that if Agnes was not home by that time she should demand that she be sent for. She rose and stood before Mrs. Dent, who looked up coolly from her embroidery.

"I've waited just as long as I'm going to," she said. "I've come 'way from Michigan to see my own sister's daughter and take her home with me. I've been here ever since yesterday—twenty-four hours—and I haven't seen her. Now I'm going to. I want her sent for."

Mrs. Dent folded her embroidery and rose.

"Well, I don't blame you," she said. "It is high time she came home. I'll go right over and get her myself."

Rebecca heaved a sigh of relief. She hardly knew what she had suspected or feared, but she knew that her position had been one of antagonism if not accusation, and she was sensible of relief.

"I wish you would," she said gratefully, and went back to her chair, while Mrs. Dent got her shawl and her little white head-tie. "I wouldn't trouble you, but I do feel as if I couldn't wait any longer to see her," she remarked apologetically.

"Oh, it ain't any trouble at all," said Mrs. Dent as she went out. "I don't blame you; you have waited long enough."

Rebecca sat at the window watching breathlessly until Mrs. Dent came stepping through the yard alone. She ran to the door and saw, hardly noticing it this time, that the rose-bush was again violently agitated, yet with no wind evident elsewhere.

"Where is she?" she cried.

Mrs. Dent laughed with stiff lips as she came up the steps over the terrace. "Girls will be girls," said she. "She's gone with Addie to Lincoln. Addie's got an uncle who's conductor on the train, and lives there, and he got 'em passes, and they're goin' to stay to Addie's Aunt Margaret's a few days. Mrs. Slocum said Agnes didn't have time to come over and ask me before the train went, but she took it on herself to say it would be all right, and—"

"Why hadn't she been over to tell you?" Rebecca was angry, though not suspicious. She even saw no reason for her anger.

"Oh, she was putting up grapes. She was coming over just as soon as she got the black off her hands. She heard I had company, and her hands were a sight. She was holding them over sulphur matches."

"You say she's going to stay a few days?" repeated Rebecca dazedly.

"Yes; till Thursday, Mrs. Slocum said."

"How far is Lincoln from here?"

"About fifty miles. It'll be a real treat to her. Mrs. Slocum's sister is a real nice woman."

"It is goin' to make it pretty late about my goin' home."

"If you don't feel as if you could wait, I'll get her ready and send her on just as soon as I can," Mrs. Dent said sweetly.

"I'm going to wait," said Rebecca grimly.

The two women sat down again, and Mrs. Dent took up her embroidery.

"Is there any sewing I can do for her?" Rebecca asked finally in a desperate way. "If I can get her sewing along some—"

Mrs. Dent arose with alacrity and fetched a mass of white from the closet. "Here," she said, "if you want to sew the lace on this nightgown. I was going to put her to it, but she'll be glad enough to get rid of it. She ought to have this and one more before she goes. I don't like to send her away without some good underclothing."

Rebecca snatched at the little white garment and sewed feverishly.

That night she wakened from a deep sleep a little after midnight and lay a minute trying to collect her faculties and explain to herself what she was listening to. At last she discovered that it was the then popular strains of "The Maiden's Prayer" floating up through the floor from the piano in the sitting-room below. She jumped up, threw a shawl over her nightgown, and hurried downstairs trembling. There was nobody in the sitting-room; the piano was silent. She ran to Mrs. Dent's bedroom and called hysterically:

"Emeline! Emeline!"

"What is it?" asked Mrs. Dent's voice from the bed. The voice was stern, but had a note of consciousness in it.

"Who—who was that playing 'The Maiden's Prayer' in the sitting-room, on the piano?"

"I didn't hear anybody."

"There was some one."

"I didn't hear anything."

"I tell you there was some one. But—*there ain't anybody there.*"

"I didn't hear anything."

"I did—somebody playing 'The Maiden's Prayer' on the piano. Has Agnes got home? I want to know."

"Of course Agnes hasn't got home," answered Mrs. Dent with rising inflection. "Be you gone crazy over that girl? The last boat from Porter's Falls was in before we went to bed. Of course she ain't come."

"I heard—"

"You were dreaming."

"I wasn't; I was broad awake."

Rebecca went back to her chamber and kept her lamp burning all night.

The next morning her eyes upon Mrs. Dent were wary and blazing with suppressed excitement. She kept opening her mouth as if to speak, then frowning, and setting her lips hard. After breakfast she went upstairs, and came down presently with her coat and bonnet.

"Now, Emeline," she said, "I want to know where the Slocums live."

Mrs. Dent gave a strange, long, half-lidded glance at her. She was finishing her coffee.

"Why?" she asked.

"I'm going over there and find out if they have heard anything from her daughter and Agnes since they went away. I don't like what I heard last night."

"You must have been dreaming."

"It don't make any odds whether I was or not. Does she play 'The Maiden's Prayer' on the piano? I want to know."

"What if she does? She plays it a little, I believe. I don't know. She don't half play it, anyhow; she ain't got an ear."

"That wasn't half played last night. I don't like such things happening. I ain't superstitious, but I don't like it. I'm going. Where do the Slocums live?"

"You go down the road over the bridge past the old grist mill, then you turn to the left; it's the only house for half a mile. You can't miss it. It has a barn with a ship in full sail on the cupola."

"Well, I'm going. I don't feel easy."

About two hours later Rebecca returned. There were red spots on her cheeks. She looked wild. "I've been there," she said, "and there isn't a soul at home. Something *has* happened."

"What has happened?"

"I don't know. Something. I had a warning last night. There wasn't a soul there. They've been sent for to Lincoln."

"Did you see anybody to ask?" asked Mrs. Dent with thinly concealed anxiety.

"I asked the woman that lives on the turn of the road. She's stone deaf. I suppose you know. She listened while I screamed at her to know where the Slocums were, and then she said, 'Mrs. Smith don't live here.' I didn't see anybody on the road, and that's the only house. What do you suppose it means?"

"I don't suppose it means much of anything," replied Mrs. Dent coolly. "Mr. Slocum is conductor on the railroad, and he'd be away anyway, and Mrs. Slocum often goes early when he does, to spend the day with her sister in Porter's Falls. She'd be more likely to go away than Addie."

"And you don't think anything has happened?" Rebecca asked with diminishing distrust before the reasonableness of it.

"Land, no!"

Rebecca went upstairs to lay aside her coat and bonnet. But she came hurrying back with them still on.

"Who's been in my room?" she gasped. Her face was pale as ashes.

Mrs. Dent also paled as she regarded her.

"What do you mean?" she asked slowly.

"I found when I went upstairs that—little nightgown of—Agnes's on—the bed, laid out. It was—*laid out.* The sleeves were folded across the bosom, and there was that little red rose between them. Emeline, what is it? Emeline, what's the matter? Oh!"

Mrs. Dent was struggling for breath in great, choking gasps. She clung to the back of a chair. Rebecca, trembling herself so she could scarcely keep on her feet, got her some water.

As soon as she recovered herself Mrs. Dent regarded her with eyes full of the strangest mixture of fear and horror and hostility.

"What do you mean talking so?" she said in a hard voice.

"It *is there.*"

"Nonsense. You threw it down and it fell that way."

"It was folded in my bureau drawer."

"It couldn't have been."

"Who picked that red rose?"

"Look on the bush," Mrs. Dent replied shortly.

Rebecca looked at her; her mouth gaped. She hurried out of the room. When she came back her eyes seemed to protrude. (She had in the meantime hastened upstairs, and come down with tottering steps, clinging to the banisters.)

"Now I want to know what all this means?" she demanded.

"What *what* means?"

"The rose is on the bush, and it's gone from the bed in my room! Is this house haunted, or what?"

"I don't know anything about a house being haunted. I don't believe in such things. Be you crazy?" Mrs. Dent spoke with gathering force. The colour flashed back to her cheeks.

"No," said Rebecca shortly. "I ain't crazy yet, but I shall be if this keeps on much longer. I'm going to find out where that girl is before night."

Mrs. Dent eyed her.

"What be you going to do?"

"I'm going to Lincoln."

A faint triumphant smile overspread Mrs. Dent's large face.

"You can't," said she; "there ain't any train."

"No train?"

"No; there ain't any afternoon train from the Falls to Lincoln."

"Then I'm going over to the Slocums' again to-night."

However, Rebecca did not go; such a rain came up as deterred even her resolution, and she had only her best dresses with her. Then in the evening came the letter from the Michigan village which she had left nearly a week ago. It was from her cousin, a single woman, who had come to keep her house while she was away. It was a pleasant unexciting letter enough, all the first of it, and related mostly how she missed Rebecca; how she hoped she was having pleasant weather and kept her health; and how her friend, Mrs. Greenaway, had come to stay with her since she had felt lonesome the first night in the house; how she hoped Rebecca would have no objections to this, although nothing had been said about it, since she had not realized that she might be nervous alone. The cousin was painfully conscientious, hence the letter. Rebecca smiled in spite of her disturbed mind as she read it, then her eye caught the postscript. That was in a different hand, purporting to be written by the friend, Mrs. Hannah Greenaway, informing her that the cousin had fallen down the cellar stairs and broken her hip, and was in a dangerous condition, and begging Rebecca to return at once, as she herself was rheumatic and unable to nurse her properly, and no one else could be obtained.

Rebecca looked at Mrs. Dent, who had come to her room with the letter quite late; it was half-past nine, and she had gone upstairs for the night.

"Where did this come from?" she asked.

"Mr. Amblecrom brought it," she replied.

"Who's he?"

"The postmaster. He often brings the letters that come on the late mail. He knows I ain't anybody to send. He brought yours about your coming. He said he and his wife came over on the ferry-boat with you."

"I remember him," Rebecca replied shortly. "There's bad news in this letter."

Mrs. Dent's face took on an expression of serious inquiry.

"Yes, my Cousin Harriet has fallen down the cellar stairs—they were always dangerous—and she's broken her hip, and I've got to take the first train home to-morrow."

"You don't say so. I'm dreadfully sorry."

"No, you ain't sorry!" said Rebecca, with a look as if she leaped. "You're glad. I don't know why, but you're glad. You've wanted to get rid of me for some reason ever since I came. I don't know why. You're a strange woman. Now you've got your way, and I hope you're satisfied."

"How you talk."

Mrs. Dent spoke in a faintly injured voice, but there was a light in her eyes.

"I talk the way it is. Well, I'm going to-morrow morning, and I want you, just as soon as Agnes Dent comes home, to send her out to me. Don't you wait for anything. You pack what clothes she's got, and don't wait

235

even to mend them, and you buy her ticket. I'll leave the money, and you send her along. She don't have to change cars. You start her off, when she gets home, on the next train!"

"Very well," replied the other woman. She had an expression of covert amusement.

"Mind you do it."

"Very well, Rebecca."

Rebecca started on her journey the next morning. When she arrived, two days later, she found her cousin in perfect health. She found, moreover, that the friend had not written the postscript in the cousin's letter. Rebecca would have returned to Ford Village the next morning, but the fatigue and nervous strain had been too much for her. She was not able to move from her bed. She had a species of low fever induced by anxiety and fatigue. But she could write, and she did, to the Slocums, and she received no answer. She also wrote to Mrs. Dent; she even sent numerous telegrams, with no response. Finally she wrote to the postmaster, and an answer arrived by the first possible mail. The letter was short, curt, and to the purpose. Mr. Amblecrom, the postmaster, was a man of few words, and especially wary as to his expressions in a letter.

"Dear madam," he wrote, "your favour rec'ed. No Slocums in Ford's Village. All dead. Addie ten years ago, her mother two years later, her father five. House vacant. Mrs. John Dent said to have neglected stepdaughter. Girl was sick. Medicine not given. Talk of taking action. Not enough evidence. House said to be haunted. Strange sights and sounds. Your niece, Agnes Dent, died a year ago, about this time.

"Yours truly,
"THOMAS AMBLECROM."

19

The Ghost of Fear

By H. G. Wells

I CAN ASSURE YOU," SAID I, "THAT IT WILL TAKE A VERY TANGIBLE GHOST to frighten me." And I stood up before the fire with my glass in my hand.

"It is your own choosing," said the man with the withered arm, and glanced at me askance.

"Eight-and-twenty years," said I, "I have lived, and never a ghost have I seen as yet."

The old woman sat staring hard into the fire, her pale eyes wide open. "Ay," she broke in, "and eight-and-twenty years you have lived, never seen the likes of this house, I reckon. There's a many things to see, when one's still but eight-and-twenty." She swayed her head slowly from side to side. "A many things to see and sorrow for."

I half suspected these old people were trying to enhance the spectral terrors of their house by this droning insistence. I put down my empty glass on the table, and, looking about the room, caught a glimpse of myself, abbreviated and broadened to an impossible sturdiness, in the queer old mirror beside the china cupboard. "Well," I said, "if I see anything to-night, I shall be so much the wiser. For I come to the business with an open mind."

"It's your own choosing," said the man with the withered arm once more.

I heard the faint sound of a stick and a shambling step on the flags in the passage outside. The door creaked on its hinges as a second old man entered, more bent, more wrinkled, more aged even than the first. He supported himself by the help of a crutch, his eyes were covered by a shade, and his lower lip, half averted, hung pale and pink from his decaying yellow teeth. He made straight for an armchair on the opposite side of the table, sat down clumsily, and began to cough. The man with the withered hand gave the newcomer a short glance of positive dislike; the old woman took no notice of his arrival, but remained with her eyes fixed steadily on the fire.

"I said—it's your own choosing," said the man with the withered hand, when the coughing had ceased for a while.

"It's my own choosing," I answered.

The man with the shade became aware of my presence for the first time, and threw his head back for a moment, and sidewise, to see me. I caught a momentary glimpse of his eyes, small and bright and inflamed. Then he began to cough and splutter again.

"Why don't you drink?" said the man with the withered arm, pushing the beer toward him. The man with the shade poured out a glassful with a shaking hand, that splashed half as much again on the deal table. A monstrous shadow of him crouched upon the wall, and mocked his action as he poured and drank. I must confess I had scarcely expected these grotesque custodians. There is, to my mind, something inhuman in senility, something crouching and atavistic: the human qualities seem to drop from old people insensibly day by day. The three of them made me feel uncomfortable with their gaunt silences, their bent carriage, their evident unfriendliness to me and to one another. And that night, perhaps, I was in the mood for uncomfortable impressions. I resolved to get away from their vague foreshadowings of the evil things upstairs.

"If," said I, "you will show me to this haunted room of yours, I will make myself comfortable there."

The old man with the cough jerked his head back so suddenly that it startled me, and shot another glance of his red eyes at me from out of the darkness under the shade, but no one answered me. I waited a minute, glancing from one to the other. The old woman stared like a dead body, glaring into the fire with the lackluster eyes.

"If," I said, a little louder, "if you will show me to this haunted room of yours, I will relieve you from the task of entertaining me."

"There's a candle on the slab outside the door," said the man with the withered hand, looking at my feet as he addressed me. "But if you go to the Red Room to-night—"

"This night of all nights!" said the old woman, softly. "—You go alone."

"Very well," I answered shortly, "and which way do I go?"

"You go along the passage for a bit," said he, nodding his head on his shoulder at the door, "until you come to a spiral staircase; and on the second landing is a door covered with green baize. Go through that, and down the long corridor to the end, and the Red Room is on your left up the steps."

"Have I got that right?" I said, and repeated his directions.

He corrected me in one particular.

"And you are really going?" said the man with the shade, looking at me again for the third time with that queer, unnatural tilting of the face.

"This night of all nights!" whispered the old woman.

"It is what I came for," I said, and moved toward the door. As I did so, the old man with the shade rose and staggered round the table, so as to be closer to the others and to the fire. At the door I turned and looked at them, and saw they were all close together, dark against the firelight, starting at me over their shoulders, with an intent expression on their ancient faces.

"Good night," I said, setting the door open.

"It's your own choosing," said the man with the withered arm.

I left the door wide open until the candle was well alight, and then I shut them in, and walked down the chilly, echoing passage.

I must confess that the oddness of these three old pensioners in whose charge their ladyship had left the castle, and the deep-toned, old-fashioned furniture of the housekeeper's room, in which they forgath-cred, had affected me curiously in spite of my effort to keep myself at a matter-of-fact phase. They seemed to belong to another age, an older age, an age when things spiritual were indeed to be feared, when common sense was uncommon, an age when omens and witches were credible, and ghosts beyond denying. Their very existence, thought I, is spectral; the cut of their clothing, fashions born in dead brains; the ornaments and conveniences in the room about them even are ghostly—the thoughts of vanished men, which still haunt rather than participate in the world of to-day. And the passage I was in, long and shadowy, with a film of moisture glistening on the walls, was as gaunt and cold as a thing that is dead and rigid. But with an effort I sent such thoughts to the right-about. The long, drafty subterranean passage was chilly and dusty, and my candle flared and made the shadows cower and quiver. The echoes rang up and down the spiral staircase, and a shadow came sweeping up after me, and another fled before me into the darkness overhead. I came to the wide landing and stopped there for a moment listening to a rustling that I fancied I heard creeping behind me, and then, satisfied of the absolute silence, pushed open the unwilling baize-covered door and stood in the silent corridor.

The effect was scarcely what I had expected, for the moonlight, coming in by the great window on the grand staircase, picked out everything in vivid black shadow or reticulated silvery illumination. Everything seemed in its proper position; the house might have been deserted on the yesterday instead of twelve months ago. There were candles in the sockets of the sconces, and whatever dust had gathered on the carpets or upon the polished flooring was distributed so evenly as to be invisible in my candlelight. A waiting stillness was over everything. I was about to advance, and stopped abruptly. A bronze group stood upon the landing hidden from me by a corner of the wall; but its shadow fell with marvelous distinctness upon the white paneling, and gave me the impression of someone crouching to waylay me. The thing jumped upon my attention suddenly. I stood rigid for half a moment, perhaps. Then, with my hand in the pocket that held the revolver, I advanced, only to discover a Ganymede and Eagle, glistening in the moonlight. That incident for a time restored my nerve, and a dim porcelain Chinaman on a buhl table, whose head rocked as I passed, scarcely startled me.

The door of the Red Room and the steps up to it were in a shadowy corner. I moved my candle from side to side in order to see clearly the nature of the recess in which I stood, before opening the door. Here it is, thought I, that my predecessor was found, and the memory of that story gave me a sudden twinge of apprehension. I glanced over my shoulder at the black Ganymede in the moonlight, and opened the door of the

Red Room rather hastily, with my face half turned to the pallid silence of the corridor.

I entered, closed the door behind me at once, turned the key I found in the lock within, and stood with the candle held aloft surveying the scene of my vigil, the great Red Room of Lorraine Castle, in which the young Duke had died; or rather in which he had begun his dying, for he had opened the door and fallen headlong down the steps I had just ascended. That had been the end of his vigil, of his gallant attempt to conquer the ghostly tradition of the place, and never, I thought, had apoplexy better served the ends of superstition. There were other and older stories that clung to the room, back to the half-incredible beginning of it all, the tale of a timid wife and the tragic end that came to her husband's jest of frightening her. And looking round that huge shadowy room with its black window bays, its recesses and alcoves, its dusty brown-red hangings and dark gigantic furniture, one could well understand the legends that had sprouted in its black corners, its germinating darkness. My candle was a little tongue of light in the vastness of the chamber; its rays failed to pierce to the opposite end of the room, and left an ocean of dull red mystery and suggestion, sentinel shadows and watching darkness beyond its island of light. And the stillness of desolation brooded over it all.

I must confess some impalpable quality of that ancient room disturbed me. I tried to fight the feeling down. I resolved to make a systematic examination of the place, and so by leaving nothing to the imagination, dispel the fanciful suggestions of the obscurity before they obtained a hold upon me. After satisfying myself of the fastening of the door, I began to walk round the room, peering round each article of furniture, tucking up the valances of the bed and opening its curtain wide. In one place there was a distinct echo to my footsteps, the noises I made seemed so little that they enhanced rather than broke the silence of the place. I pulled up the blinds and examined the fastenings of the several windows. Attracted by the fall of a particle of dust, I leaned forward and looked up the blackness of the wide chimney. Then, trying to preserve my scientific attitude of mind, I walked round and began tapping the oak paneling for any secret opening, but I desisted before reaching the alcove. I saw my face in a mirror—white.

There were two big mirrors in the room, each with a pair of sconces bearing candles, and on the mantleshelf, too, were candles in china candlesticks. All these I lit one after the other. The fire was laid—an unexpected consideration from the old housekeeper—and I lit it, to keep down any disposition to shiver, and when it was burning well I stood round with my back to it and regarded the room again. I had pulled up a chintz-covered armchair and a table to form a kind of barricade before me. On this lay my revolver, ready to hand. My precise examination had done me a little good, but I still found the remoter darkness of the place and its perfect stillness too stimulating for the imagination. The echoing of the stir and cracking of the fire was no sort of comfort to me. The shadow in the alcove at the end of the room began to display that undefinable quality of a presence, that odd suggestion of a lurking living thing that comes so easily in silence and solitude. And to reassure myself, I walked with a candle into it and satisfied myself that there was nothing tangible there. I stood that candle upon the floor of the alcove and left it in that position.

By this time I was in a state of considerable nervous tension, although to my reason there was no adequate cause for my condition. My mind, however, was perfectly clear. I postulated quite unreservedly that nothing supernatural could happen, and to pass the time I began stringing some rhymes together, Ingoldsby fashion, concerning the original legend of the place. A few I spoke aloud, but the echoes were not pleasant. For the same reason I also abandoned, after a time, a conversation with myself upon the impossibility of ghosts and haunting. My mind reverted to the three old and distorted people downstairs, and I tried to keep it upon that topic.

The somber reds and grays of the room troubled me; even with its seven candles the place was merely dim. The light in the alcove flaring in a draft, and the fire flickering, kept the shadows and penumbra perpetually shifting and stirring in a noiseless flighty dance. Casting about for a remedy, I recalled the wax candles I had seen in the corridor, and, with a slight effort, carrying a candle and leaving the door open, I walked out into the moonlight, and presently returned with as many as ten. These I put in the various knick-knacks of china with which the room was sparsely adorned, and lit and placed them where the shadows had lain deepest, some on the floor, some in the window recesses, arranging and rearranging them until at last my seventeen candles were so placed that not an inch of the room but had the direct light of at least one of them. It occurred to me that when the ghost came I could warn him not to trip over them. The room was now quite brightly illuminated. There was something very cheering and reassuring in these little silent streaming flames, and to notice their steady diminution of length offered me an occupation and gave me a reassuring sense of the passage of time.

Even with that, however, the brooding expectation of the vigil weighed heavily enough upon me. I stood watching the minute hand of my watch creep towards midnight.

Then something happened in the alcove. I did not see the candle go out, I simply turned and saw that the darkness was there, as one might start and see the unexpected presence of a stranger. The black shadow had sprung back to its place. "By Jove," said I aloud, recovering from my surprise, "that draft's a strong one"; and taking the matchbox from the table, I walked across the room in a leisurely manner to relight the corner again. My first match would not strike, and as I succeeded with the second, something seemed to blink on the wall before me. I turned my head involuntarily and saw that the two candles on the little table by the fireplace were extinguished. I rose at once to my feet.

"Odd," I said. "Did I do that myself in a flash of absentmindedness?"

I walked back, relit one, and as I did so I saw the candle on the right sconce of one of the mirrors wink and go right out, and almost immediately its companion followed it. The flames vanished as if the wick had been suddenly nipped between a finger and thumb, leaving the wick neither glowing nor smoking, but black. While I stood gaping the candle at the foot of the bed went out, and the shadows seemed to take another step toward me.

"This won't do!" said I, and first one and then another candle on the mantleshelf followed.

"What's up?" I cried, with a queer high note getting into my voice somehow. At that the candle on the corner of the wardrobe went out, and the one I had relit in the alcove followed.

"Steady on!" I said, "those candles are wanted," speaking with a half-hysterical facetiousness, and scratching away at a match the while, "for the mantel candlesticks." My hands trembled so much that twice I missed the rough paper of the matchbox. As the mantel emerged from the darkness again, two candles in the remoter end of the room were eclipsed. But with the same match I also relit the larger mirror candles, and those on the floor near the doorway, so that for a moment I seemed to gain on the extinctions. But then in a noiseless volley there vanished four lights at once in different corners of the room, and I struck another match in quivering haste, and stood hesitating whither to take it.

As I stood undecided, an invisible hand seemed to sweep out the two candles on the table. With a cry of terror I dashed at the alcove, then into the corner and then into the window, relighting three as two more vanished by the fireplace, and then, perceiving a better way I dropped matches on the iron-bound deedbox in the corner, and caught up the bedroom candlestick. With this I avoided the delay of striking matches, but for all that the steady process of extinction went on, and the shadows I feared and fought against returned, and crept in upon me, first a step gained on this side of me, then on that. I was now almost frantic with the horror of the coming darkness, and my self-possession deserted me. I leaped panting from candle to candle in a vain struggle against that remorseless advance.

I bruised myself in the thigh against a table, I sent a chair headlong, I stumbled and fell and whisked the cloth from the table in my fall. My candle rolled away from me and I snatched another as I rose. Abruptly this was blown out as I swung it off the table by the wind of my sudden movement, and immediately the two remaining candles followed. But there was light still in the room, a red light, that streamed across the ceiling and staved off the shadows from me. The fire! Of course I could still thrust my candle between the bars and relight it!

I turned to where the flames were still dancing between the glowing coals and splashing red reflections upon the furniture; made two steps toward the grate, and incontinently the flames dwindled and vanished, the glow vanished, the reflections rushed together and disappeared, and as I thrust the candle between the bars darkness closed upon me like the shutting of an eye, wrapped about me in a stifling embrace, sealed my vision, and crushed the last vestiges of self-possession from my brain.

And it was not only palpable darkness, but intolerable terror. The candle fell from my hands. I flung out my arms in a vain effort to thrust that ponderous blackness away from me, and lifting up my voice, screamed with all my might, once, twice, thrice. Then I think I must have staggered to my feet. I know I thought suddenly of the moonlit corridor, and with my head bowed and my arms over my face, made a stumbling run for the door.

But I had forgotten the exact position of the door, and I struck myself heavily against the corner of the bed. I staggered back, turned, and was either struck or struck myself against some other bulky furnishing. I have a vague memory of battering myself thus to and fro in the darkness, of a heavy blow at last upon my forehead, of a horrible sensation of falling that lasted an age, of my last frantic effort to keep my footing, and then I remember no more.

I opened my eyes in daylight. My head was roughly bandaged, and the man with the withered hand was watching my face. I looked about me trying to remember what had happened, and for a space I could not recollect. I rolled my eyes into the corner and saw the old woman, no longer abstracted, no longer terrible, pouring out some drops of medicine from a little blue phial into a glass. "Where am I?" I said. "I seem to remember you, and yet I cannot remember who you are."

They told me then, and I heard of the haunted Red Room as one who hears a tale. "We found you at dawn," said he, "and there was blood on your forehead and lips."

I wondered that I had ever disliked him. The three of them in the daylight seemed commonplace old folk enough. The man with the green shade had his head bent as one who sleeps.

It was very slowly I recovered the memory of my experience. "You believe now," said the old man with the withered hand, "that the room is haunted." He spoke no longer as one who greets an intruder, but as one who condoles a friend.

"Yes," said I, "the room is haunted."

"And you have seen it. And we who have been here all our lives have never set eyes upon it. Because we have never dared. Tell us, is it truly the old earl who—"

"No," said I, "it is not."

"I told you so," said the old lady, with the glass in her hand. "It is his poor young countess who was frightened—"

"It is not," I said. "There is neither ghost of earl nor ghost of countess in that room; there is not ghost there at all, but worse, far worse, something impalpable—"

"Well?" they said.

"The worst of all the things that haunt poor mortal men," said I; "and that is, in all its nakedness— 'Fear!' Fear that will not have light nor sound, that will not bear with reason, that deafens and darkens and overwhelms. It followed me through the corridor, it fought against me in the room—"

I stopped abruptly. There was an interval of silence. My hand went up to my bandages. "The candles went out one after another, and I fled—"

Then the man with the shade lifted his face sideways to see me and spoke.

"That is it," said he. "I knew that was it. A Power of Darkness. To put such a curse upon a home! It lurks there always. You can feel it even in the daytime, even of a bright summer's day, in the hangings, in the curtains, keeping behind you however you face about. In the dark it creeps into the corridor and follows you, so that you dare not turn. It is even as you say. Fear itself is in that room. Black Fear . . . And there it will be . . . so long as this house of sin endures."

20

Teig O'Kane and the Corpse

THERE WAS ONCE A GROWN-UP LAD IN COUNTY LEITRIM, AND HE WAS strong and lively, and the son of a rich farmer. His father had plenty of money, and he did not spare it on the son. Accordingly, when the boy grew up he liked sport better than work, and, as his father had no other children, he loved this one so much that he allowed him to do in everything just as it pleased himself. He was very extravagant, and he used to scatter the gold money as another person would scatter the white. He was seldom to be found at home, but if there was a fair, or a race, or a gathering within ten miles of him, you were dead certain to find him there. And he seldom spent a night in his father's house, but he used to be always out rambling, and there was "the love of every girl in the breast of his shirt," and many's the kiss he got and he gave, for he was very handsome, and there wasn't a girl in the country but would not fall in love with him, only for him to fasten his two eyes on her, and it was for that someone made this rann on him—

At last he became very wild and unruly. He wasn't to be seen day or night in his father's house, but always rambling or going on his kailee from place to place and from house to house, so that the old people used to shake their heads and say to one another, "It's easy seen what will happen to the land when the old man dies; his son will run through it in a year, and it won't stand him that long itself."

But it happened one day that the old man was told that the son had ruined the character of a girl in the neighborhood, and he was greatly angry, and he called the son to him, and said to him, quietly and sensibly—"Avic," says he, "you know I loved you greatly up to this, and I never stopped you from doing your choice thing whatever it was, and I kept plenty of money with you, and I always hoped to leave you the house and land, and all I had after myself would be gone; but I heard a story of you today that has disgusted me with you. I cannot tell you the grief that I felt when I heard such a thing of you, and I tell you now plainly that unless you marry that girl I'll leave house and land and everything to my brother's son. I never could leave it to anyone who would make so bad a use of it as you do yourself, deceiving women and coaxing girls. Settle with yourself now whether you'll marry that girl and get my land as a fortune with her, or refuse to marry her and give up all that was coming to you; and tell me in the morning which of the two things you have chosen."

"Och! Domnoo Sheery! Father, you wouldn't say that to me, and I such a good son as I am. Who told you I wouldn't marry the girl?"

But his father was gone, and the lad knew well enough that he would keep his word too; and he was greatly troubled in his mind, for as quiet and as kind as the father was, he never went back on a word that he had once said, and there wasn't another man in the country who was harder to bend than he was.

The boy did not know rightly what to do. He was in love with the girl indeed, and he hoped to marry her sometime or other, but he would much sooner have remained another while as he was, and follow on at his old tricks—drinking, sporting, and playing cards; and, along with that, he was angry that his father should order him to marry, and should threaten him if he did not do it.

His mind was so much excited that he remained between two notions as to what he should do. He walked out into the night at last to cool his heated blood, and went on to the road. He lit a pipe, and as the night was fine he walked and walked on, until the quick pace made him begin to forget his trouble. The night was bright, and the moon half full. There was not a breath of wind blowing, and the air was calm and mild. He walked on for nearly three hours, when he suddenly remembered that it was late in the night, and time for him to turn.

"Musha! I think I forgot myself; it must be near twelve o'clock now."

He stood listening, and he heard the voices of many people talking through others, but he could not understand what they were saying. "Oh, wirra!" says he, "I'm afraid. It's not Irish or English they have; it can't be they're Frenchmen!" He went on a couple of yards further, and he saw well enough by the light of the moon a band of little people coming towards him, and they were carrying something big and heavy with them. "Oh, murder!" says he to himself, "sure it can't be that they're the good people that's in it!" Every rib of hair that was on his head stood up, and there fell a shaking on his bones, for he saw that they were coming to him fast.

He looked at them again, and perceived that there were about twenty little men in it, and there was not a man at all of them higher than about three feet or three feet and a half, and some of them were grey, and seemed very old. He looked again, but he could not make out what was the heavy thing they were carrying until they came up to him, and then they all stood round about him. They threw the heavy thing down on the road, and he saw on the spot that it was a dead body.

He became as cold as the Death, and there was not a drop of blood running in his veins when an old little grey maneen came up to him and said, "Well, now, isn't it lucky we met you, Teig O'Kane?"

Teig could not open his lips, his blood ran so cold.

"Teig O'Kane, isn't it timely you met us?"

Teig could not answer him.

"Teig O'Kane, isn't it lucky and timely that we met you?"

But Teig remained silent, for he was afraid to return an answer, and his tongue was as if it was tied to the roof of his mouth.

The little grey man turned to his companions, and there was joy in his bright little eye. "And now," says he, "Teig O'Kane hasn't a word, we can do with him what we please. Teig, Teig," says he, "you're living a bad life, and we can make a slave of you now, and you cannot withstand us, for there's no use in trying to go against us. Lift that corpse."

Frightened as he was, Teig was still obstinate: "I won't."

"Teig O'Kane won't lift the corpse," said the little maneen, with a wicked little laugh, for all the world like the breaking of a lock of dry kippeens, and with a little harsh voice like the striking of a cracked bell. "Teig O'Kane won't lift the corpse—make him lift it"; and before the word was out of his mouth they had all gathered round poor Teig, and they all talking and laughing. And then all twenty of them bounded together, grabbing Teig, and forced the corpse on his back. The corpse must have still had some life in it, for its two strong arms seized him about the neck fiercely, and its two strong legs squeezed his hips tightly, and whatever Teig tried, he could not dislodge it.

"Now, Teigeen," says the little man, "you didn't lift the body when I told you to lift it, and see how you were made to lift it; perhaps when I tell you to bury it you won't bury it until you're made to bury it!"

He was terribly frightened then, and he thought he was lost. "Ochone! for ever," said he to himself, "it's the bad life I'm leading that has given the good people this power over me. I promise to God and Mary, Peter and Paul, Patrick and Bridget, that I'll mend my ways for as long as I have to live, if I come clear out of this danger—and I'll marry the girl."

"Listen to me now, Teig O'Kane, and if you don't obey me in all I'm telling you to do, you'll repent it. You must carry that corpse to Teampoll-Demus, and you must make a grave for it in the very middle of the church, such that no one could know a new grave had been made there.

"But perhaps there will be no room there; another man may have that grave-bed and be unwilling to share it with anyone else. In that case you must carry the corpse to Carrick-fhad-vic-Orus and bury it there; and if you cannot bury it there, take it to Teampoll-Ronan; and if not there, then Imlogue-Fada; and if not there, you must take it to Kill-Breedya. In one church or another of these you will be able to bury the corpse.

"If you do this work rightly, we will be thankful to you, and you will have no cause to grieve; but if you are slow or lazy, believe me we shall take satisfaction of you."

The other gray little men laughed and clapped their hands and cried: "Glic! Glic! Hwee! Hwee! Go on, go on, you have eight hours before you till daybreak!"

The men kicked and beat Teig until he ran off in the direction towards which they hounded him. There was not a wet path, or a dirty boreen, or a crooked, contrary road in the whole county that he did not cover that night. He eventually came upon a high wall that was in pieces broken down, and an old church on the inside of the wall. He went up to the church door and found it locked and too solidly built to knock down.

A voice in his ear said to him, "Search for the key on the top of the door, or on the wall."

"Who is that speaking to me?!"

"Search for the key on the top of the door, or on the wall."

"What's that?" said Teig, the sweat running from his forehead, "who spoke to me?!"

"It's I, the corpse, that spoke to you!" said the voice.

"Can you talk?" said Teig.

"Now and again," said the corpse.

Teig searched for the key, and he found it on top of the wall. Shaking in fear, he opened the door and went inside the church.

"Light the candle," said the corpse, for it was pitch black. Teig lit an old stump of a candle he found in a rusted candlestick by the door. He went to the middle aisle of the church, where he found a spade. He pried up the flagstones, and dug until he uncovered a body.

"You corpse, there on my back," says he, "will you be satisfied if I bury you there?" There was no response.

"That's a good sign," Teig said to himself. He thrust the spade into the earth again.

The dead man that was in the hole stood up in the grave, and gave an awful shout. "Hoo! Hoo! Hoo! Go! Go!! Go!!! or YOU'RE A DEAD, DEAD, DEAD MAN!" The corpse then fell back into the grave.

Teig's hair stood upright, the cold sweat came over his face, and a tremor ran through his bones. Still, as he calmed down, he remembered to return the earth and the flagstones to their original state.

He tried digging in another space closer to the door. Scarcely had he turned the clay away when the woman underneath sat up and began to cry, "Ho, you bodach! Ha, you bodach! Where has he been that he got no bed?"

Teig stumbled back, and the woman, seeing that she would get no answer, peacefully closed her eyes and fell back into the grave. After recovering his wits, Teig again made the grave as it was before. Tired and dejected, he left the church, locked the door, and replaced the key on the wall.

Teig sat on a tombstone that was near the church, laid his face in his hands, and cried for grief and fatigue, for at this point he was dead certain that he would never come home alive. He attempted once more to dislodge the corpse from his back, but the harder he pulled on the corpse's hands, the tighter they squeezed.

Teig gave up, and was going to sit down once more, when the cold, horrid lips of the dead man said to him, "Carrick-fhad-vic-Orus," and he remembered the command of the good people to bring the corpse with him to that place if he should be unable to bury it where he had been.

He rose up, and looked about him. "I don't know the way," he said.

As soon as he had uttered the word, the corpse stretched out suddenly its left hand that had been tightened round his neck, and kept it pointing out, showing him the road he ought to follow. Teig went in the direction that the fingers were stretched, and passed out of the churchyard. He found himself on an old rutty, stony road, and he stood still again, not knowing where to turn. The corpse stretched out its bony hand a second time, and pointed out to him another road—not the road by which he had come when approaching the old church. Teig followed that road, and whenever he came to a path or road meeting it, the corpse always stretched out its hand and pointed with its fingers, showing him the way he was to take.

Many was the cross-road he turned down, and many was the crooked boreen he walked, until he saw from him an old burying-ground at last, beside the road, but there was neither church nor chapel nor any other building in it. The corpse squeezed him tightly, and he stood. "Bury me, bury me in the burying-ground," said the voice.

Teig drew over towards the old burying-place, and he was not more than about twenty yards from it, when, raising his eyes, he saw hundreds and hundreds of ghosts—men, women, and children—sitting on the top of the wall round about, or standing on the inside of it, or running backwards and forwards, and pointing at him, while he could see their mouths opening and shutting as if they were speaking, though he heard no word, nor any sound amongst them at all.

He was afraid to go forward, so he stood where he was, and the moment he stood, all the ghosts became quiet, and ceased moving. Then Teig understood that it was trying to keep him from going in, that they were. He walked a couple of yards forwards, and immediately the whole crowd rushed together towards the spot to which he was moving, and they stood so thickly together that it seemed to him that he never could break through them, even though he had a mind to try. But he had no mind to try it. He went back broken and dispirited, and when he had gone a couple of hundred yards from the burying-ground, he stood again, for he did not know what way he was to go. He heard the voice of the corpse in his ear, saying, "Teampoll-Ronan," and the skinny hand was stretched out again, pointing him out the road.

As tired as he was, he had to walk, and the road was neither short nor even. The night was darker than ever, and it was difficult to make his way. Many was the toss he got, and many a bruise they left on his body. At last he saw Teampoll-Ronan from him in the distance, standing in the middle of the burying-ground. He moved over towards it, and thought he was all right and safe, when he saw no ghosts nor anything else on the wall, and he thought he would never be hindered now from leaving his load off him at last. He moved over to the gate, but as he was passing in, he tripped on the threshold. Before he could recover himself, something that he could not see seized him by the neck, by the hands, and by the feet, and bruised him, and shook him, and choked him, until he was nearly dead; and at last he was lifted up, and carried more than a hundred yards from that place, and then thrown down in an old dyke, with the corpse still clinging to him.

He rose up, bruised and sore, but feared to go near the place again, for he had seen nothing the time he was thrown down and carried away.

"You corpse, up on my back?" said he, "shall I go over again to the churchyard?"—but the corpse never answered him. "That's a sign you don't wish me to try it again," said Teig.

He was now in great doubt as to what he ought to do, when the corpse spoke in his ear, and said, "Imlogue-Fada."

"Oh, murder!" said Teig, "must I bring you there? If you keep me long walking like this, I tell you I'll fall under you."

He went on, however, in the direction the corpse pointed out to him. He could not have told, himself, how long he had been going, when the dead man behind suddenly squeezed him, and said, "There!"

Teig looked from him, and he saw a little low wall, that was so broken down in places that it was no wall at all. It was in a great wide field, in from the road; and only for three or four great stones at the corners, that were more like rocks than stones, there was nothing to show that there was either graveyard or burying-ground there.

"Is this Imlogue-Fada? Shall I bury you here?" said Teig.

"Yes," said the voice.

"But I see no grave or gravestone, only this pile of stones," said Teig.

The corpse did not answer, but stretched out its long fleshless hand to show Teig the direction in which he was to go. Teig went on accordingly, but he was greatly terrified, for he remembered what had happened to him at the last place. He went on, "with his heart in his mouth," as he said himself afterwards; but when he came to within fifteen or twenty yards of the little low square wall, there broke out a flash of lightning, bright yellow and red, with blue streaks in it, and went round about the wall in one course, and it swept by as fast as the swallow in the clouds, and the longer Teig remained looking at it the faster it went, till at last it became like a bright ring of flame round the old graveyard, which no one could pass without being burnt by it. Teig never saw, from the time he was born, and never saw afterwards, so wonderful or so splendid a sight as that was. Round went the flame, white and yellow and blue sparks leaping out from it as it went, and although at first it had been no more than a thin, narrow line, it increased slowly until it was at last a great broad band, and it was continually getting broader and higher, and throwing out more brilliant sparks, till there was never a color on the ridge of the earth that was not to be seen in that fire; and lightning never shone and flame never flamed that was so shining and so bright as that.

Teig was amazed; he was half dead with fatigue, and he had no courage left to approach the wall. There fell a mist over his eyes, and there came a soorawn in his head, and he was obliged to sit down upon a great stone to recover himself. He could see nothing but the light, and he could hear nothing but the whirr of it as it shot round the paddock faster than a flash of lightning.

As he sat there on the stone, the voice whispered once more in his ear, "Kill-Breedya"; and the dead man squeezed him so tightly that he cried out. He rose again, sick, tired, and trembling, and went forward as he was directed. The wind was cold, and the road was bad, and the load upon his back was heavy, and the night was dark, and he himself was nearly worn out, and if he had had very much farther to go he must have fallen dead under his burden.

At last the corpse stretched out its hand, and said to him, "Bury me there."

"This is the last burying-place," said Teig in his own mind; "and the little grey man said I'd be allowed to bury him in some of them, so it must be this; it can't be but they'll let him in here."

The first faint streak of the ring of day was appearing in the east, and the clouds were beginning to catch fire, but it was darker than ever, for the moon was set, and there were no stars.

"Make haste, make haste!" said the corpse; and Teig hurried forward as well as he could to the graveyard, which was a little place on a bare hill, with only a few graves in it. He walked boldly in through the open gate, and nothing touched him, nor did he either hear or see anything. He came to the middle of the ground, and then stood up and looked round him for a spade or shovel to make a grave. As he was turning round and searching, he suddenly perceived what startled him greatly—a newly dug grave right before him. He moved over to it, and looked down, and there at the bottom he saw a black coffin. He clambered down into the hole and lifted the lid, and found that (as he thought it would be) the coffin was empty. He had hardly mounted up out of the hole, and was standing on the brink, when the corpse, which had clung to him for more than eight hours, suddenly relaxed its hold of his neck, and loosened its shins from round his hips, and sank down with a plop into the open coffin.

Teig fell down on his two knees at the brink of the grave, and gave thanks to God. He made no delay then, but pressed down the coffin lid in its place, and threw in the clay over it with his two hands, and when the grave was filled up, he stamped and leaped on it with his feet, until it was firm and hard, and then he left the place.

All the people at his own home thought that he must have left the country, and they rejoiced greatly when they saw him come back. Everyone began asking him where he had been, but he would not tell anyone except his father.

He was a changed man from that day. He never drank too much; he never lost his money over cards; and especially he would not take the world and be out late by himself of a dark night.

He was not a fortnight at home until he married Mary, the girl he had been in love with, and it's at their wedding the sport was, and it's he was the happy man from that day forward, and it's all I wish that we may be as happy as he was.

GLOSSARY.—Rann, a stanza; kailee (céilidhe), a visit in the evening; wirra (a mhuire), "Oh, Mary!" an exclamation like the French dame; rib, a single hair (in Irish, ribe); a lock (glac), a bundle or wisp, or a little share of anything; maneen, a little person, elf, or fairy; kippeen (cipín), a rod or twig; boreen (bóithrin), a lane; bodach, a clown; soorawn (suarán), vertigo. Avic (a Mhic), my son, or rather, Oh, son. Mic is the vocative of Mac.

The Screaming Skull

By F. Marion Crawford

I HAVE OFTEN HEARD IT SCREAM. NO, I AM NOT NERVOUS, I AM NOT imaginative, and I never believed in ghosts, unless that thing is one. Whatever it is, it hates me almost as much as it hated Luke Pratt, and it screams at me.

If I were you, I would never tell ugly stories about ingenious ways of killing people, for you never can tell but that some one at the table may be tired of his or her nearest and dearest. I have always blamed myself for Mrs. Pratt's death, and I suppose I was responsible for it in a way, though heaven knows I never wished her anything but long life and happiness. If I had not told that story she might be alive yet. That is why the thing screams at me, I fancy.

She was a good little woman, with a sweet temper, all things considered, and a nice gentle voice; but I remember hearing her shriek once when she thought her little boy was killed by a pistol that went off though everyone was sure that it was not loaded. It was the same scream; exactly the same, with a sort of rising quaver to the end; do you know what I mean? Unmistakable.

The truth is, I had not realized that the doctor and his wife were not on good terms. They used to bicker a bit now and then when I was here, and I often noticed that little Mrs. Pratt got very red and bit her lip hard to keep her temper, while Luke grew pale and said the most offensive things. He was that sort when he was in the nursery, I remember, and afterwards at school. He was my cousin, you know; that is how I came by this house; after he died, and his boy Charley was killed in South Africa, there were no relations left. Yes, it's a pretty little property, just the sort of thing for an old sailor like me who has taken to gardening.

One always remembers one's mistakes much more vividly than one's cleverest things, doesn't one? I've often noticed it. I was dining with the Pratts one night, when I told them the story that afterwards made so much difference. It was a wet night in November, and the sea was moaning. Hush!—if you don't speak you will hear it now. . . .

Do you hear the tide? Gloomy sound, isn't it? Sometimes, about this time of year—hallo!—there it is! Don't be frightened, man—it won't eat you—it's only a noise, after all! But I'm glad you've heard it, because there are always people who think it's the wind, or my imagination, or something. You won't hear it again tonight, I fancy, for it doesn't often come more than once. Yes—that's right. Put another stick on the fire, and a little more stuff into that weak mixture you're so fond of. Do you remember old Blauklot the carpenter, on that German ship that picked us up when the Clontarf went to the bottom? We were hove to in a howling gale one night, snug as you please, with no land within five hundred miles, and the ship coming up and falling off as regularly as clockwork—"Biddy te boor beebles ashore tis night, poys!" old Blauklot sang out, as he went off to his quarters with the sail-maker. I often think of that, now that I'm ashore for good and all.

Yes, it was on a night like this, when I was at home for a spell, waiting to take the Olympia out on her first trip—it was on the next voyage that she broke the record, you remember—but that dates it. Ninety-two was the year, early in November.

The weather was dirty, Pratt was out of temper, and the dinner was bad, very bad indeed, which didn't improve matters, and cold, which made it worse. The poor little lady was very unhappy about it, and insisted on making a Welsh rarebit on the table to counteract the raw turnips and the half-boiled mutton. Pratt must have had a hard day. Perhaps he had lost a patient. At all events, he was in a nasty temper.

"My wife is trying to poison me, you see!" he said. "She'll succeed some day." I saw that she was hurt, and I made believe to laugh, and said that Mrs. Pratt was much too clever to get rid of her husband in such a simple way; and then I began to tell them about Japanese tricks with spun glass and chopped horsehair and the like.

Pratt was a doctor, and knew a lot more than I did about such things, but that only put me on my mettle, and I told a story about a woman in Ireland who did for three husbands before anyone suspected foul play.

Did you ever hear that tale? The fourth husband managed to keep awake and caught her, and she was hanged. How did she do it? She drugged them, and poured melted lead into their ears through a little horn funnel when they were asleep—No, that's the wind whistling. It's backing up to the southward again. I can tell by the sound. Besides, the other thing doesn't often come more than once in an evening even at this time of year—when it happened. Yes, it was in November. Poor Mrs. Pratt died suddenly in her bed not long after I dined there. I can fix the date, because I got the news in New York by the steamer that followed the Olympia when I took her out on her first trip. You had the Leofric the same year? Yes, I remember. What a pair of old duffers we are coming to be, you and I. Nearly fifty years since we were apprentices together on the Clontarf. Shall you ever forget old Blauklot? "Biddy te boor beebles ashore, poys!" Ha, ha! Take a little more, with all that water. It's the old Hulstkamp I found in the cellar when this house came to me, the same I brought Luke from Amsterdam five-and-twenty years ago. He had never touched a drop of it. Perhaps he's sorry now, poor fellow.

Where did I leave off? I told you that Mrs. Pratt died suddenly—yes. Luke must have been lonely here after she was dead, I should think; I came to see him now and then, and he looked worn and nervous, and told me that his practice was growing too heavy for him, though he wouldn't take an assistant on any account. Years went on, and his son was killed in South Africa, and after that he began to be queer. There was something about him not like other people. I believe he kept his senses in his profession to the end; there was no complaint of his having made mistakes in cases, or anything of that sort, but he had a look about him—.

Luke was a red-headed man with a pale face when he was young, and he was never stout; in middle age he turned a sandy grey, and after his son died he grew thinner and thinner, till his head looked like a skull with parchment stretched over it very tight, and his eyes had a sort of glare in them that was very disagreeable to look at.

He had an old dog that poor Mrs. Pratt had been fond of, and that used to follow her everywhere. He was a bulldog, and the sweetest tempered beast you ever saw, though he had a way of hitching his upper lip behind one of his fangs that frightened strangers a good deal. Sometimes, of an evening, Pratt and Bumble—that was the dog's name—used to sit and look at each other a long time, thinking about old times, I suppose, when Luke's wife used to sit in that chair you've got. That was always her place, and this was the doctor's, where I'm sitting. Bumble used to climb up by the footstool—he was old and fat by that time, and could not jump much, and his teeth were getting shaky. He would look steadily at Luke, and Luke looked steadily at the dog, his face growing more and more like a skull with two little coals for eyes; and after about five minutes or so, though it may have been less, old Bumble would suddenly begin to shake all over, and all on a sudden he would set up an awful howl, as if he had been shot, and tumble out of the easy-chair and trot away, and hide himself under the sideboard, and lie there making odd noises.

Considering Pratt's looks in those last months, the thing is not surprising, you know. I'm not nervous or imaginative, but I can believe that he might have sent a sensitive woman into hysterics—his head looked so much like a skull in parchment.

At last I came down one day before Christmas, when my ship was in dock and I had three weeks off. Bumble was not about, and I said casually that I supposed the old dog was dead.

"Yes," Pratt answered, and I thought there was something odd in his tone even before he went on after a little pause. "I killed him," he said presently.

"I could stand it no longer."

I asked what it was that Luke could not stand, though I guessed well enough.

"She had a way of sitting in her chair and glaring at me, and then howling." Luke shivered a little. "He didn't suffer at all, poor old Bumble," he went on in a hurry, as if he thought I might imagine he had been cruel.

"I put dionine into his drink to make him sleep soundly, and then I chloroformed him gradually, so that he could not have felt suffocated even if he was dreaming. It's been quieter since then."

I wondered what he meant, for the words slipped out as if he could not help saying them. I've understood since. He meant that he did not hear that noise so often after the dog was out of the way. Perhaps he thought at first that it was old Bumble in the yard howling at the moon, though it's not that kind of noise, is it? Besides, I know what it is, if Luke didn't. It's only a noise after all, and a noise never hurt anybody yet. But he was much more imaginative than I am. No doubt there really is something about this place that I don't understand; but when I don't understand a thing, I call it a phenomenon, and I don't take it for granted, that it's going to kill me, as he did. I don't understand everything, by long odds, nor do you, nor does any man who has been to sea. We used to talk of tidal waves, for instance, and we could not account for them; now we account for them by calling them submarine earthquakes, and we branch off into fifty theories, any one of which might make earthquakes quite comprehensible if we only knew what they were. I fell in with one of them once, and the inkstand flew straight up from the table against the ceiling of my cabin. The same thing happened to Captain Lecky—I dare say you've read about it in his "Wrinkles." Very good. If that sort of thing took place ashore, in this room for instance, a nervous person would talk about spirits and levitation and fifty things that mean nothing, instead of just quietly setting it down as a "phenomenon" that has not been explained yet. My view of that voice, you see.

Besides, what is there to prove that Luke killed his wife? I would not even suggest such a thing to anyone but you. After all, there was nothing but the coincidence that poor little Mrs. Pratt died suddenly in her bed a few days after I told that story at dinner. She was not the only woman who ever died like that. Luke got the doctor over from the next parish and they agreed that she had died of something the matter with her heart. Why not? It's common enough.

Of course, there was the ladle. I never told anybody about that, and it made me start when I found it in the cupboard in the bedroom. It was new, too—a little tinned iron ladle that had not been in the fire more than once or twice, and there was some lead in it that had not been melted, and stuck to the bottom of the bowl, all grey, with hardened dross on it. But that proves nothing. A country doctor is generally a handy man, who does everything for himself, and Luke may have had a dozen reasons for melting a little lead in a ladle. He was fond of sea-fishing, for instance, and he may have cast a sinker for a night-line; perhaps it was a weight for the hall clock, or something like that. All the same, when I found it I had a rather queer sensation, because it looked so much like the thing I had described when I told them the story. Do you understand? It affected me unpleasantly, and I threw it away; it's at the bottom of the sea a mile from the Spit, and it will be jolly well rusted beyond recognizing if it's ever washed up by the tide.

You see, Luke must have bought it in the village, years ago, for the man sells just such ladles still. I suppose they are used in cooking. In any case, there was no reason why an inquisitive housemaid should find such a thing lying about, with lead in it, and wonder what it was, and perhaps talk to the maid who heard me tell the story at dinner—for that girl married the plumber's son in the village, and may remember the whole thing.

You understand me, don't you? Now that Luke Pratt is dead and gone, and lies buried beside his wife, with an honest man's tombstone at his head, I should not care to stir up anything that could hurt his memory. They are both dead, and their son, too. There was trouble enough about Luke's death, as it was.

How? He was found dead on the beach one morning, and there was a coroner's inquest. There were marks on his throat, but he had not been robbed. The verdict was that he had come to his end "By the hands or teeth of some person or animal unknown," for half the jury thought it might have been a big dog that had thrown him down and gripped his windpipe, though the skin of his throat was not broken. No one knew at what time he had gone out, nor where he had been. He was found lying on his back above high-water mark, and an old cardboard bandbox that had belonged to his wife lay under his hand, open. The lid had fallen off. He seemed to have been carrying home a skull in the box—doctors are fond of collecting such things. It had rolled out and lay near his head, and it was a remarkably fine skull, rather small, beautifully shaped and very white, with perfect teeth. That is to say, the upper jaw was perfect, but there was no lower one at all, when I first saw it.

Yes, I found it here when I came. You see, it was very white and polished, like a thing meant to be kept under a glass case, and the people did not know where it came from, nor what to do with it; so they put it back into the bandbox and set it on the shelf of the cupboard in the best bedroom, and of course they showed it to me when I took possession. I was taken down to the beach, too, to be shown the place where Luke was found, and the old fisherman explained just how he was lying, and the skull beside him. The only point he could not explain was why the skull had rolled up the sloping sand towards Luke's head instead of rolling downhill to his feet. It did not seem odd to me at that time, but I have often thought of it since, for the place is rather steep. I'll take you there tomorrow if you like—I made a sort of cairn of stones there afterwards.

When he fell down, or was thrown down—whichever happened— the bandbox struck the sand, and the lid came off, and the thing came out and ought to have rolled down. But it didn't. It was close to his head, almost touching it, and turned with the face towards it. I say it didn't strike me as odd when the man told me; but I could not help thinking about it afterwards, again and again, till I saw a picture of it all when I closed my eyes; and then I began to ask myself why the plaguey thing had rolled up instead of down, and why it had stopped near Luke's head instead of anywhere else, a yard away, for instance.

You naturally want to know what conclusion I reached, don't you? None that at all explained the rolling, at all events. But I got something else into my head, after a time, that made me feel downright uncomfortable.

Oh, I don't mean as to anything supernatural! There may be ghosts, or there may not be. If there are, I'm not inclined to believe that they can hurt living people except by frightening them, and, for my part, I would rather face any shape of ghost than a fog in the Channel when it's crowded. No. What bothered me was just a foolish idea, that's all, and I cannot tell how it began, nor what made it grow till it turned into a certainty.

I was thinking about Luke and his poor wife one evening over my pipe and a dull book, when it occurred to me that the skull might possibly be hers, and I have never got rid of the thought since. You'll tell me there's no sense in it, no doubt, that Mrs. Pratt was buried like a Christian and is lying in the churchyard where they put her, and that it's perfectly monstrous to suppose her husband kept her skull in her old bandbox in his bedroom. All the same, in the face of reason, and common sense, and probability, I'm convinced that he did. Doctors do all sorts of queer things that would make men like you and me feel creepy, and those are just the things that don't seem probable, nor logical, nor sensible to us.

Then, don't you see?—if it really was her skull, poor woman, the only way of accounting for his having it is that he really killed her, and did it in that way, as the woman killed her husbands in the story, and that he was afraid there might be an examination some day which would betray him. You see, I told that too, and I believe it had really happened some fifty or sixty years ago. They dug up the three skulls, you know, and there was a small lump of lead rattling about in each one. That was what hanged the woman. Luke remembered that, I'm sure. I don't want to know what he did when he thought of it; my taste never ran in the direction of horrors, and I don't fancy you care for them either, do you? No. If you did, you might supply what is wanting to the story.

It must have been rather grim, eh? I wish I did not see the whole thing so distinctly, just as everything must have happened. He took it the night before she was buried, I'm sure, after the coffin had been shut, and when the servant girl was asleep. I would bet anything, that when he'd got it, he put something under the sheet in its place, to fill up and look like it. What do you suppose he put there, under the sheet?

I don't wonder you take me up on what I'm saying! First I tell you that I don't want to know what happened, and that I hate to think about horrors, and then I describe the whole thing to you as if I had seen it. I'm quite sure that it was her work-bag that he put there. I remember the bag very well, for she always used it of an evening; it was made of brown plush, and when it was stuffed full it was about the size of—you understand. Yes, there I am, at it again! You may laugh at me, but you don't live here alone, where it was done, and you didn't tell Luke the story about the melted lead. I'm not nervous, I tell you, but sometimes I begin to feel that I understand why some people are. I dwell on all this when I'm alone, and

I dream of it, and when that thing screams—well, frankly, I don't like the noise any more than you do, though I should be used to it by this time.

I ought not to be nervous. I've sailed in a haunted ship. There was a Man in the Top, and two-thirds of the crew died of the West Coast fever inside of ten days after we anchored; but I was all right, then and afterwards. I have seen some ugly sights, too, just as you have, and all the rest of us. But nothing ever stuck in my head in the way this does.

You see, I've tried to get rid of the thing, but it doesn't like that. It wants to be there in its place, in Mrs. Pratt's bandbox in the cupboard in the best bedroom. It's not happy anywhere else. How do I know that? Because I've tried it. You don't suppose that I've not tried, do you? As long as it's there, it only screams now and then, generally at this time of year, but if I put it out of the house it goes on all night, and no servant will stay here twenty-four hours. As it is, I've often been left alone and have been obliged to shift for myself for a fortnight at a time. No one from the village would ever pass a night under the roof now, and as for selling the place, or even letting it, that's out of the question. The old women say that if I stay here I shall come to a bad end myself before long.

I'm not afraid of that. You smile at the mere idea that anyone could take such nonsense seriously. Quite right. It's utterly blatant nonsense, I agree with you. Didn't I tell you that it's only a noise after all when you started and looked round as if you expected to see a ghost standing behind your chair?

I may be all wrong about the skull, and I like to think that I am when I can. It may be just a fine specimen which Luke got somewhere long ago, and what rattles about inside when you shake it may be nothing but a pebble, or a bit of hard clay, or anything. Skulls that have lain long in the ground generally have something inside them that rattles, don't they? No, I've never tried to get it out, whatever it is; I'm afraid it might be lead, don't you see? And if it is, I don't want to know the face, for I'd much rather not be sure. If it really is lead, I killed her quite as much as if I had done the deed myself. Anybody must see that, I should think. As long as I don't know for certain, I have the consolation of saying that it's all utterly ridiculous nonsense, that Mrs. Pratt died a natural death and that the beautiful skull belonged to Luke when he was a student in London. But if I were quite sure, I believe I should have to leave the house; indeed I do, most certainly. As it is, I had to give up trying to sleep in the best bedroom where the cupboard is.

You ask me why I don't throw it into the pond—yes, but please don't call it a "confounded bugbear"—it doesn't like being called names.

There! Lord, what a shriek! I told you so! You're quite pale, man. Fill up your pipe and draw your chair nearer to the fire, and take some more drink. Old Holland's never hurt anybody yet. I've seen a Dutchman in Java drink half a jug of Hulstkamp in a morning without turning a hair. I don't take much rum myself, because it doesn't agree with my rheumatism, but you are not rheumatic and it won't damage you. Besides, it's a very damp night outside. The wind is howling again, and it will soon be in the south-west; do you hear how the windows rattle? The tide must have turned too, by the moaning.

We should not have heard the thing again if you had not said that. I'm pretty sure we should not. Oh yes, if you choose to describe it as a coincidence, you are quite welcome, but I would rather that you should not call the thing names again, if you don't mind. It may be that the poor little woman hears, and perhaps it hurts her, don't you know? Ghosts? No! You don't call anything a ghost that you can take in your hands and look at in broad daylight, and that rattles when you shake it, do you, now? But it's something that hears and understands; there's no doubt about that.

I tried sleeping in the best bedroom when I first came to the house just because it was the best and most comfortable, but I had to give it up. It was their room, and there's the big bed she died in, and the cupboard is in the thickness of the wall, near the head, on the left. That's where it likes to be kept, in its bandbox. I only used the room for a fortnight after I came, and then I turned out and took the little room downstairs, next to the surgery, where Luke used to sleep when he expected to be called to a patient during the night.

I was always a good sleeper ashore; eight hours is my dose, eleven to seven when I'm alone, twelve to eight when I have a friend with me. But I could not sleep after three o'clock in the morning in that room—a quarter past, to be accurate—as a matter of fact, I timed it with my old pocket chronometer, which still keeps good time, and it was always at exactly seventeen minutes past three. I wonder whether that was the hour when she died?

It was not what you have heard. If it had been that, I could not have stood it two nights. It was just a start and a moan and hard breathing for a few seconds in the cupboard, and it could never have waked me under ordinary circumstances, I'm sure. I suppose you are like me in that, and we are just like other people who have been to sea. No natural sounds disturb us at all, not all the racket of a square-rigger hove to in a heavy gale, or rolling on her beam ends before the wind. But if a lead pencil gets adrift and rattles in the drawer of your cabin table you are awake in a moment. Just so—you always understand. Very well, the noise in the cupboard was no louder than that, but it waked me instantly.

I said it was like a "start." I know what I mean, but it's hard to explain without seeming to talk nonsense. Of course you cannot exactly "hear" a person "start"; at the most, you might hear the quick drawing of the breath between the parted lips and closed teeth, and the almost imperceptible sound of clothing that moved suddenly though very slightly. It was like that.

You know how one feels what a sailing vessel is going to do, two or three seconds before she does it, when one has the wheel. Riders say the same of a horse, but that's less strange, because the horse is a live animal with feelings of its own, and only poets and landsmen talk about a ship being alive, and all that. But I have always felt somehow that besides being a steaming instrument or a sailing machine for carrying weights, a vessel at sea is a sensitive instrument, and a means of communication between nature and man, and most particularly the man at the wheel, if she is steered by hand. She takes her impressions directly from wind and sea, tide and stream, and transmits them to the man's hands, just as the wireless telegraphy picks up the interrupted currents aloft and turns them out below in the form of a message.

You see what I am driving at; I felt that something started in the cupboard, and I felt it so vividly that I heard it, though there may have been nothing to hear, and the sound inside my head waked me suddenly. But I really heard the other noise. It was as if it were muffled inside a box, as far away as if it came through a long-distance telephone; and yet I knew that it was inside the cupboard near the head of my bed. My hair did not bristle and my blood did not run cold that time. I simply resented being waked up by something that had no business to make a noise, any more than a pencil should rattle in the drawer of my cabin table on board ship. For I did not understand; I just supposed that the cupboard had some communication with the outside air, and that the wind had got in and was moaning through it with a sort of very faint screech. I struck a light and looked at my watch, and it was seventeen minutes past three. Then I turned over and went to sleep on my right ear. That's my good one; I'm pretty deaf with the other, for I struck the water with it when I was a lad diving from the fore-topsail yard. Silly thing to do, it was, but the result is very convenient when I want to go to sleep when there's a noise.

That was the first night, and the same thing happened again and several times afterwards, but not regularly, though it was always at the same time, to a second; perhaps I was sometimes sleeping on my good ear, and sometimes not. I overhauled the cupboard and there was no way by which the wind could get in, or anything else, for the door makes a good fit, having been meant to keep out moths, I suppose; Mrs. Pratt must have kept her winter things in it, for it still smells of camphor and turpentine.

After about a fortnight I had had enough of the noises. So far I had said to myself that it would be silly to yield to it and take the skull out of the room. Things always look differently by daylight, don't they? But the voice grew louder—I suppose one may call it a voice—and it got inside my deaf ear, too, one night. I realized that when I was wide awake, for my good ear was jammed down on the pillow, and I ought not to have heard a foghorn in that position. But I heard that, and it made me lose my temper, unless it scared me, for sometimes the two are not far apart. I struck a light and got up, and I opened the cupboard, grabbed the bandbox and threw it out the window, as far as I could.

Then my hair stood on end. The thing screamed in the air, like a shell from a twelve-inch gun. It fell on the other side of the road. The night was very dark, and I could not see it fall, but I know it fell beyond the road. The window is just over the front door, it's fifteen yards to the fence, more or less, and the road is ten yards wide. There's a thick-set hedge beyond, along the glebe that belongs to the vicarage.

I did not sleep much more that night. It was not more than half an hour after I had thrown the bandbox out when I heard a shriek outside— like what we've had tonight, but worse, more despairing, I should call it; and it may have been my imagination, but I could have sworn that the screams came nearer and nearer each time. I lit a pipe, and walked up and down for a bit, and then took a book and sat up reading, but I'll be hanged if I can remember what I read nor even what the book was, for every now and then a shriek came up that would have made a dead man turn in his coffin.

A little before dawn someone knocked at the front door. There was no mistaking that for anything else, and I opened my window and looked down, for I guessed that someone wanted the doctor, supposing that the new man had taken Luke's house. It was rather a relief to hear a human knock after that awful noise.

You cannot see the door from above, owing to the little porch. The knocking came again, and I called out, asking who was there, but nobody answered, though the knock was repeated. I sang out again, and said that the doctor did not live here any longer. There was no answer, but it occurred to me that it might be some old countryman who was stone deaf. So I took my candle and went down to open the door. Upon my word, I was not thinking of the thing yet, and I had almost forgotten the other noises. I went down convinced that I should find somebody outside, on the doorstep, with a message. I set the candle on the hall table, so that the wind should not blow it out when I opened. While I was drawing the old-fashioned bolt I heard the knocking again. It was not loud, and it had a queer, hollow sound, now that I was close to it, I remember, but I certainly thought it was made by some person who wanted to get in.

It wasn't. There was nobody there, but as I opened the door inward, standing a little on one side, so as to see out at once, something rolled across the threshold and stopped against my foot.

I drew back as I felt it, for I knew what it was before I looked down. I cannot tell you how I knew, and it seemed unreasonable, for I am still quite sure that I had thrown it across the road. It's a French window, that opens wide, and I got a good swing when I flung it out. Besides, when I went out early in the morning, I found the bandbox beyond the thick hedge.

You may think it opened when I threw it, and that the skull dropped out; but that's impossible, for nobody could throw an empty cardboard box so far. It's out of the question; you might as well try to fling a ball of paper twenty-five yards, or a blown bird's egg.

To go back, I shut and bolted the hall door, picked the thing up carefully, and put it on the table beside the candle. I did that mechanically, as one instinctively does the right thing in danger without thinking at all—unless one does the opposite. It may seem odd, but I believe my first thought had been that somebody might come and find me there on the threshold while it was resting against my foot, lying a little on its side, and turning one hollow eye up at my face, as if it meant to accuse me. And the light and shadow from the candle played in the hollows of the eyes as it stood on the table, so that they seemed to open and shut at me. Then the candle went out quite unexpectedly, though the door was fastened and there was not the least draught; and I used up at least half a dozen matches before it would burn again.

I sat down rather suddenly, without quite knowing why. Probably I had been badly frightened, and perhaps you will admit there was no great shame in being scared. The thing had come home, and it wanted to go upstairs, back to its cupboard. I sat still and stared at it for a bit till I began to feel very cold; then I took it and carried it up and set it in its place, and I remember that I spoke to it, and promised that it should have its bandbox again in the morning.

You want to know whether I stayed in the room till daybreak? Yes, but I kept a light burning, and sat up smoking and reading, most likely out of fright; plain, undeniable fear, and you need not call it cowardice either, for that's not the same thing. I could not have stayed alone with that thing in the cupboard; I should have been scared to death, though I'm not more timid than other people. Confound it all, man, it had crossed the road alone, and had got up on the doorstep and had knocked to be let in.

When the dawn came, I put on my boots and went out to find the bandbox. I had to go a good way round, by the gate near the high road, and I found the box open and hanging on the other side of the hedge. It had caught on the twigs by the string, and the lid had fallen off and was lying on the ground below it. That shows it did not open till it was well over; and if it had not opened as soon as it left my hand, what was inside must have gone beyond the road too.

That's all. I took the box upstairs to the cupboard, and put the skull back and locked it up. When the girl brought me my breakfast she said she was sorry, but that she must go, and she did not care if she lost her month's wages. I looked at her, and her face was a sort of greenish yellowish white. I pretended to be surprised, and asked what was the matter; but that was of no use, for she just turned on me and wanted to know whether I meant to stay in a haunted house, and how long I expected to live if I did, for though she noticed I was sometimes a little hard of hearing, she did not believe that even I could sleep through those screams again—and if I could, why had I been moving about the house and opening and shutting the front door, between three and four in the morning? There was no answering that, since she had heard me, so off she went, and I was left to myself. I went down to the village during the morning and found a woman who was willing to come and do the little work there is and cook my dinner, on condition that she might go home every night. As for me, I moved downstairs that day, and I have never tried to sleep in the best bedroom since. After a little while I got a brace of middle-aged Scotch servants from London, and things were quiet enough for a long time. I began by telling them that the house was in a very exposed position, and that the wind whistled round it a good deal in the autumn and winter, which had given it a bad name in the village, the Cornish people being inclined to superstition and telling ghost stories. The two hard-faced, sandy-haired sisters almost smiled, and they answered with great contempt that they had no great opinion of any Southern bogey whatsoever, having been in service in two English haunted houses, where they had never seen so much as the Boy in Grey, whom they reckoned no very particular rarity in Forfarshire.

They stayed with me several months, and while they were in the house we had peace and quiet. One of them is here again now, but she went away with her sister within the year. This one—she was the cook—married the sexton, who works in my garden. That's the way of it. It's a small village and he has not much to do, and he knows enough about flowers to help me nicely, besides doing most of the hard work; for though I'm fond of exercise, I'm getting a little stiff in the hinges. He's a sober, silent sort of fellow, who minds his own business, and he was a widower when I came here—Trehearn is his name, James Trehearn. The Scottish sisters would not admit that there was anything wrong about the house, but when November came they gave me warning that they were going, on the ground that the chapel was such a long walk from here, being in the next parish, and that they could not possibly go to our church. But the younger one came back in the spring, and as soon as the banns could be published she was married to James Trehearn by the vicar, and she seems to have had no scruples about hearing him preach since then. I'm quite satisfied, if she is! The couple live in a small cottage that looks over the churchyard.

I suppose you are wondering what all this has to do with what I was talking about. I'm alone so much that when an old friend comes to see me, I sometimes go on talking just for the sake of hearing my own voice. But in this case there is really a connection of ideas. It was James Trehearn who buried poor Mrs. Pratt, and her husband after her in the same grave, and it's not far from the back of his cottage. That's the connection in my mind, you see. It's plain enough. He knows something; I'm quite sure that he does, though he's such a reticent beggar.

Yes, I'm alone in the house at night now, for Mrs. Trehearn does everything herself, and when I have a friend the sexton's niece comes in to wait on the table. He takes his wife home every evening in winter, but in summer, when there's light, she goes by herself. She's not a nervous woman, but she's less sure than she used to be that there are no bogies in England worth a Scotch-woman's notice. Isn't it amusing, the idea that Scotland has a monopoly on the supernatural? Odd sort of national pride, I call that, don't you?

That's a good fire, isn't it? When driftwood gets started at last there's nothing like it, I think. Yes, we get lots of it, for I'm sorry to say there are still a great many wrecks about here. It's a lonely coast, and you may have all the wood you want for the trouble of bringing it in. Trehearn and I borrow a cart now and then, and load it between here and the Spit. I hate a coal fire when I can get wood of any sort. A log is company, even if it's only a piece of a deck beam or timber sawn off, and the salt in it makes pretty sparks. See how they fly, like Japanese hand-fireworks! Upon my word, with an old friend and a good fire and a pipe, one forgets all about that thing upstairs, especially now that the wind has moderated. It's only a lull, though, and it will blow a gale before morning.

You think you would like to see the skull? I've no objection. There's no reason why you shouldn't have a look at it, and you never saw a more perfect one in your life, except that there are two front teeth missing in the lower.

Oh yes—I had not told you about the jaw yet. Trehearn found it in the garden last spring when he was digging a pit for a new asparagus bed. You know we make asparagus beds six or eight feet deep here. Yes, yes—I had forgotten to tell you that. He was digging straight down, just as he digs a grave; if you want a good asparagus bed made, I advise you to get a sexton to make it for you. Those fellows have a wonderful knack at that sort of digging.

Trehearn had got down about three feet when he cut into a mass of white lime in the side of the trench. He had noticed that the earth was a little looser there, though he says it had not been disturbed for a number of years. I suppose he thought that even old lime might not be good for asparagus, so he broke it out and threw it up. It was pretty hard, he says, in biggish lumps, and out of sheer force of habit he cracked the lumps with his spade as they lay outside the pit beside him; the jaw bone of the skull dropped out of one of the pieces. He thinks he must have knocked out the two front teeth in breaking up the lime, but he did not see them anywhere. He's a very experienced man in such things, as you may imagine, and he said at once that the jaw had probably belonged to a young woman, and that the teeth had been complete when she died. He brought it to me, and asked me if I wanted to keep it; if I did not, he said he would drop it into the next grave he made in the churchyard, as he supposed it was a Christian jaw, and ought to have decent burial, wherever the rest of the body might be. I told him that doctors often put bones into quicklime to whiten them nicely, and that I supposed Dr. Pratt had once had a little lime pit in the garden for that purpose, and had forgotten the jaw. Trehearn looked at me quietly.

"Maybe it fitted that skull that used to be in the cupboard upstairs, sir," he said. "Maybe Dr. Pratt had put the skull into the lime to clean it, or something, and when he took it out he left the lower jaw behind. There's some human hair sticking in the lime, sir."

I saw there was, and that was what Trehearn said. If he did not suspect something, why in the world should he have suggested that the jaw might fit the skull? Besides, it did. That's proof that he knows more than he cares to tell. Do you suppose he looked before she was buried? Or perhaps—when he buried Luke in the same grave—.

Well, well, it's of no use to go over that, is it? I said I would keep the jaw with the skull, and I took it upstairs and fitted it into its place. There's not the slightest doubt about the two belonging together, and together they are.

Trehearn knows several things. We were talking about plastering the kitchen a while ago, and he happened to remember that it had not been done since the very week when Mrs. Pratt died. He did not say that the mason must have left some lime on the place, but he thought it, and that it was the very same lime he had found in the asparagus pit. He knows a lot. Trehearn is one of your silent beggars who can put two and two together. That grave is very near the back of his cottage, too, and he's one of the quickest men with a spade I ever saw. If he wanted to know the truth, he could, and no one else would ever be the wiser unless he chose to tell. In a quiet village like ours, people don't go and spend the night in the churchyard to see whether the sexton potters about by himself between ten o'clock and daylight.

What is awful to think of, is Luke's deliberation, if he did it; his cool certainty that no one would find him out; above all, his nerve, for that must have been extraordinary. I sometimes think it's bad enough to live in the place where it was done, if it really was done. I always put in the condition, you see, for the sake of his memory, and a little bit of my own sake, too.

I'll go upstairs and fetch the box in a minute. Let me light my pipe; there's no hurry! We had supper early, and it's only half-past nine o'clock. I never let a friend go to bed before twelve, or with less than three glasses—you may have as many more as you like, but you shan't have less, for the sake of old times.

It's breezing up again, do you hear? That was only a lull just now, and we are going to have a bad night.

A thing happened that made me start a little when I found the jaw fitted exactly. I'm not very easily startled in that way myself, but I have seen people make a quick movement, drawing their breath sharply, when they had thought they were alone and suddenly turned and saw someone very near them. Nobody can call that fear. You wouldn't, would you? No. Well, just when I had set the jaw in its place under the skull, the teeth closed sharply on my finger. It felt exactly as if it were biting me hard, and I confess that I jumped before I realized that I had been pressing the jaw and skull together with my other hand. I assure you I was not at all nervous. It was broad daylight, too, and a fine day, and the sun was streaming into the best bedroom. It would have been absurd to be nervous, and it was only a quick mistaken impression, but it really made me feel queer. Somehow it made me think of the funny verdict of the coroner's jury on Luke's death, "by the hand or teeth of some person or animal unknown." Ever since then I've wished I had seen those marks on his throat, though the lower jaw was missing then.

I have often seen a man do insane things with his hands that he does not realize at all. I once saw a man hanging on by an old awning stop with one hand, leaning backward, outboard, with all his weight on it, and he was just cutting the stop with his knife in his other hand when I got my arms round him. We were in mid-ocean, going twenty knots. He had not the smallest idea what he was doing; neither had I when I managed to pinch my finger between the teeth of that thing. I can feel it now. It was exactly as if it were alive and were trying to bite me. It would if it could, for I know it hates me, poor thing! Do you suppose that what rattles about inside is really a bit of lead? Well, I'll get the box down presently, and if whatever it is happens to drop out into your hands, that's your affair. If it's only a clod of earth or a pebble, the whole matter would be off my mind, and I don't believe I should ever think of the skull again; but somehow I cannot bring myself to shake out the bit of hard stuff myself. The mere idea that it may be lead makes me confoundedly uncomfortable, yet I've got the conviction that I shall know before long. I shall certainly know. I'm sure Trehearn knows, but he's such a silent beggar.

I'll go upstairs now and get it. What? You had better go with me? Ha, ha! Do you think I'm afraid of a bandbox and a noise? Nonsense!

Bother the candle, it won't light! As if the ridiculous thing understood what it's wanted for! Look at that—the third match. They light fast enough for my pipe. There, don't you see? It's a fresh box, just out of the tin safe where I keep the supply on account of the dampness. Oh, you think the wick of the candle may be damp, do you? All right, I'll light the beastly thing in the fire. That won't go out, at all events. Yes, it sputters a bit, but it will keep lighted now. It burns just like any other candle, doesn't it? The fact is, candles are not very good about here. I don't know where they come from, but they have a way of burning low occasionally, with a greenish flame that spits tiny sparks, and I'm often annoyed by their going out of themselves. It cannot be helped, for it will be long before we have electricity in our village. It really is rather a poor light, isn't it?

You think I had better leave you the candle and take the lamp, do you? I don't like to carry lamps about, that's the truth. I never dropped one in my life, but I have always thought I might, and it's so confoundedly dangerous if you do. Besides, I am pretty well used to these rotten candles by this time.

You may as well finish that glass while I'm getting it, for I don't mean to let you off with less than three before you go to bed. You won't have to go upstairs, either, for I've put you in the old study next to the surgery—that's where I live myself. The fact is, I never ask a friend to sleep upstairs now. The last man who did was Crackenthorpe, and he said he was kept awake all night. You remember old Crack, don't you? He stuck to the Service, and they've just made him an admiral. Yes, I'm off now—unless the candle goes out. I couldn't help asking if you remembered Crackenthorpe. If anyone had told us that the skinny little idiot he used to be was to turn out the most successful of the lot of us, we should have laughed at the idea, shouldn't we? You and I did not do badly, it's true—but I'm really going now. I don't mean to let you think that I've been putting it off by talking! As if there were anything to be afraid of! If I were scared, I should tell you so quite frankly, and get you to go upstairs with me.

Here's the box. I brought it down very carefully, so as not to disturb it, poor thing. You see, if it were shaken, the jaw might get separated from it again, and I'm sure it wouldn't like that. Yes, the candle went out as I was coming downstairs, but that was the draught from the leaky window on the landing. Did you hear anything? Yes, there was another scream. Am I pale, do you say? That's nothing. My heart is a little queer sometimes, and I went upstairs too fast. In fact, that's one reason why I really prefer to live altogether on the ground floor.

Wherever the shriek came from, it was not from the skull, for I had the box in my hand when I heard the noise, and here it is now; so we have proved definitely that the screams are produced by something else. I've no doubt I shall find out some day what makes them. Some crevice in the wall, of course, or a crack in a chimney, or a chink in the frame of a window. That's the way all ghost stories end in real life. Do you know, I'm jolly glad I thought of going up and bringing it down for you to see, for that last shriek settles the question. To think that I should have been so weak as to fancy that the poor skull could really cry out like a living thing!

Now I'll open the box, and we'll take it out and look at it under the bright light. It's rather awful to think that the poor lady used to sit there, in your chair, evening after evening, in just the same light, isn't it? But then—I've made up my mind that it's all rubbish from beginning to end, and that it's just an old skull that Luke had when he was a student and perhaps he put it into the lime merely to whiten it, and could not find the jaw.

I made a seal on the string, you see, after I had put the jaw in its place, and I wrote on the cover. There's the old white label on it still, from the milliner's, addressed to Mrs. Pratt when the hat was sent to her, and as there was room I wrote on the edge: "A skull, once the property of the late Luke Pratt, MD." I don't quite know why I wrote that, unless it was with the idea of explaining how the thing happened to be in my possession. I cannot help wondering sometimes what sort of hat it was that came in the bandbox. What colour was it, do you think? Was it a gay spring hat with a bobbing feather and pretty ribands? Strange that the very same box should hold the head that wore the finery—perhaps. No—we made up our minds that it just came from the hospital in London where Luke did his time. It's far better to look at it in that light, isn't it? There's no more connection between that skull and poor Mrs. Pratt than there was between my story about the lead and—.

Good Lord! Take the lamp—don't let it go out, if you can help it—I'll have the window fastened again in a second—I say, what a gale! There, it's out! I told you so! Never mind, there's the firelight—I've got the window shut—the bolt was only half down.

Was the box blown off the table? Where the deuce is it? There! That won't open again, for I've put up the bar. Good dodge, an old-fashioned bar—there's nothing like it. Now, you find the bandbox while I light the lamp. Confound those wretched matches! Yes, a pipe spill is better—it must light the fire—hadn't thought of it—thank you—there we are again. Now, where's the box? Yes, put it back on the table, and we'll open it.

That's the first time I have ever known the wind to burst that window open; but it was partly carelessness on my part when I last shut it. Yes, of course I heard the scream. It seemed to go all round the house before it broke in at the window. That proves that it's always been the wind and nothing else, doesn't it? When it was not the wind, it was my imagination. I've always been a very imaginative man; I must have been, though I did not know it. As we grow older we understand ourselves better, don't you know?

I'll have a drop of the Hulstkamp neat, by way of an exception, since you are filling up your glass. That damp gust chilled me, and with my rheumatic tendency I'm very much afraid of chills, for the cold sometimes seems to stick in my joints all winter when it once gets in.

By George, that's good stuff! I'll just light a fresh pipe, now that everything is snug again, and then we'll open the box. I'm so glad we heard that last scream together, with the skull here on the table between us, for the thing cannot possibly be in two places at the same time, and the noise most certainly came from outside, as any noise the wind makes must. You thought you heard it scream through the room after the window was burst open? Oh yes, so did I, but that was natural enough when everything was open. Of course we heard the wind. What could one expect?

Look here, please. I want you to see that the seal is intact before we open the box together. Will you take my glasses? No, you have your own. All right. The seal is sound, you see, and you can read the words of the motto easily. "Sweet and low"—that's it—because the poem goes on "Wind of the Western Sea," and says, "blow him again to me," and all that. Here is the seal on my watch chain, where it's hung for more than forty years. My poor little wife gave it to me when I was courting, and I never had any other. It was just like her to think of those words—she was always fond of Tennyson.

It's no use to cut the string, for it's fastened to the box, so I'll just break the wax and untie the knot, and afterwards we'll seal it up again. You see, I like to feel that the thing is safe in its place, and that nobody can take it out. Not that I should suspect Trehearn of meddling with it, but I always felt that he knows a lot more than he tells.

You see, I've managed it without breaking the string, though when I fastened it I never expected to open the bandbox again. The lid comes off easily enough. There! Now look!

What! Nothing in it! Empty! It's gone, man, the skull is gone!

No, there's nothing the matter with me. I'm only trying to collect my thoughts. It's so strange. I'm positively certain that it was inside when I put on the seal last spring. I can't have imagined that; it's utterly impossible. If I ever took a stiff glass with a friend now and then, I would admit that I might have made some idiotic mistake when I had taken too much. But I don't, and I never did. A pint of ale at supper and half a go of rum at bedtime was the most I ever took in my good days. I believe it's always we sober fellows who get rheumatism and gout! Yet there was my seal, and there is the empty bandbox. That's plain enough.

I say, I don't half like this. It's not right. There's something wrong about it, in my opinion. You needn't talk to me about supernatural manifestations, for I don't believe in them, not a little bit! Somebody must have tampered with the seal and stolen the skull. Sometimes, when I go out to work in the garden in summer, I leave my watch and chain on the table. Trehearn must have taken the seal then, and used it, for he would be quite sure that I should not come in for at least an hour.

If it was not Trehearn—oh, don't talk to me about the possibility that the thing has got out by itself!

If it has, it must be somewhere about the house, in some out-of-the-way corner, waiting. We may come upon it anywhere, waiting for us, don't you know?—just waiting in the dark. Then it will scream at me; it will shriek at me in the dark, for it hates me, I tell you!

The bandbox is quite empty. We are not dreaming, either of us. There, I turn it upside down.

What's that? Something fell out as I turned it over. It's on the floor, it's near your feet. I know it is, and we must find it. Help me to find it, man. Have you got it? For God's sake, give it to me, quickly!

Lead! I knew it when I heard it fall. I knew it couldn't be anything else by the little thud it made on the hearthrug. So it was lead after all and Luke did it.

I feel a bit shaken up—not exactly nervous, you know, but badly shaken up, that's the fact. Anybody would, I should think. After all, you cannot say that it's fear of the thing, for I went up and brought it down—at least I believed I was bringing it down, and that's the same thing, and by George, rather than give in to such silly nonsense, I'll take the box upstairs again and put it back in its place. It's not that. It's the certainty that the poor little woman came to her end in that way, by my fault, because I told the story. That's what is so dreadful. Somehow, I had always hoped that I should never be quite sure of it, but there is no doubting it now. Look at that!

Look at it! That little lump of lead with no particular shape. Think of what it did, man! Doesn't it make you shiver? He gave her something to make her sleep, of course, but there must have been one moment of awful agony. Think of having boiling lead poured into your brain. Think of it. She was dead before she could scream, but only think of—oh! There it is again—it's just outside—I know it's just outside—I can't keep it out of my head!—oh!—oh!

You thought I had fainted? No, I wish I had, for it would have stopped sooner. It's all very well to say that it's only a noise, and that a noise never hurt anybody—you're as white as a shroud yourself. There's only one thing to be done, if we hope to close an eye tonight. We must find it and put it back into its bandbox and shut it up in the cupboard, where it likes to be. I don't know how it got out, but it wants to get in again. That's why it screams so awfully tonight—it was never so bad as this—never since I first—.

Bury it? Yes, if we can find it, we'll bury it, if it takes us all night. We'll bury it six feet deep and ram down the earth over it, so that it shall never get out again, and if it screams, we shall hardly hear it so deep down. Quick, we'll get the lantern and look for it. It cannot be far away; I'm sure it's just outside—it was coming in when I shut the window, I know it.

Yes, you're quite right. I'm losing my senses, and I must get hold of myself. Don't speak to me for a minute or two; I'll sit quite still and keep my eyes shut and repeat something I know. That's the best way.

"All together the altitude, the latitude, and the polar distance, divide by two and subtract the altitude from the half-sum; then add the logarithm of the secant of the latitude, the cosecant of the polar distance, the cosine of the half-sum and the sine of the half-sum minus the altitude"—there! Don't say that I'm out of my senses, for my memory is all right, isn't it?

Of course, you may say that it's mechanical, and that we never forget the things we learned when we were boys and have used almost every day for a lifetime. But that's the very point. When a man is going crazy, it's the mechanical part of his mind that gets out of order and won't work right; he remembers things that never happened or he sees things that aren't real or he hears noises when there is perfect silence. That's not what is the matter with either of us, is it?

Come on, we'll get the lantern and go round the house. It's not raining—only blowing like old boots, as we used to say. The lantern is in the cupboard under the stairs in the hall, and I always keep it trimmed in case of a wreck.

No use to look for the thing? I don't see how you can say that. It was nonsense to talk of burying it, of course, for it doesn't want to be buried;

it wants to go back to its bandbox and be taken upstairs, poor thing! Trehearn took it out, I know, and made the seal over again. Perhaps he took it to the churchyard, and he may have meant well. I dare say he thought that it would not scream any more if it were quietly laid in consecrated ground, near where it belongs. But it has come home. Yes, that's it. He's not half a bad fellow, Trehearn, and rather religiously inclined, I think. Does not that sound natural, and reasonable, and well meant? He supposed it screamed because it was not decently buried—with the rest. But he was wrong. How should he know that it screams at me because it hates me, and because it's my fault that there was that little lump of lead in it?

No use to look for it, anyhow? Nonsense! I tell you it wants to be found—Hark! What's that knocking? Do you hear it? Knock—knock—knock—three times, then a pause, and then again. It has a hollow sound, hasn't it?

It has come home. I've heard that knock before. It wants to come in and be taken upstairs in its box. It's at the front door.

Will you come with me? We'll take it in. Yes, I own that I don't like to go alone and open the door. The thing will roll in and stop against my foot, just as it did before, and the light will go out. I'm a good deal shaken by finding that bit of lead, and, besides, my heart isn't quite right—too much strong tobacco, perhaps. Besides, I'm quite willing to own that I'm a bit nervous tonight, if I never was before in my life.

That's right, come along! I'll take the box with me, so as not to come back. Do you hear the knocking? It's not like any other knocking I ever heard. If you will hold this door open, I can find the lantern under the stairs by the light from this room without bringing the lamp into the hall—it would only go out.

The thing knows we are coming—hark! It's impatient to get in. Don't shut the door till the lantern is ready, whatever you do. There will be the usual trouble with the matches, I suppose—no, the first one, by Jove! I tell you it wants to get in, so there's no trouble. All right with that door now; shut it, please. Now come and hold the lantern, for it's blowing so hard outside that I shall have to use both hands. That's it, hold the light low. Do you hear the knocking still? Here goes—I'll open just enough with my foot against the bottom of the door—now!

Catch it! It's only the wind that blows it across the floor, that's all—there's half a hurricane outside, I tell you! Have you got it? The bandbox is on the table. One minute, and I'll have the bar up. There!

Why did you throw it into the box so roughly? It doesn't like that, you know.

What do you say? Bitten your hand? Nonsense, man! You did just what I did. You pressed the jaws together with your other hand and pinched yourself. Let me see. You don't mean to say you have drawn blood? You must have squeezed hard, by Jove, for the skin is certainly torn. I'll give you some carbolic solution for it before we go to bed, for they say a scratch from a skull's tooth may go bad and give trouble.

Come inside again and let me see it by the lamp. I'll bring the band-box—never mind the lantern, it may just as well burn in the hall for I shall need it presently when I go up the stairs. Yes, shut the door if you will; it makes it more cheerful and bright. Is your finger still bleeding? I'll get you the carbolic in an instant; just let me see the thing.

Strange that the jaw should stick to it so closely, isn't it? I suppose it's the dampness, for it shuts like a vice—I have wiped off the drop of blood, for it was not nice to look at. I'm not going to try to open the jaws, don't be afraid! I shall not play any tricks with the poor thing, but I'll just seal the box again, and we'll take it upstairs and put it away where it wants to be. The wax is on the writing-table by the window. Thank you. It will be long before I leave my seal lying about again, for Trehearn to use, I can tell you. Explain? I don't explain natural phenomena, but if you choose to think that Trehearn had hidden it somewhere in the bushes, and that the gale blew it to the house against the door, and made it knock, as if it wanted to be let in, you're not thinking the impossible, and I'm quite ready to agree with you.

Do you see that? You can swear that you've actually seen me seal it this time, in case anything of the kind should occur again. The wax fastens the strings to the lid, which cannot possibly be lifted, even enough to get in one finger. You're quite satisfied, aren't you? Yes. Besides, I shall lock the cupboard and keep the key in my pocket hereafter.

Now we can take the lantern and go upstairs. Do you know? I'm very much inclined to agree with your theory that the wind blew it against the house. I'll go ahead, for I know the stairs; just hold the lantern near my feet as we go up. How the wind howls and whistles! Did you feel the sand on the floor under your shoes as we crossed the hall?

Yes—this is the door of the best bedroom. Hold up the lantern, please. This side, by the head of the bed. I left the cupboard open when I got the box. Isn't it queer how the faint odour of women's dresses will hang about an old closet for years? This is the shelf. You've seen me set the box there, and now you see me turn the key and put it into my pocket. So that's done!

Goodnight. Are you sure you're quite comfortable? It's not much of a room, but I dare say you would as soon sleep here as upstairs tonight. If you want anything, sing out; there's only a lath and plaster partition between us. There's not so much wind on this side by half. There's the Hollands on the table, if you'll have one more nightcap. No? Well, do as you please. Goodnight again, and don't dream about that thing, if you can.

The following paragraph appeared in the *Penraddon News*, 23 November 1906:

MYSTERIOUS DEATH OF A RETIRED SEA CAPTAIN

The village of Tredcombe is much disturbed by the strange death of Captain Charles Braddock, and all sorts of impossible stories are circulating with regard to the circumstances, which certainly seem difficult of explanation. The retired captain, who had successfully commanded in his time the largest and fastest liners belonging to one of the principal transatlantic steamship companies, was found dead in his bed on Tuesday morning in his own cottage, a quarter of a mile from the village. An examination was made at once by the local practitioner, which revealed the horrible fact that the deceased had been bitten in the throat by a human assailant, with such amazing force as to crush the windpipe and cause death. The marks of the teeth of both jaws were so plainly visible on the skin that they could be counted, but the perpetrator of the deed had evidently lost the two lower middle incisors. It is hoped that this peculiarity may help to identify the murderer, who can only be a dangerous escaped maniac. The deceased, though over sixty-five years of age, is said to have been a hale man of considerable physical strength, and it is remarkable that no signs of any struggle were visible in the room, nor could it be ascertained how the murderer had entered the house. Warning has been sent to all the insane asylums in the United Kingdom, but as yet no information has been received regarding the escape of any dangerous patient.

The coroner's Jury returned the somewhat singular verdict that Captain Braddock came to his death "by the hands or teeth of some person unknown." The local surgeon is said to have expressed privately the opinion that the maniac is a woman, a view he deduces from the small size of the jaws, as shown by the marks of the teeth. The whole affair is shrouded in mystery. Captain Braddock was a widower, and lived alone. He leaves no children.

AUTHOR'S NOTE—Students of ghost lore and haunted houses will find the foundation of the foregoing story in the legends about a skull which is still preserved in the farmhouse called Bettiscombe Manor, situated, I believe, on the Dorsetshire coast.

22

Canon Alberic's Scrap-Book

By M. R. James

St. Bertrand de Comminges is a decayed town on the spurs of the Pyrenees, not very far from Toulouse, and still nearer to Bagnères-de-Luchon. It was the site of a bishopric until the Revolution, and has a cathedral which is visited by a certain number of tourists. In the spring of 1883 an Englishman arrived at this old-world place—I can hardly dignify it with the name of city, for there are not a thousand inhabitants. He was a Cambridge man, who had come specially from Toulouse to see St. Bertrand's Church, and had left two friends, who were less keen archaeologists than himself, in their hotel at Toulouse, under promise to join him on the following morning. Half an hour at the church would satisfy them, and all three could then pursue their journey in the direction of Auch.

But our Englishman had come early on the day in question, and proposed to himself to fill a notebook and to use several dozens of plates in the process of describing and photographing every corner of the wonderful church that dominates the little hill of Comminges. In order to carry out this design satisfactorily, it was necessary to monopolize the verger of the church for the day. The verger or sacristan (I prefer the latter appellation, inaccurate as it may be) was accordingly sent for by the somewhat brusque lady who keeps the inn of the Chapeau Rouge; and when he came, the Englishman found him an unexpectedly interesting object of study. It was not in the personal appearance of the little, dry, wizened old man that the interest lay, for he was precisely like dozens of other church-guardians in France, but in a curious furtive, or rather hunted and oppressed, air which he had. He was perpetually half glancing behind him; the muscles of his back and shoulders seemed to be hunched in a continual nervous contraction, as if he were expecting every moment to find himself in the clutch of an enemy. The Englishman hardly knew whether to put him down as a man haunted by a fixed delusion, or as one oppressed by a guilty conscience, or as an unbearably henpecked husband. The probabilities, when reckoned up, certainly pointed to the last idea; but, still, the impression conveyed was that of a more formidable persecutor even than a termagant wife.

However, the Englishman (let us call him Dennistoun) was soon too deep in his notebook and too busy with his camera to give more than an occasional glance to the sacristan. Whenever he did look at him, he found him at no great distance, either huddling himself back against the wall or crouching in one of the gorgeous stalls. Dennistoun became rather fidgety after a time. Mingled suspicions that he was keeping the old man away from his déjeuner, that he was regarded as likely to make away with St. Bertrand's ivory crozier, or with the dusty stuffed crocodile that hangs over the font, began to torment him. "Won't you go home?" he said at last; "I'm quite well able to finish my notes alone; you can lock me in if you like. I shall want at least two hours more here, and it must be cold for you, isn't it?"

"Good Heavens!" said the little man, whom the suggestion seemed to throw into a state of unaccountable terror, "such a thing cannot be thought of for a moment. Leave monsieur alone in the church? No, no; two hours, three hours, all will be the same to me. I have breakfasted, I am not at all cold, with many thanks to monsieur."

"Very well, my little man," quoth Dennistoun to himself. "You have been warned, and must take the consequences."

Before the expiration of two hours, the stalls, the enormous dilapidated organ, the choir-screen of Bishop Jean de Mauléon, the remnants of glass and tapestry, and the objects in the treasure-chamber, had been well and truly examined; the sacristan still keeping at Dennistoun's heels, and every now and then whipping round as if he had been stung, when one or other of the strange noises that trouble a large empty building fell on his ear. Curious noises they were sometimes.

"Once," Dennistoun said to me, "I could have sworn I heard a thin metallic voice laughing high up in the tower. I darted an inquiring glance at my sacristan. He was white to the lips. 'It is he—that is—it is no one; the door is locked,' was all he said, and we looked at each other for a full minute."

Another little incident puzzled Dennistoun a good deal. He was examining a large dark picture that hangs behind the altar, one of a series illustrating the miracles of St. Bertrand. The composition of the picture is well-nigh indecipherable, but there is a Latin legend below, which runs thus: Qualiter S. Bertrandus liberavit hominem quem diabolus diu volebat strangulare. [How St. Bertrand delivered a man whom the Devil long sought to strangle.]

Dennistoun was turning to the sacristan with a smile and a jocular remark of some sort on his lips, but he was confounded to see the old man on his knees, gazing at the picture with the eye of a suppliant in agony, his hands clasped, and a rain of tears on his cheeks. Dennistoun naturally pretended to have noticed nothing, but the question would not away from him, "Why should a daub of this kind affect anyone so strongly?" He seemed to himself to be getting some sort of clue to the reason of the strange look that had been puzzling him all day; the man must be a monomaniac; but what was his monomania?

It was nearly five o'clock; the short day was drawing in, and the church began to fill with shadows, while the curious noises—the muffled footfalls and distant talking voices that had been perceptible all day—seemed, no doubt because of the fading light and the consequently quickened sense of hearing, to become more frequent and insistent.

The sacristan began for the first time to show signs of hurry and impatience. He heaved a sigh of relief when camera and notebook were finally packed and stowed away, and hurriedly beckoned Dennistoun to the western door of the church, under the tower. It was time to ring the Angelus. A few pulls at the reluctant rope, and the great bell Bertrande, high in the tower, began to speak, and swung her voice up among the pines and down to the valleys, loud with mountain-streams, calling the dwellers on those lonely hills to remember and repeat the salutation of the angel to her whom He called Blessed among women. With that a profound quiet seemed to fall for the first time that day upon the little town, and Dennistoun and the sacristan went out of the church.

On the doorstep they fell into conversation. "Monsieur seemed to interest himself in the old choir-books in the sacristy."

"Undoubtedly. I was going to ask you if there were a library in the town."

"No, monsieur; perhaps there used to be one belonging to the Chapter, but it is now such a small place—" Here came a strange pause of irresolution, as it seemed; then, with a sort of plunge, he went on: "But if monsieur is amateur des vieux livres [a lover of old books], I have at home something that might interest him. It is not a hundred yards."

At once all Dennistoun's cherished dreams of finding priceless manuscripts in untrodden corners of France flashed up, to die down again the next moment. It was probably a stupid missal of Plantin's printing, about 1580. Where was the likelihood that a place so near Toulouse would not have been ransacked long ago by collectors? However, it would be foolish not to go; he would reproach himself for ever after if he refused. So they set off. On the way the curious irresolution and sudden determination of the sacristan recurred to Dennistoun, and he wondered in a shamefaced way whether he was being decoyed into some purlieu to be made away with as a supposed rich Englishman. He contrived, therefore, to begin talking to his guide, and to drag in, in a rather clumsy fashion, the fact that he expected two friends to join him early the next morning. To his surprise, the announcement seemed to relieve the sacristan of some of the anxiety that oppressed him.

"That is well," he said quite brightly—"that is very well. Monsieur will travel in company with his friends; they will be always near him. It is a good thing to travel thus in company—sometimes."

The last word appeared to be added as an afterthought, and to bring with it a relapse into gloom for the poor little man.

They were soon at the house, which was one rather larger than its neighbors, stone-built, with a shield carved over the door, the shield of Alberic de Mauléon, a collateral descendant, Dennistoun tells me, of Bishop John de Mauléon. This Alberic was a Canon of Comminges from

1680 to 1701. The upper windows of the mansion were boarded up, and the whole place bore, as does the rest of Comminges, the aspect of decaying age. Arrived on his doorstep, the sacristan paused a moment. "Perhaps," he said, "perhaps, after all, monsieur has not the time?"

"Not at all—lots of time—nothing to do till tomorrow. Let us see what it is you have got."

The door was opened at this point, and a face looked out, a face younger than the sacristan's but bearing something of the same distressing look; only here it seemed to be the mark, not so much of fear for personal safety as of acute anxiety on behalf of another. Plainly, the owner of the face was the sacristan's daughter; and, but for the expression I have described, she was a handsome girl enough. She brightened up considerably on seeing her father accompanied by an able-bodied stranger. A few remarks passed between father and daughter, of which Dennistoun only caught these words, said by the sacristan, "He was laughing in the church," words which were answered only by a look of terror from the girl.

But in another minute they were in the sitting-room of the house, a small, high chamber with a stone floor, full of moving shadows cast by a wood-fire that flickered on a great hearth. Something of the character of an oratory was imparted to it by a tall crucifix, which reached almost to the ceiling on one side; the figure was painted of the natural colours, the cross was black. Under this stood a chest of some age and solidity, and when a lamp had been brought, and chairs set, the sacristan went to this chest, and produced therefrom, with growing excitement and nervousness, as Dennistoun thought, a large book, wrapped in a white cloth, on which cloth a cross was embroidered in red thread.

Even before the wrapping had been removed, Dennistoun began to be interested by the size and shape of the volume. "Too large for a missal," he thought, "and not the shape of an antiphoner; perhaps it may be something good, after all." The next moment the book was open, and Dennistoun felt that he had at last lit upon something better than good. Before him lay a large folio, bound, perhaps, late in the seventeenth century, with the arms of Canon Alberic de Mauléon stamped in gold on the sides. There may have been a hundred and fifty leaves of paper in the book, and on almost every one of them was fastened a leaf from an illuminated manuscript. Such a collection Dennistoun had hardly dreamed of in his wildest moments. Here were ten leaves from a copy of Genesis, illustrated with pictures, which could not be later than a.d. 700. Further on was a complete set of pictures from a Psalter, of English execution, of the very finest kind that the thirteenth century could produce; and, perhaps best of all, there were twenty leaves of uncial writing in Latin, which, as a few words seen here and there told him at once, must belong to some very early unknown patristic treatise. Could it possibly be a fragment of the copy of Papias's 'On the Words of Our Lord,' which was known to have existed as late as the twelfth century at Nîmes?

In any case, his mind was made up; that book must return to Cambridge with him, even if he had to draw the whole of his balance from the bank and stay at St. Bertrand till the money came. He glanced up at the sacristan to see if his face yielded any hint that the book was for sale. The sacristan was pale, and his lips were working. "If monsieur will turn on to the end," he said. So monsieur turned on, meeting new treasures at every rise of a leaf; and at the end of the book he came upon two sheets of paper, of much more recent date than anything he had yet seen, which puzzled him considerably. They must be contemporary, he decided, with the unprincipled Canon Alberic, who had doubtless plundered the Chapter library of St. Bertrand to form this priceless scrap-book. On the first of the paper sheets was a plan, carefully drawn and instantly recognizable by a person who knew the ground, of the south aisle and cloisters of St. Bertrand's. There were curious signs looking like planetary symbols, and a few Hebrew words, in the corners; and in the north-west angle of the cloister was a cross drawn in gold paint. Below the plan were some lines of writing in Latin, which ran thus:

Responsa 12mi Dec. 1694. Interrogatum est: Inveniamne? Respon-sum est: invenenies. Fiamne dives? Fies. Vivamne invidendus? Vives. Moriarne in lecto meo? Ita. [Answers of the 12th of December, 1694. It was asked: Shall I find it? Answer: Thou shalt. Shall I become rich? Thou wilt. Shall I live an object of envy? Thou wilt. Shall I die in my bed? Thou wilt.]

"A good specimen of the treasure-hunter's record—quite reminds one of Mr. Minor-Canon Quatremain in Old St. Paul's," was Dennistoun's comment, and he turned the leaf.

What he then saw impressed him, as he has often told me, more than he could have conceived any drawing or picture capable of impressing him. And, though the drawing he saw is no longer in existence, there is a photograph of it (which I possess) which fully bears out that statement. The picture in question was a sepia drawing at the end of the seventeenth century, representing, one would say at first sight, a Biblical scene; for the architecture (the picture represented an interior) and the figures had that semi-classical flavour about them which the artists of two hundred years ago thought appropriate to illustrations of the Bible. On the right was a King on his throne, the throne elevated on twelve steps, a canopy overhead, lions on either side—evidently King Solomon. He was bending forward with outstretched sceptre, in attitude of command; his face expressed horror and disgust, yet there was in it also the mark of imperious will and confident power. The left half of the picture was the strangest, however. The interest plainly centered there. On the pavement before the throne were grouped four soldiers, surrounding a crouching figure which must be described in a moment. A fifth soldier lay dead on the pavement, his neck distorted, and his eyeballs starting from his head. The four surrounding guards were looking at the King. In their faces the sentiment of horror was intensified; they seemed, in fact, only restrained from flight by their implicit trust in their master. All this terror was plainly excited by the being that crouched in their midst.

I entirely despair of conveying by any words the impression which this figure makes upon anyone who looks at it. I recollect once showing the photograph of the drawing to a lecturer on morphology—a person of, I was going to say, abnormally sane and unimaginative habits of mind. He absolutely refused to be alone for the rest of that evening, and he told me afterwards that for many nights he had not dared to put out his light before going to sleep. However, the main traits of the figure I can at least indicate. At first you saw only a mass of coarse, matted black hair; presently it was seen that this covered a body of fearful thinness, almost a skeleton, but with the muscles standing out like wires. The hands were of a dusky pallor, covered, like the body, with long, coarse hairs, and hideously taloned. The eyes, touched in with a burning yellow, had intensely black pupils, and were fixed upon the throned King with a look of beast-like hate. Imagine one of the awful bird-catching spiders of South America translated into human form, and endowed with intelligence just less than human, and you will have some faint conception of the terror inspired by this appalling effigy. One remark is universally made by those to whom I have shown the picture: "It was drawn from the life."

As soon as the first shock of his irresistible fright had subsided, Dennistoun stole a look at his hosts. The sacristan's hands were pressed upon his eyes; his daughter, looking up at the cross on the wall, was telling her beads feverishly.

At last the question was asked, "Is this book for sale?"

There was the same hesitation, the same plunge of determination that he had noticed before, and then came the welcome answer, "If monsieur pleases."

"How much do you ask for it?"

"I will take two hundred and fifty francs."

This was confounding. Even a collector's conscience is sometimes stirred, and Dennistoun's conscience was tenderer than a collector's.

"My good man!" he said again and again, "your book is worth far more than two hundred and fifty francs, I assure you—far more."

But the answer did not vary: "I will take two hundred and fifty francs, not more."

There was really no possibility of refusing such a chance. The money was paid, the receipt signed, a glass of wine drunk over the transaction, and then the sacristan seemed to become a new man. He stood upright, he ceased to throw those suspicious glances behind him, he actually laughed or tried to laugh. Dennistoun rose to go.

"I shall have the honour of accompanying monsieur to his hotel?" said the sacristan.

"Oh no, thanks! It isn't a hundred yards. I know the way perfectly, and there is a moon."

The offer was pressed three or four times, and refused as often.

"Then, monsieur will summon me if—if he finds occasion; he will keep the middle of the road, the sides are so rough."

"Certainly, certainly," said Dennistoun, who was impatient to examine his prize by himself; and he stepped out into the passage with the book under his arm.

Here he was met by the daughter; she, it appeared, was anxious to do a business on her own account; perhaps, like Gehazi, to "take somewhat" from the foreigner whom her father had spared.

"A silver crucifix and chain for the neck; monsieur would perhaps be good enough to accept it?"

Well, really, Dennistoun hadn't much use for these things. What did mademoiselle want for it?

"Nothing—nothing in the world. Monsieur is more than welcome to it."

The tone in which this and much more was said was unmistakably genuine, so that Dennistoun was reduced to profuse thanks, and submitted to have the chain put round his neck. It really seemed as if he had rendered the father and daughter some service which they hardly knew how to repay. As he set off with his book they stood at the door looking after him, and they were still looking when he waved them a last good night from the steps of the Chapeau Rouge.

Dinner was over, and Dennistoun was in his bedroom, shut up alone with his acquisition. The landlady had manifested a particular interest in him since he had told her that he had paid a visit to the sacristan and bought an old book from him. He thought, too, that he had heard a hurried dialogue between her and the said sacristan in the passage outside the salle à manger; some words to the effect that "Pierre and Bertrand would be sleeping in the house" had closed the conversation.

All this time a growing feeling of discomfort had been creeping over him—a nervous reaction, perhaps, after the delight of his discovery. Whatever it was, it resulted in a conviction that there was someone behind him, and that he was far more comfortable with his back to the wall. All this, of course, weighed light in the balance as against the obvious value of the collection he had acquired. And now, as I said, he was alone in his bedroom, taking stock of Canon Alberic's treasures, in which every moment revealed something more charming.

"Bless Canon Alberic!" said Dennistoun, who had an inveterate habit of talking to himself. "I wonder where he is now? Dear me! I wish that landlady would learn to laugh in a more cheering manner; it makes one feel as if there was someone dead in the house. Half a pipe more, did you say? I think perhaps you are right. I wonder what that crucifix is that the young woman insisted on giving me? Last century, I suppose. Yes, probably. It is rather a nuisance of a thing to have round one's neck—just too heavy. Most likely her father has been wearing it for years. I think I might give it a clean-up before I put it away."

He had taken the crucifix off, and laid it on the table, when his attention was caught by an object lying on the red cloth just by his left elbow. Two or three ideas of what it might be flitted through his brain with their own incalculable quickness.

"A penwiper? No, no such thing in the house. A rat? No, too black. A large spider? I trust to goodness not—no. Good God! A hand like the hand in that picture!"

In another infinitesimal flash he had taken it in. Pale, dusky skin, covering nothing but bones and tendons of appalling strength; coarse black hairs, longer than ever grew on a human hand; nails rising from the ends of the fingers and curving sharply downward and forward, grey, horny, and wrinkled.

He flew out of his chair with deadly, inconceivable terror clutching at his heart. The shape, whose left hand rested on the table, was rising to a standing posture behind his seat, its right hand crooked above his scalp. There was black and tattered drapery about it; the coarse hair covered it as in the drawing. The lower jaw was thin—what can I call it?—shallow, like a beast's; teeth showed behind the black lips; there was no nose; the eyes, of a fiery yellow, against which the pupils showed black and intense, and the exulting hate and thirst to destroy life which shone there, were the most horrifying features in the whole vision. There was intelligence of a kind in them—intelligence beyond that of a beast, below that of a man.

The feelings which this horror stirred in Dennistoun were the intensest physical fear and the most profound mental loathing. What did he do? What could he do? He has never been quite certain what words he said, but he knows that he spoke, that he grasped blindly at the silver crucifix, that he was conscious of a movement towards him on the part of the demon, and that he screamed with the voice of an animal in hideous pain.

Pierre and Bertrand, the two sturdy little serving-men, who rushed in, saw nothing, but felt themselves thrust aside by something that passed out between them, and found Dennistoun in a swoon. They sat up with him that night, and his two friends were at St. Bertrand by nine o'clock next morning. He himself, though still shaken and nervous, was almost himself by that time, and his story found credence with them, though not until they had seen the drawing and talked with the sacristan.

Almost at dawn the little man had come to the inn on some pretence, and had listened with the deepest interest to the story detailed by the landlady. He showed no surprise.

"It is he—it is he! I have seen him myself," was his only comment; and to questionings but one reply was vouchsafed: "Deux fois je l'ai vu; mille fois je l'ai senti." [Twice I have seen him. A thousand times I have felt him.] He would tell them nothing of the provenance of the book, nor any details of his experiences. "I shall soon sleep, and my rest will be sweet. Why should you trouble me?" he said.

We shall never know what he or Canon Alberic de Mauléon suffered. At the back of that fateful drawing were some lines of writing, which may suppose to throw light on the situation:

Contradictio Salomonis cum demonio nocturno.
Albericus de Mauleone delineavit.
V. Deus in adiutorium. Ps. Qui habitat.
Sancte Bertrande, demoniorum effugator,
intercede pro me miserrimo.
Primum uidi nocte 12mi Dec. 1694: uidebo mox
ultimum. Peccaui et passus sum, plura adhuc
passurus. Dec. 29, 1701.

I have never quite understood what was Dennistoun's view of the events I have narrated. He quoted to me once a text from Ecclesiasticus: "Some spirits there be that are created for vengeance, and in their fury lay on sore strokes." On another occasion he said, "Isaiah was a very sensible man; doesn't he say something about night monsters living in the ruins of Babylon? These things are rather beyond us at present."

Another confidence of his impressed me rather, and I sympathized with it. We had been, last year, to Comminges, to see Canon Alberic's tomb. It is a great marble erection with an effigy of the Canon in a large wig and soutane, and an elaborate eulogy of his learning below. I saw Dennistoun talking for some time with the Vicar of St. Bertrand's, and as we drove away he said to me: "I hope it isn't wrong; you know I am a Presbyterian—but I—I believe there will be 'saying of Mass and singing of dirges' for Alberic de Mauléon's rest." Then he added, with a touch of the Northern British in his tone, "I had no notion they came so dear."

The book is in the Wentworth Collection at Cambridge. The drawing was photographed and then burnt by Dennistoun on the day when he left Comminges on the occasion of his first visit.

He died that summer; his daughter married, and settled at St. Papoul. She never understood the circumstances of her father's "obsession."

The dispute of Solomon with a demon of the night. Drawn by Alberic de Mauléon. Versicle.

> *O Lord, make haste to help me. Psalm. Whoso dwelleth (xci).*
> *Saint Bertrand, who puttest devils to flight, pray for me most unhappy.*
> *I saw it first on the night of Dec. 12, 1694; soon I shall see it for the last time.*
> *I have sinned and suffered, and have more to suffer yet.*
> DECEMBER 29, 1701

The Gallia Christiana gives the date of the Canon's death as December 31, 1701, "in bed, of a sudden seizure." Details of this kind are not common in the great work of the Sammarthani.

23

A True Story

By Benjamin Disraeli

SIR,—WHEN I WAS A YOUNG BOY, I HAD DELICATE HEALTH, AND WAS somewhat of a pensive and contemplative turn of mind; it was my delight in the long summer evenings to slip away from my noisy and more robust companions, that I might walk in the shade of a venerable wood, my favourite haunt, and listen to the cawing of the old rooks, who seemed as fond of this retreat as I was.

One evening I sat later than usual, though the distant sound of the cathedral clock had more than once warned me to my home. There was a stillness in all nature that I was unwilling to disturb by the least motion. From this reverie I was suddenly startled by the sight of a tall, slender female who was standing by me, looking sorrowfully and steadily in my face. She was dressed in white, from head to foot, in a fashion I had never seen before; her garments were unusually long and flowing, and rustled as she glided through the low shrubs near me as if they were made of the richest silk. My heart beat as if I were dying, and I knew not that I could have stirred from the spot; but she seemed so very mild and beautiful, I did not attempt it. Her pale brown hair was braided round her head, but there were some locks that strayed upon her neck; and altogether she looked like a lovely picture, but not like a living woman. I closed my eyes forcibly with my hands, and when I looked again she had vanished.

I cannot exactly say why I did not on my return speak of this beautiful appearance, nor why, with a strange mixture of hope and fear, I went again and again to the same spot that I might see her. She always came, and often in the storm and plashing rain, that never seemed to touch or to annoy her, and looked sweetly at me, and silently passed on; and though she was so near to me, that once the wind lifted these light straying locks, and I felt them against my cheek, yet I never could move or speak to her. I fell ill, and when I recovered, my mother closely questioned me of the tall lady, of whom, in the height of my fever, I had so often spoken.

I cannot tell you what a weight was taken from my boyish spirits when I learned that this was no apparition, but a most lovely woman; not young, though she had kept her young looks, for the grief which had broken her heart seemed to have spared her beauty.

When the rebel troops were retreating after their total defeat, in that very wood I was so fond of, a young officer, unable any longer to endure the anguish of his wounds, sunk from his horse, and laid himself down to die. He was found there by the daughter of Sir Henry R——, and conveyed by a trusty domestic to her father's mansion. Sir Henry was a loyalist; but the officer's desperate condition excited his compassion, and his many wounds spoke a language a brave man could not misunderstand. Sir Henry's daughter, with many tears, pleaded for him and pronounced that he should be carefully and secretly attended. And well she kept that promise, for she waited upon him (her mother being long dead) for many weeks, and anxiously watched for the first opening of eyes, that, languid as he was, looked brightly and gratefully upon his nurse.

You may fancy better than I can tell you, as he slowly recovered, all the moments that were spent in reading, and low-voiced singing, and gentle playing on the lute, and how many fresh flowers were brought to one whose wounded limbs would not bear him to gather them for himself, and how calmly the days glided on in blessedness of returning health, and in that sweet silence so carefully enjoined him. I will pass by this to speak of one day, which brighter and pleasanter than others, did not seem more bright or more lovely than the looks of the young maiden, as she gaily spoke of "a little festival which (though it must bear an unworthier name) she meant really to give in honour of her guest's recovery." "And it is time, lady," said he, "for that guest so tended and honoured, to tell you his whole story, and speak to you of one who will help him to thank you; may I ask you, fair lady, to write a little billet for me, which even in these times of danger I may find some means to forward?" To his mother, no doubt, she thought, as with light steps and a lighter heart she seated herself by his couch, and smilingly bade him dictate; but when he said "My dear wife," and lifted up his eyes to be asked for more, he saw before him a pale statue, that gave him one look of utter despair, and fell—for he had no power to help her—heavily at his feet. Those eyes never truly reflected the pure soul again, or answered by answering looks the fond enquiries of her poor old father. She lived to be as I saw her,—sweet and gentle, and delicate always; but reason returned no more. She visited till the day of her death the spot where she first saw that young soldier, and dressed herself in the very clothes that he said so well became her.

24

The Phantom 'Rickshaw

By Rudyard Kipling

May no ill dreams disturb my rest,
Nor Powers of Darkness me molest.

—EVENING HYMN

ONE OF THE FEW ADVANTAGES THAT INDIA HAS OVER ENGLAND IS A certain great Knowability. After five years' service a man is directly or indirectly acquainted with the two or three hundred Civilians in his Province, all the Messes of ten or twelve Regiments and Batteries, and some fifteen hundred other people of the non-official castes. In ten years his knowledge should be doubled, and at the end of twenty he knows, or knows something about, almost every Englishman in the Empire, and may travel anywhere and everywhere without paying hotel bills.

Globe-trotters who expect entertainment as a right, have, even within my memory, blunted this open-heartedness, but, none the less, to-day if you belong to the Inner Circle and are neither a bear nor a black sheep all houses are open to you and our small world is very kind and helpful.

Rickett of Kamartha stayed with Polder of Kumaon, some fifteen years ago. He meant to stay two nights only, but was knocked down by rheumatic fever, and for six weeks disorganized Polder's establishment, stopped Polder's work, and nearly died in Polder's bedroom. Polder behaves as though he had been placed under eternal obligation by Rickett, and yearly sends the little Ricketts a box of presents and toys. It is the same everywhere. The men who do not take the trouble to conceal from you their opinion that you are an incompetent ass, and the women who blacken your character and misunderstand your wife's amusements, will work themselves to the bone on your behalf if you fall sick or into serious trouble.

Heatherlegh, the doctor, kept, in addition to his regular practice, a hospital on his private account—an arrangement of loose-boxes for Incurables, his friends called it—but it was really a sort of fitting-up shed for craft that had been damaged by stress of weather. The weather in India is often sultry, and since the tale of bricks is a fixed quantity, and the only liberty allowed is permission to work overtime and get no thanks, men occasionally break down and become as mixed as the metaphors in this sentence.

Heatherlegh is the nicest doctor that ever was, and his invariable prescription to all his patients is "lie low, go slow, and keep cool." He says that more men are killed by overwork than the importance of this world justifies. He maintains that overwork slew Pansay who died under his hands about three years ago. He has, of course, the right to speak authoritatively, and he laughs at my theory that there was a crack in Pansay's head and a little bit of the Dark World came through and pressed him to death. "Pansay went off the handle," says Heatherlegh, "after the stimulus of long leave at Home. He may or he may not have behaved like a blackguard to Mrs. Keith-Wessington. My notion is that the work of the Katabundi Settlement ran him off his legs, and that he took to brooding and making much of an ordinary P. & O. flirtation. He certainly was engaged to Miss Mannering, and she certainly broke off the engagement. Then he took a feverish chill and all that nonsense about ghosts developed itself. Overwork started his illness, kept it alight, and killed him, poor devil. Write him off to the System—one man to do the work of two-and-a-half men."

I do not believe this. I used to sit up with Pansay sometimes when Heatherlegh was called out to visit patients and I happened to be within claim. The man would make me most unhappy by describing in a low, even voice the procession of men, women, children, and devils that was always passing at the bottom of his bed. He had a sick man's command of language. When he recovered I suggested that he should write out the whole affair from beginning to end, knowing that ink might assist him to ease his mind. When little boys have learned a new bad word they are never happy till they have chalked it up on a door. And this also is Literature.

He was in high fever while he was writing, and the blood-and-thunder Magazine style he adopted did not calm him. Two months afterwards he was reported fit for duty, but, in spite of the fact that he was urgently needed to help an undermanned Commission stagger through a deficit, he preferred to die; vowing at the last that he was hag-ridden. I secured his manuscript before he died, and this is his version of the affair, dated 1885:

My doctor tells me that I need rest and change of air. It is not improbable that I shall get both ere long—rest that neither the red-coated orderly nor the mid-day gun can break, and change of air far beyond that which any homeward-bound steamer can give me. In the meantime I am resolved to stay where I am; and, in flat defiance of my doctor's orders, to take all the world into my confidence. You shall learn for yourselves the precise nature of my malady; and shall, too, judge for yourselves whether any man born of woman on this weary earth was ever so tormented as I.

Speaking now as a condemned criminal might speak ere the drop-bolts are drawn, my story, wild and hideously improbable as it may appear, demands at least attention. That it will ever receive credence I utterly disbelieve. Two months ago I should have scouted as mad or drunk the man who had dared tell me the like. Two months ago I was the happiest man in India. To-day, from Peshawar to the sea, there is no one more wretched. My doctor and I are the only two who know this. His explanation is that my brain, digestion, and eyesight are all slightly affected; giving rise to my frequent and persistent "delusions." Delusions, indeed! I call him a fool; but he attends me still with the same unwearied smile, the same bland professional manner, the same neatly trimmed red whiskers, till I begin to suspect that I am an ungrateful, evil-tempered invalid. But you shall judge for yourselves.

Three years ago it was my fortune—my great misfortune—to sail from Gravesend to Bombay, on return from long leave, with one Agnes Keith-Wessington, wife of an officer on the Bombay side. It does not in the least concern you to know what manner of woman she was. Be content with the knowledge that ere the voyage had ended, both she and I were desperately and unreasoningly in love with one another. Heaven knows that I can make the admission now without one particle of vanity. In matters of this sort there is always one who gives and another who accepts. From the first day of our ill-omened attachment, I was conscious that Agnes's passion was a stronger, a more dominant, and—if I may use the expression—a purer sentiment than mine. Whether she recognized the fact then, I do not know. Afterwards it was bitterly plain to both of us.

Arrived at Bombay in the spring of the year, we went our respective ways, to meet no more for the next three or four months, when my leave and her love took us both to Simla. There we spent the season together; and there my fire of straw burnt itself out to a pitiful end with the closing year. I attempt no excuse. I make no apology. Mrs. Wessington had given up much for my sake, and was prepared to give up all. From my own lips in August, 1882, she learnt that I was sick of her presence, tired of her company, and weary of the sound of her voice. Ninety-nine women out of a hundred would have wearied of me as I wearied of them; seventy-five of that number would have promptly avenged themselves by active and obtrusive flirtation with other men. Mrs. Wessington was the hundredth. On her neither my openly expressed aversion, nor the cutting brutalities with which I garnished our interviews had the least effect.

"Jack, darling!" was her eternal cuckoo-cry, "I'm sure it's all a mistake—a hideous mistake; and we'll be good friends again some day. Please forgive me, Jack, dear."

I was the offender, and I knew it. That knowledge transformed my pity into passive endurance, and eventually, into blind hate—the same instinct, I suppose, which prompts a man to savagely stamp on the spider he has but half killed. And with this hate in my bosom the season of 1882 came to an end.

Next year we met again at Simla—she with her monotonous face and timid attempts at reconciliation, and I with loathing of her in every fiber of my frame. Several times I could not avoid meeting her alone; and on each occasion her words were identically the same. Still the unreasoning wail that it was all a "mistake"; and still the hope of eventually "making friends." I might have seen, had I cared to look, that that hope only was keeping her alive. She grew more wan and thin month by month. You will agree with me, at least, that such conduct would have driven any one to despair. It was uncalled for, childish, unwomanly. I maintain that she was much to blame. And again, sometimes, in the black, fever-stricken night watches, I have begun to think that I might have been a little kinder to her. But that really is a "delusion." I could not have continued pretending to love her when I didn't; could I? It would have been unfair to us both.

Last year we met again—on the same terms as before. The same weary appeals, and the same curt answers from my lips. At least I would make her see how wholly wrong and hopeless were her attempts at resuming the old relationship. As the season wore on, we fell apart—that is to say, she found it difficult to meet me, for I had other and more absorbing interests to attend to. When I think it over quietly in my sick-room, the season of 1884 seems a confused nightmare wherein light and shade were fantastically intermingled—my courtship of little Kitty Mannering; my hopes, doubts and fears; our long rides together; my trembling avowal of attachment; her reply; and now and again a vision of a white face flitting by in the 'rickshaw with the black and white liveries I once watched for so earnestly; the wave of Mrs. Wessington's gloved hand; and, when she met me alone, which was but seldom, the irksome monotony of her appeal. I loved Kitty Mannering, honestly, heartily loved her, and with my love for her grew my hatred for Agnes. In August Kitty and I were engaged. The next day I met those accursed "magpie" jhampanies at the back of Jakko, and moved by some passing sentiment of pity, stopped to tell Mrs. Wessington everything. She knew it already.

"So I hear you're engaged, Jack, dear." Then, without a moment's pause: "I'm sure it's all a mistake—a hideous mistake. We shall be as good friends some day, Jack, as we ever were."

My answer might have made even a man wince. It cut the dying woman before me like the blow of a whip. "Please forgive me, Jack; I didn't mean to make you angry; but it's true, it's true!"

And Mrs. Wessington broke down completely. I turned away and left her to finish her journey in peace, feeling, but only for a moment or two, that I had been an unutterably mean hound. I looked back, and saw that she had turned her 'rickshaw with the idea, I suppose, of overtaking me.

The scene and its surroundings were photo-graphed on my memory. The rain-swept sky (we were at the end of the wet weather), the sodden, dingy pines, the muddy road, and the black powder-driven cliffs formed a gloomy background against which the black and white liveries of the jhampanies, the yellow-paneled 'rickshaw and Mrs. Wessington's down-bowed golden head stood out clearly. She was holding her handkerchief in her left hand and was leaning back exhausted against the 'rickshaw cushions. I turned my horse up a bypath near the Sanjowlie Reservoir and literally ran away. Once I fancied I heard a faint call of "Jack!" This may have been imagination. I never stopped to verify it. Ten minutes later I came across Kitty on horseback; and, in the delight of a long ride with her, forgot all about the interview.

A week later Mrs. Wessington died, and the inexpressible burden of her existence was removed from my life. I went Plainsward perfectly happy. Before three months were over I had forgotten all about her, except that at times the discovery of some of her old letters reminded me unpleasantly of our bygone relationship. By January I had disinterred what was left of our correspondence from among my scattered belongings and had burnt it. At the beginning of April of this year, 1885, I was at Simla—semi-deserted Simla—once more, and was deep in lover's talks and walks with Kitty. It was decided that we should be married at the end of June. You will understand, therefore, that, loving Kitty as I did, I am not saying too much when I pronounce myself to have been, at the time, the happiest man in India.

Fourteen delightful days passed almost before I noticed their flight. Then, aroused to the sense of what was proper among mortals circumstanced as we were, I pointed out to Kitty that an engagement-ring was the outward and visible sign of her dignity as an engaged girl; and that she must forthwith come to Hamilton's to be measured for one. Up to that moment, I give you my word, we had completely forgotten so trivial a matter. To Hamilton's we accordingly went on the 15th of April, 1885. Remember that—whatever my doctor may say to the contrary—I was then in perfect health, enjoying a well-balanced mind and an absolutely tranquil spirit. Kitty and I entered Hamilton's shop together, and there, regardless of the order of affairs, I measured Kitty's finger for the ring in the presence of the amused assistant. The ring was a sapphire with two diamonds. We then rode out down the slope that leads to the Combermere Bridge and Peliti's shop.

While my Waler was cautiously feeling his way over the loose shale, and Kitty was laughing and chattering at my side—while all Simla, that is to say as much of it as had then come from the Plains, was grouped round the Reading-room and Peliti's veranda—I was aware that some one, apparently at a vast distance, was calling me by my Christian name. It struck me that I had heard the voice before, but when and where I could not at once determine. In the short space it took to cover the road between the path from Hamilton's shop and the first plank of the Combermere Bridge I had thought over half-a-dozen people who might have committed such a solecism, and had eventually decided that it must have been some singing in my ears. Immediately opposite Peliti's shop my eye was arrested by the sight of four jhampanies in black and white livery, pulling a yellow-paneled, cheap, bazar 'rickshaw. In a moment my mind flew back to the previous season and Mrs. Wessington with a sense of irritation and disgust. Was it not enough that the woman was dead and done with, without her black and white servitors reappearing to spoil the day's happiness?

Whoever employed them now I thought I would call upon, and ask as a personal favor to change her jhampanies' livery. I would hire the men myself, and, if necessary, buy their coats from off their backs. It is impossible to say here what a flood of undesirable memories their presence evoked.

"Kitty," I cried, "there are poor Mrs. Wessington's jhampanies turned up again! I wonder who has them now?"

Kitty had known Mrs. Wessington slightly last season, and had always been interested in the sickly woman.

"What? Where?" she asked. "I can't see them anywhere."

Even as she spoke, her horse, swerving from a laden mule, threw himself directly in front of the advancing 'rickshaw. I had scarcely time to utter a word of warning when, to my unutterable horror, horse and rider passed through men and carriage as if they had been thin air.

"What's the matter?" cried Kitty; "what made you call out so foolishly, Jack? If I am engaged I don't want all creation to know about it. There was lots of space between the mule and the veranda; and, if you think I can't ride—There!"

Whereupon willful Kitty set off, her dainty little head in the air, at a hand-gallop in the direction of the Band-stand; fully expecting, as she herself afterwards told me, that I should follow her. What was the matter? Nothing, indeed. Either that I was mad or drunk, or that Simla was haunted with devils. I reined in my impatient cob, and turned round. The 'rickshaw had turned, too, and now stood immediately facing me, near the left railing of the Combermere Bridge.

"Jack! Jack, darling." (There was no mistake about the words this time: they rang through my brain as if they had been shouted in my ear.) "It's some hideous mistake, I'm sure. Please forgive me, Jack, and let's be friends again."

The 'rickshaw-hood had fallen back, and inside, as I hope and pray daily for the death I dread by night, sat Mrs. Keith-Wessington, handkerchief in hand, and golden head bowed on her breast.

How long I stared motionless I do not know. Finally, I was aroused by my groom taking the Waler's bridle and asking whether I was ill. I tumbled off my horse and dashed, half fainting, into Peliti's for a glass of cherry-brandy. There two or three couples were gathered round the coffee-tables discussing the gossip of the day. Their trivialities were more comforting to me just then than the consolations of religion could have been. I plunged into the midst of the conversation at once; chatted, laughed and jested with a face (when I caught a glimpse of it in a mirror) as white and drawn as that of a corpse. Three or four men noticed my condition; and, evidently setting it down to the results of over many pegs, charitably endeavored to draw me apart from the rest of the loungers. But I refused to be led away. I wanted the company of my kind—as a child rushes into the midst of the dinner-party after a fright in the dark. I must have talked for about ten minutes or so, though it seemed an eternity to me, when I heard Kitty's clear voice outside inquiring for me. In another minute she had entered the shop, prepared to upbraid me roundly for failing so signally in my duties. Something in my face stopped her.

"Why, Jack," she cried, "what have you been doing? What has happened? Are you ill?" Thus driven into a direct lie, I said that the sun had been a little too much for me. It was close upon five o'clock of a cloudy April afternoon, and the sun had been hidden all day. I saw my mistake as soon as the words were out of my mouth; attempted to recover it; blundered hopelessly and followed Kitty, in a regal rage, out of doors, amid the smiles of my acquaintances. I made some excuse (I have forgotten what) on the score of my feeling faint; and cantered away to my hotel, leaving Kitty to finish the ride by herself.

In my room I sat down and tried calmly to reason out the matter. Here was I, Theobald Jack Pansay, a well-educated Bengal Civilian in the year of grace 1885, presumably sane, certainly healthy, driven in terror from my sweetheart's side by the apparition of a woman who had been dead and buried eight months ago. These were facts that I could not blink. Nothing was further from my thought than any memory of Mrs. Wessington when Kitty and I left Hamilton's shop. Nothing was more utterly commonplace than the stretch of wall opposite Peliti's. It was broad daylight. The road was full of people; and yet here, look you, in defiance of every law of probability, in direct outrage of Nature's ordinance, there had appeared to me a face from the grave.

Kitty's Arab had gone through the 'rickshaw; so that my first hope that some woman marvelously like Mrs. Wessington had hired the carriage and the coolies with their old livery was lost. Again and again I went round this treadmill of thought; and again and again gave up baffled and in despair. The voice was as inexplicable as the apparition. I had originally some wild notion of confiding it all to Kitty; of begging her to marry me at once; and in her arms defying the ghostly occupant of the 'rickshaw. "After all," I argued, "the presence of the 'rickshaw is in itself enough to prove the existence of a spectral illusion. One may see ghosts of men and women, but surely never of coolies and carriages. The whole thing is absurd. Fancy the ghost of a hill-man!"

Next morning I sent a penitent note to Kitty, imploring her to overlook my strange conduct of the previous afternoon. My Divinity was still very wroth, and a personal apology was necessary. I explained, with a fluency born of night-long pondering over a falsehood, that I had been attacked with a sudden palpitation of the heart—the result of indigestion. This eminently practical solution had its effect; and Kitty and I rode out that afternoon with the shadow of my first lie dividing us.

Nothing would please her save a canter round Jakko. With my nerves still unstrung from the previous night I feebly protested against the notion, suggesting Observatory Hill, Jutogh, the Boileaugunge road—anything rather than the Jakko round. Kitty was angry and a little hurt, so I yielded from fear of provoking further misunderstanding, and we set out together towards Chota Simla. We walked a greater part of the way, and, according to our custom, cantered from a mile or so below the Convent to the stretch of level road by the Sanjowlie Reservoir. The wretched horses appeared to fly, and my heart beat quicker and quicker as we neared the crest of the ascent. My mind had been full of Mrs. Wessington all the afternoon; and every inch of the Jakko road bore witness to our old-time walks and talks. The boulders were full of it; the pines sang it aloud overhead; the rain-fed torrents giggled and chuckled unseen over the shameful story; and the wind in my ears chanted the iniquity aloud.

As a fitting climax, in the middle of the level men call the Ladies' Mile, the Horror was awaiting me. No other 'rickshaw was in sight—only the four black and white jhampanies, the yellow-paneled carriage, and the golden head of the woman within—all apparently just as I had left them eight months and one fortnight ago! For an instant I fancied that Kitty must see what I saw—we were so marvelously sympathetic in all things. Her next words undeceived me— "Not a soul in sight! Come along, Jack, and I'll race you to the Reservoir buildings!" Her wiry little Arab was off like a bird, my Waler following close behind, and in this order we dashed under the cliffs. Half a minute brought us within fifty yards of the 'rickshaw. I pulled my Waler and fell back a little. The 'rickshaw was directly in the middle of the road: and once more the Arab passed through, my horse following. "Jack, Jack, dear! Please forgive me," rang with a wail in my ears, and, after an interval: "It's all a mistake, a hideous mistake!"

I spurred my horse like a man possessed. When I turned my head at the Reservoir works the black and white liveries were still waiting—patiently waiting—under the gray hillside, and the wind brought me a mocking echo of the words I had just heard. Kitty bantered me a good deal on my silence throughout the remainder of the ride. I had been talking up till then wildly and at random. To save my life I could not speak afterwards naturally, and from Sanjowlie to the Church wisely held my tongue.

I was to dine with the Mannerings that night and had barely time to canter home to dress. On the road to Elysium Hill I overheard two men talking together in the dusk—"It's a curious thing," said one, "how completely all trace of it disappeared. You know my wife was insanely fond of the woman (never could see anything in her myself) and wanted me to pick up her old 'rickshaw and coolies if they were to be got for love or money. Morbid sort of fancy I call it, but I've got to do what the Memsahib tells me. Would you believe that the man she hired it from tells me that all four of the men, they were brothers, died of cholera, on the way to Hardwár, poor devils; and the 'rickshaw has been broken up by the man himself. Told me he never used a dead Memsahib's 'rickshaw. Spoilt his luck. Queer notion, wasn't it? Fancy poor little Mrs. Wessington spoiling any one's luck except her own!" I laughed aloud at this point; and my laugh jarred on me as I uttered it. So there were ghosts of 'rickshaws after all, and ghostly employments in the other world! How much did Mrs. Wessington give her men? What were their hours? Where did they go?

And for visible answer to my last question I saw the infernal thing blocking my path in the twilight. The dead travel fast and by short-cuts unknown to ordinary coolies. I laughed aloud a second time and checked my laughter suddenly, for I was afraid I was going mad. Mad to a certain extent I must have been, for I recollect that I reined in my horse at the head of the 'rickshaw, and politely wished Mrs. Wessington "good evening." Her answer was one I knew only too well. I listened to the end; and replied that I had heard it all before, but should be delighted if she had anything further to say. Some malignant devil stronger than I must have entered into me that evening, for I have a dim recollection of talking the commonplaces of the day for five minutes to the thing in front of me.

"Mad as a hatter, poor devil—or drunk. Max, try and get him to come home."

Surely that was not Mrs. Wessington's voice! The two men had overheard me speaking to the empty air, and had returned to look after me.

They were very kind and considerate, and from their words evidently gathered that I was extremely drunk. I thanked them confusedly and cantered away to my hotel, there changed, and arrived at the Mannerings' ten minutes late. I pleaded the darkness of the night as an excuse; was rebuked by Kitty for my unlover-like tardiness; and sat down.

The conversation had already become general; and, under cover of it, I was addressing some tender small talk to my sweetheart when I was aware that at the further end of the table a short red-whiskered man was describing with much broidery his encounter with a mad unknown that evening. A few sentences convinced me that he was repeating the incident of half an hour ago. In the middle of the story he looked round for applause, as professional story-tellers do, caught my eye, and straightaway collapsed. There was a moment's awkward silence, and the red-whiskered man muttered something to the effect that he had "forgotten the rest"; thereby sacrificing a reputation as a good story-teller which he had built up for six seasons past. I blessed him from the bottom of my heart and— went on with my fish.

In the fullness of time that dinner came to an end; and with genuine regret I tore myself away from Kitty—as certain as I was of my own existence that It would be waiting for me outside the door. The red-whiskered man, who had been introduced to me as Dr. Heatherlegh of Simla, volunteered to bear me company as far as our roads lay together. I accepted his offer with gratitude.

My instinct had not deceived me. It lay in readiness in the Mall, and, in what seemed devilish mockery of our ways, with a lighted headlamp. The red-whiskered man went to the point at once, in a manner that showed he had been thinking over it all dinner time.

"I say, Pansay, what the deuce was the matter with you this evening on the Elysium road?" The suddenness of the question wrenched an answer from me before I was aware.

"That!" said I, pointing to It.

"That may be either D. T. or eyes for aught I know. Now you don't liquor. I saw as much at dinner, so it can't be D. T. There's nothing whatever where you're pointing, though you're sweating and trembling with fright like a scared pony. Therefore, I conclude that it's eyes. And I ought to understand all about them. Come along home with me. I'm on the Blessington lower road."

To my intense delight the 'rickshaw instead of waiting for us kept about twenty yards ahead—and this, too, whether we walked, trotted, or cantered. In the course of that long night ride I had told my companion almost as much as I have told you here.

"Well, you've spoilt one of the best tales I've ever laid tongue to," said he, "but I'll forgive you for the sake of what you've gone through. Now come home and do what I tell you; and when I've cured you, young man, let this be a lesson to you to steer clear of women and indigestible food till the day of your death."

The 'rickshaw kept steadily in front; and my red-whiskered friend seemed to derive great pleasure from my account of its exact whereabouts.

"Eyes, Pansay—all eyes, brain, and stomach; and the greatest of these three is stomach. You've too much conceited brain, too little stomach, and thoroughly unhealthy eyes. Get your stomach straight and the rest follows. And all that's French for a liver pill. I'll take sole medical charge of you from this hour; for you're too interesting a phenomenon to be passed over."

By this time we were deep in the shadow of the Blessington lower road and the 'rickshaw came to a dead stop under a pine-clad overhanging shale cliff. Instinctively I halted too, giving my reason. Heatherlegh rapped out an oath.

"Now, if you think I'm going to spend a cold night on the hillside for the sake of a stomach-cum-brain-cum-eye illusion . . . Lord ha' mercy! What's that?"

There was a muffled report, a blinding smother of dust just in front of us, a crack, the noise of rent boughs, and about ten yards of the cliffside—pines, undergrowth, and all—slid down into the road below, completely blocking it up. The uprooted trees swayed and tottered for a moment like drunken giants in the gloom, and then fell prone among their fellows with a thunderous crash. Our two horses stood motionless and sweating with fear. As soon as the rattle of falling earth and stone had subsided, my companion muttered: "Man, if we'd gone forward we should have been ten feet deep in our graves by now! 'There are more things in heaven and earth' . . . Come home, Pansay, and thank God. I want a drink badly."

We retraced our way over the Church Ridge, and I arrived at Dr. Heatherlegh's house shortly after midnight.

His attempts towards my cure commenced almost immediately, and for a week I never left his sight. Many a time in the course of that week did I bless the good fortune which had thrown me in contact with Simla's best and kindest doctor. Day by day my spirits grew lighter and more equable. Day by day, too, I became more and more inclined to fall in with Heatherlegh's "spectral illusion" theory, implicating eyes, brain, and stomach. I wrote to Kitty, telling her that a slight sprain caused by a fall from my horse kept me indoors for a few days; and that I should be recovered before she had time to regret my absence.

Heatherlegh's treatment was simple to a degree. It consisted of liver-pills, cold-water baths and strong exercise, taken in the dusk or at early dawn—for, as he sagely observed: "A man with a sprained ankle doesn't walk a dozen miles a day, and your young woman might be wondering if she saw you."

At the end of the week, after much examination of pupil and pulse and strict injunctions as to diet and pedestrianism, Heatherlegh dismissed me as brusquely as he had taken charge of me. Here is his parting benediction: "Man, I certify to your mental cure, and that's as much as to say I've cured most of your bodily ailments. Now, get your traps out of this as soon as you can; and be off to make love to Miss Kitty."

I was endeavoring to express my thanks for his kindness. He cut me short:

"Don't think I did this because I like you. I gather that you've behaved like a blackguard all through. But, all the same you're a phenomenon, and as queer a phenomenon as you are a blackguard. Now, go out and see if you can find the eyes-brain-and-stomach business again. I'll give you a lakh for each time you see it."

Half an hour later I was in the Mannering's drawing-room with Kitty—drunk with the intoxication of present happiness and the foreknowledge that I should never more be troubled with Its hideous presence. Strong in the sense of my newfound security, I proposed a ride at once; and, by preference, a canter round Jakko.

Never have I felt so well, so overladen with vitality and mere animal spirits as I did on the afternoon of the 30th of April. Kitty was delighted at the change in my appearance, and complimented me on it in her delightfully frank and outspoken manner. We left the Mannering's house together, laughing and talking, and cantered along the Chota Simla road as of old.

I was in haste to reach the Sanjowlie Reservoir and there make my assurance doubly sure. The horses did their best, but seemed all too slow to my impatient mind. Kitty was astonished at my boisterousness. "Why, Jack!" she cried at last, "you are behaving like a child! What are you doing?"

We were just below the Convent, and from sheer wantonness I was making my Waler plunge and curvet across the road as I tickled it with the loop of my riding-whip.

"Doing," I answered, "nothing, dear. That's just it. If you'd been doing nothing for a week except lie up, you'd be as riotous as I.

'Singing and murmuring in your feastful mirth,
Joying to feel yourself alive;
Lord over nature, Lord of the visible Earth,
Lord of the senses five.'"

My quotation was hardly out of my lips before we had rounded the corner above the Convent; and a few yards further on could see across to Sanjowlie. In the center of the level road stood the black and white liveries, the yellow-paneled 'rickshaw and Mrs. Keith-Wessington. I pulled up, looked, rubbed my eyes, and, I believe, must have said something. The next thing I knew was that I was lying face downward on the road, with Kitty kneeling above me in tears.

"Has it gone, child?" I gasped. Kitty only wept more bitterly.

"Has what gone? Jack dear: what does it all mean? There must be a mistake somewhere, Jack. A hid-eous mistake." Her last words brought me to my feet—mad—raving for the time being.

"Yes, there is a mistake somewhere," I repeated, "a hideous mistake. Come and look at It!"

I have an indistinct idea that I dragged Kitty by the wrist along the road up to where It stood, and implored her for pity's sake to speak to It; to tell It that we were betrothed! That neither Death nor Hell could break the tie between us; and Kitty only knows how much more to the same effect. Now and again I appealed passionately to the Terror in the 'rickshaw to bear witness to all I had said, and to release me from a torture that was killing me. As I talked I suppose I must have told Kitty of my old relations with Mrs. Wessington, for I saw her listen intently with white face and blazing eyes.

"Thank you, Mr. Pansay," she said, "that's quite enough. Bring my horse."

The grooms, impassive as Orientals always are, had come up with the recaptured horses; and as Kitty sprang into her saddle I caught hold of the bridle entreating her to hear me out and forgive. My answer was the cut of her riding-whip across my face from mouth to eye, and a word or two of farewell that even now I cannot write down. So I judged, and judged rightly, that Kitty knew all; and I staggered back to the side of the 'rickshaw. My face was cut and bleeding, and the blow of the riding-whip had raised a livid blue weal on it. I had no self-respect. Just then, Heatherlegh, who must have been following Kitty and me at a distance, cantered up.

"Doctor," I said, pointing to my face, "here's Miss Mannering's signature to my order of dismissal and . . . I'll thank you for that lakh as soon as convenient."

Heatherlegh's face, even in my abject misery, moved me to laugh.

"I'll stake my professional reputation," he began. "Don't be a fool," I whispered. "I've lost my life's happiness and you'd better take me home."

As I spoke the 'rickshaw was gone. Then I lost all knowledge of what was passing. The crest of Jakko seemed to heave and roll like the crest of a cloud and fall in upon me.

Seven days later (on the 7th of May, that is to say) I was aware that I was lying in Heatherlegh's room as weak as a little child. Heatherlegh was watching me intently from behind the papers on his writing table. His first words were not very encouraging; but I was too far spent to be much moved by them.

"Here's Miss Kitty has sent back your letters. You corresponded a good deal, you young people. Here's a packet that looks like a ring, and a cheerful sort of note from Mannering Papa, which I've taken the liberty of reading and burning. The old gentleman's not pleased with you."

"And Kitty?" I asked dully.

"Rather more drawn than her father from what she says. By the same token you must have been letting out any number of queer reminiscences just before I met you. Says that a man who would have behaved to a woman as you did to Mrs. Wessington ought to kill himself out of sheer pity for his kind. She's a hot-headed little virago, your mash. Will have it too that you were suffering from D. T. when that row on the Jakko road turned up. Says she'll die before she ever speaks to you again."

I groaned and turned over on the other side.

"Now you've got your choice, my friend. This engagement has to be broken off; and the Mannerings don't want to be too hard on you. Was it broken through D.T. or epileptic fits? Sorry I can't offer you a better exchange unless you'd prefer hereditary insanity. Say the word and I'll tell 'em it's fits. All Simla knows about that scene on the Ladies' Mile. Come! I'll give you five minutes to think over it."

During those five minutes I believe that I explored thoroughly the lowest circles of the Inferno which it is permitted man to tread on earth. And at the same time I myself was watching myself faltering through the dark labyrinths of doubt, misery, and utter despair. I wondered, as Heatherlegh in his chair might have wondered, which dreadful alternative I should adopt. Presently I heard myself answering in a voice that I hardly recognized:

"They're confoundedly particular about morality in these parts. Give 'em fits, Heatherlegh, and my love. Now let me sleep a bit longer."

Then my two selves joined, and it was only I (half-crazed, devil-driven I) that tossed in my bed, tracing step by step the history of the past month.

"But I am in Simla," I kept repeating to myself. "I, Jack Pansay, am in Simla, and there are no ghosts here. It's unreasonable of that woman to pretend there are. Why couldn't Agnes have left me alone? I never did her any harm. It might just as well have been me as Agnes. Only I'd never have come back on purpose to kill her. Why can't I be left alone—left alone and happy?"

It was high noon when I first awoke; and the sun was low in the sky before I slept—slept as the tortured criminal sleeps on his rack, too worn to feel further pain.

Next day I could not leave my bed. Heatherlegh told me in the morning that he had received an answer from Mr. Mannering, and that, thanks to his (Heatherlegh's) friendly offices, the story of my affliction had traveled through the length and breadth of Simla, where I was on all sides much pitied.

"And that's rather more than you deserve," he concluded pleasantly, "though the Lord knows you've been going through a pretty severe mill. Never mind; we'll cure you yet, you perverse phenomenon."

I declined firmly to be cured. "You've been much too good to me already, old man," said I; "but I don't think I need trouble you further."

In my heart I knew that nothing Heatherlegh could do would lighten the burden that had been laid upon me.

With that knowledge came also a sense of hopeless, impotent rebellion against the unreasonableness of it all. There were scores of men no better than I whose punishments had at least been reserved for another world and I felt that it was bitterly, cruelly unfair that I alone should have been singled out for so hideous a fate. This mood would in time give place to another where it seemed that the 'rickshaw and I were the only realities in a world of shadows; that Kitty was a ghost; that Mannering, Heatherlegh, and all the other men and women I knew were all ghosts and the great, gray hills themselves but vain shadows devised to torture me. From mood to mood I tossed backwards and forwards for seven weary days, my body growing daily stronger and stronger, until the bedroom looking-glass told me that I had returned to everyday life, and was as other men once more. Curiously enough, my face showed no signs of the struggle I had gone through. It was pale indeed, but as expressionless and commonplace as ever. I had expected some permanent alteration—visible evidence of the disease that was eating me away. I found nothing.

On the 15th of May I left Heatherlegh's house at eleven o'clock in the morning; and the instinct of the bachelor drove me to the Club. There I found that every man knew my story as told by Heatherlegh, and was, in clumsy fashion, abnormally kind and attentive. Nevertheless I recognized that for the rest of my natural life I should be among, but not of, my fellows; and I envied very bitterly indeed the laughing coolies on the Mall below. I lunched at the Club, and at four o'clock wandered aimlessly down the Mall in the vague hope of meeting Kitty. Close to the Band-stand the black and white liveries joined me; and I heard Mrs. Wessington's old appeal at my side. I had been expecting this ever since I came out; and was only surprised at her delay. The phantom 'rickshaw and I went side by side along the Chota Simla road in silence. Close to the bazaar, Kitty and a man on horseback overtook and passed us. For any sign she gave I might have been a dog in the road. She did not even pay me the compliment of quickening her pace; though the rainy afternoon had served for an excuse.

So Kitty and her companion, and I and my ghostly Light-o'-Love, crept round Jakko in couples. The road was streaming with water; the pines dripped like roof-pipes on the rocks below, and the air was full of fine, driving rain. Two or three times I found myself saying to myself almost aloud: "I'm Jack Pansay on leave at Simla—at Simla! Everyday, ordinary Simla. I mustn't forget that—I mustn't forget that." Then I would try to recollect some of the gossip I had heard at the Club; the price of So-and-So's horses—anything, in fact, that related to the work-a-day Anglo-Indian world I knew so well. I even repeated the multiplication-table rapidly to myself, to make quite sure that I was not taking leave of my senses. It gave me much comfort; and must have prevented my hearing Mrs. Wessington for a time.

Once more I wearily climbed the Convent slope and entered the level road. Here Kitty and the man started off at a canter, and I was left alone with Mrs. Wessington. "Agnes," said I, "will you put back your hood and tell me what it all means?" The hood dropped noiselessly and I was face to face with my dead and buried mistress. She was wearing the dress in which I had last seen her alive: carried the same tiny handkerchief in her right hand; and the same card-case in her left. (A woman eight months dead with a card-case!) I had to pin myself down to the multiplication-table, and to set both hands on the stone parapet of the road to assure myself that that at least was real.

"Agnes," I repeated, "for pity's sake tell me what it all means." Mrs. Wessington leant forward, with that odd, quick turn of the head I used to know so well, and spoke.

If my story had not already so madly overleaped the bounds of all human belief I should apologize to you now. As I know that no one—no, not even Kitty, for whom it is written as some sort of justification of my conduct—will believe me, I will go on. Mrs. Wessington spoke and I walked with her from the Sanjowlie road to the turning below the Commander-in-Chief's house as I might walk by the side of any living woman's 'rickshaw, deep in conversation. The second and most torment-ing of my moods of sickness had suddenly laid hold upon me, and like a prince in Tennyson's poem, "I seemed to move amid a world of ghosts." There had been a garden-party at the Commander-in-Chief's, and we two joined the crowd of homeward-bound folk. As I saw them then it seemed that they were the shadows—impalpable fantastic shadows—that divided for Mrs. Wessington's 'rickshaw to pass through. What we said during the course of that weird interview I cannot—indeed, I dare not—tell. Heatherlegh's comment would have been a short laugh and a remark that I had been "mashing a brain-eye-and-stomach chimera." It was a ghastly and yet in some indefinable way a marvelously dear experience. Could it be possible, I wondered, that I was in this life to woo a second time the woman I had killed by my own neglect and cruelty?

I met Kitty on the homeward road—a shadow among shadows.

If I were to describe all the incidents of the next fortnight in their order, my story would never come to an end; and your patience would be exhausted. Morning after morning and evening after evening the ghostly 'rickshaw and I used to wander through Simla together. Wherever I went, there the four black and white liveries followed me and bore me com-pany to and from my hotel. At the theater I found them amid the crowd of yelling jhampanies; outside the Club veranda, after a long evening of whist; at the birthday ball, waiting patiently for my reappearance; and in broad daylight when I went calling. Save that it cast no shadow, the 'rickshaw was in every respect as real to look upon as one of wood and iron. More than once, indeed, I have had to check myself from warning some hard-riding friend against cantering over it. More than once I have walked down the Mall deep in conversation with Mrs. Wessington to the unspeakable amazement of the passers-by.

Before I had been out and about a week I learnt that the "fit" theory had been discarded in favor of insanity. However, I made no change in my mode of life. I called, rode, and dined out as freely as ever. I had a passion for the society of my kind which I had never felt before; I hungered to be among the realities of life; and at the same time I felt vaguely unhappy when I had been separated too long from my ghostly companion. It would be almost impossible to describe my varying moods from the 15th of May up to to-day.

The presence of the 'rickshaw filled me by turns with horror, blind fear, a dim sort of pleasure, and utter despair. I dared not leave Simla; and I knew that my stay there was killing me. I knew, moreover, that it was my destiny to die slowly and a little every day. My only anxiety was to get the penance over as quietly as might be. Alternately I hungered for a sight of Kitty and watched her outrageous flirtations with my successor—to speak more accurately, my successors—with amused interest. She was as much out of my life as I was out of hers. By day I wandered with Mrs. Wessington almost content. By night I implored Heaven to let me return to the world as I used to know it. Above all these varying moods lay the sensation of dull, numbing wonder that the seen and the unseen should mingle so strangely on this earth to hound one poor soul to its grave.

August 27th—Heatherlegh has been indefatigable in his attendance on me; and only yesterday told me that I ought to send in an application for sick-leave. An application to escape the company of a phantom! A request that the Government would graciously permit me to get rid of five ghosts and an airy 'rickshaw by going to England! Heatherlegh's proposition moved me to almost hysterical laughter. I told him that I should await the end quietly at Simla; and I am sure that the end is not far off. Believe me that I dread its advent more than any word can say; and I torture myself nightly with a thousand speculations as to the manner of my death.

Shall I die in my bed decently and as an English gentleman should die; or, in one last walk on the Mall, will my soul be wrenched from me to take its place for ever and ever by the side of that ghastly phantasm? Shall I return to my old lost allegiance in the next world, or shall I meet Agnes loathing her and bound to her side through all eternity? Shall we two hover over the scene of our lives till the end of time? As the day of my death draws nearer, the intense horror that all living flesh feels towards escaped spirits from beyond the grave grows more and more powerful. It is an awful thing to go down quick among the dead with scarcely one half of your life completed. It is a thousand times more awful to wait as I do in your midst, for I know not what unimaginable terror. Pity me, at least on the score of my "delusion," for I know you will never believe what I have written here. Yet as surely as ever a man was done to death by the Powers of Darkness I am that man.

In justice, too, pity her. For as surely as ever woman was killed by man, I killed Mrs. Wessington. And the last portion of my punishment is even now upon me.

25

The Lagoon

By Joseph Conrad

THE WHITE MAN, LEANING WITH BOTH ARMS OVER THE ROOF OF THE little house in the stern of the boat, said to the steersman—

"We will pass the night in Arsat's clearing. It is late."

The Malay only grunted, and went on looking fixedly at the river. The white man rested his chin on his crossed arms and gazed at the wake of the boat. At the end of the straight avenue of forests cut by the intense glitter of the river, the sun appeared unclouded and dazzling, poised low over the water that shone smoothly like a band of metal. The forests, sombre and dull, stood motionless and silent on each side of the broad stream. At the foot of big, towering trees, trunkless nipa palms rose from the mud of the bank, in bunches of leaves enormous and heavy, that hung unstirring over the brown swirl of eddies. In the stillness of the air every tree, every leaf, every bough, every tendril of creeper and every petal of minute blossoms seemed to have been bewitched into an immobility perfect and final. Nothing moved on the river but the eight paddles that rose flashing regularly, dipped together with a single splash; while the steersman swept right and left with a periodic and sudden flourish of his blade describing a glinting semicircle above his head. The churned-up water frothed alongside with a confused murmur. And the white man's canoe, advancing upstream in the short-lived disturbance of its own making, seemed to enter the portals of a land from which the very memory of motion had forever departed.

The white man, turning his back upon the setting sun, looked along the empty and broad expanse of the sea-reach. For the last three miles of its course the wandering, hesitating river, as if enticed irresistibly by the freedom of an open horizon, flows straight into the sea, flows straight to the east—to the east that harbours both light and darkness. Astern of the boat the repeated call of some bird, a cry discordant and feeble, skipped along over the smooth water and lost itself, before it could reach the other shore, in the breathless silence of the world.

The steersman dug his paddle into the stream, and held hard with stiffened arms, his body thrown forward. The water gurgled aloud; and suddenly the long straight reach seemed to pivot on its centre, the forests swung in a semicircle, and the slanting beams of sunset touched the broadside of the canoe with a fiery glow, throwing the slender and distorted shadows of its crew upon the streaked glitter of the river. The white man turned to look ahead. The course of the boat had been altered at right-angles to the stream, and the carved dragon-head of its prow was pointing now at a gap in the fringing bushes of the bank. It glided through, brushing the overhanging twigs, and disappeared from the river like some slim and amphibious creature leaving the water for its lair in the forests.

The narrow creek was like a ditch: tortuous, fabulously deep; filled with gloom under the thin strip of pure and shining blue of the heaven. Immense trees soared up, invisible behind the festooned draperies of creepers. Here and there, near the glistening blackness of the water, a twisted root of some tall tree showed amongst the tracery of small ferns, black and dull, writhing and motionless, like an arrested snake. The short words of the paddlers reverberated loudly between the thick and sombre walls of vegetation. Darkness oozed out from between the trees, through the tangled maze of the creepers, from behind the great fantastic and unstirring leaves; the darkness, mysterious and invincible; the darkness scented and poisonous of impenetrable forests.

The men poled in the shoaling water. The creek broadened, opening out into a wide sweep of a stagnant lagoon. The forests receded from the marshy bank, leaving a level strip of bright green, reedy grass to frame the reflected blueness of the sky. A fleecy pink cloud drifted high above, trailing the delicate colouring of its image under the floating leaves and the silvery blossoms of the lotus. A little house, perched on high piles, appeared black in the distance. Near it, two tall nibong palms, that seemed to have come out of the forests in the background, leaned slightly over the ragged roof, with a suggestion of sad tenderness and care in the droop of their leafy and soaring heads.

The steersman, pointing with his paddle, said, "Arsat is there. I see his canoe fast between the piles."

The polers ran along the sides of the boat glancing over their shoulders at the end of the day's journey. They would have preferred to spend the night somewhere else than on this lagoon of weird aspect and ghostly reputation. Moreover, they disliked Arsat, first as a stranger, and also because he who repairs a ruined house, and dwells in it, proclaims that he is not afraid to live amongst the spirits that haunt the places abandoned by mankind. Such a man can disturb the course of fate by glances or words; while his familiar ghosts are not easy to propitiate by casual wayfarers upon whom they long to wreak the malice of their human master. White men care not for such things, being unbelievers and in league with the Father of Evil, who leads them unharmed through the invisible dangers of this world. To the warnings of the righteous they oppose an offensive pretence of disbelief. What is there to be done?

So they thought, throwing their weight on the end of their long poles. The big canoe glided on swiftly, noiselessly, and smoothly, towards Arsat's clearing, till, in a great rattling of poles thrown down, and the loud murmurs of "Allah be praised!" it came with a gentle knock against the crooked piles below the house.

The boatmen with uplifted faces shouted discordantly, "Arsat! O Arsat!" Nobody came. The white man began to climb the rude ladder giving access to the bamboo platform before the house. The juragan of the boat said sulkily, "We will cook in the sampan, and sleep on the water."

"Pass my blankets and the basket," said the white man, curtly.

He knelt on the edge of the platform to receive the bundle. Then the boat shoved off, and the white man, standing up, confronted Arsat, who had come out through the low door of his hut. He was a man young, powerful, with broad chest and muscular arms. He had nothing on but his sarong. His head was bare. His big, soft eyes stared eagerly at the white man, but his voice and demeanour were composed as he asked, without any words of greeting—

"Have you medicine, Tuan?"

"No," said the visitor in a startled tone. "No. Why? Is there sickness in the house?"

"Enter and see," replied Arsat, in the same calm manner, and turning short round, passed again through the small doorway. The white man, dropping his bundles, followed.

In the dim light of the dwelling he made out on a couch of bamboos a woman stretched on her back under a broad sheet of red cotton cloth. She lay still, as if dead; but her big eyes, wide open, glittered in the gloom, staring upwards at the slender rafters, motionless and unseeing. She was in a high fever, and evidently unconscious. Her cheeks were sunk slightly, her lips were partly open, and on the young face there was the ominous and fixed expression—the absorbed, contemplating expression of the unconscious who are going to die. The two men stood looking down at her in silence.

"Has she been long ill?" asked the traveller.

"I have not slept for five nights," answered the Malay, in a deliberate tone. "At first she heard voices calling her from the water and struggled against me who held her. But since the sun of to-day rose she hears nothing—she hears not me. She sees nothing. She sees not me—me!"

He remained silent for a minute, then asked softly—

"Tuan, will she die?"

"I fear so," said the white man, sorrowfully. He had known Arsat years ago, in a far country in times of trouble and danger, when no friendship is to be despised. And since his Malay friend had come unexpectedly to dwell in the hut on the lagoon with a strange woman, he had slept many times there, in his journeys up and down the river. He liked the man who knew how to keep faith in council and how to fight without fear by the side of his white friend. He liked him—not so much perhaps as a man likes his favourite dog—but still he liked him well enough to help and ask no questions, to think sometimes vaguely and hazily in the midst of his own pursuits, about the lonely man and the long-haired woman with audacious face and triumphant eyes, who lived together hidden by the forests—alone and feared.

The white man came out of the hut in time to see the enormous conflagration of sunset put out by the swift and stealthy shadows that, rising like a black and impalpable vapour above the tree-tops, spread over the heaven, extinguishing the crimson glow of floating clouds and the red brilliance of departing daylight. In a few moments all the stars came out above the intense blackness of the earth and the great lagoon gleaming suddenly with reflected lights resembled an oval patch of night sky flung down into the hopeless and abysmal night of the wilderness. The white man had some supper out of the basket, then collecting a few sticks that lay about the platform, made up a small fire, not for warmth, but for the sake of the smoke, which would keep off the mosquitoes. He wrapped himself in the blankets and sat with his back against the reed wall of the house, smoking thoughtfully.

Arsat came through the doorway with noiseless steps and squatted down by the fire. The white man moved his outstretched legs a little.

"She breathes," said Arsat in a low voice, anticipating the expected question. "She breathes and burns as if with a great fire. She speaks not; she hears not—and burns!"

He paused for a moment, then asked in a quiet, incurious tone—

"Tuan . . . will she die?"

The white man moved his shoulders uneasily and muttered in a hesitating manner—

"If such is her fate."

"No, Tuan," said Arsat, calmly. "If such is my fate. I hear, I see, I wait. I remember . . . Tuan, do you remember the old days? Do you remember my brother?"

"Yes," said the white man. The Malay rose suddenly and went in. The other, sitting still outside, could hear the voice in the hut. Arsat said: "Hear me! Speak!" His words were succeeded by a complete silence. "O Diamelen!" he cried, suddenly. After that cry there was a deep sigh. Arsat came out and sank down again in his old place.

They sat in silence before the fire. There was no sound within the house, there was no sound near them; but far away on the lagoon they could hear the voices of the boatmen ringing fitful and distinct on the calm water. The fire in the bows of the sampan shone faintly in the distance with a hazy red glow. Then it died out. The voices ceased. The land and the water slept invisible, unstirring and mute. It was as though there had been nothing left in the world but the glitter of stars streaming, ceaseless and vain, through the black stillness of the night.

The white man gazed straight before him into the darkness with wide-open eyes. The fear and fascination, the inspiration and the wonder of death—of death near, unavoidable, and unseen, soothed the unrest of his race and stirred the most indistinct, the most intimate of his thoughts. The ever-ready suspicion of evil, the gnawing suspicion that lurks in our hearts, flowed out into the stillness round him—into the stillness profound and dumb, and made it appear untrustworthy and infamous, like the placid and impenetrable mask of an unjustifiable violence. In that fleeting and powerful disturbance of his being the earth enfolded in the starlight peace became a shadowy country of inhuman strife, a battlefield of phantoms terrible and charming, august or ignoble, struggling ardently for the possession of our helpless hearts. An unquiet and mysterious country of inextinguishable desires and fears.

A plaintive murmur rose in the night; a murmur saddening and startling, as if the great solitudes of surrounding woods had tried to whisper into his ear the wisdom of their immense and lofty indifference. Sounds hesitating and vague floated in the air round him, shaped themselves slowly into words; and at last flowed on gently in a murmuring stream of soft and monotonous sentences. He stirred like a man waking up and changed his position slightly. Arsat, motionless and shadowy, sitting with bowed head under the stars, was speaking in a low and dreamy tone—

". . . for where can we lay down the heaviness of our trouble but in a friend's heart? A man must speak of war and of love. You, Tuan, know what war is, and you have seen me in time of danger seek death as other men seek life! A writing may be lost; a lie may be written; but what the eye has seen is truth and remains in the mind!"

"I remember," said the white man, quietly. Arsat went on with mournful composure—

"Therefore I shall speak to you of love. Speak in the night. Speak before both night and love are gone—and the eye of day looks upon my sorrow and my shame; upon my blackened face; upon my burnt-up heart."

A sigh, short and faint, marked an almost imperceptible pause, and then his words flowed on, without a stir, without a gesture.

"After the time of trouble and war was over and you went away from my country in the pursuit of your desires, which we, men of the islands, cannot understand, I and my brother became again, as we had been before, the sword-bearers of the Ruler. You know we were men of family, belonging to a ruling race, and more fit than any to carry on our right shoulder the emblem of power. And in the time of prosperity Si Dendring showed us favour, as we, in time of sorrow, had showed to him the faithfulness of our courage. It was a time of peace. A time of deer-hunts and cock-fights; of idle talks and foolish squabbles between men whose bellies are full and weapons are rusty. But the sower watched the young rice-shoots grow up without fear, and the traders came and went, departed lean and returned fat into the river of peace. They brought news, too. Brought lies and truth mixed together, so that no man knew when to rejoice and when to be sorry. We heard from them about you also. They had seen you here and had seen you there. And I was glad to hear, for I remembered the stirring times, and I always remembered you, Tuan, till the time came when my eyes could see nothing in the past, because they had looked upon the one who is dying there—in the house."

He stopped to exclaim in an intense whisper, "O Mara bahia! O Calamity!" then went on speaking a little louder:

"There's no worse enemy and no better friend than a brother, Tuan, for one brother knows another, and in perfect knowledge is strength for good or evil. I loved my brother. I went to him and told him that I could see nothing but one face, hear nothing but one voice. He told me: 'Open your heart so that she can see what is in it—and wait. Patience is wisdom. Inchi Midah may die or our Ruler may throw off his fear of a woman!' ... I waited! ... You remember the lady with the veiled face, Tuan, and the fear of our Ruler before her cunning and temper. And if she wanted her servant, what could I do? But I fed the hunger of my heart on short glances and stealthy words. I loitered on the path to the bath-houses in the daytime, and when the sun had fallen behind the forest I crept along the jasmine hedges of the women's courtyard. Unseeing, we spoke to one another through the scent of flowers, through the veil of leaves, through the blades of long grass that stood still before our lips; so great was our prudence, so faint was the murmur of our great longing. The time passed swiftly . . . and there were whispers amongst women—and our enemies watched—my brother was gloomy, and I began to think of killing and of a fierce death. . . . We are of a people who take what they want—like you whites. There is a time when a man should forget loyalty and respect. Might and authority are given to rulers, but to all men is given love and strength and courage. My brother said, 'You shall take her from their midst. We are two who are like one.' And I answered, 'Let it be soon, for I find no warmth in sunlight that does not shine upon her.' Our time came when the Ruler and all the great people went to the mouth of the river to fish by torchlight. There were hundreds of boats, and on the white sand, between the water and the forests, dwellings of leaves were built for the households of the Rajahs. The smoke of cooking-fires was like a blue mist of the evening, and many voices rang in it joyfully. While they were making the boats ready to beat up the fish, my brother came to me and said, 'To-night!' I looked to my weapons, and when the time came our canoe took its place in the circle of boats carrying the torches. The lights blazed on the water, but behind the boats there was darkness. When the shouting began and the excitement made them like mad we dropped out. The water swallowed our fire, and we floated back to the shore that was dark with only here and there the glimmer of embers. We could hear the talk of slave-girls amongst the sheds. Then we found a place deserted and silent. We waited there. She came. She came running along the shore, rapid and leaving no trace, like a leaf driven by the wind into the sea. My brother said gloomily, 'Go and take her; carry her into our boat.' I lifted her in my arms. She panted. Her heart was beating against my breast. I said, 'I take you from those people. You came to the cry of my heart, but my arms take you into my boat against the will of the great!' 'It is right,' said my brother. 'We are men who take what we want and can hold it against many. We should have taken her in daylight.' I said, 'Let us be off'; for since she was in my boat I began to think of our Ruler's many men. 'Yes. Let us be off,' said my brother. 'We are cast out and this boat is our country now—and the sea is our refuge.' He lingered with his foot on the shore, and I entreated him to hasten, for I remembered the strokes of her heart against my breast and thought that two men cannot withstand a hundred. We left, paddling downstream close to the bank; and as we passed by the creek where they were fishing, the great shouting had ceased, but the murmur of voices was loud like the humming of insects flying at noonday. The boats floated, clustered together, in the red light of torches, under a black roof of smoke; and men talked of their sport. Men that boasted, and praised, and jeered—men that would have been our friends in the morning, but on that night were already our enemies. We paddled swiftly past. We had no more friends in the country of our birth. She sat in the middle of the canoe with covered face; silent as she is now; unseeing as she is now—and I had no regret at what I was leaving because I could hear her breathing close to me—as I can hear her now."

He paused, listened with his ear turned to the doorway, then shook his head and went on:

"My brother wanted to shout the cry of challenge—one cry only—to let the people know we were freeborn robbers who trusted our arms and the great sea. And again I begged him in the name of our love to be silent. Could I not hear her breathing close to me? I knew the pursuit would come quick enough. My brother loved me. He dipped his paddle without a splash. He only said, 'There is half a man in you now—the other half is in that woman. I can wait. When you are a whole man again, you will come back with me here to shout defiance. We are sons of the same mother.' I made no answer. All my strength and all my spirit were in my hands that held the paddle—for I longed to be with her in a safe place beyond the reach of men's anger and of women's spite. My love was so great, that I thought it could guide me to a country where death was unknown, if I could only escape from Inchi Midah's fury and from our Ruler's sword. We paddled with haste, breathing through our teeth. The blades bit deep into the smooth water. We passed out of the river; we flew in clear channels amongst the shallows. We skirted the black coast; we skirted the sand beaches where the sea speaks in whispers to the land;

and the gleam of white sand flashed back past our boat, so swiftly she ran upon the water. We spoke not. Only once I said, 'Sleep, Diamelen, for soon you may want all your strength.' I heard the sweetness of her voice, but I never turned my head. The sun rose and still we went on. Water fell from my face like rain from a cloud. We flew in the light and heat. I never looked back, but I knew that my brother's eyes, behind me, were looking steadily ahead, for the boat went as straight as a bushman's dart, when it leaves the end of the sumpitan. There was no better paddler, no better steersman than my brother. Many times, together, we had won races in that canoe. But we never had put out our strength as we did then—then, when for the last time we paddled together! There was no braver or stronger man in our country than my brother. I could not spare the strength to turn my head and look at him, but every moment I heard the hiss of his breath getting louder behind me. Still he did not speak. The sun was high. The heat clung to my back like a flame of fire. My ribs were ready to burst, but I could no longer get enough air into my chest. And then I felt I must cry out with my last breath, 'Let us rest!' . . . 'Good!' he answered; and his voice was firm. He was strong. He was brave. He knew no fear and no fatigue . . . My brother!"

A murmur powerful and gentle, a murmur vast and faint; the murmur of trembling leaves, of stirring boughs, ran through the tangled depths of the forests, ran over the starry smoothness of the lagoon, and the water between the piles lapped the slimy timber once with a sudden splash. A breath of warm air touched the two men's faces and passed on with a mournful sound—a breath loud and short like an uneasy sigh of the dreaming earth.

Arsat went on in an even, low voice.

"We ran our canoe on the white beach of a little bay close to a long tongue of land that seemed to bar our road; a long wooded cape going far into the sea. My brother knew that place. Beyond the cape a river has its entrance, and through the jungle of that land there is a narrow path. We made a fire and cooked rice. Then we lay down to sleep on the soft sand in the shade of our canoe, while she watched. No sooner had I closed my eyes than I heard her cry of alarm. We leaped up. The sun was halfway down the sky already, and coming in sight in the opening of the bay we saw a prau manned by many paddlers. We knew it at once; it was one of our Rajah's praus. They were watching the shore, and saw us. They beat the gong, and turned the head of the prau into the bay. I felt my heart become weak within my breast. Diamelen sat on the sand and covered her face. There was no escape by sea. My brother laughed. He had the gun you had given him, Tuan, before you went away, but there was only a handful of powder. He spoke to me quickly: 'Run with her along the path. I shall keep them back, for they have no firearms, and landing in the face of a man with a gun is certain death for some. Run with her. On the other side of that wood there is a fisherman's house —and a canoe. When I have fired all the shots I will follow. I am a great runner, and before they can come up we shall be gone. I will hold out as long as I can, for she is but a woman—that can neither run nor fight, but she has your heart in her weak hands.' He dropped behind the canoe. The prau was coming. She and I ran, and as we rushed along the path I heard shots. My brother fired—once—twice—and the booming of the gong ceased. There was silence behind us. That neck of land is narrow. Before I heard my brother fire the third shot I saw the shelving shore, and I saw the water again; the mouth of a broad river. We crossed a grassy glade. We ran down to the water. I saw a low hut above the black mud, and a small canoe hauled up. I heard another shot behind me. I thought, 'That is his last charge.' We rushed down to the canoe; a man came running from the hut, but I leaped on him, and we rolled together in the mud. Then I got up, and he lay still at my feet. I don't know whether I had killed him or not. I and Diamelen pushed the canoe afloat. I heard yells behind me, and I saw my brother run across the glade. Many men were bounding after him. I took her in my arms and threw her into the boat, then leaped in myself. When I looked back I saw that my brother had fallen. He fell and was up again, but the men were closing round him. He shouted, 'I am coming!' The men were close to him. I looked. Many men. Then I looked at her. Tuan, I pushed the canoe! I pushed it into deep water. She was kneeling forward looking at me, and I said, 'Take your paddle,' while I struck the water with mine. Tuan, I heard him cry. I heard him cry my name twice; and I heard voices shouting, 'Kill! Strike!' I never turned back. I heard him calling my name again with a great shriek, as when life is going out

335

together with the voice—and I never turned my head. My own name! . . . My brother! Three times he called—but I was not afraid of life. Was she not there in that canoe? And could I not with her find a country where death is forgotten—where death is unknown!"

The white man sat up. Arsat rose and stood, an indistinct and silent figure above the dying embers of the fire. Over the lagoon a mist drifting and low had crept, erasing slowly the glittering images of the stars. And now a great expanse of white vapour covered the land: it flowed cold and gray in the darkness, eddied in noiseless whirls round the tree-trunks and about the platform of the house, which seemed to float upon a restless and impalpable illusion of a sea. Only far away the tops of the trees stood outlined on the twinkle of heaven, like a sombre and forbidding shore—a coast deceptive, pitiless and black.

Arsat's voice vibrated loudly in the profound peace.

"I had her there! I had her! To get her I would have faced all mankind. But I had her—and—"

His words went out ringing into the empty distances. He paused, and seemed to listen to them dying away very far—beyond help and beyond recall. Then he said quietly—

"Tuan, I loved my brother."

A breath of wind made him shiver. High above his head, high above the silent sea of mist the drooping leaves of the palms rattled together with a mournful and expiring sound. The white man stretched his legs. His chin rested on his chest, and he murmured sadly without lifting his head—

"We all love our brothers."

Arsat burst out with an intense whispering violence—

"What did I care who died? I wanted peace in my own heart."

He seemed to hear a stir in the house—listened—then stepped in noiselessly. The white man stood up. A breeze was coming in fitful puffs. The stars shone paler as if they had retreated into the frozen depths of immense space. After a chill gust of wind there were a few seconds of perfect calm and absolute silence. Then from behind the black and wavy line of the forests a column of golden light shot up into the heavens and spread over the semicircle of the eastern horizon. The sun had risen. The mist lifted, broke into drifting patches, vanished into thin flying wreaths; and the unveiled lagoon lay, polished and black, in the heavy shadows at the foot of the wall of trees. A white eagle rose over it with a slanting and ponderous flight, reached the clear sunshine and appeared dazzlingly brilliant for a moment, then soaring higher, became a dark and motionless speck before it vanished into the blue as if it had left the earth forever. The white man, standing gazing upwards before the doorway, heard in the hut a confused and broken murmur of distracted words ending with a loud groan. Suddenly Arsat stumbled out with outstretched hands, shivered, and stood still for some time with fixed eyes. Then he said—

"She burns no more."

Before his face the sun showed its edge above the tree-tops rising steadily. The breeze freshened; a great brilliance burst upon the lagoon, sparkled on the rippling water. The forests came out of the clear shadows of the morning, became distinct, as if they had rushed nearer—to stop short in a great stir of leaves, of nodding boughs, of swaying branches. In the merciless sunshine the whisper of unconscious life grew louder, speaking in an incomprehensible voice round the dumb darkness of that human sorrow. Arsat's eyes wandered slowly, then stared at the rising sun.

"I can see nothing," he said half aloud to himself.

"There is nothing," said the white man, moving to the edge of the platform and waving his hand to his boat. A shout came faintly over the lagoon and the sampan began to glide towards the abode of the friend of ghosts.

"If you want to come with me, I will wait all the morning," said the white man, looking away upon the water.

"No, Tuan," said Arsat, softly. "I shall not eat or sleep in this house, but I must first see my road. Now I can see nothing—see nothing! There is no light and no peace in the world; but there is death—death for many. We are sons of the same mother—and I left him in the midst of enemies; but I am going back now."

He drew a long breath and went on in a dreamy tone: "In a little while I shall see clear enough to strike—to strike. But she has died, and . . . now . . . darkness."

He flung his arms wide open, let them fall along his body, then stood still with unmoved face and stony eyes, staring at the sun. The white man got down into his canoe. The polers ran smartly along the sides of the boat, looking over their shoulders at the beginning of a weary journey. High in the stern, his head muffled up in white rags, the juragan sat moody, letting his paddle trail in the water. The white man, leaning with both arms over the grass roof of the little cabin, looked back at the shining ripple of the boat's wake. Before the sampan passed out of the lagoon into the creek he lifted his eyes. Arsat had not moved. He stood lonely in the searching sunshine; and he looked beyond the great light of a cloudless day into the darkness of a world of illusions.

26

On the Water

By Guy de Maupassant

Translated from the French by Bill Bowers

I HAD RENTED, LAST SUMMER, A LITTLE COUNTRY HOUSE ON THE BANKS of the Seine several leagues from Paris, and I went there to sleep every night. After a few days I made the acquaintance of one of my neighbors, a man between thirty and forty, who was certainly the most curious fellow I had ever met. He was an old hand at boating, passionate about boating, always near the water, always on the water, always in the water. He must have been born in a boat, and he would certainly die in a boat.

One night, while we were walking together on the bank of the Seine, I asked him to tell me some stories about his life on the water; and at that the good man suddenly became animated, transfigured, eloquent, almost poetical. He had in his heart one great passion, devouring and irresistible: the river.

"Ah!" said he to me, "how many memories I have of that river you see flowing there near us. You people who live on streets, you don't know what the river is. But just listen to a fisherman simply pronouncing that word. For him it is the thing mysterious, profound, unknown, the place of mirage and of phantasmagoria, where one sees, at night, things that do not exist, where one hears unfamiliar noises, where one trembles without knowing why, as though crossing a cemetery. And it is, indeed, the most sinister of cemeteries—a cemetery where there are no tombs.

"To the fisherman the land seems limited, but in the dark, when there is no moon, the river seems limitless. A sailor has no such feeling for the sea. She is often hard and wicked, it's true; but she cries, she screams, she is loyal, the great sea, while the river is silent and treacherous. She never even mutters, she flows always noiselessly, and this eternal movement of flowing water is far more terrifying for me than high seas on the ocean.

"Dreamers claim that the sea hides in her bosom great blue regions where the drowned roll among the great fish, in the midst of strange forests and in crystal grottos. The river has only black depths where one rots in the slime. For all that, she is beautiful when she gleams in the rising sun or washes softly along between her banks covered with murmuring reeds.

"The poet says of the ocean:

> Oh seas, you know sad stories!
> Deep seas, feared by kneeling mothers,
> You tell the stories to one another at flood tides!
> And that is why you have such despairing voices
> When at night you come towards us nearer and nearer.

"Well, I think that the stories whispered by the slender reeds with their soft little voices must be still more sinister than the gloomy dramas told by the howling of the high seas.

"But, since you ask me for some of my memories, I will tell you a singular adventure which I had here about ten years ago:"

I lived then, as I still do, in the house of the old lady Lafon, and one of my best friends, Louis Bernet, who has now given up his oars to join the civil service, along with his low shoes and his sleeveless jersey, lived in the village of C——, two leagues farther down. We dined together every day—sometimes at his place, sometimes at mine.

One evening as I was returning home alone and rather tired, painfully pulling my heavy boat, a twelve-footer that I always used at night, I stopped for a few seconds to catch my breath near the point where so many reeds grow, down there about two hundred meters before you come to the railroad bridge. The weather was magnificent; the moon was resplendent, the river gleamed, the air was calm and soft. The tranquility of it all tempted me; I told myself that it would be extremely nice to smoke a pipe just here. Action followed the thought; I seized my anchor and threw it into the river.

The boat, which floated down again with the current, pulled the chain out to its full length, then stopped; and I seated myself in the stern on my sheepskin, as comfortable as possible. I heard nothing—nothing; only sometimes I thought I caught a low, almost insensible lapping of water along the bank, and I made out a few clumps of reeds which, taller than most, took on surprising shapes, and seemed from time to time to stir.

The river was perfectly still, but I felt myself moved by the extraordinary silence which surrounded me. All the animals—the frogs and toads, those nocturnal singers of the marshes—were silent. Suddenly on my right, near me, a frog croaked; I started; it fell silent; I heard nothing more, and I resolved to smoke a little by way of distraction. But though I am a regular blackener of pipes, I could not smoke that night; after the second puff I sickened of it and I stopped. I began to hum; the sound of my voice was painful to me; so I stretched myself out in the bottom of the boat and I looked at the sky. For some time I remained quiet, but soon the slight movements of the boat made me uneasy. It seemed to me that it was yawing tremendously, striking now this riverbank, and now the other; then I thought that a being or invisible force was dragging it down gently to the bottom, and then was lifting it up simply to let it fall again. I was tossed about as if in the middle of a storm; I heard noises around me; I sat up with a sudden start; the water gleamed, everything was calm.

I understood that my nerves were unsettled, and I resolved to get out of there. I pulled on my chain; the boat started moving, then I felt resistance; I pulled harder. The anchor did not come up; it had caught on something at the bottom of the river and I could not lift it. I started pulling again—in vain.

So, with my oars I turned the boat upstream to change the position of the anchor. It was no use; it still held. I got angry, and I shook the chain in a rage. Nothing moved. I sat down discouraged and thought about my position. There was no hope of breaking that chain, or of getting it loose from my craft, because it was very heavy, and riveted at the bow into a piece of wood thicker than my arm; but since the weather remained quite nice, I thought that I should doubtless not have to wait long before meeting some fisherman who would come to my rescue. My misadventure had calmed me; I sat down and was finally able to smoke my pipe. I had a flask of brandy with me; I drank two or three glasses, and my situation made me laugh. It was very hot, so that, if need be, I could spend the night under the stars without great inconvenience.

Suddenly a little knock sounded against the side. I shivered, and a cold sweat froze me from head to toe. The noise came, no doubt, from some piece of wood drawn along by the current, but that was enough, and I felt myself again overcome by a strange nervous agitation. I seized my chain, and I stiffened myself in a desperate effort. The anchor held solidly. I sat down, exhausted.

But, little by little, the river had become covered with a very thick white mist, which crept very low over the water, so that, standing up, I could no longer see the stream or my feet or my boat, and saw only the tips of the reeds, and then, beyond them, the plain, all pale in the moonlight, and with great black stains that rose into the sky, and which were made by clumps of Italian poplars. I was as though wrapped to the waist in a cotton sheet of strange whiteness, and there began to come to me fantastic imaginings.

I imagined that someone was trying to climb into my boat, since I could no longer make it out, and that the river, hidden by this opaque mist, must be full of strange beings swimming around me. I experienced a horrible uneasiness, my jaws clenched, my heart beat to the point of suffocation; and, losing my head, I thought of saving myself by swimming; then in an instant the very idea made me shiver with fear. I saw myself, lost, drifting aimlessly in this impenetrable mist, struggling among the grasses and the reeds that I would not be able to avoid, with a rattle in my throat from fear, not seeing the shore, never finding my boat again. And it seemed to me as though I felt myself being drawn by the feet down to the bottom of that black water.

In fact, since I should have had to swim upstream at least five hundred meters before finding a point clear of rushes and reeds, where I could regain my footing, there were nine chances in ten that I should lose my bearings in the fog and drown, however good a swimmer I might be. I tried to reason with myself. I realized that my will was firmly enough resolved to be fearless; but there was something in me besides my will, and this other thing was afraid. I asked myself what it could be that I dreaded; that part of me that was courageous railed at that part of me that was cowardly; and I had never understood so well before the opposition between those two beings which exist within us, the one willing, the other resisting, and each in turn the master.

This stupid and inexplicable fear kept growing until it became terror. I remained motionless, eyes wide open, with a straining and expectant ear. Expecting—what? I did not know, but only that it had to be terrible. I'm sure that if a fish, as often happens, had felt like jumping out of the water, it would have taken only that to make me faint and fall flat on my back.

Finally, by a violent effort, I very nearly recovered the reason which had been escaping me. I again took my brandy flask, and I drank from it in great gulps. Then an idea came to me, and I began to shout with all my might, turning in succession towards all four points of the horizon. When my throat was at last completely paralyzed, I listened. A dog was howling, a long way off.

I drank again; and I stretched out on my back in the bottom of the boat. I stayed that way for an hour, perhaps for two, without sleeping, my eyes wide open, with nightmares all around me. I did not dare to sit up, and yet I had a wild desire to do so; so I kept putting it off from minute to minute. I would say to myself: "Come on! Get up!" and I was afraid to make a move. At last I raised myself with infinite precaution, as if life depended on the slightest sound I might make, and I peered over the edge of the boat.

I was dazzled by the most marvelous, the most astonishing spectacle that it is possible to see. It was one of those phantasmagorias from fairy-land, one of those visions told by travelers returning from far away, and which we hear without believing them.

The mist, which two hours before was floating over the water, had little by little withdrawn and piled itself upon the banks. Leaving the river absolutely clear, it had formed, along each shore, long low hills about six or seven meters high, which gleamed beneath the moon with the brilliance of snow, so that one saw nothing except this river of fire between those two white mountains; and up there, high above my head, a great, luminous moon, full and large, glowed in a blue and milky sky.

All the animals of the water had awakened; the bullfrogs croaked furiously, while, from instant to instant, sometimes on my right, sometimes on my left, I heard those short, mournful, sad notes that the brassy voices of the marsh frogs direct at the sky. Strangely enough, I was no longer afraid; I was in the midst of such an extraordinary landscape that the most unusual things could not have astonished me. How long this sight lasted I do not know, because at last I had grown drowsy. When I again opened my eyes the moon had set, the sky was full of clouds. The water lashed mournfully, the wind whispered, it grew cold; the darkness was profound.

I drank all the brandy I had left; then I listened, shivering, to the rustling of the reeds and to the sinister noise of the river. I tried to see, but I could not make out my boat or even my own hands, though I brought them close to my eyes.

Little by little, however, the density of the blackness diminished. Suddenly I thought I felt a shadow slipping along near me; I cried out; a voice replied—it was a fisherman. I hailed him; he approached, and I told him of my misadventure. He pulled his boat alongside, and both of us heaved on the chain. The anchor did not budge. The day was coming on—somber, gray, rainy, cold—one of those days that always bring sorrow and misfortune. I made out another craft; we hailed it. The man aboard joined his efforts to ours, then, little by little, the anchor yielded. It came up, slowly, slowly, and weighted down by something very heavy. At last we made out a black mass, and we pulled it alongside.

It was the corpse of an old woman with a great stone around her neck.

27

The Erl-King

By Johann Wolfgang von Goethe

WHO'S RIDING SO LATE WHERE WINDS BLOW WILD
It is the father grasping his child;
He holds the boy embraced in his arm,
He clasps him snugly, he keeps him warm.

"My son, why cover your face in such fear?"
"You see the erl-king, father?
He's near! The king of the elves with crown
and train!"
"My son, the mist is on the plain."

'Sweet lad, O come and join me, do!
Such pretty games I will play with you;
On the shore gay flowers their color unfold,
My mother has many garments of gold.'

"My father, my father, and can you not hear
The promise the elf-king breathes in my ear?"
"Be calm, stay calm, my child, lie low:
In withered leaves the night-winds blow."

'Will you, sweet lad, come along with me?
My daughters shall care for you tenderly;

In the night my daughters their revelry keep
They'll rock you and dance you and sing you to sleep.'

"My father, my father, O can you not trace
The elf-king's daughters in that gloomy place?"
"My son, my son, I see it clear
How grey the ancient willows appear."

'I love you, your comeliness charms me, my boy!
And if you're not willing, my force I'll employ.'
"Now father, now father, he's seizing my arm.
Elf-king has done me a cruel harm."

The father shudders, his ride is wild,
In his arms he's holding the groaning child,
Reaches the court with toil and dread.
The child he held in his arms was dead.

28

The Body-Snatcher

By Robert Louis Stevenson

EVERY NIGHT IN THE YEAR, FOUR OF US SAT IN THE SMALL PARLOUR OF the George at Debenham—the undertaker, and the landlord, and Fettes, and myself. Sometimes there would be more; but blow high, blow low, come rain or snow or frost, we four would be each planted in his own particular armchair. Fettes was an old drunken Scotchman, a man of education obviously, and a man of some property, since he lived in idleness. He had come to Debenham years ago, while still young, and by a mere continuance of living had grown to be an adopted townsman. His blue camlet cloak was a local antiquity, like the church-spire. His place in the parlour at the George, his absence from church, his old, crapulous, disreputable vices, were all things of course in Debenham. He had some vague Radical opinions and some fleeting infidelities, which he would now and again set forth and emphasise with tottering slaps upon the table. He drank rum—five glasses regularly every evening; and for the greater portion of his nightly visit to the George sat, with his glass in his right hand, in a state of melancholy alcoholic saturation. We called him the Doctor, for he was supposed to have some special knowledge of medicine, and had been known, upon a pinch, to set a fracture or reduce a dislocation; but beyond these slight particulars, we had no knowledge of his character and antecedents.

One dark winter night—it had struck nine some time before the landlord joined us—there was a sick man in the George, a great neighboring proprietor suddenly struck down with apoplexy on his way to Parliament; and the great man's still greater London doctor had been telegraphed to his bedside. It was the first time that such a thing had happened in Debenham, for the railway was newly open, and we were all proportionately moved by the occurrence.

"He's come," said the landlord, after he had filled and lighted his pipe.

"He?" said I. "Who?—not the doctor?"

"Himself," replied our host.

"What is his name?"

"Dr. Macfarlane," said the landlord.

Fettes was far through his third tumblers stupidly fuddled, now nodding over, now staring mazily around him; but at the last word he seemed to awaken, and repeated the name "Macfarlane" twice, quietly enough the first time, but with sudden emotion at the second.

"Yes," said the landlord, "that's his name, Doctor Wolfe Macfarlane."

Fettes became instantly sober; his eyes awoke, his voice became clear, loud, and steady, his language forcible and earnest. We were all startled by the transformation, as if a man had risen from the dead.

"I beg your pardon," he said. "I am afraid I have not been paying much attention to your talk. Who is this Wolfe Macfarlane?" And then, when he had heard the landlord out, "It cannot be, it cannot be," he added; "and yet I would like well to see him face to face."

"Do you know him, Doctor?" asked the undertaker, with a gasp.

"God forbid!" was the reply. "And yet the name is a strange one; it were too much to fancy two. Tell me, landlord, is he old?"

"Well," said the host, "he's not a young man, to be sure, and his hair is white; but he looks younger than you."

"He is older, though; years older. But," with a slap upon the table, "it's the rum you see in my face—rum and sin. This man, perhaps, may have an easy conscience and a good digestion. Conscience! Hear me speak. You would think I was some good, old, decent Christian, would you not? But no, not I; I never canted. Voltaire might have canted if he'd stood in my shoes; but the brains"—with a rattling fillip on his bald head— "the brains were clear and active, and I saw and made no deductions."

"If you know this doctor," I ventured to remark, after a somewhat awful pause, "I should gather that you do not share the landlord's good opinion."

Fettes paid no regard to me.

"Yes," he said, with sudden decision, "I must see him face to face."

There was another pause, and then a door was closed rather sharply on the first floor, and a step was heard upon the stair.

"That's the doctor," cried the landlord. "Look sharp, and you can catch him."

It was but two steps from the small parlour to the door of the old George Inn; the wide oak staircase landed almost in the street; there was room for a Turkey rug and nothing more between the threshold and the last round of the descent; but this little space was every evening brilliantly lit up, not only by the light upon the stair and the great signal-lamp below the sign, but by the warm radiance of the barroom window. The George thus brightly advertised itself to passers-by in the cold street. Fettes walked steadily to the spot, and we, who were hanging behind, beheld the two men meet, as one of them had phrased it, face to face. Dr. Macfarlane was alert and vigorous. His white hair set off his pale and placid, though energetic, countenance. He was richly dressed in the finest of broadcloth and the whitest of linen, with a great gold watch-chain, and studs and spectacles of the same precious material. He wore a broad-folded tie, white and speckled with lilac, and he carried on his arm a comfortable driving-coat of fur. There was no doubt but he became his years, breathing, as he did, of wealth and consideration; and it was a surprising contrast to see our parlour sot—bald, dirty, pimpled, and robed in his old camlet cloak—confront him at the bottom of the stairs.

"Macfarlane!" he said somewhat loudly, more like a herald than a friend.

The great doctor pulled up short on the fourth step, as though the familiarity of the address surprised and somewhat shocked his dignity.

"Toddy Macfarlane!" repeated Fettes.

The London man almost staggered. He stared for the swiftest of seconds at the man before him, glanced behind him with a sort of scare, and then in a startled whisper, "Fettes!" he said, "you!"

"Ay," said the other, "me! Did you think I was dead, too? We are not so easy shut of our acquaintance."

"Hush, hush!" exclaimed the doctor. "Hush, hush! This meeting is so unexpected—I can see you are unmanned I hardly knew you, I confess, at first; but I am overjoyed—overjoyed to have this opportunity. For the present it must be how-d'ye-do and good-by in one, for my fly is waiting, and I must not fail the train; but you shall—let me see—yes—you shall give me your address, and you can count on early news of me. We must do something for you, Fettes. I fear you are out at elbows; but we must see to that for auld lang syne, as once we sang at suppers."

"Money!" cried Fettes; "money from you! The money that I had from you is lying where I cast it in the rain."

Dr. Macfarlane had talked himself into some measure of superiority and confidence, but the uncommon energy of his refusal cast him back into his first confusion.

A horrible, ugly look came and went across his almost venerable countenance. "My dear fellow," he said, "be it as you please; my last thought is to offend you. I would intrude on none. I will leave you my address however—"

"I do not wish it—I do not wish to know the roof that shelters you," interrupted the other. "I heard your name; I feared it might be you; I wished to know if, after all, there were a God; I know now that there is none. Begone!"

He stood still in the middle of the rug, between the stair and doorway; and the great London physician, in order to escape, would be forced to step to one side. It was plain that he hesitated before the thought of this humiliation. White as he was, there was a dangerous glitter in his spectacles; but while he still paused uncertain, he became aware that the driver of his fly was peering in from the street at this unusual scene, and caught a glimpse at the same time of our little body from the parlour, huddled by the corner of the bar. The presence of so many witnesses decided him at once to flee. He crouched together, brushing on the wainscot, and made a dart like a serpent, striking for the door. But his tribulation was not yet entirely at an end, for even as he was passing Fettes clutched him by the arm and these words came in a whisper, and yet painfully distinct, "Have you seen it again?"

The great rich London doctor cried out aloud with a sharp, throttling cry; he dashed his questioner across the open space, and, with his hands over his head, fled out of the door like a detected thief. Before it had occurred to one of us to make a movement the fly was already rattling toward the station. The scene was over like a dream, but the dream had left proofs and traces of its passage. Next day the servant found the fine gold spectacles broken on the threshold, and that very night we were all standing breathless by the barroom window, and Fettes at our side, sober, pale, and resolute in look.

"God protect us, Mr. Fettes!" said the landlord, coming first into possession of his customary senses. "What in the universe is all this? These are strange things you have been saying."

Fettes turned toward us; he looked us each in succession in the face. "See if you can hold your tongues," said he. "That man Macfarlane is not safe to cross; those that have done so already have repented it too late."

And then, without so much as finishing his third glass, far less waiting for the other two, he bade us good-by and went forth, under the lamp of the hotel, into the black night.

We three turned to our places in the parlour, with the big red fire and four clear candles; and as we recapitulated what had passed the first chill of our surprise soon changed into a glow of curiosity. We sat late; it was the latest session I have known in the old George. Each man, before we parted, had his theory that he was bound to prove; and none of us had any nearer business in this world than to track out the past of our condemned companion, and surprise the secret that he shared with the great London doctor. It is no great boast, but I believe I was a better hand at worming out a story than either of my fellows at the George; and perhaps there is now no other man alive who could narrate to you the following foul and unnatural events.

In his young days Fettes studied medicine in the schools of Edinburgh. He had a talent of a kind, the talent that picks up swiftly what it hears and readily retails it for its own. He worked little at home; but he was civil, attentive, and intelligent in the presence of his masters. They soon picked him out as a lad who listened closely and remembered well; nay, strange as it seemed to me when I first heard it, he was in those days well favored, and pleased by his exterior. There was, at that period, a certain extramural teacher of anatomy, whom I shall here designate by the letter K. His name was subsequently too well known. The man who bore it skulked through the streets of Edinburgh in disguise, while the mob that applauded at the execution of Burke called loudly for the blood of his employer. But Mr. K— was then at the top of his vogue; he enjoyed a popularity due partly to his own talent and address, partly to the incapacity of his rival, the university professor. The students, at least, swore by his name, and Fettes believed himself, and was believed by others, to have laid the foundations of success when he had acquired the favour of this meteorically famous man. Mr. K— was a bon vivant as well as an accomplished teacher; he liked a sly allusion no less than a careful preparation. In both capacities, Fettes enjoyed and deserved his notice, and by the second year of his attendance he held the half-regular position of second demonstrator or sub-assistant in his class.

In this capacity, the charge of the theatre and lecturer-dom devolved in particular upon his shoulders. He had to answer for the cleanliness of the premises and the conduct of the other students, and it was a part of his duty to supply, receive, and divide the various subjects. It was with a view to this last—at that time very delicate—affair that he was lodged by Mr. K— in the same wynd, and at last in the same building, with the dissecting-room. Here, after a night of turbulent pleasures, his hand still tottering, his sight still misty and confused, he would be called out of bed in the black hours before the winter dawn by the unclean and desperate interlopers who supplied the table. He would open the door to these men, since infamous throughout the land. He would help them with their tragic burden, pay them their sordid price, and remain alone, when they were gone, with the unfriendly relics of humanity. From such a scene he would return to snatch another hour or two of slumber, to repair the abuses of the night, and refresh himself for the labours of the day.

Few lads could have been more insensible to the impressions of a life thus passed among the ensigns of mortality. His mind was closed against all general considerations. He was incapable of interest in the fate and fortunes of another, the slave of his own desires and low ambitions. Cold, light, and selfish in the last resort, he had that modicum of prudence, miscalled morality, which keeps a man from inconvenient drunkenness or punishable theft. He coveted, besides, a measure of consideration from his masters and his fellow-pupils, and he had no desire to fall conspicuously in the external parts of life. Thus he made it his pleasure to gain some distinction in his studies, and day after day rendered unimpeachable eye-service to his employer, Mr. K—. For his day of work he indemnified himself by nights of roaring, blackguardly enjoyment; and when that balance had been struck, the organ that he called his conscience declared itself content.

The supply of subjects was a continual trouble to him as well as to his master. In that large and busy class, the raw material of the anatomists kept perpetually running out; and the business thus rendered necessary was not only unpleasant in itself, but threatened dangerous consequences to all who were concerned. It was the policy of Mr. K— to ask no questions in his dealings with the trade. "They bring the body, and we pay the price," he used to say, dwelling on the alliteration—"quid pro quo." And again, and somewhat profanely, "Ask no questions," he would tell his assistants, "for conscience sake." There was no understanding that the subjects were provided by the crime of murder. Had that idea been broached to him in words, he would have recoiled in horror; but the lightness of his speech upon so grave a matter was, in itself, an offence against good manners, and a temptation to the men with whom he dealt. Fettes, for instance, had often remarked to himself upon the singular freshness of the bodies. He had been struck again and again by the hang-dog, abominable looks of the ruffians who came to him before dawn; and putting things together clearly in his private thoughts, he perhaps attributed a meaning too immoral and too categorical to the unguarded counsels of his master. He understood his duty, in short, to have three branches: to take what was brought, to pay the price, and to avert the eye from any evidence of crime.

One November morning this policy of silence was put sharply to the test. He had been awake all night with a racking toothache—pacing his room like a caged beast or throwing himself in fury on his bed—and had fallen at last into that profound, uneasy slumber that so often follows on a night of pain, when he was awakened by the third or fourth angry repetition of the concerted signal. There was a thin, bright moonshine; it was bitter cold, windy, and frosty; the town had not yet awakened, but an indefinable stir already preluded the noise and business of the day. The ghouls had come later than usual, and they seemed more than usually eager to be gone. Fettes, sick with sleep, lighted them upstairs. He heard their grumbling Irish voices through a dream; and as they stripped the sack from their sad merchandise he leaned dozing, with his shoulder propped against the wall; he had to shake himself to find the men their money. As he did so his eyes lighted on the dead face. He started; he took two steps nearer, with the candle raised.

"God Almighty!" he cried. "That is Jane Galbraith!" The men answered nothing, but they shuffled nearer the door.

"I know her, I tell you," he continued. "She was alive and hearty yesterday. It's impossible she can be dead; it's impossible you should have got this body fairly."

"Sure, sir, you're mistaken entirely," said one of the men.

But the other looked Fettes darkly in the eyes, and demanded the money on the spot.

It was impossible to misconceive the threat or to exaggerate the danger. The lad's heart failed him. He stammered some excuses, counted out the sum, and saw his hateful visitors depart. No sooner were they gone than he hastened to confirm his doubts. By a dozen unquestionable marks he identified the girl he had jested with the day before. He saw, with horror, marks upon her body that might well betoken violence. A panic seized him, and he took refuge in his room. There he reflected at length over the discovery that he had made; considered soberly the bearing of Mr. K—'s instructions and the danger to himself of interference in so serious a business, and at last, in sore perplexity, determined to wait for the advice of his immediate supervisor, the class assistant.

This was a young doctor, Wolfe Macfarlane, a high favourite among all the reckless students, clever, dissipated, and unscrupulous to the last degree. He had traveled and studied abroad. His manners were agreeable and a little forward. He was an authority on the stage, skilful on the ice or the links with skate or golf-club; he dressed with nice audacity, and, to put the finishing touch upon his glory, he kept a gig and a strong trotting-horse. With Fettes he was on terms of intimacy; indeed, their relative positions called for some community of life; and when subjects were scarce the pair would drive far into the country in Macfarlane's gig, visit and desecrate some lonely graveyard, and return before dawn with their booty to the door of the dissecting-room.

On that particular morning Macfarlane arrived somewhat earlier than his wont. Fettes heard him, and met him on the stairs, told him his story, and showed him the cause of his alarm. Macfarlane examined the marks on her body.

"Yes," he said with a nod, "it looks fishy."

"Well, what should I do?" asked Fettes.

"Do?" repeated the other. "Do you want to do anything? Least said soonest mended, I should say."

"Someone else might recognise her," objected Fettes. "She was as well known as the Castle Rock.

"We'll hope not," said Macfarlane, "and if anybody does—well, you didn't, don't you see, and there's an end. The fact is, this has been going on too long. Stir up the mud, and you'll get K— into the most unholy trouble; you'll be in a shocking box yourself. So will I, if you come to that. I should like to know how any one of us would look, or what the devil we should have to say for ourselves in any Christian witness-box. For me, you know there's one thing certain—that, practically speaking, all our subjects have been murdered."

"Macfarlane!" cried Fettes.

"Come now!" sneered the other. "As if you hadn't suspected it yourself!"

"Suspecting is one thing—"

"And proof another. Yes, I know; and I'm as sorry as you are this should have come here," tapping the body with his cane. "The next best thing for me is not to recognise it; and," he added coolly, "I don't. You may, if you please. I don't dictate, but I think a man of the world would do as I do; and I may add, I fancy that is what K— would look for at our hands. The question is, Why did he choose us two for his assistants? And I answer, because he didn't want old wives."

This was the tone of all others to affect the mind of a lad like Fettes. He agreed to imitate Macfarlane. The body of the unfortunate girl was duly dissected, and no one remarked or appeared to recognize her.

One afternoon, when his day's work was over, Fettes dropped into a popular tavern and found Macfarlane sitting with a stranger. This was a small man, very pale and dark, with coal-black eyes. The cut of his features gave a promise of intellect and refinement which was but feebly realized in his manners, for he proved, upon a nearer acquaintance, coarse, vulgar, and stupid. He exercised, however, a very remarkable control over Macfarlane; issued orders like the Great Bashaw; became inflamed at the least discussion or delay, and commented rudely on the servility with which he was obeyed. This most offensive person took a fancy to Fettes on the spot, plied him with drinks, and honored him with unusual confidences on his past career. If a tenth part of what he confessed to me were true, he was a very loathsome rogue; and the lad's vanity was tickled by the attention of so experienced a man.

"I'm a pretty bad fellow myself," the stranger remarked, "but Macfarlane is the boy—Toddy Macfarlane, I call him. Toddy, order your friend another glass." Or it might be, "Toddy, you jump up and shut the door." "Toddy hates me," he said again. "Oh yes, Toddy, you do!"

"Don't you call me that confounded name," growled Macfarlane.

"Hear him! Did you ever see the lads play knife? He would like to do that all over my body," remarked the stranger.

"We medicals have a better way than that," said Fettes. "When we dislike a dead friend of ours, we dissect him."

Marfarlane looked up sharply, as though this jest was scarcely to his mind.

The afternoon passed. Gray, for that was the stranger's name, invited Fettes to join them at dinner, ordered a feast so sumptuous that the tavern was thrown in commotion, and when all was done commanded Macfarlane to settle the bill. It was late before they separated; the man Gray was incapably drunk. Macfarlane, sobered by his fury, chewed the cud of the money he had been forced to squander and the slights he had been obliged to swallow. Fettes, with various liquours singling in his head, returned home with devious footsteps and a mind entirely in abeyance. Next day Macfarlane was absent from the class, and Fettes smiled to himself as he imagined him still squiring the intolerable Gray from tavern to tavern. As soon as the hour of liberty had struck he posted from place to place in quest of his last night's companions. He could find them, however, nowhere; so returned early to his rooms, went early to bed, and slept the sleep of the just.

At four in the morning he was awakened by the well-known signal. Descending to the door, he was filled with astonishment to find Macfarlane with his gig, and in the gig one of those long and ghastly packages with which he was so well acquainted.

"What?" he cried. "Have you been out alone? How did you manage?"

But Macfarlane silenced him roughly, bidding him turn to business. When they had got the body upstairs and laid it on the table, Macfarlane made at first as if he were going away. Then he paused and seemed to hesitate; and then, "You had better look at the face," says he, in tones of some constraint. "You had better," he repeated, as Fettes only stared at him in wonder.

"But where, and how, and when did you come by it?" cried the other.

"Look at the face," was the only answer.

Fettes was staggered; strange doubts assailed him. He looked from the young doctor to the body, and then back again. At last, with a start, he did as he was bidden. He had almost expected the sight that met his eyes, and yet the shock was cruel. To see, fixed in the rigidity of death and naked on that coarse layer of sackcloth, the man whom he had left well clad and full of meat and sin upon the threshold of a tavern, awoke, even in the thoughtless Fettes, some of the terrors of the conscience. It was a *cras tibi* which re-echoed in his soul, that two whom he had known should have come to lie upon these icy tables. Yet these were only secondary thoughts. His first concern regarded Wolfe.

Unprepared for a challenge so momentous, he knew not how to look at his comrade in the face. He durst not meet his eye, and he had neither words nor voice at his command.

It was Macfarlane himself who made the first advance. He came up quietly behind and laid his hand gently but firmly on the other's shoulder.

"Richardson," said he, "may have the head."

Now Richardson was a student who had long been anxious for that portion of the human subject to dissect. There was no answer, and the murderer resumed: "Talking of business, you must pay me; your accounts, you see, must tally."

Fettes found a voice, the ghost of his own: "Pay you!" he cried. "Pay you for that?"

"Why, yes, of course you must. By all means and on every possible account, you must," returned the other. "I dare not give it for nothing, you dare not take it for nothing; it would compromise us both. This is another case like Jane Galbraith's. The more things are wrong the more we must act as if all were right. Where does old K— keep his money?"

"There," answered Fettes, hoarsely, pointing to a cupboard in the corner.

"Give me the key, then," said the other, calmly, holding out his hand.

There was an instant's hesitation, and the die was cast. Macfarlane could not suppress a nervous twitch, the infinitesimal mark of an immense relief, as he felt the key between his fingers. He opened the cupboard, brought out pen and ink and a paper-book that stood in one compartment, and separated from the funds in a drawer a sum suitable to the occasion.

"Now, look here," he said, "there is the payment made—first proof of your good faith; first step to your security. You have now to clinch it by a second. Enter the payment in your book, and then you for your part may defy the devil."

The next few seconds were for Fettes an agony of thought; but in balancing his terrors it was the most immediate that triumphed. Any future difficulty seemed almost welcome if he could avoid a present quarrel with Macfarlane. He set down the candle which he had been carrying all this time, and with a steady hand entered the date, the nature, and the amount of the transaction.

"And now," said Macfarlane, "it's only fair that you should pocket the lucre. I've had my share already. By the bye, when a man of the world falls into a bit of luck, has a few shillings extra in his pocket—I'm ashamed to speak of it, but there's a rule of conduct in the case. No treating, no purchase of expensive class-books, no squaring of old debts; borrow, don't lend."

"Macfarlane," began Fettes, still somewhat hoarsely, "I have put my neck in a halter to oblige you."

"To oblige me?" cried Wolfe. "Oh, come! You did, as near as I can see the matter, what you downright had to do in self-defence. Suppose I got in trouble, where would you be? This second little matter flows clearly from the first. Mr. Gray is the continuation of Miss Galbraith. You can't begin and then stop. If you begin, you must keep on beginning; that's the truth. No rest for the wicked."

A horrible sense of blackness and the treachery of fate seized hold upon the soul of the unhappy student.

"My God!" he cried, "but what have I done? And when did I begin? To be made a class assistant—in the name of reason, where's the harm in that? Service wanted the position; Service might have got it. Would he have been where I am now?"

"My dear fellow," said Macfarlane, "what a boy you are! What harm has come to you? What harm can come to you if you hold your tongue? Why, man, do you know what this life is? There are two squads of us—the lions, and the lambs. If you're a lamb, you'll come to lie upon these tables like Gray or Jane Galbraith; if you're a lion, you'll live and drive a horse like me, like K—, like all the world with any wit or courage. You're staggered at the first. But look at K—! My dear fellow, you're clever, you have pluck. I like you, and K—likes you. You were born to lead the hunt; and I tell you, on my honour and my experience of life, three days from now you'll laugh at all these scarecrows like a high school boy at a farce."

And with that Macfarlane took his departure and drove off up the wynd in his gig to get under cover before daylight. Fettes was thus left alone with his regrets. He saw the miserable peril in which he stood involved. He saw, with inexpressible dismay, that there was no limit to his weakness, and that, from concession to concession, he had fallen from the arbiter of Macfarlane's destiny to his paid and helpless accomplice. He would have given the world to have been a little braver at the time, but it did not occur to him that he might still be brave. The secret of Jane Galbraith and the cursed entry in the daybook closed his mouth.

Hours passed; the class begins to arrive; the members of the unhappy Gray were dealt out to one and to another, and received without remark. Richardson was made happy with the head; and before the hour of freedom rang Fettes trembled with exultation to perceive how far they had already gone toward safety.

For two days he continued to watch, with increasing joy, the dreadful process of disguise.

On the third day Macfarlane made his appearance. He had been ill, he said; but he made up for lost time by the energy with which he directed the students. To Richardson in particular he extended the most valuable assistance and advice, and that student, encouraged by the praise of the demonstrator, burned high with ambitious hopes, and saw the medal already in his grasp.

Before the week was out Macfarlane's prophecy had been fulfilled. Fettes had outlived his terrors and had forgotten his baseness. He began to plume himself upon his courage, and had so arranged the story in his mind that he could look back on these events with an unhealthy pride. Of his accomplice he saw but little. They met, of course, in the business of the class; they received their orders together from Mr. K—. At times they had a word or two in private, and Macfarlane was from first to last particularly kind and jovial. But it was plain that he avoided any reference to their common secret; and even when Fettes whispered to him that he had cast in his lot with the lions and foresworn the lambs, he only signed to him smilingly to hold his peace.

At length an occasion arose which threw the pair once more into a closer union. Mr. K— was again short of subjects; pupils were eager, and it was a part of this teacher's pretensions to be always well supplied. At the same time there came the news of a burial in the rustic graveyard of Glencorse. Time had little changed the place in question. It stood then, as now, upon a cross road, out of call of human habitations, and buried fathoms deep in the foliage of six cedar trees. The cries of the sheep upon the neighboring hills, the streamlets upon either hand, one loudly singing among pebbles, the other dripping furtively from pond to pond, the stir of the wind in mountainous old flowering chestnuts, and once in seven days the voice of the bell and the old tunes of the precentor, were the only sounds that disturbed the silence around the rural church. The Resurrection Man—to use a byname of the period—was not to be deterred by any of the sanctities of customary piety. It was part of his trade to despise and desecrate the scrolls and trumpets of old tombs, the paths worn by the feet of worshippers and mourners, and the offerings and the inscriptions of bereaved affection. To rustic neighborhoods, where love is more than commonly tenacious, and where some bonds of blood or fellowship unite the entire society of a parish, the body-snatcher, far from being repelled by natural respect, was attracted by the ease and safety of the task. To bodies that had been laid in earth, in joyful expectation of a far different awakening, there came that hasty, lamp-lit, terror-haunted resurrection of the spade and mattock. The coffin was forced, the cerements torn, and the melancholy relics, clad in sackcloth, after being rattled for hours on moonless byways, were at length exposed to uttermost indignities before a class of gaping boys.

Somewhat as two vultures may swoop upon a dying lamb, Fettes and Macfarlane were to be let loose upon a grave in that green and quiet resting place. The wife of a farmer, a woman who had lived for sixty years, and been known for nothing but good butter and a godly conversation, was to be rooted from her grave at midnight and carried, dead and naked to that far-away city that she had always honored with her Sunday's best; the place beside her family was to be empty till the crack of doom; her innocent and almost venerable members to be exposed to that last curiosity of the anatomist.

Late one afternoon the pair set forth, well wrapped in cloaks and furnished with a formidable bottle. It rained without remission—a cold, dense, lashing rain. Now and again there blew a puff of wind, but these sheets of falling water kept it down. Bottle and all, it was a sad and silent drive as far as Penicuik, where they were to spend the evening. They stopped once, to hide their implements in a thick bush not far from the churchyard, and once again at the Fisher's Tryst, to have a toast before the kitchen fire and vary their nips of whiskey with a glass of ale. When they reached their journey's end the gig was housed, the horse was fed and comforted, and the two young doctors in a private room sat down to the best dinner and the best wine the house afforded. The lights, the fire, the beating rain upon the window, the cold, incongruous work that lay before them, added zest to their enjoyment of the meal. With every glass their cordiality increased. Soon Macfarlane handed a little pile of gold to his companion.

"A compliment," he said. "Between friends these little d——d accommodations ought to fly like pipe-lights."

Fettes pocketed the money, and applauded the sentiment to the echo. "You are a philosopher," he cried. "I was an ass till I knew you. You and K—between you, by the Lord Harry! But you'll make a man of me."

"Of course, we shall," applauded Macfarlane. "A man? I tell you, it required a man to back me up the other morning. There are some big, brawling, forty-year-old cowards who would have turned sick at the look of the d——d thing; but not you—you kept your head. I watched you."

"Well, and why not?" Fettes thus vaunted himself. "It was no affair of mine. There was nothing to gain on the one side but disturbance, and on the other I could count on your gratitude, don't you see?" And he slapped his pocket till the gold pieces rang.

Macfarlane somehow felt a certain touch of alarm at these unpleasant words. He may have regretted that he had taught his young companion so successfully, but he had no time to interfere, for the other noisily continued in this boastful strain:

"The great thing is not to be afraid. Now, between you and me, I don't want to hang—that's practical; but for all cant, Macfarlane, I was born with a contempt. Hell, God, Devil, right, wrong, sin, crime, all the old gallery of curiosities—they may frighten boys, but men of the world, like you and me, despise them. Here's to the memory of Gray!"

It was by this time growing somewhat late. The gig, according to order, was brought round to the door with both lamps brightly shining, and the young men had to pay their bill and take the road. They announced that they were bound for Peebles, and drove in that direction till they were clear of the last houses of town; then, extinguishing the lamps, returned upon their course, and followed a by-road toward Glencorse. There was no sound but that of their own passage, and the incessant, strident pouring of the rain. It was pitch dark; here and there a white gate or a white stone in the wall guided them for a short space across the night; but for the most part it was at a foot pace, and almost groping, that they picked their way through that resonant blackness to their solemn and isolated destination. In the sunken woods that traverse the neighbourhood of the burying ground the last glimmer failed them, and it became necessary to kindle a match and reillumine one of the lanterns of the gig. Thus, under dripping trees, and environed by huge and moving shadows, they reached the scene of their unhallowed labours.

They were both experienced in such affairs, and powerful with the spade; and they had scarce been twenty minutes at their task before they were rewarded by a dull rattle on the coffin lid. At the same moment Macfarlane, having hurt his hand upon a stone, flung it carelessly above his head. The grave, in which they now stood almost to the shoulders, was close to the edge of the plateau of the graveyard; and a gig lamp had been propped, the better to illuminate their labours, against a tree, and on the immediate verge of the steep bank descending to the stream. Chance had taken a sure aim with the stone. Then came a clang of broken glass; night fell upon them; sounds alternately dull and ringing announced the bounding of the lantern down the bank, and its occasional collision with the trees. A stone or two, which it had dislodged in its descent, rattled behind it into the profundities of the glen; and then silence, like night, resumed its sway; and they might bend their hearing to its utmost pitch, but naught was to be heard except the rain, now marching to the wind, now steadily falling over miles of open country.

They were so nearly at an end of their abhorred task that they judged it wisest to complete it in the dark. The coffin was exhumed and broken open; the body inserted in the dripping sack and carried between them to the gig; one mounted to keep it in its place, and the other, taking the horse by the mouth, groped along by wall and bush until they reached the wider road by the Fisher's Tryst. Here was a faint, diffused radiancy, which they hailed like daylight; by that they pushed the horse to a good place and began to rattle along merrily in the direction of the town.

They had both been wetted to the skin during their operations, and now, as the gig jumped among the deep ruts, the thing that stood propped between them fell now upon one and now upon the other. At every repetition of the horrid contact each instinctively repelled it with the greater haste; and the process, natural although it was, began to tell upon the nerves of the companions. Macfarlane made some ill-favored jest about the farmer's wife, but it came hollowly from his lips, and was allowed to drop in silence. Still their unnatural burden bumped from side to side; and now the head would be laid, as if in confidence, upon their shoulders, and now the drenching sackcloth would flap icily about their faces. A creeping chill began to possess the soul of Fettes. He peered at the bundle, and it seemed somehow larger than at first. All over the countryside, and from every degree of distance, the farm dogs accompanied their passage with tragic ululations; and it grew and grew upon his mind that some unnatural miracle had been accomplished, that some nameless change had befallen the dead body, and that it was in fear of their unholy burden that the dogs were howling.

"For God's sake," said he, making a great effort to arrive at speech, "for God's sake, let's have a light!"

Seemingly Macfarlane was affected in the same direction; for, though he made no reply, he stopped the horse, passed the reins to his companion, got down, and proceeded to kindle the remaining lamp. They had by that time got no further than the cross-road down to Auchenclinny. The rain still poured as though the deluge were returning, and it was no easy matter to make a light in such a world of wet and darkness. When at last the flickering blue flame had been transferred to the wick and began to expand and clarify, and shed a wide circle of misty brightness round the gig, it became possible for the two young men to see each other and the thing they had along with them. The rain had moulded the rough sacking to the outlines of the body underneath; the head was distinct from the trunk, the shoulders plainly modeled; something at once spectral and human riveted their eyes upon the ghastly comrade of their drive.

For some time Macfarlane stood motionless, holding up the lamp. A nameless dread was swathed, like a wet sheet, about the body, and tightened the white skin upon the face of Fettes; a fear that was meaningless, a horror of what could not be, kept mounting to his brain. Another beat of the watch, and he had spoken. But his comrade forestalled him.

"That is not a woman," said Macfarlane in a hushed voice.

"It was a woman when we put her in," whispered Fettes.

"Hold that lamp," said the other. "I must see her face."

And as Fettes took the lamp his companion untied the fastenings of the sack and drew down the cover from the head. The light fell very clear upon the dark, well-moulded features and smooth-shaven cheeks of a too familiar countenance, often beheld in dreams of both of these young men. A wild yell rang up into the night; each leaped from his own side into the roadway; the lamp fell, broke, and was extinguished; and the horse, terrified by this unusual commotion, bounded and went off toward Edinburgh at a gallop, bearing along with it, sole occupant of the gig, the body of the dead and long-dissected Gray.

29

The Phantom Coach

By Amelia B. Edwards

THE CIRCUMSTANCES I AM ABOUT TO RELATE TO YOU HAVE TRUTH TO recommend them. They happened to myself, and my recollection of them is as vivid as if they had taken place only yesterday. Twenty years, however, have gone by since that night. During those twenty years I have told the story to but one other person. I tell it now with a reluctance which I find difficult to overcome. All I entreat, meanwhile, is that you will abstain from forcing your own conclusions upon me. I want nothing explained away. I desire no arguments. My mind on this subject is quite made up, and having the testimony of my own senses to rely upon, I prefer to abide by it.

Well! It was just twenty years ago, and within a day or two of the end of the grouse season. I had been out all day with my gun, and had had no sport to speak of. The wind was due east; the month, December; the place, a bleak wide moor in the far north of England. And I had lost my way. It was not a pleasant place in which to lose one's way, with the first feathery flakes of a coming snowstorm just fluttering down upon the heather, and the leaden evening closing in all around. I shaded my eyes with my hand, and stared anxiously into the gathering darkness, where the purple moorland melted into a range of low hills, some ten or twelve miles distant. Not the faintest smoke-wreath, not the tiniest cultivated patch, or fence, or sheep-track, met my eyes in any direction. There was nothing for it but to walk on, and take my chance of finding what shelter I could, by the way. So I shouldered my gun again and pushed wearily forward, for I had been on foot since an hour before daybreak and had eaten nothing since breakfast.

Meanwhile, the snow began to come down with ominous steadiness, and the wind fell. After this, the cold became more intense, and the night came rapidly up. As for me, my prospects darkened with the darkening sky, and my heart grew heavy as I thought how my young wife was already watching for me through the window of our little inn parlour, and thought of all the suffering in store for her throughout this weary night. We had been married four months, and, having spent our autumn in the Highlands, were now lodging in a remote little village situated just on the verge of the great English moorlands. We were very much in love, and, of course, very happy. This morning, when we parted, she had implored me to return before dusk, and I had promised her that I would. What would I not have given to have kept my word!

Even now, weary as I was, I felt that with a supper, an hour's rest, and a guide, I might still get back to her before midnight, if only guide and shelter could be found.

And all this time the snow fell and the night thickened. I stopped and shouted every now and then, but my shouts seemed only to make the silence deeper. Then a vague sense of uneasiness came upon me, and I began to remember stories of travelers who had walked on and on in the falling snow until, wearied out, they were fain to lie down and sleep their lives away. Would it be possible, I asked myself, to keep on thus through all the long dark night? Would there not come a time when my limbs must fail, and my resolution give way? When I, too, must sleep the sleep of death. Death! I shuddered. How hard to die just now, when life lay all so bright before me! How hard for my darling, whose whole loving heart— but that thought was not to be borne! To banish it, I shouted again, louder and longer, and then listened eagerly. Was my shout answered, or did I only fancy that I heard a far-off cry? I halloed again, and again the echo followed. Then a wavering speck of light came suddenly out of the dark, shifting, disappearing, growing momentarily nearer and brighter. Running towards it at full speed, I found myself, to my great joy, face to face with an old man and a lantern.

"Thank God!" was the exclamation that burst involuntarily from my lips.

Blinking and frowning, he lifted his lantern and peered into my face. "What for?" growled he, sulkily.

"Well—for you. I began to fear I should be lost in the snow."

"Eh, then, folks do get cast away hereabouts fra' time to time, an' what's to hinder you from bein' cast away likewise, if the Lord's so minded?"

"If the Lord is so minded that you and I shall be lost together my friend, we must submit," I replied; "but I don't mean to be lost without you. How far am I now from Dwolding?"

"A gude twenty mile, more or less."

"And the nearest village?"

"The nearest village is Wyke, an' that's twelve miles t'other side."

"Where do you live, then?"

"Out yonder," said he, with a vague jerk of the lantern.

"You're going home, I presume?"

"Maybe I am."

"Then I'm going with you."

The old man shook his head, and rubbed his nose reflectively with the handle of the lantern.

"It ain't no use," growled he. "He 'ont let you in—not he."

"We'll see about that," I replied, briskly. "Who is he?"

"The master."

"Who is the master?"

"That's nowt to you," was the unceremonious reply.

"Well, well; you lead the way, and I'll engage that the master shall give me shelter and a supper tonight."

"Eh, you can try him!" muttered my reluctant guide; and, still shaking his head, he hobbled gnome-like, away through the falling snow. A large mass loomed up presently out of the darkness, and a huge dog rushed out barking furiously.

"Is this the house?" I asked.

"Ay, it's the house. Down, Bey!" And he fumbled in his pocket for the key.

I drew up close behind him, prepared to lose no chance of entrance, and saw in the little circle of light shed by the lantern that the door was heavily studded with iron nails, like the door of a prison. In another minute he had turned the key and I had pushed past him into the house.

Once inside, I looked round with curiosity and found myself in a great raftered hall, which served, apparently, a variety of uses. One end was piled to the roof with corn, like a barn. The other was stored with flour-sacks, agricultural implements, casks, and all kinds of miscellaneous lumber; while from the beams overhead hung rows of hams, flitches, and bunches of dried herbs for winter use. In the centre of the floor stood some huge object gauntly dressed in a dingy wrapping-cloth, and reaching halfway to the rafters. Lifting a corner of this, I saw, to my surprise, a telescope of very considerable size, mounted on a rude movable platform, with four small wheels. The tube was made of painted wood bound round with bands of metal rudely fashioned; the speculum, so far as I could estimate its size in the dim light, measured at least fifteen inches in diameter. While I was yet examining the instrument, and asking myself whether it was not the work of some self-taught optician, a bell rang sharply.

"That's for you," said my guide, with a malicious grin. "Yonder's his room."

He pointed to a low black door at the opposite side of the hall. I crossed over, rapped somewhat loudly, and went in, without waiting for an invitation. A huge, white-haired old man rose from a table covered with books and paper, and confronted me sternly.

"Who are you?" said he. "How came you here? What do you want?"

"James Murray, barrister-at-law. On foot across the moor. Meat, drink, and sleep."

He bent his bushy brows into a portentous frown.

"Mine is not a house of entertainment," he said haughtily. "Jacob, how dare you admit this stranger?"

"I didn't admit him," grumbled the old man. "He followed me over the muir, and shouldered his way in before me. I'm no match for six foot two."

"And pray, sir, by what right have your forced an entrance into my house?"

"The same by which I should have clung to your boat, if I were drowning. The right of self-preservation."

"Self-preservation?"

"There's an inch of snow on the ground already," I replied, briefly; "and it would be deep enough to cover my body before daybreak."

He strode to the window, pulled aside a heavy black curtain, and looked out.

"It is true," he said. "You can stay, if you choose, till morning. Jacob, serve the supper."

With this he waved me to a seat, resumed his own, and became at once absorbed in the studies from which I had disturbed him.

I placed my gun in a corner, drew my chair to the hearth, and examined my quarters at leisure. Smaller and less incongruous in its arrangements than the hall, this room contained, nevertheless, much to awaken my curiosity. The floor was carpetless. The whitewashed walls were in parts scrawled over with strange diagrams, and in others covered with shelves crowded with philosophical instruments, the uses of many of which were unknown to me. On one side of the fireplace stood a bookcase filled with dingy folios; on the other, a small organ, fantastically decorated with painted carvings of medieval saints and devils. Through the half-opened door of cupboard at the further end of the room I saw a long array of geological specimens, surgical preparations, crucibles, retorts, and jars of chemicals; while on the mantleshelf beside me, amid a number of small objects stood a model of the solar system, a small galvanic battery, and a microscope. Every chair had its burden. Every corner was heaped high with books. The very floor was littered over with maps, casts, papers, tracings, and learned lumber of all conceivable kinds.

I stared about me with an amazement increased by every fresh object upon which my eyes chanced to rest. So strange a room I had never seen; yet seemed it stranger still, to find such a room in a lone farmhouse amid those wild and solitary moors! Over and over again I looked from my host to his surroundings, and from his surroundings back to my host, asking myself who and what he could be? His head was singularly fine; but it was more the head of a poet than of a philosopher. Broad in the temples, prominent over the eyes, and clothed with a rough profusion of perfectly white hair, it had all the ideality and much of the ruggedness that characterizes the head of Louis von Beethoven. There were the same deep lines about the mouth, and the same stern furrows in the brow. There was the same concentration of expression. While I was yet observing him, the door opened and Jacob brought in the supper. His master then closed his book, rose, and with more courtesy of manner than he had yet shown, invited me to the table.

A dish of ham and eggs, a loaf of brown bread, and a bottle of admirable sherry were placed before me.

"I have but the homeliest farmhouse fare to offer you, sir," said my entertainer. "Your appetite, I trust, will make up for the deficiencies of our larder."

I had already fallen upon the viands, and now protested, with the enthusiasm of a starving sportsman, that I had never eaten anything so delicious.

He bowed stiffly, and sat down to his own supper, which consisted, primitively, of a jug of milk and a basin of porridge. We ate in silence, and, when we had done, Jacob removed the tray. I then drew my chair back to the fireside. My host, somewhat to my surprise, did the same, and turning abruptly towards me, said:

"Sir, I have lived here in strict retirement for three-and-twenty years. During that time I have not seen as many strange faces and I have not read a single newspaper. You are the first stranger who has crossed my threshold for more than four years. Will you favour me with a few words of information respecting that outer world from which I have parted company so long?"

"Pray interrogate me," I replied. "I am heartily at your service."

He bent his head in acknowledgement; leaned forward, with his elbow resting on his knees and his chin supported in the palms of his hands; stared fixedly into the fire; and proceeded to question me.

His inquiries related chiefly to scientific matters, with the later progress of which, as applied to the practical purposes of life, he was almost wholly unacquainted. No student of science myself, I replied as well as my slight information permitted; but the task was far from easy, and I was much relieved when, passing from interrogation to discussion, he began pouring forth his own conclusions upon the facts which I had been attempting to place before him. He talked, and I listened spellbound. He talked till I believe he almost forgot my presence, and only thought aloud. I had never heard anything like it then; I have never heard anything like it since.

Familiar with all systems of all philosophies, subtle in analysis, bold in generalization, he poured forth his thoughts in an uninterrupted stream, and, still leaning forward in the same moody attitude with his eyes fixed upon the fire, wandered from topic to topic, from speculation to speculation, like an inspired dreamer. From practical science to mental philosophy; from electricity in the wire to electricity in the nerve; from Watts to Mesmer, from Mesmer to Reichenbach, from Reichenbach to Swedenborg, Spinoza, Condillac, Descartes, Berkeley, Aristotle, Plato, and the Magi and mystics of the East, were transitions which, however bewildering in their variety and scope, seemed easy and harmonious upon his lips as sequences in music. By and by—I forget now by which link of conjecture or illustration—he passed on to that field which lies beyond the boundary line of even conjectural philosophy, and reaches no man knows hither. He spoke of the soul and its aspirations; of the spirit and its powers; of second sight; of prophecy; of those phenomena which, under the names of ghosts, specters, and supernatural appearances, have been denied by the skeptics and attested by the credulous of all ages.

"The world," he said, "grows hourly more and more skeptical of all that lies beyond its own narrow radius; and our men of science foster the fatal tendency. They condemn as fable all that resists experiment. They reject as false all that cannot be brought to the test of the laboratory or the dissecting-room. Against what superstition have they waged so long and obstinate a war, as against the belief in apparitions? And yet what superstition has maintained its hold upon the minds of men so long and so firmly? Show me any facts in physics, in history, in archaeology, which is supported by testimony so wide and so various. Attested by all races of men, in all ages, and in all climates, by the soberest sages of antiquity, by the rudest savage of today, by the Christian, the Pagan, the Pantheist, the Materialist, this phenomenon is treated as a nursery tale by the philosophers of our century. Circumstantial evidence weighs with them as a feather in the balance. The comparison of causes with effects, however valuable in physical science, is put aside as worthless and unreliable. The evidence of competent witnesses, however conclusive in a court of justice, counts for nothing. He who pauses before he pronounces, is condemned as a trifler. He who believes, is a dreamer or a fool."

He spoke with bitterness, and having said thus, relapsed for some minutes into silence. Presently he raised his head from his hands, and added, with an altered voice and manner:

"I, sir, paused, investigated, believed, and was not ashamed to state my convictions to the world. I, too, was branded as a visionary, held up to ridicule by my contemporaries, and hooted from that field of science in which I had laboured with honour during all the best years of my life. These things happened just three-and-twenty years ago. Since then I have lived as you see me living now, and the world has forgotten me, as I have forgotten the world. You have my history."

"It is a very common one," he replied. "I have only suffered for the truth, as many a better and wiser man has suffered before me."

He rose, as if desirous of ending the conversation, and went over to the window.

"It has ceased snowing," he observed, as he dropped the curtain and came back to the fireside.

"Ceased!" I exclaimed, starting eagerly to my feet, "Oh, if it were only possible—but no! It is hopeless. Even if I could find my way across the moor, I could not walk twenty miles tonight."

"Walk twenty miles tonight!" repeated my host. "What are you thinking of?"

"Of my wife," I replied impatiently. "Of my young wife, who does not know that I have lost my way, and who is at this moment breaking her heart with suspense and terror."

"Where is she?"

"At Dwolding, twenty miles away."

"At Dwolding," he echoed, thoughtfully. "Yes, the distance, it is true, is twenty miles; but—are you so very anxious to save the next six or eight hours?"

"So very, very anxious, that I would give ten guineas at this moment for a guide and a horse."

"Your wish can be gratified at a less costly rate," said he, smiling. "The night mail from the north, which changes horses at Dwolding, passes within five miles of this spot, and will be due at a certain cross-road in about an hour and a quarter. If Jacob were to go with you across the moor and put you into the old coach-road, you could find your way, I suppose, to where it joins the new one?"

"Easily—gladly."

He smiled again, rang the bell, gave the old servant his directions, and, taking a bottle of whiskey and wineglass from the cupboard in which he kept his chemicals, said:

"The snow lies deep and it will be difficult walking tonight on the moor. A glass of usquebaugh before you start?"

I would have declined the spirit, but he pressed it on me, and I drank it. It went down my throat like liquid flame and almost took my breath away.

"It is strong," he said; "but it will help to keep out the cold. And now you have no moments to spare. Good night!"

I thanked him for his hospitality and would have shaken hands but that he had turned away before I could finish my sentence. In another minute I had traversed the hall, Jacob had locked the outer door behind me, and we were out on the wide white moor.

Although the wind had fallen, it was still bitterly cold. Not a star glimmered in the black vault overhead. Not a sound, save the rapid crunching of the snow beneath our feet, disturbed the heavy stillness of the night. Jacob, not too well pleased with his mission, shambled on before in sullen silence, his lantern in his hand and his shadow at his feet. I followed, with my gun over my shoulder, as little inclined for conversation as himself. My thoughts were full of my late host. His voice yet rang in my ears. His eloquence yet held my imagination captive. I remember to this day, with surprise, how my over-excited brain retained whole sentences and parts of sentences, troops of brilliant images, and fragments of splendid reasoning, in the very words in which he had uttered them. Musing thus over what

375

I had heard, and striving to recall a lost link here and there, I strode on at the heel of my guide, absorbed and unobservant. Presently—at the end, as it seemed to me, of only a few minutes—he came to a sudden halt, and said:

"Yon's your road. Keep the stone fence to your right hand and you can't fail of the way."

"This, then, is the old coach-road?"

"Ay, 'tis the old coach-road."

"And how far do I go before I reach the cross-roads?"

"Nigh upon three mile."

I pulled out my purse, and he became more communicative.

"The road's a fair road enough," said he, "for foot passengers; but 'twas over-steep and narrow for the northern traffic. You'll mind where the parpet's broken away, close again' the signpost. It's never been mended since the accident."

"What accident?"

"Eh, the night mail pitched right over into the valley below—a gude fifty feet an' more—just at the worst bit o' road in the whole county."

"Horrible! Were many lives lost?"

"All. Four were found dead, and t'other two died next morning."

"How long is it since this happened?"

"Just nine year."

"Near the sign-post, you say? I will bear it in mind. Good night."

"Gude night, sir, and thankee." Jacob pocketed his half-crown, made a faint pretence of touching his hat, and trudged back by the way he had come.

I watched the light of his lantern till it quite disappeared, and then turned to pursue my way alone. This was no longer a matter of the slightest difficulty, for, despite the dead darkness overhead, the line of stone fence showed distinctly enough against the pale gleam of snow. How silent it seemed now, with only my footsteps to listen to; how silent and how solitary! A strange disagreeable sense of loneliness stole over me. I walked faster. I hummed a fragment of a tune. I cast up enormous sums in my head, and accumulated them at compound interest. I did my best, in short, to forget the startling speculations to which I had but just been listening, and, to some extent, I succeeded.

Meanwhile, the night air seemed to become colder and colder; and though I walked fast I found it impossible to keep myself warm. My feet were like ice. I lost sensation in my hands, and grasped my gun mechanically. I even breathed with difficulty, as though, instead of traversing a quiet North-country highway, I were scaling the uppermost heights of some gigantic alp. This last symptom became presently so distressing that I was forced to stop for a few minutes and lean against the stone fence. As I did so I chanced to look back up the road, and there, to my infinite relief, I saw a distant point of light, like the gleam of an approaching lantern. I at first concluded that Jacob had retraced his steps and followed me; but even as the conjecture presented itself, a second light flashed into sight— a light evidently parallel with the first, and approaching at the same rate of motion. It needed no second thought to show me that these must be the carriage-lamps of some private vehicle, though it seemed strange that any private vehicle should take a road professedly disused and dangerous.

There could be no doubt, however, of the fact, for the lamps grew larger and brighter every moment, and I even fancied I could already see the dark outline of the carriage between them. It was coming up very fast, and quite noiselessly, the snow being nearly a foot deep under the wheels.

And now the body of the vehicle became distinctly visible behind the lamps. It looked strangely lofty. A sudden suspicion flashed upon me. Was it possible that I had passed the cross-roads in the dark without observing the sign-post and could this be the very coach which I had come to meet?

No need to ask myself that question a second time, for here it came round the bend of the road, guard and driver, one outside passenger, and four steaming greys, all wrapped in a soft haze of light, through which the lamps blazed out, like a pair of fiery meteors.

I jumped forward, waved my hat, and shouted. The mail came down at full speed and passed me. For a moment I feared that I had not been seen or heard, but it was only for a moment. The coachman pulled up; the guard, muffled to the eyes in capes and comforters, and apparently sound asleep in the rumble, neither answered my hail nor made the slightest effort to dismount; the outside passenger did not even turn his head. I opened the door for myself, and looked in. There were but three travelers inside, so I stepped in, shut the door, slipped into the vacant corner, and congratulated myself of my good fortune.

The atmosphere of the coach seemed, if possible, colder than that of the outer air and was pervaded by a singularly damp and disagreeable smell. I looked round at my fellow-passengers. They were all three, men, and all silent. They did not seem to be asleep, but each leaned back in his corner of the vehicle, as if absorbed in his own reflections. I attempted to open a conversation.

"How intensely cold it is tonight," I said, addressing my opposite neighbor.

He lifted his head, looked at me, but made no reply.

"The winter," I added, "seems to have begun in earnest."

Although the corner in which he sat was so dim that I could distinguish none of his features very clearly, I saw that his eyes were still turned full upon me. And yet he answered never a word.

At any other time I should have felt, and perhaps expressed, some annoyance, but at the moment I felt too ill to do either. The icy coldness of the night air had struck a chill to my very marrow, and the strange smell inside the coach was affecting me with an intolerable nausea. I shivered from head to foot, and, turning to my left-hand neighbour, asked if he had any objection to an open window?

He neither spoke nor stirred.

I repeated the question somewhat more loudly, but with the same result. Then I lost my patience and let the sash down. As I did so, the leather strap broke in my hand, and I observed that the glass was covered with a thick coat of mildew, the accumulation, apparently, of years. My attention being thus drawn to the condition of the coach, I examined it more narrowly, and saw by the uncertain light of the outer lamps that it was in the last state of dilapidation. Every part of it was not only out of repair but in a condition of decay. The sashes splintered at a touch. The leather fittings were crusted over with mould, and literally rotting from the woodwork. The floor was almost breaking away beneath my feet. The whole machine, in short, was foul with damp, and had evidently been dragged from some outhouse in which it had been moldering away for years, to do another day or two of duty on the road.

I turned to the third passenger, whom I had not yet addressed, and hazarded one more remark.

"This coach," I said, "is in deplorable condition. The regular mail, I suppose, is under repair."

He moved his head slowly, and looked me in the face, without speaking a word. I shall never forget that look while I live. I turned cold at heart under it. I turn cold at heart even now when I recall it. His eyes glowed with a fiery unnatural luster. His face was livid as the face of a corpse. His bloodless lips were drawn back as if in the agony of death, and showed the gleaming teeth between.

The words that I was about to utter died upon my lips, and a strange horror—a dreadful horror—came upon me. My sight had by this time become used to the gloom of the coach and I could see with tolerable distinctness. I turned to my opposite neighbour. He, too, was looking at me with the same startling pallor in his face and the same stony glitter in his eyes. I passed my hand across my brow. I turned to the passenger on the seat beside my own, and saw—oh, Heaven! How shall I describe what I saw? I saw that he was no living man—that none of them were living men, like myself! A pale phosphorescent light—the light of putrefaction—played upon their awful faces; upon their hair, dank with the dews of the grave; upon their clothes, earth stained and dropping to pieces; upon their hands, which were as the hands of corpses long buried. Only their eyes, their terrible eyes, were living; and those eyes were all turned menacingly upon me!

A shriek of terror, a wild, unintelligible cry for help and mercy, burst from my lips as I flung myself against the door and strove in vain to open it.

In that single instant, brief and vivid as a landscape beheld in the flash of summer lightning, I saw the moon shining down through a rift of stormy cloud—the ghastly sign-post rearing its warning finger by the wayside—the broken parapet—the plunging horses—the black gulf below. Then the coach reeled like a ship at sea. Then came a mighty crash—a sense of crushing pain—and then darkness.

It seemed as if years had gone by when I awoke one morning from a deep sleep and found my wife watching by my bedside. I will pass over the scene that ensued and give you, in half a dozen words, the tale she told me with tears of thanksgiving. I had fallen over a precipice, close against the junction of the old coach-road and the new, and had only been saved from certain death by lighting upon a deep snowdrift that had accumulated at the foot of the rock beneath. In this snowdrift I was discovered at daybreak by a couple of shepherds, who carried me to the nearest shelter and brought a surgeon to my aid. The surgeon found me in a state of raving delirium, with a broken arm and a compound fracture of the skull. The letters in my pocket-book showed my name and address; my wife was summoned to nurse me; and, thanks to youth and a fine constitution, I came out of danger at last. The place of my fall, I need scarcely say, was precisely that at which a frightful accident had happened to the north mail nine years before.

I never told my wife the fearful events which I have just related to you. I told the surgeon who attended me; but he treated the whole adventure as a mere dream born of the fever in my brain. We discussed the question over and over again until we found that we could discuss it with temper no longer, and then we dropped it. Others may form what conclusions they please—I know that twenty years ago I was the fourth inside passenger in that Phantom Coach.

30

Ligeia

By Edgar Allan Poe

*And the will therein lieth, which dieth not. Who knoweth the myster-
ies of the will, with its vigor? For God is but a great will pervading
all things by nature of its intentness. Man doth not yield himself to the
angels, nor unto death utterly, save only through the weakness of his
feeble will.*

—JOSEPH GLANVILL

I CANNOT, FOR MY SOUL, REMEMBER HOW, WHEN, OR EVEN PRECISELY
where, I first became acquainted with the lady Ligeia. Long years have
since elapsed, and my memory is feeble through much suffering. Or, perhaps, I cannot now bring these points to mind, because, in truth, the
character of my beloved, her rare learning, her singular yet placid cast of
beauty, and the thrilling and enthralling eloquence of her low musical
language, made their way into my heart by paces so steadily and stealthily progressive, that they must have been unnoticed and unknown. Yet I
believe that I met her first and most frequently in some large, old, decaying city near the Rhine. Of her family—I have surely heard her speak.
That it is of a remotely ancient date cannot be doubted. Ligeia! Ligeia!
Buried in studies of a nature more than all else adapted to deaden impressions of the outward world, it is by that sweet word alone—by Ligeia—
that I bring before mine eyes in fancy the image of her who is no more.
And now, while I write, a recollection flashes upon me that I have never

known the paternal name of her who was my friend and my betrothed, and who became the partner of my studies, and finally the wife of my bosom. Was it a playful charge on the part of my Ligeia?

Or was it a test of my strength of affection, that I should institute no inquiries upon this point? Or was it rather a caprice of my own—a wildly romantic offering on the shrine of the most passionate devotion? I but indistinctly recall the fact itself—what wonder that I have utterly forgotten the circumstances which originated or attended it?

And, indeed, if ever that spirit which is entitled Romance—if ever she, the wan and misty-winged Ashtophet of idolatrous Egypt, presided, as they tell, over marriages ill-omened, then most surely she presided over mine.

There is one dear topic, however, on which my memory fails me not. It is the person of Ligeia. In stature she was tall, somewhat slender, and, in her latter days, even emaciated. I would in vain attempt to portray the majesty, the quiet ease of her demeanor, or the incomprehensible lightness and elasticity of her footfall. She came and departed as a shadow. I was never made aware of her entrance into my closed study, save by the dear music of her low sweet voice, as she placed her marble hand upon my shoulder. In beauty of face no maiden ever equaled her. It was the radiance of an opium-dream—an airy and spirit-lifting vision more wildly divine than the phantasies which hovered about the slumbering souls of the daughters of Delos. Yet her features were not of that regular mold which we have been falsely taught to worship in the classical labors of the heathen. 'There is no exquisite beauty,' says Bacon, Lord Verulam, speaking truly of all the forms and genera of beauty, 'without some strangeness in the proportion.' Yet, although I saw that the features of Ligeia were not of a classic regularity—although I perceived that her loveliness was indeed 'exquisite,' and felt that there was much of 'strangeness' pervading it, yet I have tried in vain to detect the irregularity and to trace home my own perception of 'the strange.' I examined the contour of the lofty and pale forehead—it was faultless—how cold indeed that word when applied to a majesty so divine!—the skin rivaling the purest ivory, the commanding extent and repose, the gentle prominence of the regions above the temples; and then the raven-black, the glossy, the luxuriant, and naturally curling tresses, setting forth the full force of the Homeric epithet, 'hyacinthine!' I looked at the delicate outlines of the nose—and nowhere but in the graceful medallions of the Hebrews had I beheld a similar perfection. There were the same luxurious smoothness of surface, the same scarcely perceptible tendency to the aquiline, the same harmoniously curved nostrils speaking the free spirit. I regarded the sweet mouth. Here was indeed the triumph of all things heavenly—the magnificent turn of the short upper lip—the soft, voluptuous slumber of the under — the dimples which sported, and the color which spoke—the teeth glancing back, and with a brilliancy almost startling, every ray of the holy light which fell upon them in her serene and placid yet most exultingly radiant of all smiles. I scrutinized the formation of the chin—and, here too, I found the gentleness of breadth, the softness and the majesty, the fullness and the spirituality, of the Greek—the contour which the god Apollo revealed but in a dream, to Cleomenes, the son of the Athenian. And then I peered into the large eyes of Ligeia.

For eyes we have no models in the remotely antique. It might have been, too, that in these eyes of my beloved lay the secret to which Lord Verulam alludes. They were, I must believe, far larger than the ordinary eyes of our own race. They were even fuller than the fullest of gazelle eyes of the tribe of the valley of Nourjahad. Yet it was only at intervals—in moments of intense excitement—that this peculiarity became more than slightly noticeable in Ligeia. And at such moments was her beauty—in my heated fancy thus it appeared perhaps—the beauty of beings either above or apart from the earth—the beauty of the fabulous Houri of the Turk. The hue of the orbs was the most brilliant of black, and, far over them, hung jetty lashes of the same length. The brows, slightly irregular in outline, had the same tint. The 'strangeness,' however, which I found in the eyes was of a nature distinct from the formation, or the color, or the brilliancy of the features, and must, after all, be referred to the expression. Ah, word of no meaning! Behind whose vast latitude of mere sound we entrench our ignorance of so much of the spiritual. The expression of the eyes of Ligeia! How for long hours have I pondered upon it! How have I, through the whole of a midsummer night, struggled to fathom it! What was it—that something more profound than the well of

Democritus—which lay far within the pupils of my beloved! What was it? I was possessed with a passion to discover. Those eyes! Those large, those shining, those divine orbs! They became to me twin stars of Leda, and I to them devoutest of astrologers.

There is no point, among the many incomprehensible anomalies of the science of mind, more thrillingly exciting than the fact—never, I believe, noticed in the schools—that in our endeavors to recall to memory something long forgotten, we often find ourselves upon the very verge of remembrance, without being able, in the end, to remember. And thus how frequently, in my intense scrutiny of Ligeia's eyes, have I felt approaching the full knowledge of their expression—felt it approaching—yet not quite be mine—and so at length entirely depart! And (strange, oh, strangest mystery of all!) I found, in the commonest objects of the universe, a circle of analogies to that expression. I mean to say that, subsequently to the period when Ligeia's beauty passed into my spirit, there dwelling as in a shrine, I derived, from many existences in the material world, a sentiment such as I felt always around, within me, by her large and luminous orbs. Yet not the more could I define that sentiment, or analyze, or even steadily view it. I recognized it, let me repeat, sometimes in the survey of a rapidly growing vine—in the contemplation of a moth, a butterfly, a chrysalis, a stream of running water. I have felt it in the ocean—in the falling of a meteor. I have felt it in the glances of unusually aged people. And there are one or two stars in heaven (one especially, a star of the sixth magnitude, double and changeable, to be found near the large star in Lyra) in a telescopic scrutiny of which I have been made aware of the feeling. I have been filled with it by certain sounds from stringed instruments, and not infrequently by passages from books. Among innumerable other instances, I well remember something in a volume of Joseph Glanvill, which (perhaps merely from its quaintness—who shall say?) never failed to inspire me with the sentiment: 'And the will therein lieth, which dieth not. Who knoweth the mysteries of the will, with its vigor? For God is but a great will pervading all things by nature of its intentness. Man doth not yield him to the angels, nor unto death utterly, save only through the weakness of his feeble will.'

Length of years and subsequent reflection have enabled me to trace, indeed, some remote connection between this passage in the English moralist and a portion of the character of Ligeia. An intensity in thought, action, or speech was possibly, in her, a result, or at least an index, of that gigantic volition which, during our long intercourse, failed to give other and more immediate evidence of its existence. Of all the women whom I have ever known, she, the outwardly calm, the ever-placid Ligeia, was the most violently a prey to the tumultuous vultures of stern passion. And of such passion I could form no estimate, save by the miraculous expansion of those eyes which at once so delighted and appalled me—by the almost magical melody, modulation, distinctness, and placidity of her very low voice—and by the fierce energy (rendered doubly effective by contrast with her manner of utterance) of the wild words which she habitually uttered.

I have spoken of the learning of Ligeia: it was immense—such as I have never known in woman. In the classical tongues was she deeply proficient, and as far as my own acquaintance extended in regard to the modern dialects of Europe, I had never known her at fault. Indeed upon any theme of the most admired because simply the most abstruse of the boasted erudition of the Academy, have I ever found Ligeia at fault? How singularly—how thrillingly, this one point in the nature of my wife has forced itself, at this late period only, upon my attention! I said her knowledge was such as I have never known in woman—but where breathes the man who has traversed, and successfully, all the wide areas of moral, physical, and mathematical science! I saw not then what I now clearly perceive, that the acquisitions of Ligeia were gigantic, were astounding; yet I was sufficiently aware of her infinite supremacy to resign myself, with a child-like confidence, to her guidance through the chaotic world of metaphysical investigation at which I was most busily occupied during the earlier years of our marriage. With how vast a triumph—with how vivid a delight—with how much of all that is ethereal in hope did I feel, as she bent over me in studies but little sought—but less known—that delicious vista by slow degrees expanding before me, down whose long, gorgeous, and all untrodden path, I might at length pass onward to the goal of a wisdom too divinely precious not to be forbidden!

How poignant, then, must have been the grief with which, after some years, I beheld my well-grounded expectations take wings to themselves and fly away! Without Ligeia I was but as a child groping benighted. Her presence, her readings alone, rendered vividly luminous the many mysteries of the transcendentalism in which we were immersed. Wanting the radiant luster of her eyes, letters, lambent and golden, grew duller than Saturnian lead. And now those eyes shone less and less frequently upon the pages over which I pored. Ligeia grew ill. The wild eyes blazed with a too—too glorious effulgence; the pale fingers became of the transparent waxen hue of the grave; and the blue veins upon the lofty forehead swelled and sank impetuously with the tides of the most gentle emotion. I saw that she must die—and I struggled desperately in spirit with the grim Azrael. And the struggles of the passionate wife were, to my astonishment, even more energetic than my own. There had been much in her stern nature to impress me with the belief that, to her, death would have come without its terrors; but not so. Words are impotent to convey any just idea of the fierceness of resistance with which she wrestled with the Shadow. I groaned in anguish at the pitiable spectacle. I would have soothed—I would have reasoned; but in the intensity of her wild desire for life—for life—but for life—solace and reason were alike the uttermost of folly. Yet not until the last instance, amid the most convulsive writhings of her fierce spirit, was shaken the external placidity of her demeanor. Her voice grew more gentle—grew more low—yet I would not wish to dwell upon the wild meaning of the quietly uttered words. My brain reeled as I hearkened, entranced to a melody more than mortal—to assumptions and aspirations which mortality had never before known.

That she loved me I should not have doubted; and I might have been easily aware that, in a bosom such as hers, love would have reigned no ordinary passion. But in death only was I fully impressed with the strength of her affection. For long hours, detaining my hand, would she pour out before me the overflowing of a heart whose more than passionate devotion amounted to idolatry. How had I deserved to be so blessed by such confessions?—how had I deserved to be so cursed with the removal of my beloved in the hour of my making them? But upon this subject I cannot bear to dilate. Let me say only, that in Ligeia's more than womanly abandonment to a love, alas! All unmerited, all unworthily bestowed, I at length recognized the principle of her longing, with so wildly earnest a desire, for the life which was now fleeing so rapidly away. It is this wild longing—it is this eager vehemence of desire for life—but for life—that I have no power to portray—no utterance capable of expressing.

At high noon of the night in which she departed, beckoning me, peremptorily, to her side, she bade me repeat certain verses composed by herself not many days before. I obeyed her. They were these:—

Lo! 'tis a gala night
Within the lonesome latter years!
An angel throng, bewinged, bedight
In veils, and drowned in tears,
Sit in a theatre, to see
A play of hopes and fears,
While the orchestra breathes fitfully
The music of the spheres.

Mimes, in the form of God on high,
Mutter and mumble low,
And hither and thither fly;
Mere puppets they, who come and go
At bidding of vast formless things
That shift the scenery to and fro,
Flapping from out their
Condor wings invisible woe!

That motley drama!—oh, be sure
It shall not be forgot!
With its Phantom chased for evermore,
By a crowd that seize it not,
Through a circle that ever returneth in
To the self-same spot;
And much of Madness, and more of Sin
And Horror, the soul of the plot!

But see, amid the mimic rout
A crawling shape intrude!
A blood-red thing that writhes from out
The scenic solitude!
It writhes!—it writhes!—with mortal pangs
The mimes become its food,
And the seraphs sob at vermin fangs
In human gore imbued.

Out—out are the lights—out all!
And over each quivering form,
The curtain, a funeral pall,
Comes down with the rush of a storm—
And the angels, all pallid and wan,
Uprising, unveiling, affirm
That the play is the tragedy 'Man,'
And its hero, the conqueror Worm.

'Oh God!' half shrieked Ligeia, leaping to her feet and extending her arms aloft with a spasmodic movement, as I made an end of these lines— 'Oh God! O Divine Father!—shall these things be undeviatingly so?— shall this conqueror be not once conquered? Are we not part and parcel in Thee? Who—who knoweth the mysteries of the will with its vigor? Man doth not yield him to the angels, nor unto death utterly, save only through the weakness of his feeble will.'

And now, as if exhausted with emotion, she suffered her white arms to fall, and returned solemnly to her bed of death. And as she breathed her last sighs, they came mingled with them a low murmur from her lips. I bent to them my ear, and distinguished again, the concluding words of the passage in Glanvill: 'Man doth not yield him to the angels, nor unto death utterly, save only through the weakness of his feeble will.'

She died: and I, crushed into the very dust with sorrow, could no longer endure the lonely desolation of my dwelling in the dim and decaying city by the Rhine. I had no lack of what the world calls wealth. Ligeia had brought me far more, very far more, than ordinarily falls to the lot of mortals. After a few months, therefore, of weary and aimless wandering,

I purchased and put in some repair, an abbey, which I shall not name, in one of the wildest and least frequented portions of fair England. The gloomy and dreary grandeur of the building, the almost savage aspect of the domain, the many melancholy and time-honored memories connected with both, had much in unison with the feelings of utter abandonment, which had driven me into that remote and unsocial region of the country. Yet although the external abbey, with its verdant decay hanging about it, suffered but little alteration, I gave way, with a child-like perversity, and perchance with a faint hope of alleviating my sorrows, to a display of more than regal magnificence within. For such follies, even in childhood, I had imbibed a taste, and now they came back to me as if in the dotage of grief. Alas, I feel how much even of incipient madness might have been discovered in the gorgeous and fantastic draperies, in the solemn carvings of Egypt, in the wild cornices and furniture, in the Bedlam patterns of the carpets of tufted gold! I had become a bounden slave in the trammels of opium, and my labors and my orders had taken a coloring from my dreams. But these absurdities I must not pause to detail. Let me speak only of that one chamber, ever accursed, whither, in a moment of mental alienation, I led from the altar as my bride—as the successor of the unforgotten Ligeia—the fair-haired and blue-eyed Lady Rowena Trevanion, of Tremaine.

There is no individual portion of the architecture and decoration of that bridal chamber which is not now visibly before me. Where were the souls of the haughty family of the bride, when, through thirst of gold, they permitted to pass the threshold of an apartment so bedecked, a maiden and a daughter so beloved? I have said, that I minutely remember the details of the chamber—yet I am sadly forgetful on topics of deep moment; and here there was no system, no keeping, in the fantastic display, to take hold upon the memory. The room lay in a high turret of the castellated abbey, was pentagonal in shape, and of capacious size. Occupying the whole southern face of the pentagon was the sole window—an immense sheet of unbroken glass from Venice—a single pane, and tinted of a leaden hue, so that the rays of either the sun or moon passing through it, fell with a ghastly luster on the objects within. Over the upper portion of this huge window, extended the trellis-work of an aged vine, which clambered up the massy walls of the turret. The ceiling, of gloomy-looking oak, was excessively lofty, vaulted, and elaborately fretted with the wildest and most grotesque specimens of a semi-Gothic, semi-Druidical device. From out the most central recess of this melancholy vaulting, depended, by a single chain of gold with long links, a huge censer of the same metal, Saracenic in pattern, and with many perforations so contrived that there writhed in and out of them, as if endued with a serpent vitality, a continual succession of parti-colored fires.

Some few ottomans and golden candelabra, of Eastern figure, were in various stations about; and there was the couch, too—the bridal couch—of an Indian model, and low, and sculptured of solid ebony, with a pall-like canopy above. In each of the angles of the chamber stood on end a giant sarcophagus of black granite, from the tombs of the kings over against Luxor, with their aged lids full of immemorial sculpture. But in the draping of the apartment lay, alas! The chief phantasy of all. The lofty walls, gigantic in height—even unproportionably so—were hung from summit to foot, in vast folds, with a heavy and massive looking tapestry—tapestry of a material which was found alike as a carpet on the floor, as a covering for the ottomans and the ebony bed, as a canopy for the bed and as the gorgeous volutes of the curtains which partially shaded the window. The material was the richest cloth of gold. It was spotted all over, at irregular intervals, with arabesque figures, about a foot in diameter, and wrought upon the cloth in patterns of the most jetty black. But these figures partook of the true character of the arabesque only when regarded from a single point of view. By a contrivance now common, and indeed traceable to a very remote period of antiquity, they were made changeable in aspect. To one entering the room, they bore the appearance of simple monstrosities; but upon a farther advance, this appearance gradually departed; and, step by step, as the visitor moved his station in the chamber, he saw himself surrounded by an endless succession of the ghastly forms which belong to the superstition of the Norman, or arise in the guilty slumbers of the monk. The phantasmagoric effect was vastly heightened by the artificial introduction of a strong continual current of wind behind the draperies—giving a hideous and uneasy animation to the whole.

In halls such as these—in a bridal chamber such as this—I passed, with the Lady of Tremaine, the unhallowed hours of the first month of our marriage—passed them with but little disquietude. That my wife dreaded the fierce moodiness of my temper—that she shunned me, and loved me but little—I could not help perceiving; but it gave me rather pleasure than otherwise. I loathed her with a hatred belonging more to demon than to man. My memory flew back (oh, with what intensity of regret!) to Ligeia, the beloved, the august, the beautiful, the entombed. I revelled in recollections of her purity, of her wisdom, of her lofty—her ethereal nature, of her passionate, her idolatrous love. Now, then, did my spirit fully and freely burn with more than all the fires of her own. In the excitement of my opium dreams (for I was habitually fettered in the shackles of the drug), I would call aloud upon her name, during the silence of the night, or among the sheltered recesses of the glens by day, as if, through the wild eagerness, the solemn passion, the consuming ardor of my longing for the departed, I could restore her to the pathways she had abandoned—ah, could it be for ever?—upon the earth.

About the commencement of the second month of the marriage, the Lady Rowena was attacked with sudden illness, from which her recovery was slow. The fever which consumed her rendered her nights uneasy; and in her perturbed state of half-slumber, she spoke of sounds, and of motions, in and about the chamber of the turret, which I concluded had no origin save in the distemper of her fancy, or perhaps in the phantasmagoric influences of the chamber itself. She became at length convalescent—finally, well. Yet but a brief period elapsed, ere a second more violent disorder again threw her upon a bed of suffering; and from this attack her frame, at all times feeble, never altogether recovered. Her illnesses were, after this epoch, of alarming character, and of more alarming recurrence, defying alike the knowledge and the great exertions of her physicians. With the increase of the chronic disease, which had thus, apparently, taken too sure hold upon her constitution to be eradicated by human means, I could not fail to observe a similar increase in the nervous irritation of her temperament, and in her excitability by trivial causes of fear. She spoke again, and now more frequently and pertinaciously, of the sounds—of the light sounds—and of the unusual motions among the tapestries, to which she had formerly alluded.

One night, near the closing in of September, she pressed this distressing subject with more than usual emphasis upon my attention. She had just awakened from an unquiet slumber, and I had been watching, with feelings half of anxiety, half of vague terror, the workings of her emaciated countenance. I sat by the side of her ebony bed, upon one of the ottomans of India. She partly arose, and spoke, in an earnest low whisper, of sounds which she then heard, but which I could not hear—of motions which she then saw, but which I could not perceive. The wind was rushing hurriedly behind the tapestries, and I wished to show her (what, let me confess it, I could not all believe) that those almost inarticulate breathings, and those very gentle variations of the figures upon the wall, were but the natural effects of that customary rushing of the wind. But a deadly pallor, overspreading her face, had proved to me that my exertions to reassure her would be fruitless. She appeared to be fainting, and no attendants were within call. I remembered where was deposited a decanter of light wine which had been ordered by her physicians, and hastened across the chamber to procure it. But, as I stepped beneath the light of the censer, two circumstances of a startling nature attracted my attention. I had felt that some palpable although invisible object had passed lightly by my person; and I saw that there lay upon the golden carpet, in the very middle of the rich luster thrown from the censer, a shadow—a faint, indefinite shadow of angelic aspect—such as might be fancied for the shadow of a shade. But I was wild with the excitement of an immoderate dose of opium, and heeded these things but little, nor spoke of them to Rowena. Having found the wine, I recrossed the chamber, and poured out a gobletful, which I held to the lips of the fainting lady. She had now partially recovered, however, and took the vessel herself, which I sank upon an ottoman near me, with my eyes fastened upon her person. It was then that I became distinctly aware of a gentle foot-fall upon the carpet, and near the couch; and in a second thereafter, as Rowena was in the act of raising the wine to her lips, I saw, or may have dreamed that I saw, fall within the goblet, as if from some invisible spring in the atmosphere of the room, three or four large drops of a brilliant and ruby colored fluid. If this I saw—not so

Rowena. She swallowed the wine unhesitatingly, and I forbore to speak to her of a circumstance which must, after all, I considered, have been but the suggestion of a vivid imagination, rendered morbidly active by the terror of the lady, by the opium, and by the hour.

Yet I cannot conceal it from my own perception that, immediately subsequent to the fall of the ruby-drops, a rapid change for the worse took place in the disorder of my wife; so that, on the third subsequent night, the hands of her menials prepared her for the tomb, and on the fourth, I sat alone, with her shrouded body, in that fantastic chamber which had received her as my bride. Wild visions, opium-engendered, flitted, shadow-like, before me. I gazed with unquiet eye upon the sarcophagi in the angles of the room, upon the varying figures of the drapery, and upon the writhing of the parti-colored fires in the censer overhead. My eyes then fell, as I called to mind the circumstances of a former night, to the spot beneath the glare of the censer where I had seen the faint traces of shadow. It was there, however, no longer; and breathing with greater freedom, I turned my glances to the pallid and rigid figure in the bed. Then rushed upon me a thousand memories of Ligeia—and then came back upon my heart, with the turbulent violence of a flood, the whole of that unutterable woe with which I had regarded her thus enshrouded. The night waned; and still, with a bosom full of bitter thoughts of the one only and supremely beloved, I remained gazing upon the body of Rowena.

It might have been midnight, or perhaps earlier, or later, for I had taken no note of time, when a sob, low, gentle, but very distinct, startled me from my revery. I felt that it came from the bed of ebony—the bed of death. I listened in an agony of superstitious terror—but there was no repetition of the sound. I strained my vision to detect any motion in the corpse—but there was not the slightest perceptible. Yet I could not have been deceived. I had heard the noise, however faint, and my soul was awakened within me. I resolutely and perseveringly kept my attention riveted upon the body. Many minutes elapsed before any circumstance occurred tending to throw light upon the mystery. At length it became evident that a slight, a very feeble, and barely noticeable tinge of color had flushed up within the cheeks, and along the sunken small veins of the eyelids. Through a species of unutterable horror and awe, for which the language of mortality has no sufficiently energetic expression, I felt my heart cease to beat, my limbs grow rigid where I sat. Yet a sense of duty finally operated to restore my self-possession. I could no longer doubt that we had been precipitate in our preparations—that Rowena still lived. It was necessary that some immediate exertion be made; yet the turret was altogether apart from the portion of the abbey tenanted by the servants—there were none within call—I had no means of summoning them to my aid without leaving the room for many minutes—and this I could not venture to do. I therefore struggled alone in my endeavors to call back the spirit still hovering. In a short period it was certain, however, that a relapse had taken place; the color disappeared from both eyelid and cheek, leaving a wanness even more than that of marble; the lips became doubly shriveled and pinched up in the ghastly expression of death; a repulsive clamminess and coldness overspread rapidly at the surface of the body; and all the usual rigorous stiffness immediately supervened. I fell back with a shudder upon the couch from which I had been so startlingly aroused, and again gave myself up to passionate waking visions of Ligeia.

An hour thus elapsed, when (could it be possible?) I was a second time aware of some vague sound issuing from the region of the bed. I listened—in extremity of horror. The sound came again—it was a sigh. Rushing to the corpse, I saw—distinctly saw—a tremor upon the lips. In a minute afterward they relaxed, disclosing a bright line of the pearly teeth. Amazement now struggled in my bosom with the profound awe which had hitherto reigned there alone. I felt that my vision grew dim, that my reason wandered; and it was only by a violent effort that I at length succeeded in nerving myself to the task which duty thus once more had pointed out. There was now a partial glow upon the forehead and upon the cheek and throat; a perceptible warmth pervaded the whole frame; there was even a slight pulsation at the heart. The lady lived; and with redoubled ardor I betook myself to the task of restoration. I chafed and bathed the temples and the hands, and used every exertion which experience, and no little medical reading, could suggest. But in vain. Suddenly, the color fled, the pulsation ceased, the lips resumed the expression of the dead, and, in an instant afterward, the whole body took upon itself the icy chilliness, the livid hue, the intense rigidity, the sunken outline, and all the loathsome peculiarities of that which has been, for many days, a tenant of the tomb.

And again I sunk into visions of Ligeia—and again (what marvel that I shudder while I write?), again there reached my ears a low sob from the region of the ebony bed. But why shall I pause to relate how, time after time, until near the period of the gray dawn, this hideous drama of revivification was repeated; how each terrific relapse was only into a sterner and apparently more irredeemable death; how each agony wore the aspect of a struggle with some invisible foe; and how each struggle was succeeded by I know not what of wild change in the personal appearance of the corpse? Let me hurry to a conclusion.

The greater part of the fearful night had worn away, and she who had been dead once again stirred—and now more vigorously than hitherto, although arousing from a dissolution more appalling in its utter hopelessness than any. I had long ceased to struggle or to move, and remained sitting rigidly upon the ottoman, a helpless prey to a whirl of violent emotions, of which extreme awe was perhaps the least terrible, the least consuming. The corpse, I repeat, stirred, and now more vigorously than before. The hues of life flushed up with unwonted energy into the countenance—the limbs relaxed—and, save that the eyelids were yet pressed heavily together, and that the bandages and draperies of the grave still imparted their charnel character to the figure, I might have dreamed that Rowena had indeed shaken off, utterly, the fetters of Death. But if this idea was not, even then, altogether adopted, I could at least doubt no longer, when, arising from the bed, tottering, with feeble steps, with closed eyes, and with the manner of one bewildered in a dream, the thing that was enshrouded advanced boldly and palpably into the middle of the apartment.

I trembled not—I stirred not—for a crowd of unutterable fancies connected with the air, the stature, the demeanor, of the figure, rushing hurriedly through my brain, had paralyzed—had chilled me into stone. I stirred not—but gazed upon the apparition. There was a mad disorder in my thoughts—a tumult unappeasable. Could it, indeed, be the living Rowena who confronted me? Could it, indeed, be Rowena at all?—the fair-haired, the blue-eyed Lady Rowena Trevanion of Tremaine? Why,

why should I doubt it? The bandage lay heavily about the mouth—but then might it not be the mouth of the breathing Lady of Tremaine? And the cheeks—there were the roses as in her noon of life—yes, these might indeed be the fair cheeks of the living Lady of Tremaine. And the chin, with its dimples, as in health, might it not be hers?—but had she then grown taller since her malady? What inexpressible madness seized me with that thought? One bound, and I had reached her feet! Shrinking from my touch, she let fall from her head, unloosed, the ghastly cerements which had confined it, and there streamed forth into the rushing atmosphere of the chamber huge masses of long and disheveled hair; it was blacker than the raven wings of midnight! And now slowly opened the eyes of the figure which stood before me. 'Here then, at least,' I shrieked aloud, 'can I never—can I never be mistaken—these are the full, and the black, and the wild eyes—of my lost love—of the Lady—of the Lady Ligeia.'

The Secret of Macarger's Gulch

By Ambrose Bierce

NORTHWESTWARDLY FROM INDIAN HILL, ABOUT NINE MILES AS THE crow flies, is Macarger's Gulch. It is not much of a gulch—a mere depression between two wooded ridges of inconsiderable height. From its mouth up to its head—for gulches, like rivers, have an anatomy of their own—the distance does not exceed two miles, and the width at bottom is at only one place more than a dozen yards; for most of the distance on either side of the little brook which drains it in the winter, and goes dry in the early spring, there is no level ground at all; the steep slopes of the hills covered with an almost impenetrable growth of manzanita and chemisal, are parted by nothing but the width of the watercourse. No one but an occasional enterprising hunter of the vicinity ever goes into Macarger's Gulch, and five miles away it is unknown, even by name. Within that distance in any direction are far more conspicuous topographical features without names, and one might try in vain to ascertain by local inquiry the origin of the name of this one.

About midway between the head and the mouth of Macarger's Gulch, the hill on the right as you ascend is cloven by another gulch, a short dry one, and at the junction of the two is a level space of two or three acres, and there a few years ago stood an old board house containing one small room. How the component parts of the house, few and simple as they were, had been assembled at that almost inaccessible point is a problem in the solution of which there would be greater satisfaction than advantage. Possibly the creek bed is a reformed road. It is certain that the gulch was at one time pretty thoroughly prospected by miners, who must have had some means of getting in with at least pack animals carrying tools and supplies; their profits, apparently, were not such as would have justified any considerable outlay to connect Macarger's Gulch with any centre of civilization enjoying the distinction of a saw-mill. The house, however, was there, most of it. It lacked a door and a window frame, and the chimney of mud and stones had fallen into an unlovely heap, over-grown with rank weeds. Such humble furniture as there may once have been and much of the lower weather-boarding, had served as fuel in the camp fires of hunters; as had also, probably, the kerbing of an old well, which at the time I write of existed in the form of a rather wide but not very deep depression nearby.

One afternoon in the summer of 1874, I passed up Macarger's Gulch from the narrow valley into which it opens, by following the dry bed of the brook. I was quail-shooting and had made a bag of about a dozen birds by the time I had reached the house described, of whose existence I was until then unaware. After rather carelessly inspecting the ruin I resumed my sport, and having fairly good success prolonged it until near sunset, when it occurred to me that I was a long way from any human habitation—too far to reach one by nightfall. But in my game bag was food, and the old house would afford shelter, if shelter were needed on a warm and dewless night in the foothills of the Sierra Nevada, where one may sleep in comfort on the pine needles, without covering. I am fond of solitude and love the night, so my resolution to "camp out" was soon taken, and by the time that it was dark I had made my bed of boughs and grasses in a corner of the room and was roasting a quail at a fire that I had kindled on the hearth. The smoke escaped out of the ruined chimney, the light illuminated the room with a kindly glow, and as I ate my simple meal of plain bird and drank the remains of a bottle of red wine which had served me all the afternoon in place of water, which the region did not supply, I experienced a sense of comfort which better fare and accom-modations do not always give.

Nevertheless, there was something lacking. I had a sense of comfort, but not of security. I detected myself staring more frequently at the open doorway and blank window than I could find warrant for doing. Outside these apertures all was black, and I was unable to repress a certain feeling of apprehension as my fancy pictured the outer world and filled it with unfriendly entities, natural and supernatural—chief among which, in their respective classes, were the grizzly bear, which I knew was occasionally still seen in that region, and the ghost, which I had reason to think was not. Unfortunately, our feelings do not always respect the law of probabilities, and to me that evening, the possible and the impossible were equally disquieting.

Every one who has had experience in the matter must have observed that one confronts the actual and imaginary perils of the night with far less apprehension in the open air than in a house with an open doorway. I felt this now as I lay on my leafy couch in a corner of the room next to the chimney and permitted my fire to die out. So strong became my sense of the presence of something malign and menacing in the place, that I found myself almost unable to withdraw my eyes from the opening, as in the deepening darkness it became more and more indistinct. And when the last little flame flickered and went out I grasped the shotgun which I had laid at my side and actually turned the muzzle in the direction of the now invisible entrance, my thumb on one of the hammers, ready to cock the piece, my breath suspended, my muscles rigid and tense. But later I laid down the weapon with a sense of shame and mortification. What did I fear, and why?—I, to whom the night had been a more familiar face than that of man—I, in whom that element of hereditary superstition from which none of us is altogether free had given to solitude and darkness and silence only a more alluring interest and charm! I was unable to comprehend my folly, and losing in the conjecture the thing conjectured of, I fell asleep. And then I dreamed.

I was in a great city in a foreign land—a city whose people were of my own race, with minor differences of speech and costume; yet precisely what these were I could not say; my sense of them was indistinct. The city was dominated by a great castle upon an overlooking height whose name I knew but could not speak. I walked through many streets, some broad and straight with high, modern buildings, some narrow, gloomy, and tortuous, between the gables of quaint old houses whose overhanging stories, elaborately ornamented with carvings in wood and stone, almost met above my head.

I sought someone whom I had never seen, yet knew that I should recognize when found. My quest was not aimless and fortuitous; it had a definite method. I turned from one street into another without hesitation and threaded a maze of intricate passages, devoid of the fear of losing my way.

Presently I stopped before a low door in a plain stone house which might have been the dwelling of an artisan of the better sort, and without announcing myself, entered. The room, rather sparsely furnished, and lighted by a single window with small diamond-shaped panes, had but two occupants: a man and a woman. They took no notice of my intrusion, a circumstance which, in the manner of dreams, appeared entirely natural. They were not conversing; they sat apart, unoccupied and sullen.

The woman was young and rather stout, with fine large eyes and a certain grave beauty; my memory of her expression is exceedingly vivid, but in dreams one does not observe the details of faces. About her shoulders was a plaid shawl. The man was older, dark, with an evil face made more forbidding by a long scar extending from near the left temple diagonally downward into the black moustache; though in my dreams it seemed rather to haunt the face as a thing apart—I can express it no otherwise—than to belong to it. The moment that I found the man and woman I knew them to be husband and wife.

What followed, I remember indistinctly; all was confused and inconsistent—made so, I think, by gleams of consciousness. It was as if two pictures, the scene of my dream, and my actual surroundings, had been blended, one overlying the other, until the former, gradually fading, disappeared, and I was broad awake in the deserted cabin entirely and tranquilly conscious of my situation.

My foolish fear was gone, and opening my eyes I saw that my fire, not altogether burned out, had revived by the falling of a stick and was again lighting the room. I had probably slept only a few minutes, but my commonplace dream had somehow so strongly impressed me that I was no longer drowsy; and after a little while I rose, pushed the embers of my fire together, and lighting my pipe proceeded in a rather ludicrously methodical way to meditate upon my vision.

It would have puzzled me then to say in what respect it was worth attention. In the first moment of serious thought that I gave to the matter I recognized the city of my dream as Edinburgh, where I had never been; so if the dream was a memory it was a memory of pictures and description. The recognition somehow deeply impressed me; it was as if something in my mind insisted rebelliously against will and reason on the importance of all this. And that faculty, whatever it was, asserted also a control of my speech. "Surely," I said aloud, quite involuntarily, "the Mac-Gregors must have come here from Edinburgh."

At the moment, neither the substance of this remark nor the fact of my making it, surprised me in the least; it seemed entirely natural that I should know the name of my dreamfolk and something of their history. But the absurdity of it all soon dawned upon me; I laughed aloud, knocked the ashes from my pipe and again stretched myself upon my bed of boughs and grass, where I lay staring absently into my failing fire, with no further thought of either my dream or my surroundings. Suddenly the single remaining flame crouched for a moment, then, springing upward, lifted itself clear of its embers and expired in air. The darkness was absolute.

At that instant—almost, it seemed, before the gleam of the blaze had faded from my eyes—there was a dull, dead sound, as of some heavy body falling upon the floor, which shook beneath me as I lay. I sprang to a sitting posture and groped at my side for my gun; my notion was that some wild beast had leaped in through the open window. While the flimsy structure was still shaking from the impact I heard the sound of blows, the scuffling of feet upon the floor, and then—it seemed to come from almost within reach of my hand—the sharp shrieking of a woman in mortal agony. So horrible a cry I had never heard nor conceived; it utterly unnerved me; I was conscious for a moment of nothing but my own terror! Fortunately my hand now found the weapon of which it was in search, and the familiar touch somewhat restored me. I leaped to my feet, straining my eyes to pierce the darkness. The violent sounds had ceased, but more terrible than these, I heard, at what seemed long intervals, the faint intermittent gasping of some living, dying thing!

As my eyes grew accustomed to the dim light of the coals in the fireplace, I saw first the shapes of the door and window looking blacker than the black of the walls. Next, the distinction between wall and floor became discernible, and at last I was sensible to the form and full expanse of the floor from end to end and side to side. Nothing was visible, and the silence was unbroken.

With a hand that shook a little, the other still grasping my gun, I restored my fire and made a critical examination of the place. There was nowhere any sign that the cabin had been entered. My own tracks were visible in the dust covering the floor, but there were no others. I relit my pipe, provided fresh fuel by ripping a thin board or two from the inside of the house—I did not care to go into the darkness out of doors—and passed the rest of the night smoking and thinking, and feeding my fire; not for added years of life would I have permitted that little flame to expire again.

Some years afterward I met in Sacramento a man named Morgan, to whom I had a note of introduction from a friend in San Francisco. Dining with him one evening at his home I observed various "trophies" upon the wall, indicating that he was fond of shooting. It turned out that he was, and in relating some of his feats he mentioned having been in the region of my adventure.

"Mr. Morgan," I asked abruptly, "do you know a place up there called Macarger's Gulch?"

"I have good reason to," he replied. "It was I who gave to the newspapers, last year, the accounts of the finding of the skeleton there."

I had not heard of it; the accounts had been published, it appeared, while I was absent in the East.

"By the way," said Morgan, "the name of the gulch is a corruption; it should have been called 'MacGregor's.' My dear," he added, speaking to his wife, "Mr. Elderson has upset his wine."

That was hardly accurate—I had simply dropped it, glass and all.

"There was an old shanty once in the gulch," Morgan resumed when the ruin wrought by my awkwardness had been repaired, "but just previously to my visit it had been blown down, or rather blown away, for its debris was scattered all about, the very floor being parted, plank from plank. Between two of the sleepers still in position I and my companion observed the remnant of a plaid shawl, and examining it found that it was wrapped about the shoulders of the body of a woman; of course but little remained besides the bones, partly covered with fragments of clothing, and brown dry skin. But we will spare Mrs. Morgan," he added with a smile. The lady had indeed exhibited signs of disgust rather than sympathy.

"It is necessary to say, however," he went on, "that the skull was fractured in several places, as by blows of some blunt instrument; and that instrument itself—a pick-handle, still stained with blood—lay under the boards nearby."

Mr. Morgan turned to his wife. "Pardon me, my dear," he said with affected solemnity, "for mentioning these disagreeable particulars, the natural though regrettable incidents of a conjugal quarrel—resulting, doubtless, from the luckless wife's insubordination."

"I ought to be able to overlook it," the lady replied with composure; "you have so many times asked me to in those very words."

I thought he seemed rather glad to go on with his story.

"From these and other circumstances," he said, "the coroner's jury found that the deceased, Janet MacGregor, came to her death from blows inflicted by some person to the jury unknown; but it was added that the evidence pointed strongly to her husband, Thomas MacGregor, as the guilty person. But Thomas MacGregor has never been found nor heard of. It was learned that the couple came from Edinburgh, but not—my dear, do you not observe that Mr. Elderson's bone plate has water in it?"

I had deposited a chicken bone in my finger bowl.

"In a little cupboard I found a photograph of MacGregor, but it did not lead to his capture."

"Will you let me see it?" I said.

The picture showed a dark man with an evil face made more forbidding by a long scar extending from near the temple diagonally downward into the black moustache.

"By the way, Mr. Elderson," said my affable host, "may I know why you asked about 'Macarger's Gulch'?"

"I lost a mule near there once," I replied, "and the mischance has—has quite—upset me."

"My dear," said Mr. Morgan, with the mechanical intonation of an interpreter translating, "the loss of Mr. Elderson's mule has peppered his coffee."

32

The Old Nurse's Story

Elizabeth Gaskell

YOU KNOW, MY DEARS, THAT YOUR MOTHER WAS AN ORPHAN, AND AN only child; and I dare say you have heard that your grandfather was a clergyman up in Westmoreland, where I come from. I was just a girl in the village school, when, one day, your grandmother came in to ask the mistress if there was any scholar there who would do for a nursemaid; and mighty proud I was, I can tell ye, when the mistress called me up, and spoke to my being a good girl at my needle, and a steady, honest girl, and one whose parents were very respectable, though they might be poor. I thought I should like nothing better than to serve the pretty, young lady, who was blushing as deep as I was, as she spoke of the coming baby, and what I should have to do with it. However, I see you don't care so much for this part of my story, as for what you think is to come, so I'll tell you at once. I was engaged and settled at the parsonage before Miss Rosamond (that was the baby, who is now your mother) was born. To be sure, I had little enough to do with her when she came, for she was never out of her mother's arms, and slept by her all night long; and proud enough was I sometimes when missis trusted her to me. There never was such a baby before or since, though you've all of you been fine enough in your turns; but for sweet, winning ways, you've none of you come up to your mother. She took after her mother, who was a real lady born; a Miss Furnivall, a granddaughter of Lord Furnivall's, in Northumberland. I believe she had neither brother nor sister, and had been brought up in my lord's family till she had married your grandfather, who was just a curate, son to a shopkeeper in Carlisle—but a clever, fine gentleman as ever was—and one who was a right-down hard worker in his parish, which was very wide, and scattered ill abroad over the Westmoreland Fells. When your mother, little Miss Rosamond, was about four or five years old, both her parents died in a fortnight—one after the other. Ah! that was a sad time. My pretty young mistress and me was looking for another baby, when my master came home from one of his long rides, wet, and tired, and took the fever he died of; and then she never held up her head again, but lived just to see her dead baby, and have it laid on her breast before she sighed away her life. My mistress had asked me, on her death-bed, never to leave Miss Rosamond; but if she had never spoken a word, I would have gone with the little child to the end of the world.

The next thing, and before we had well stilled our sobs, the executors and guardians came to settle the affairs. They were my poor young mistress's own cousin, Lord Furnivall, and Mr. Esthwaite, my master's brother, a shopkeeper in Manchester; not so well to do then, as he was afterwards, and with a large family rising about him. Well! I don't know if it were their settling, or because of a letter my mistress wrote on her death-bed to her cousin, my lord; but somehow it was settled that Miss Rosamond and me were to go to Furnivall Manor House, in Northumberland, and my lord spoke as if it had been her mother's wish that she should live with his family, and as if he had no objections, for that one or two more or less could make no difference in so grand a household. So, though that was not the way in which I should have wished the coming of my bright and pretty pet to have been looked at—who was like a sunbeam in any family, be it never so grand—I was well pleased that all the folks in the Dale should stare and admire, when they heard I was going to be young lady's maid at my Lord Furnivall's at Furnivall Manor.

But I made a mistake in thinking we were to go and live where my lord did. It turned out that the family had left Furnivall Manor House fifty years or more. I could not hear that my poor young mistress had ever been there, though she had been brought up in the family; and I was sorry for that, for I should have liked Miss Rosamond's youth to have passed where her mother's had been.

My lord's gentleman, from whom I asked as many questions as I durst, said that the Manor House was at the foot of the Cumberland Fells, and a very grand place; that an old Miss Furnivall, a great-aunt of my lord's, lived there, with only a few servants; but that it was a very healthy place, and my lord had thought that it would suit Miss Rosamond very well for a few years, and that her being there might perhaps amuse his old aunt.

I was bidden by my lord to have Miss Rosamond's things ready by a certain day. He was a stern proud man, as they say all the Lords Furnivall were; and he never spoke a word more than was necessary. Folk did say he had loved my young mistress; but that, because she knew that his father would object, she would never listen to him, and married Esthwaite; but I don't know. He never married at any rate. But he never took much notice of Miss Rosamond; which I thought he might have done if he had cared for her dead mother. He sent his gentleman with us to the Manor House, telling him to join him at Newcastle that same evening; so there was no great length of time for him to make us known to all the strangers before he, too, shook us off; and we were left, two lonely young things (I was not eighteen), in the great old Manor House. It seems like yesterday that we drove there. We had left our own dear parsonage very early, and we had both cried as if our hearts would break, though we were travelling in my lord's carriage, which I thought so much of once. And now it was long past noon on a September day, and we stopped to change horses for the last time at a little, smoky town, all full of colliers and miners. Miss Rosamond had fallen asleep, but Mr. Henry told me to waken her, that she might see the park and the Manor House as we drove up. I thought it rather a pity; but I did what he bade me, for fear he should complain of me to my lord. We had left all signs of a town, or even a village, and were then inside the gates of a large, wild park—not like the parks here in the south, but with rocks, and the noise of running water, and gnarled thorn-trees, and old oaks, all white and peeled with age.

The road went up about two miles, and then we saw a great and stately house, with many trees close around it, so close that in some places their branches dragged against the walls when the wind blew; and some hung broken down; for no one seemed to take much charge of the place; —to lop the wood, or to keep the moss-covered carriage-way in order. Only in front of the house all was clear. The great oval drive was without a weed; and neither tree nor creeper was allowed to grow over the long, many-windowed front; at both sides of which a wing projected, which were each the ends of other side fronts; for the house, although it was so desolate, was even grander than I expected. Behind it rose the Fells, which seemed unenclosed and bare enough; and on the left hand of the house, as you stood facing it, was a little, old-fashioned flower-garden, as I found out afterwards. A door opened out upon it from the west front; it had been scooped out of the thick dark wood for some old Lady Furnivall; but the branches of the great forest trees had grown and overshadowed it again, and there were very few flowers that would live there at that time.

When we drove up to the great front entrance, and went into the hall I thought we should be lost—it was so large, and vast, and grand. There was a chandelier all of bronze, hung down from the middle of the ceiling; and I had never seen one before, and looked at it all in amazement. Then, at one end of the hall, was a great fireplace, as large as the sides of the houses in my country, with massy andirons and dogs to hold the wood; and by it were heavy, old-fashioned sofas. At the opposite end of the hall, to the left as you went in—on the western side—was an organ built into the wall, and so large that it filled up the best part of that end. Beyond it, on the same side, was a door; and opposite, on each side of the fireplace, were also doors leading to the east front; but those I never went through as long as I stayed in the house, so I can't tell you what lay beyond.

The afternoon was closing in and the hall, which had no fire lighted in it, looked dark and gloomy, but we did not stay there a moment. The old servant, who had opened the door for us, bowed to Mr. Henry, and took us in through the door at the further side of the great organ, and led us through several smaller halls and passages into the west drawing-room, where he said that Miss Furnivall was sitting. Poor little Miss Rosamond held very tight to me, as if she were scared and lost in that great place, and as for myself, I was not much better. The west drawing-room was very cheerful-looking, with a warm fire in it, and plenty of good, comfortable furniture about. Miss Furnivall was an old lady not far from eighty, I should think, but I do not know. She was thin and tall, and had a face as full of fine wrinkles as if they had been drawn all over it with a needle's point. Her eyes were very watchful to make up, I suppose, for her being so deaf as to be obliged to use a trumpet. Sitting with her, working at the same great piece of tapestry, was Mrs. Stark, her maid and companion, and almost as old as she was. She had lived with Miss Furnivall ever since they both were young, and now she seemed more like a friend than a servant; she looked so cold, and grey, and stony, as if she had never loved or cared for any one; and I don't suppose she did care for any one, except her mistress; and, owing to the great deafness of the latter, Mrs. Stark treated her very much as if she were a child. Mr. Henry gave some message from my lord, and then he bowed good-bye to us all,—taking no notice of my sweet little Miss Rosamond's outstretched hand—and left us standing there, being looked at by the two old ladies through their spectacles.

I was right glad when they rung for the old footman who had shown us in at first, and told him to take us to our rooms. So we went out of that great drawing-room, and into another sitting-room, and out of that, and then up a great flight of stairs, and along a broad gallery—which was something like a library, having books all down one side, and windows and writing-tables all down the other—till we came to our rooms, which I was not sorry to hear were just over the kitchens; for I began to think I should be lost in that wilderness of a house. There was an old nursery, that had been used for all the little lords and ladies long ago, with a pleasant fire burning in the grate, and the kettle boiling on the hob, and tea things spread out on the table; and out of that room was the night-nursery, with a little crib for Miss Rosamond close to my bed. And old James called up Dorothy, his wife, to bid us welcome; and both he and she were so hospitable and kind, that by and by Miss Rosamond and me felt quite at home; and by the time tea was over, she was sitting on Dorothy's knee, and chattering away as fast as her little tongue could go. I soon found out that Dorothy was from Westmoreland, and that bound her and me together, as it were; and I would never wish to meet with kinder people than were old James and his wife. James had lived pretty nearly all his life in my lord's family, and thought there was no one so grand as they. He even looked down a little on his wife; because, till he had married her, she had never lived in any but a farmer's household. But he was very fond of her, as well he might be. They had one servant under them, to do all the rough work. Agnes they called her; and she and me, and James and Dorothy, with Miss Furnivall and Mrs. Stark, made up the family; always remembering my sweet little Miss Rosamond! I used to wonder what they had done before she came, they thought so much of her now. Kitchen and drawing-room, it was all the same. The hard, sad Miss Furnivall, and the cold Mrs. Stark, looked pleased when she came fluttering in like a bird, playing and pranking hither and thither, with a continual murmur, and pretty prattle of gladness. I am sure, they were sorry many a time when she flitted away into the kitchen, though they were too proud to ask her to stay with them, and were a little surprised at her taste; though to be sure, as Mrs. Stark said, it was not to be wondered at, remembering what stock her father had come of. The great, old rambling house was a famous place for little Miss Rosamond. She made expeditions all over it, with me at her heels; all, except the east wing, which was never opened, and whither we never thought of going. But in the western and northern part was many a pleasant room; full of things that were curiosities to us, though they might not have been to people who had seen more. The windows were darkened by the sweeping boughs of the trees, and the ivy which had overgrown them: but, in the green gloom, we could manage to see old China jars and carved ivory boxes, and great, heavy books, and, above all, the old pictures!

Once, I remember, my darling would have Dorothy go with us to tell us who they all were; for they were all portraits of some of my lord's family, though Dorothy could not tell us the names of every one. We had gone through most of the rooms, when we came to the old state drawing-room over the hall, and there was a picture of Miss Furnivall; or, as she was called in those days, Miss Grace, for she was the younger sister. Such a beauty she must have been! but with such a set, proud look, and such scorn looking out of her handsome eyes, with her eyebrows just a little raised, as if she wondered how any one could have the impertinence to look at her; and her lip curled at us, as we stood there gazing. She had a dress on, the like of which I had never seen before, but it was all the fashion when she was young: a hat of some soft, white stuff like beaver, pulled a little over her brows, and a beautiful plume of feathers sweeping round it on one side; and her gown of blue satin was open in front to a quilted, white stomacher.

'Well, to be sure!' said I, when I had gazed my fill. 'Flesh is grass, they do say; but who would have thought that Miss Furnivall had been such an out-and-out beauty, to see her now?'

'Yes,' said Dorothy. 'Folks change sadly. But if what my master's father used to say was true, Miss Furnivall, the elder sister, was handsomer than Miss Grace. Her picture is here somewhere; but, if I show it you, you must never let on, even to James, that you have seen it. Can the little lady hold her tongue, think you?' asked she.

I was not so sure, for she was such a little, sweet, bold, open-spoken child, so I set her to hide herself; and then I helped Dorothy to turn a great picture, that leaned with its face towards the wall, and was not hung up as the others were. To be sure, it beat Miss Grace for beauty; and, I think, for scornful pride, too, though in that matter it might be hard to choose. I could have looked at it an hour, but Dorothy seemed half frightened at having shown it to me, and hurried it back again, and bade me run and find Miss Rosamond, for that there were some ugly places about the house, where she should like ill for the child to go. I was a brave, high-spirited girl, and thought little of what the old woman said, for I liked hide-and-seek as well as any child in the parish; so off I ran to find my little one.

As winter drew on, and the days grew shorter, I was sometimes almost certain that I heard a noise as if some one was playing on the great organ in the hall. I did not hear it every evening; but, certainly, I did very often; usually when I was sitting with Miss Rosamond, after I had put her to bed, and keeping quite still and silent in the bedroom. Then I used to hear it booming and swelling away in the distance. The first night, when I went down to my supper, I asked Dorothy who had been playing music, and James said very shortly that I was a gowk to take the wind soughing among the trees for music: but I saw Dorothy look at him very fearfully, and Agnes, the kitchen-maid, said something beneath her breath, and went quite white. I saw they did not like my question, so I held my peace till I was with Dorothy alone, when I knew I could get a good deal out of her. So, the next day, I watched my time, and I coaxed and asked her who it was that played the organ; for I knew that it was the organ and not the wind well enough, for all I had kept silence before James. But Dorothy had had her lesson I'll warrant, and never a word could I get from her. So then I tried Agnes, though I had always held my head rather above her, as I was even to James and Dorothy, and she was little better than their servant. So she said I must never, never tell; and if I ever told, I was never to say she had told me; but it was a very strange noise, and she had heard it many a time, but most of all on winter nights, and before storms; and folks did say, it was the old lord playing on the great organ in the hall, just as he used to do when he was alive; but who the old lord was, or why he played, and why he played on stormy winter evenings in particular, she either could not or would not tell me. Well! I told you I had a brave heart; and I thought it was rather pleasant to have that grand music rolling about the house, let who would be the player; for now it rose above the great gusts of wind, and wailed and triumphed just like a living creature, and then it fell to a softness most complete; only it was always music, and tunes, so it was nonsense to call it the wind. I thought at first, that it might be Miss Furnivall who played, unknown to Agnes; but, one day when I was in the hall by myself, I opened the organ and peeped all about it and around it, as I had done to the organ in Crosthwaite Church once before, and I saw it was all broken and destroyed inside, though it looked so brave and fine; and then, though it was noon-day, my flesh began to creep a little, and I shut it up, and run away pretty quickly to my own bright nursery; and I did not like hearing the music for some time after that, any more than James and Dorothy did. All this time Miss Rosamond was making herself more and more beloved. The old ladies liked her to dine with them at their early dinner; James stood behind Miss Furnivall's chair, and I behind Miss Rosamond's all in state; and, after dinner, she would play about in a corner of the great drawing-room, as still as any mouse, while Miss Furnivall slept, and I had my dinner in the kitchen. But she was glad enough to come to me in the nursery afterwards; for, as she said, Miss Furnivall was so sad, and Mrs. Stark so dull; but she and I were merry enough; and, by-and-by, I got not to care for that weird rolling music, which did one no harm, if we did not know where it came from.

That winter was very cold. In the middle of October the frosts began, and lasted many, many weeks. I remember, one day at dinner, Miss Furnivall lifted up her sad, heavy eyes, and said to Mrs. Stark, 'I am afraid we shall have a terrible winter,' in a strange kind of meaning way. But Mrs. Stark pretended not to hear, and talked very loud of something else. My little lady and I did not care for the frost; not we! As long as it was dry we climbed up the steep brows, behind the house, and went up on the Fells, which were bleak, and bare enough, and there we ran races in the fresh, sharp air; and once we came down by a new path that took us past the two old, gnarled holly-trees, which grew about half-way down by the east side of the house. But the days grew shorter, and shorter; and the old lord, if it was he, played away more, and more stormily and sadly on the great organ. One Sunday afternoon,—it must have been towards the end of November—I asked Dorothy to take charge of little Missey when she came out of the drawing-room, after Miss Furnivall had had her nap; for it was too cold to take her with me to church, and yet I wanted to go. And Dorothy was glad enough to promise, and was so fond of the child that all seemed well; and Agnes and I set off very briskly, though the sky hung heavy and black over the white earth, as if the night had never fully gone away; and the air, though still, was very biting and keen.

'We shall have a fall of snow,' said Agnes to me. And sure enough, even while we were in church, it came down thick, in great, large flakes, so thick it almost darkened the windows. It had stopped snowing before we came out, but it lay soft, thick and deep beneath our feet, as we tramped home. Before we got to the hall the moon rose, and I think it was lighter then,—what with the moon, and what with the white dazzling snow— than it had been when we went to church, between two and three o'clock. I have not told you that Miss Furnivall and Mrs. Stark never went to church: they used to read the prayers together, in their quiet, gloomy way; they seemed to feel the Sunday very long without their tapestry-work to be busy at. So when I went to Dorothy in the kitchen, to fetch Miss Rosamond and take her upstairs with me, I did not much wonder when the old woman told me that the ladies had kept the child with them, and that she had never come to the kitchen, as I had bidden her, when she was tired of behaving pretty in the drawing-room. So I took off my things and went to find her, and bring her her supper in the nursery. But when I went into the best drawing-room, there sat the two old ladies, very still and quiet, dropping out a word now and then, but looking as if nothing so bright and merry as Miss Rosamond had ever been near them. Still I thought she might be hiding from me; it was one of her pretty ways; and that she had persuaded them to look as if they knew nothing about her; so I went softly peeping under this sofa, and behind that chair, making believe I was sadly frightened at not finding her.

'What's the matter, Hester?' said Mrs. Stark sharply. I don't know if Miss Furnivall had seen me, for, as I told you, she was very deaf, and she sat quite still, idly staring into the fire, with her hopeless face. 'I'm only looking for my little Rosy-Posy,' replied I, still thinking that the child was there, and near me, though I could not see her.

'Miss Rosamond is not here,' said Mrs Stark. 'She went away more than an hour ago to find Dorothy.' And she too turned and went on looking into the fire.

My heart sank at this, and I began to wish I had never left my darling. I went back to Dorothy and told her. James was gone out for the day, but she and me and Agnes took lights and went up into the nursery first, and then we roamed over the great large house, calling and entreating Miss Rosamond to come out of her hiding place, and not frighten us to death in that way. But there was no answer; no sound.

'Oh!' said I at last. 'Can she have got into the east wing and hidden there?'

But Dorothy said it was not possible, for that she herself had never been in there; that the doors were always locked, and my lord's steward had the keys, she believed; at any rate, neither she nor James had ever seen them: so, I said I would go back, and see if, after all, she was not hidden in the drawing-room, unknown to the old ladies; and if I found her there, I said, I would whip her well for the fright she had given me; but I never meant to do it. Well, I went back to the west drawing-room, and I told Mrs. Stark we could not find her anywhere, and asked for leave to look all about the furniture there, for I thought now, that she might have fallen asleep in some warm, hidden corner; but no! We looked, Miss

Furnivall got up and looked, trembling all over, and she was nowhere there; then we set off again, every one in the house, and looked in all the places we had searched before, but we could not find her. Miss Furnivall shivered and shook so much, that Mrs. Stark took her back into the warm drawing-room; but not before they had made me promise to bring her to them when she was found. Well-a-day! I began to think she never would be found, when I bethought me to look out into the great front court, all covered with snow. I was upstairs when I looked out; but, it was such dear moonlight, I could see quite plain two little footprints, which might be traced from the hall door, and round the corner of the east wing. I don't know how I got down, but I tugged open the great, stiff hall door; and, throwing the skirt of my gown over head for a cloak, I ran out. I turned the east corner, and there a black shadow fell on the snow; but when I came again into the moonlight, there were the little footmarks going up—up to the Fells. It was bitter cold; so cold that the air almost took the skin off my face as I ran, but I ran on, crying to think how my poor little darling must be perished, and frightened. I was within sight of the holly-trees, when I saw a shepherd coming down the hill, bearing something in his arms wrapped in his maud. He shouted to me, and asked me if I had lost a bairn; and, when I could not speak for crying, he bore towards me, and I saw my wee bairnie lying still, and white, and stiff, in his arms, as if she had been dead. He told me he had been up the Fells to gather in his sheep, before the deep cold of night came on, and that under the holly-trees (black marks on the hillside, where no other bush was for miles around) he had found my little lady—my lamb—my queen—my darling—stiff, and cold, in the terrible sleep which is frost-begotten. Oh! the joy, and the tears, of having her in my arms once again! for I would not let him carry her; but took her, maud and all, into my own arms, and held her near my own warm neck, and heart, and felt the life stealing slowly back again into her little, gentle limbs. But she was still insensible when we reached the hall, and I had no breath for speech. We went in by the kitchen door.

'Bring the warming-pan,' said I; and I carried her upstairs and began undressing her by the nursery fire, which Agnes had kept up. I called my little lammie all the sweet and playful names I could think of,—even while my eyes were blinded by my tears; and at last, oh! at length she opened her large, blue eyes. Then I put her into her warm bed, and sent Dorothy down to tell Miss Furnivall that all was well; and I made up my mind to sit by my darling's bedside the live-long night. She fell away into a soft sleep as soon as her pretty head had touched the pillow, and I watched by her till morning light; when she wakened up bright and clear—or so I thought at first—and, my dears, so I think now.

She said, that she had fancied that she should like to go to Dorothy, for that both the old ladies were asleep, and it was very dull in the draw-ing-room; and that, as she was going through the west lobby, she saw the snow through the high window failing—falling—soft and steady; but she wanted to see it lying pretty and white on the ground; so she made her way into the great hall; and then, going to the window, she saw it bright and soft upon the drive; but while she stood there, she saw a little girl, not as old as she was, 'but so pretty,' said my darling, 'and this little girl beckoned to me to come out; and oh, she was so pretty and so sweet, I could not choose but go.' And then this other little girl had taken her by the hand, and side by side the two had gone round the east corner.

'Now, you are a naughty little girl, and telling stories,' said I. 'What would your good mamma, that is in heaven, and never told a story in her life, say to her little Rosamond, if she heard her—and I dare say she does—telling stories!'

'Indeed, Hester,' sobbed out my child, 'I'm telling you true. Indeed I am.'

'Don't tell me!' said I, very stern. 'I tracked you by your foot-marks through the snow; there were only yours to be seen: and if you had had a little girl to go hand-in-hand with you up the hill, don't you think the foot-prints would have gone along with yours?'

'I can't help it, dear, dear Hester,' said she, crying, 'if they did not; I never looked at her feet, but she held my hand fast and tight in her little one, and it was very, very cold. She took me up the Fell-path, up to the holly trees; and there I saw a lady weeping and crying; but when she saw me, she hushed her weeping, and smiled very proud and grand, and took me on her knee, and began to lull me to sleep; and that's all, Hes-ter—but that is true; and my dear mamma knows it is,' said she, crying.

So I thought the child was in a fever, and pretended to believe her, as she went over her story—over and over again, and always the same. At last Dorothy knocked at the door with Miss Rosamond's breakfast; and she told me the old ladies were down in the eating parlour, and that they wanted to speak to me. They had both been into the night-nursery the evening before, but it was after Miss Rosamond was asleep; so they had only looked at her—not asked me any questions.

'I shall catch it,' thought I to myself, as I went along the north gallery. 'And yet,' I thought, taking courage, 'it was in their charge I left her; and it's they that's to blame for letting her steal away unknown and unwatched.' So I went in boldly, and told my story. I told it all to Miss Furnivall, shouting it close to her ear; but when I came to the mention of the other little girl out in the snow, coaxing and tempting her out, and her up to the grand and beautiful lady by the holly-tree, she threw her arms up—her old and withered arms—and cried aloud, 'Oh! Heaven, forgive! Have mercy!'

Mrs. Stark took hold of her; roughly enough, I thought; but she was past Mrs. Stark's management, and spoke to me, in a kind of wild warning and authority.

'Hester! keep her from that child! It will lure her to her death! That evil child! Tell her it is a wicked, naughty child.' Then, Mrs. Stark hurried me out of the room; where, indeed, I was glad enough to go; but Miss Furnivall kept shrieking out, 'Oh! have mercy! Wilt Thou never forgive! It is many a long year ago—'

I was very uneasy in my mind after that. I durst never leave Miss Rosamond, night or day, for fear lest she might slip off again, after some fancy or other; and all the more, because I thought I could make out that Miss Furnivall was crazy, from their odd ways about her; and I was afraid lest something of the same kind (which might be in the family, you know) hung over my darling. And the great frost never ceased all this time; and, whenever it was a more stormy night than usual, between the gusts, and through the wind, we heard the old lord playing on the great organ. But, old lord, or not, wherever Miss Rosamond went, there I followed; for my love for her, pretty, helpless orphan, was stronger than my fear for the grand and terrible sound. Besides, it rested with me to keep her cheerful and merry, as beseemed her age. So we played together, and wandered together, here and there, and everywhere; for I never dared to lose sight of her again in that large and rambling house. And so it happened, that one afternoon, not long before Christmas day, we were playing together on the billiard-table in the great hall (not that we knew the right way of playing, but she liked to roll the smooth ivory balls with her pretty hands, and I liked to do whatever she did); and, by-and-by, without our noticing it, it grew dusk indoors, though it was still light in the open air, and I was thinking of taking her back into the nursery, when, all of sudden, she cried out,—

'Look, Hester! look! there is my poor little girl out in the snow!'

I turned towards the long, narrow windows, and there, sure enough, I saw a little girl, less than my Miss Rosamond dressed all unfit to be out-of-doors such a bitter night—crying, and beating against the window-panes, as if she wanted to be let in. She seemed to sob and wail, till Miss Rosamond could bear it no longer, and was flying to the door to open it, when, all of a sudden, and close upon us, the great organ pealed out so loud and thundering, it fairly made me tremble; and all the more, when I remembered me that, even in the stillness of that dead-cold weather, I had heard no sound of little battering hands upon the window-glass, although the Phantom Child had seemed to put forth all its force; and, although I had seen it wail and cry, no faintest touch of sound had fallen upon my ears. Whether I remembered all this at the very moment, I do not know; the great organ sound had so stunned me into terror; but this I know, I caught up Miss Rosamond before she got the hall-door opened, and clutched her, and carried her away, kicking and screaming, into the large, bright kitchen, where Dorothy and Agnes were busy with their mince-pies.

'What is the matter with my sweet one?' cried Dorothy, as I bore in Miss Rosamond, who was sobbing as if her heart would break.

'She won't let me open the door for my little girl to come in; and she'll die if she is out on the Fells all night. Cruel, naughty Hester,' she said, slapping me; but she might have struck harder, for I had seen a look of ghastly terror on Dorothy's face, which made my very blood run cold.

'Shut the back kitchen door fast, and bolt it well,' said she to Agnes. She said no more; she gave me raisins and almonds to quiet Miss Rosamond: but she sobbed about the little girl in the snow, and would not touch any of the good things. I was thankful when she cried herself to sleep in bed. Then I stole down to the kitchen, and told Dorothy I had made up my mind I would carry my darling back to my father's house in Applethwaite; where, if we lived humbly, we lived at peace. I said I had been frightened enough with the old lord's organ-playing; but now that I had seen for myself this little, moaning child, all decked out as no child in the neighbourhood could be, beating and battering to get in, yet always without any sound or noise—with the dark wound on its right shoulder; and that Miss Rosamond had known it again for the phantom that had nearly lured her to her death (which Dorothy knew was true); I would stand it no longer.

I saw Dorothy change colour once or twice. When I had done, she told me she did not think I could take Miss Rosamond with me, for that she was my lord's ward, and I had no right over her; and she asked me, would I leave the child that I was so fond of, just for sounds and sights that could do me no harm; and that they had all had to get used to in their turns? I was all in a hot, trembling passion; and I said it was very well for her to talk, that knew what these sights and noises betokened, and that had, perhaps, had something to do with the Spectre-Child while it was alive. And I taunted her so, that she told me all she knew, at last; and then I wished I had never been told, for it only made me more afraid than ever.

She said she had heard the tale from old neighbours, that were alive when she was first married; when folks used to come to the hall sometimes, before it had got such a bad name on the countryside: it might not be true, or it might, what she had been told.

The old lord was Miss Furnivall's father—Miss Grace, as Dorothy called her, for Miss Maude was the elder, and Miss Furnivall by rights. The old lord was eaten up with pride. Such a proud man was never seen or heard of; and his daughters were like him. No one was good enough to wed them, although they had choice enough; for they were the great beauties of their day, as I had seen by their portraits, where they hung in the state drawing-room. But, as the old saying is, 'Pride will have a fall'; and these two haughty beauties fell in love with the same man, and he no better than a foreign musician, whom their father had down from London to play music with him at the Manor House. For, above all things, next to his pride, the old lord loved music. He could play on nearly every instrument that ever was heard of: and it was a strange thing it did not soften him; but he was a fierce, dour, old man, and had broken his poor wife's heart with his cruelty, they said. He was mad after music, and would pay any money for it. So he got this foreigner to come; who made such beautiful music, that they said the very birds on the trees stopped their singing to listen. And, by degrees, this foreign gentleman got such a hold over the old lord, that nothing would serve him but that he must come every year; and it was he that had the great organ brought from Holland, and built up in the hall, where it stood now. He taught the old lord to play on it; but many and many a time, when Lord Furnivall was thinking of nothing but his fine organ, and his finer music, the dark foreigner was walking abroad in the woods with one of the young ladies; now Miss Maude, and then Miss Grace.

Miss Maude won the day and carried off the prize, such as it was; and he and she were married, all unknown to any one; and before he made his next yearly visit, she had been confined of a little girl at a farmhouse on the Moors, while her father and Miss Grace thought she was away at Doncaster Races. But though she was a wife and a mother, she was not a bit softened, but as haughty and as passionate as ever; and perhaps more so, for she was jealous of Miss Grace, to whom her foreign husband paid a deal of court—by way of blinding her—as he told his wife. But Miss Grace triumphed over Miss Maude, and Miss Maude grew fiercer and fiercer, both with her husband and with her sister; and the former, who could easily shake off what was disagreeable, and hide himself in foreign countries, went away a month before his usual time that summer, and half-threatened that he would never come back again. Meanwhile, the little girl was left at the farmhouse, and her mother used to have her horse saddled and gallop wildly over the hills to see her once every week, at the very least—for where she loved, she loved; and where she hated, she hated.

And the old lord went on playing—playing on his organ; and the servants thought the sweet music he made had soothed down his awful temper, of which (Dorothy said) some terrible tales could be told. He grew infirm too, and had to walk with a crutch; and his son—that was the present Lord Furnivall's father—was with the army in America, and the other son at sea; so Miss Maude had it pretty much her own way, and she and Miss Grace grew colder and bitterer to each other every day; till at last they hardly ever spoke, except when the old lord was by. The foreign musician came again the next summer, but it was for the last time; for they led him such a life with their jealousy and their passions, that he grew weary, and went away, and never was heard of again. And Miss Maude, who had always meant to have her marriage acknowledged when her father should be dead, was left now a deserted wife—whom nobody knew to have been married—with a child that she dared not own, although she loved it to distraction; living with a father whom she feared, and a sister whom she hated. When the next summer passed over and the dark foreigner never came, both Miss Maude and Miss Grace grew gloomy and sad; they had a haggard look about them, though they looked handsome as ever. But by-and-by Miss Maude brightened; for her father grew more and more infirm, and more than ever carried away by his music; and she and Miss Grace lived almost entirely apart, having separate rooms, the one on the west side, Miss Maude on the east—those very rooms which were now shut up. So she thought she might have her little girl with her, and no one need ever know except those who dared not speak about it, and were bound to believe that it was, as she said, a cottager's child she had taken a fancy to. All this Dorothy said, was pretty well known; but what came afterwards no one knew, except Miss Grace, and Mrs. Stark, who was even then her maid, and much more of a friend to her than ever her sister had been. But the servants supposed, from words that were dropped, that Miss Maude had triumphed over Miss Grace, and told her that all the time the dark foreigner had been mocking her with pretended love—he was her own husband; the colour left Miss Grace's cheek and lips that very day for ever, and she was heard to say many a time that sooner or later she would have her revenge; and Mrs. Stark was forever spying about the east rooms.

One fearful night, just after the New Year had come in, when the snow was lying thick and deep, and the flakes were still falling—fast enough to blind any one who might be out and abroad—there was a great and violent noise heard, and the old lord's voice above all, cursing and swearing awfully,—and the cries of a little child,—and the proud defiance of a fierce woman,—and the sound of a blow,—and a dead still-ness,—and moans and wailings dying away on the hillside! Then the old lord summoned all his servants, and told them, with terrible oaths, and words more terrible, that his daughter had disgraced herself, and that he had turned her out of doors,—her, and her child,—and that if ever they gave her help,—or food,—or shelter,—he prayed that they might never enter Heaven. And, all the while, Miss Grace stood by him, white and still as any stone; and when he had ended she heaved a great sigh, as much as to say her work was done, and her end was accomplished. But the old lord never touched his organ again, and died within the year; and no wonder! for, on the morrow of that wild and fearful night, the shepherds, com-ing down the Fell-side, found Miss Maude sitting, all crazy and smiling, under the holly-trees, nursing a dead child,—with a terrible mark on its right shoulder. 'But that was not what killed it,' she said; 'it was the frost and the cold;—every wild creature was in its hole, and every beast in its fold,—while the child and its mother were turned out to wander on the Fells! And now you know all! and I wonder if you are less frightened now?'

I was more frightened than ever; but I said I was not. I wished Miss Rosamond and myself well out of that dreadful house forever; but I would not leave her, and I dared not take her away. But oh! how I watched her, and guarded her! We bolted the doors, and shut the window-shutters fast, an hour or more before dark, rather than leave them open five minutes too late. But my little lady still heard the weird child crying and mourning; and not all we could do or say, could keep her from wanting to go to her, and let her in from the cruel wind and the snow. All this time, I kept away from Miss Furnivall and Mrs. Stark, as much as ever I could; for I feared them—I knew no good could be about them, with their grey hard faces, and their dreamy eyes, looking back into the ghastly years that were gone. But, even in my fear, I had a kind of pity—for Miss Furnivall, at least. Those gone down to the pit can hardly have a more hopeless look than that which was ever on her face. At last I even got so sorry for her—who never said a word but what was quite forced from her—that I prayed for her; and I taught Miss Rosamond to pray for one who had done a deadly sin; but often when she came to those words, she would listen, and start up from her knees, and say, 'I hear my little girl plaining and crying very sad—Oh! let her in, or she will die!'

One night—just after New Year's Day had come at last, and the long winter had taken a turn, as I hoped—I heard the west drawing-room bell ring three times, which was the signal for me. I would not leave Miss Rosamond alone, for all she was asleep—for the old lord had been playing wilder than ever—and I feared lest my darling should waken to hear the spectre child; see her I knew she could not. I had fastened the windows too well for that. So, I took her out of her bed and wrapped her up in such outer clothes as were most handy, and carried her down to the drawing-room, where the old ladies sat at their tapestry work as usual. They looked up when I came in, and Mrs. Stark asked, quite astounded, 'Why did I bring Miss Rosamond there, out of her warm bed?' I had begun to whisper, 'Because I was afraid of her being tempted out while I was away, by the wild child in the snow,' when she stopped me short (with a glance at Miss Furnivall), and said Miss Furnivall wanted me to undo some work she had done wrong, and which neither of them could see to unpick. So, I laid my pretty dear on the sofa, and sat down on a stool by them, and hardened my heart against them, as I heard the wind rising and howling.

Miss Rosamond slept on sound, for all the wind blew so; and Miss Furnivall said never a word, nor looked round when the gusts shook the windows. All at once she started up to her full height, and put up one hand, as if to bid us listen.

'I hear voices!' said she. 'I hear terrible screams—I hear my father's voice!'

Just at that moment, my darling wakened with a sudden start: 'My little girl is crying, oh, how she is crying!' and she tried to get up and go to her, but she got her feet entangled in the blanket, and I caught her up; for my flesh had begun to creep at these noises, which they heard while we could catch no sound. In a minute or two the noises came, and gathered fast, and filled our ears; we, too, heard voices and screams, and no longer heard the winter's wind that raged abroad. Mrs. Stark looked at me, and I at her, but we dared not speak. Suddenly Miss Furnivall went towards the door, out into the ante-room, through the west lobby, and opened the door into the great hall. Mrs. Stark followed, and I durst not be left, though my heart almost stopped beating for fear. I wrapped my darling tight in my arms, and went out with them. In the hall the screams were louder than ever; they sounded to come from the east wing—nearer and nearer—close on the other side of the locked-up doors—close behind them. Then I noticed that the great bronze chandelier seemed all alight, though the hall was dim, and that a fire was blazing in the vast hearthplace, though it gave no heat; and I shuddered up with terror, and folded my darling closer to me. But as I did so, the east door shook, and she, suddenly struggling to get free from me, cried, 'Hester! I must go! My little girl is there; I hear her; she is coming! Hester, I must go!'

I held her tight with all my strength; with a set will, I held her. If I had died, my hands would have grasped her still, I was so resolved in my mind. Miss Furnivall stood listening, and paid no regard to my darling, who had got down to the ground, and whom I, upon my knees now, was holding with both my arms clasped round her neck; she still striving and crying to get free.

All at once, the east door gave way with a thundering crash, as if torn open in a violent passion, and there came into that broad and mysterious light, the figure of a tall, old man, with grey hair and gleaming eyes. He drove before him, with many a relentless gesture of abhorrence, a stern and beautiful woman, with a little child clinging to her dress.

'Oh, Hester! Hester!' cried Miss Rosamond. 'It's the lady! the lady below the holly-trees; and my little girl is with her. Hester! Hester! let me go to her; they are drawing me to them. I feel them—I feel them. I must go!'

Again she was almost convulsed by her efforts to get away; but I held her tighter and tighter, till I feared I should do her a hurt; but rather that than let her go towards those terrible phantoms. They passed along towards the great hall-door, where the winds howled and ravened for their prey; but before they reached that, the lady turned; and I could see that she defied the old man with a fierce and proud defiance; but then she quailed—and then she threw her arms wildly and piteously to save her child—her little child—from a blow from his uplifted crutch.

And Miss Rosamond was torn as by a power stronger than mine, and writhed in my arms, and sobbed (for by this time the poor darling was growing faint).

'They want me to go with them on to the Fells—they are drawing me to them. Oh, my little girl! I would come, but cruel, wicked Hester holds me very tight.' But when she saw the uplifted crutch she swooned away, and I thanked God for it. Just at this moment—when the tall, old man, his hair streaming as in the blast of a furnace, was going to strike the little, shrinking child—Miss Furnivall, the old woman by my side, cried out, 'Oh, father! father! spare the little, innocent child!' But just then I saw— we all saw—another phantom shape itself, and grow clear out of the blue and misty light that filled the hall; we had not seen her till now, for it was another lady who stood by the old man, with a look of relentless hate and triumphant scorn. That figure was very beautiful to look upon, with a soft, white hat drawn down over the proud brows, and a red and curling lip. It was dressed in an open robe of blue satin. I had seen that figure before. It was the likeness of Miss Furnivall in her youth; and the terrible phantoms moved on, regardless of old Miss Furnivall's wild entreaty, and the uplifted crutch fell on the right shoulder of the little child, and the younger sister looked on, stony and deadly serene. But at that moment, the dim lights, and the fire that gave no heat, went out of themselves, and Miss Furnivall lay at our feet stricken down by the palsy—death-stricken.

Yes! she was carried to her bed that night never to rise again. She lay with her face to the wall, muttering low, but muttering always: 'Alas! alas! what is done in youth can never be undone in age! what is done in youth can never be undone in age!'

33

August Heat

By W. F. Harvey

PHENISTONE ROAD, CLAPHAM, AUGUST 20, 190—.

I have had what I believe to be the most remarkable day in my life, and while the events are still fresh in my mind, I wish to put them down on paper as clearly as possible.

Let me say at the outset that my name is James Clarence Withencroft.

I am forty years old, in perfect health, never having known a day's illness.

By profession I am an artist, not a very successful one, but I earn enough money by my black-and-white work to satisfy my necessary wants.

My only near relative, a sister, died five years ago, so that I am independent.

I breakfasted this morning at nine, and after glancing through the morning paper I lighted my pipe and proceeded to let my mind wander in the hope that I might chance upon some subject for my pencil.

The room, though door and windows were open, was oppressively hot, and I had just made up my mind that the coolest and most comfortable place in the neighborhood would be the deep end of the public swimming bath, when the idea came.

I began to draw. So intent was I on my work that I left my lunch untouched, only stopping work when the clock of St. Jude's struck four.

The final result, for a hurried sketch, was, I felt sure, the best thing I had done.

It showed a criminal in the dock immediately after the judge had pronounced sentence. The man was fat—enormously fat. The flesh hung in rolls about his chin; it creased his huge, stumpy neck. He was clean shaven (perhaps I should say a few days before he must have been clean shaven) and almost bald. He stood in the dock, his short, stumpy fingers clasping the rail, looking straight in front of him. The feeling that his expression conveyed was not so much one of horror as of utter, absolute collapse.

There seemed nothing in the man strong enough to sustain that mountain of flesh.

I rolled up the sketch, and without quite knowing why, placed it in my pocket. Then with the rare sense of happiness which the knowledge of a good thing well done gives, I left the house.

I believe that I set out with the idea of calling upon Trenton, for I remember walking along Lytton Street and turning to the right along Gilchrist Road at the bottom of the hill where the men were at work on the new tram lines.

From there onward I have only the vaguest recollections of where I went. The one thing of which I was fully conscious was the awful heat, that came up from the dusty asphalt pavement as an almost palpable wave. I longed for the thunder promised by the great banks of copper-colored cloud that hung low over the western sky.

I must have walked five or six miles, when a small boy roused me from my reverie by asking the time.

It was twenty minutes to seven.

When he left me I began to take stock of my bearings. I found myself standing before a gate that led into a yard bordered by a strip of thirsty earth, where there were flowers, purple stock and scarlet geranium. Above the entrance was a board with the inscription—

CHAS. ATKINSON
MONUMENTAL MASON
WORKER IN ENGLISH AND ITALIAN MARBLES

From the yard itself came a cheery whistle, the noise of hammer blows, and the cold sound of steel meeting stone.

A sudden impulse made me enter.

A man was sitting with his back toward me, busy at work on a slab of curiously veined marble. He turned round as he heard my steps and stopped short.

It was the man I had been drawing, whose portrait lay in my pocket.

He sat there, huge and elephantine, the sweat pouring from his scalp, which he wiped with a red silk handkerchief. But though the face was the same, the expression was absolutely different.

He greeted me smiling, as if we were old friends, and shook my hand.

I apologized for my intrusion.

"Everything is hot and glary outside," I said. "This seems an oasis in the wilderness."

"I don't know about the oasis," he replied, "but it certainly is hot, as hot as hell. Take a seat, sir!"

He pointed to the end of the gravestone on which he was at work, and I sat down.

"That's a beautiful piece of stone you've got hold of," I said.

He shook his head. "In a way it is," he answered; "the surface here is as fine as anything you could wish, but there's a big flaw at the back, though I don't expect you'd ever notice it. I could never make really a good job of a bit of marble like that. It would be all right in the summer like this; it wouldn't mind the blasted heat. But wait till the winter comes. There's nothing like frost to find out the weak points in stone."

"Then what's it for?" I asked.

The man burst out laughing.

"You'd hardly believe me if I was to tell you it's for an exhibition, but it's the truth. Artists have exhibitions; so do grocers and butchers; we have them too. All the latest little things in headstones, you know."

He went on to talk of marbles, which sort best withstood wind and rain, and which were easiest to work; then of his garden and a new sort of carnation he had bought. At the end of every other minute he would drop his tools, wipe his shining head, and curse the heat.

I said little, for I felt uneasy. There was something unnatural, uncanny, in meeting this man.

I tried at first to persuade myself that I had seen him before, that his face, unknown to me, had found a place in some out-of-the-way corner of my memory, but I knew that I was practicing little more than a plausible piece of self-deception.

Mr. Atkinson finished his work, spat on the ground, and got up with a sigh of relief.

"There! What do you think of that?" he said, with an air of evident pride.

The inscription which I read for the first time was this—

SACRED TO THE MEMORY OF
JAMES CLARENCE WITHENCROFT
BORN JAN. 18TH, 1860
HE PASSED AWAY VERY SUDDENLY
ON AUGUST 20TH, 190—
"In the midst of life we are in death."

For some time I sat in silence. Then a cold shudder ran down my spine. I asked him where he had seen the name.

"Oh, I didn't see it anywhere," replied Mr. Atkinson. "I wanted some name, and I put down the first that came into my head. Why do you want to know?"

"It's a strange coincidence, but it happens to be mine."

He gave a long, low whistle.

"And the dates?"

"I can only answer for one of them, and that's correct."

"It's a rum go!" he said.

But he knew less than I did. I told him of my morning's work. I took the sketch from my pocket and showed it to him. As he looked, the expression of his face altered until it became more and more like that of the man I had drawn.

"And it was only the day before yesterday," he said, "that I told Maria there were no such things as ghosts!"

Neither of us had seen a ghost, but I knew what he meant.

"You probably heard my name," I said.

"And you must have seen me somewhere and have forgotten it! Were you at Clacton-on-Sea last July?"

I had never been to Clacton in my life. We were silent for some time. We were both looking at the same thing, the two dates on the gravestone, and one was right.

"Come inside and have some supper," said Mr. Atkinson.

His wife was a cheerful little woman, with the flaky red cheeks of the country-bred. Her husband introduced me as a friend of his who was an artist. The result was unfortunate, for after the sardines and watercress had been removed, she brought me out a Doré Bible, and I had to sit and express my admiration for nearly half an hour.

I went outside, and found Atkinson sitting on the gravestone smoking.

We resumed the conversation at the point we had left off.

"You must excuse my asking," I said, "but do you know of anything you've done for which you could be put on trial?"

He shook his head.

"I'm not a bankrupt, the business is prosperous enough. Three years ago I gave turkeys to some of the guardians at Christmas, but that's all I can think of. And they were small ones, too," he added as an afterthought.

He got up, fetched a can from the porch, and began to water the flowers. "Twice a day regular in the hot weather," he said, "and then the heat sometimes gets the better of the delicate ones. And ferns, good Lord! They could never stand it. Where do you live?"

I told him my address. It would take an hour's quick walk to get back home.

"It's like this," he said. "We'll look at the matter straight. If you go back home to-night, you take your chance of accidents. A cart may run over you, and there's always banana skins and orange peel, to say nothing of fallen ladders."

He spoke of the improbable with an intense seriousness that would have been laughable six hours before. But I did not laugh.

"The best thing we can do," he continued, "is for you to stay here till twelve o'clock. We'll go upstairs and smoke; it may be cooler inside."

To my surprise, I agreed.

We are sitting in a long, low room beneath the eaves. Atkinson has sent his wife to bed. He himself is busy sharpening some tools at a little oil-stone, smoking one of my cigars the while.

The air seems charged with thunder. I am writing this at a shaky table before the open window. The leg is cracked, and Atkinson, who seems a handy man with his tools, is going to mend it as soon as he has finished putting an edge on his chisel.

It is after eleven now. I shall be gone in less than an hour.

But the heat is stifling.

It is enough to send a man mad.

34

How He Left the Hotel

By Louisa Baldwin

I USED TO WORK THE PASSENGER-LIFT IN THE EMPIRE HOTEL, THAT BIG block of building in lines of red and white brick like streaky bacon, that stands at the corner of _____ Street. I'd served my time in the army, and got my discharge with good-conduct stripes; and how I got the job was in this way. The hotel was a big company affair with a managing committee of retired officers and such-like; gentlemen with a bit o' money in the concern, and nothing to do but fidget about it, and my late Colonel was one of 'em. He was as good-tempered a man as ever stepped when his will wasn't crossed, and when I asked him for a job, "Mole," says he, "you're the very man to work the lift at our big hotel. Soldiers are civil and businesslike, and the public like 'em only second best to sailors. We've had to give our last man the sack, and you can take his place."

I liked my work well enough and my pay, and kept my place a year, and I should have been there still if it hadn't been for a circumstance—but don't let me anticipate. Ours was a hydraulic lift. None o' them rickety things swung up like a poll parrot's cage in a well staircase that I shouldn't dare to trust my neck to. It ran as smooth as oil, a child might have worked it, and safe as standing on the ground. Instead of being stuck full of advertisements like an omnibus, we'd mirrors in it, and the ladies would look at themselves, and pat their hair, and set their mouths when I was taking 'em downstairs dressed of an evening. It was a little sitting-room, with red velvet cushions to sit down on, and you'd nothing to do but get into it, and it 'ud float you up or float you down light as a bird.

All the visitors used the lift one time or another, going up or coming down. Some of them was French, and they called the lift the "assenser," and good enough for them in their language, no doubt; but why the Americans, that can speak English when they choose, and are always finding out ways of doing things quicker than other folks, should waste time and breath calling a lift an elevator, I can't make out.

I was in charge of the lift from noon until midnight. By that time the theatre and dining-out folks had come in, and anyone returning late walked upstairs, for my day's work was done. One of the porters worked the lift till I come on duty in the morning; but before twelve there was nothing particular going on, and not much till after two o'clock. Then it was pretty hot work with visitors going up and down constant, and the electric bell ringing you from one floor to another like a house on fire. Then came a quiet spell while dinner was on, and I'd sit down comfortable in the lift and read my paper, only I mightn't smoke. But nobody else might neither, and I had to ask furren gentlemen to please not smoke in it, it was against the rule. I hadn't so often to tell English gentlemen, they're not like furreners that seem as if their cigars was glued to their lips.

I always noticed faces as folks got into the lift, for I've sharp sight and a good memory, and none of the visitors needed to tell me twice where to take them. I knew them and I knew their floors as well as they did themselves.

It was in November that Colonel Saxby came to the Empire Hotel. I noticed him particularly, because you could see at once that he was a soldier. He was a tall, thin man about fifty, with a hawk nose, keen eyes, and a grey moustache, and walked stiff from a gunshot wound in the knee. But what I noticed most was the scar of a sabrecut across the right side of his face. As he got into the lift to go to his room on the fourth floor, I thought what a difference there is among officers. Colonel Saxby put me in mind of a telegraph-post for height and thinness; and my old Colonel was like a barrel in uniform, but a brave soldier and a gentleman all the same. Colonel Saxby's room was number 210, just opposite the glass door leading to the lift, and every time I stopped on the fourth floor number 210 stared me in the face. The Colonel used to go up in the lift every day regular, though he never came down in it till—but I'm coming to that presently.

Sometimes, when he was alone in the lift, he'd speak to me. He asked me in what regiment I'd served, and said he knew the officers in it. But I can't say he was comfortable to talk to. There was something stand-offish about him, and he always seemed deep in his own thoughts. He never sat down in the lift. Whether it was empty or full he stood bolt upright under the lamp, where the light fell on his pale face and scarred cheek.

One day in February I didn't take the Colonel up in the lift, and as he was regular as clockwork I noticed it, but I supposed he'd gone away for a few days, and I thought no more about it. Whenever I stopped on the fourth floor the door of 210 was shut, and as he often left it open, I made sure the Colonel was away. At the end of a week I heard a chambermaid say that Colonel Saxby was ill; so, thinks I, that's why he hasn't been in the lift lately.

It was a Tuesday night, and I'd had an uncommonly busy time of it. It was one stream of traffic up and down, and so it went the whole evening. It was on the strike of midnight, and I was about to put out the light in the lift, lock the door, and leave the key in the office for the man in the morning, when the electric bell rang out sharp; I looked at the dial, and saw I was wanted on the fourth floor. It struck twelve as I stepped into the lift. As I passed the second and third floors, I wondered who it was that had rung so late, and thought it must be a stranger that didn't know the rule of the house. But when I stopped at the fourth floor and flung open the door of the lift, Colonel Saxby was standing there wrapped in a military cloak. The door of his room was shut behind him, for I read the number on it. I thought he was ill in his bed, and ill enough he looked, but he had his hat on, and what could a man that had been in bed ten days want with going out on a winter midnight? I don't think he saw me, but when I'd set the lift in motion, I looked at him standing under the lamp, with the shadow of his hat hiding his eyes, and the light full on the lower part of his face, that was deadly pale, the scar on his cheek showing still paler.

"Glad to see you're better, sir," said I; but he said nothing, and I didn't like to look at him again. He stood like a statue with his cloak about him, and I was downright glad when I opened the door of the lift for him to step out into the hall. I saluted as he got out, and he went past me towards the front door.

"The Colonel wants to go out," I said to the porter who stood staring, and he opened the door and Colonel Saxby walked out into the snow.

"That's a queer go!" he said.

"It is," said I. "I don't like the Colonel's looks, he doesn't seem himself at all. He's ill enough to be in his bed, and there he is gone out on a night like this."

"Anyhow, he's got a famous cloak to keep him warm. I say, supposing he's gone to a fancy ball, and got that cloak on to hide his dress," said the porter, laughing uneasily, for we both felt queerer than we cared to say, and as we spoke there came a loud ring at the doorbell.

"No more passengers for me!" I said; and I was really putting the light out this time, when Joe opened the door, and two gentlemen entered that I knew at a glance were doctors. One was tall, and the other was short and stout, and they both came to the lift.

"Sorry, gentlemen, but it's against the rule for the lift to go up after midnight."

"Nonsense!" said the stout gentleman; "it's only just past twelve, and a matter of life and death. Take us up at once to the fourth floor," and they were in the lift like a shot; so up we went, and when I opened the door, they walked straight to number 210. A nurse came out to meet them, and the stout doctor said: "No change for the worse, I hope?"

And I heard her reply: "The patient died five minutes ago, sir."

Though I'd no business to speak, that was more than I could stand. I followed the doctors to the door and said: "There's some mistake here, gentlemen, I took the Colonel down in the lift since the clock struck twelve, and he went out."

The stout doctor said sharply: "A case of mistaken identity. It was someone else who you took for the Colonel."

"Begging your pardon, gentlemen, it was the Colonel himself, and the night porter that opened the front door for him knew him as well as me. He was dressed for a night like this, with his military cloak wrapped round him."

"Step in and see for yourself," said the nurse.

I followed the doctor into the room, and there lay Colonel Saxby looking just as I had seen him a few minutes before. There he lay, dead as his forefathers, and the great cloak spread over the bed to keep him warm that would feel heat and cold no more. I never slept that night. I sat up with Joe, expecting every minute to hear the Colonel ring the front doorbell. Next day, every time the bell for the lift rang sharp and sudden, the sweat broke out on me and I shook again. I felt as bad as I did the first time I was in action. Me and Joe told the manager all about it, and he said we'd been dreaming; but, said he, "Mind you don't talk about it, or the house'll be empty in a week."

The Colonel's coffin was smuggled into the house the next night. Me and the manager and the undertaker's men took it up in the lift, and it lay right across it, and not an inch to spare. They carried it into number 210, and while I waited for them to come out again, a queer feeling came over me. Then the door opened softly, and four men carried out the long coffin straight across the passage, and set it down with its foot towards the door of the lift, and the manager looked round for me.

"I can't do it, sir," I said. "I can't take the Colonel down again. I took him down at midnight yesterday, and that was enough for me."

"Push it in," said the manager, speaking short and sharp, and they ran the coffin into the lift without a sound. The manager got in last, and before he closed the door he said, "Mole, you've worked this lift for the last time, it strikes me." And I had, for I wouldn't have stayed on at the Empire Hotel after what had happened, not if they'd doubled my wages; and me and the night porter left together.

35

The Man Who Went Too Far

By E. F. Benson

THE LITTLE VILLAGE OF ST. FAITH'S NESTLES IN A HOLLOW OF WOODED
hill up on the north bank of the river Fawn in the county of Hampshire,
huddling close round its gray Norman church as if for spiritual protec-
tion against the fays and fairies, the trolls and "little people," who might
be supposed still to linger in the vast empty spaces of the New Forest,
and to come after dusk and do their doubtful businesses. Once outside
the hamlet you may walk in any direction (so long as you avoid the high
road which leads to Brockenhurst) for a length of a summer afternoon
without seeing sign of human habitation, or possibly even catching sight
of another human being. Shaggy wild ponies may stop their feeding for
a moment as you pass, the white scuts of rabbits will vanish into their
burrows, a brown viper perhaps will glide from your path into a clump
of heather, and unseen birds will chuckle in the bushes, but it may easily
happen that for a long day you will see nothing human. But you will not
feel in the least lonely; in summer, at any rate, the sunlight will be gay
with butterflies, and the air thick with all those woodland sounds which
like instruments in an orchestra combine to play the great symphony of
the yearly festival of June. Winds whisper in the birches, and sigh among
the firs; bees are busy with their redolent labor among the heather, myriad
birds chirp in the green temples of the forest trees, and the voice of the
river prattling over stony places, bubbling into pools, chuckling and gulp-
ing round corners, gives you the sense that many presences and companions are near at hand.

Yet, oddly enough, though one would have thought that these benign and cheerful influences of wholesome air and spaciousness of forest were very healthful comrades for a man, in so far as nature can really influence this wonderful human genus which has in these centuries learned to defy her most violent storms in its well-established houses, to bridle her torrents and make them light its streets, to tunnel her mountains and plow her seas, the inhabitants of St. Faith's will not willingly venture into the forest after dark. For in spite of the silence and loneliness of the hooded night it seems that a man is not sure in what company he may suddenly find himself, and though it is difficult to get from these villagers any very clear story of occult appearances, the feeling is widespread. One story indeed I have heard with some definiteness, the tale of a monstrous goat that has been seen to skip with hellish glee about the woods and shady places, and this perhaps is connected with the story which I have here attempted to piece together. It too is well-known to them; for all remember the young artist who died here not long ago, a young man, or so he struck the beholder, of great personal beauty, with something about him that made men's faces to smile and brighten when they looked on him. His ghost they will tell you "walks" constantly by the stream and through the woods which he loved so, and in especial it haunts a certain house, the last of the village, where he lived, and its garden in which he was done to death. For my part I am inclined to think that the terror of the Forest dates chiefly from that day. So, such as the story is, I have set it forth in connected form. It is based partly on the accounts of the villagers, but mainly on that of Darcy, a friend of mine and a friend of the man with whom these events were chiefly concerned.

The day had been one of untarnished midsummer splendor, and as the sun drew near to its setting, the glory of the evening grew every moment more crystalline, more miraculous. Westward from St. Faith's the beech-wood which stretched for some miles toward the heathery upland beyond already cast its veil of clear shadow over the red roofs of the village, but the spire of the gray church, overtopping all, still pointed a flaming orange finger into the sky. The river Fawn, which runs below, lay in sheets of sky-reflected blue, and wound its dreamy devious course round the edge of this wood, where a rough two-planked bridge crossed from the bottom of the garden of the last house in the village, and communicated by means of a little wicker gate with the wood itself. Then once out of the shadow of the wood the stream lay in flaming pools of the molten crimson of the sunset, and lost itself in the haze of woodland distances.

This house at the end of the village stood outside the shadow, and the lawn which sloped down to the river was still flecked with sunlight. Garden-beds of dazzling color lined its gravel walks, and down the middle of it ran a brick pergola, half-hidden in clusters of rambler-rose and purple with starry clematis. At the bottom end of it, between two of its pillars, was slung a hammock containing a shirt-sleeved figure.

The house itself lay somewhat remote from the rest of the village, and a footpath leading across two fields, now tall and fragrant with hay, was its only communication with the high road. It was low-built, only two stories in height, and like the garden, its walls were a mass of flowering roses. A narrow stone terrace ran along the garden front, over which was stretched an awning, and on the terrace a young silent-footed man-servant was busied with the laying of the table for dinner. He was neat-handed and quick with his job, and having finished it he went back into the house, and reappeared again with a large rough bath-towel on his arm. With this he went to the hammock in the pergola.

"Nearly eight, sir," he said.

"Has Mr. Darcy come yet?" asked a voice from the hammock.

"No, sir."

"If I'm not back when he comes, tell him that I'm just having a bathe before dinner."

The servant went back to the house, and after a moment or two Frank Halton struggled to a sitting posture, and slipped out on to the grass. He was of medium height and rather slender in build, but the supple ease and grace of his movements gave the impression of great physical strength; even his descent from the hammock was not an awkward performance. His face and hands were of very dark complexion, either from constant exposure to wind and sun, or, as his black hair and dark eyes tended to show, from some strain of southern blood. His head was small, his face of an exquisite beauty of modeling, while the smoothness of its contour would have led you to believe that he was a beardless lad still in his teens. But something, some look which living and experience alone can give, seemed to contradict that, and finding yourself completely puzzled as to his age, you would next moment probably cease to think about that, and only look at this glorious specimen of young manhood with wondering satisfaction.

He was dressed as became the season and the heat, and wore only a shirt open at the neck, and a pair of flannel trousers. His head, covered very thickly with a somewhat rebellious crop of short curly hair, was bare as he strolled across the lawn to the bathing-place that lay below. Then for a moment there was silence, then the sound of splashed and divided waters, and presently after, a great shout of ecstatic joy, as he swam upstream with the foamed water standing in a frill round his neck. Then after some five minutes of limb-stretching struggle with the flood, he turned over on his back, and with arms thrown wide, floated downstream, ripple-cradled and inert. His eyes were shut, and between half-parted lips he talked gently to himself.

"I am one with it," he said to himself, "the river and I, I and the river. The coolness and splash of it is I, and the water-herbs that wave in it are I also. And my strength and my limbs are not mine but the river's. It is all one, all one, dear Fawn."

A quarter of an hour later he appeared again at the bottom of the lawn, dressed as before, his wet hair already drying into its crisp short curls again. There he paused a moment, looking back at the stream with the smile with which men look on the face of a friend, then turned towards the house. Simultaneously his servant came to the door leading on to the terrace, followed by a man who appeared to be some halfway through the fourth decade of his years. Frank and he saw each other across the bushes and garden-beds, and each quickening his step, they met suddenly face to face round an angle of the garden walk, in the fragrance of syringa.

"My dear Darcy," cried Frank, "I am charmed to see you."

But the other stared at him in amazement.

"Frank!" he exclaimed.

"Yes, that is my name," he said laughing, "what is the matter?"

Darcy took his hand.

"What have you done to yourself?" he asked. "You are a boy again."

"Ah, I have a lot to tell you," said Frank. "Lots that you will hardly believe, but I shall convince you—"

He broke off suddenly, and held up his hand.

"Hush, there is my nightingale," he said.

The smile of recognition and welcome with which he had greeted his friend faded from his face, and a look of rapt wonder took its place, as of a lover listening to the voice of his beloved. His mouth parted slightly, showing the white line of teeth, and his eyes looked out and out till they seemed to Darcy to be focused on things beyond the vision of man. Then something perhaps startled the bird, for the song ceased.

"Yes, lots to tell you," he said. "Really I am delighted to see you. But you look rather white and pulled down; no wonder after that fever. And there is to be no nonsense about this visit. It is June now, you stop here till you are fit to begin work again. Two months at least."

"Ah, I can't trespass quite to that extent."

Frank took his arm and walked him down the grass.

"Trespass? Who talks of trespass? I shall tell you quite openly when I am tired of you, but you know when we had the studio together, we used not to bore each other. However, it is ill talking of going away on the moment of your arrival. Just a stroll to the river, and then it will be dinner-time."

Darcy took out his cigarette case, and offered it to the other.

Frank laughed.

"No, not for me. Dear me, I suppose I used to smoke once. How very odd!"

"Given it up?"

"I don't know. I suppose I must have. Anyhow I don't do it now. I would as soon think of eating meat."

"Another victim on the smoking altar of vegetarianism?"

"Victim?" asked Frank. "Do I strike you as such?"

He paused on the margin of the stream and whistled softly. Next moment a moor-hen made its splashing flight across the river, and ran up the bank. Frank took it very gently in his hands and stroked its head, as the creature lay against his shirt.

"And is the house among the reeds still secure?" he half-crooned to it. "And is the missus quite well, and are the neighbors flourishing? There, dear, home with you," and he flung it into the air.

"That bird's very tame," said Darcy, slightly bewildered.

"It is rather," said Frank, following its flight.

During dinner Frank chiefly occupied himself in bringing himself up-to-date in the movements and achievements of this old friend whom he had not seen for six years. Those six years, it now appeared, had been full of incident and success for Darcy; he had made a name for himself as a portrait painter which bade fair to outlast the vogue of a couple of seasons, and his leisure time had been brief. Then some four months previously he had been through a severe attack of typhoid, the result of which as concerns this story was that he had come down to this sequestered place to recruit.

"Yes, you've got on," said Frank at the end. "I always knew you would. A.R.A. with more in prospect. Money? You roll in it, I suppose, and, O Darcy, how much happiness have you had all these years? That is the only imperishable possession. And how much have you learned? Oh, I don't mean in Art. Even I could have done well in that."

Darcy laughed.

"Done well? My dear fellow, all I have learned in these six years you knew, so to speak, in your cradle. Your old pictures fetch huge prices. Do you never paint now?"

Frank shook his head.

"No, I'm too busy," he said.

"Doing what? Please tell me. That is what every one is forever asking me."

"Doing? I suppose you would say I do nothing."

Darcy glanced up at the brilliant young face opposite him.

"It seems to suit you, that way of being busy," he said. "Now, it's your turn. Do you read? Do you study? I remember you saying that it would do us all—all us artists, I mean—a great deal of good if we would study any one human face carefully for a year, without recording a line. Have you been doing that?"

Frank shook his head again.

"I mean exactly what I say," he said. "I have been doing nothing. And I have never been so occupied. Look at me; have I not done something to myself to begin with?"

"You are two years younger than I," said Darcy, "at least you used to be. You therefore are thirty-five. But had I never seen you before I should say that you were just twenty. But was it worth while to spend six years of greatly occupied life in order to look twenty? Seems rather like a woman of fashion."

Frank laughed boisterously.

"First time I've ever been compared to that particular bird of prey," he said. "No, that has not been my occupation—in fact I am only very rarely conscious that one effect of my occupation has been that. Of course, it must have been if one comes to think of it. It is not very important. Quite true my body has become young. But that is very little; I have become young."

Darcy pushed back his chair and sat sideways to the table looking at the other.

"Has that been your occupation then?" he asked.

"Yes, that anyhow is one aspect of it. Think what youth means! It is the capacity for growth, mind, body, spirit, all grow, all get stronger, all have a fuller, firmer life every day. That is something, considering that every day that passes after the ordinary man reaches the full-blown flower of his strength, weakens his hold on life. A man reaches his prime, and remains, we say, in his prime, for ten years, or perhaps twenty. But after his primest prime is reached, he slowly, insensibly weakens. These are the signs of age in you, in your body, in your art probably, in your mind. You are less electric than you were. But I, when I reach my prime—I am nearing it—ah, you shall see."

The stars had begun to appear in the blue velvet of the sky, and to the east the horizon seen above the black silhouette of the village was growing dove-colored with the approach of moonrise. White moths hovered dimly over the garden-beds, and the footsteps of night tiptoed through the bushes. Suddenly Frank rose.

"Ah, it is the supreme moment," he said softly. "Now more than at any other time the current of life, the eternal imperishable current runs so close to me that I am almost enveloped in it. Be silent a minute."

He advanced to the edge of the terrace and looked out standing stretched with arms outspread. Darcy heard him draw a long breath into his lungs, and after many seconds expel it again. Six or eight times he did this, then turned back into the lamplight.

"It will sound to you quite mad, I expect," he said, "but if you want to hear the soberest truth I have ever spoken and shall ever speak, I will tell you about myself. But come into the garden if it is not too damp for you. I have never told any one yet, but I shall like to tell you. It is long, in fact, since I have even tried to classify what I have learned."

They wandered into the fragrant dimness of the pergola, and sat down. Then Frank began:

"Years ago, do you remember," he said, "we used often to talk about the decay of joy in the world. Many impulses, we settled, had contributed to this decay, some of which were good in themselves, others that were quite completely bad. Among the good things, I put what we may call certain Christian virtues, renunciation, resignation, sympathy with suffering, and the desire to relieve sufferers. But out of those things spring very bad ones, useless renunciations, asceticism for its own sake, mortification of the flesh with nothing to follow, no corresponding gain that is, and that awful and terrible disease which devastated England some centuries ago, and from which by heredity of spirit we suffer now, Puritanism. That was a dreadful plague, the brutes held and taught that joy and laughter and merriment were evil: it was a doctrine the most profane and wicked. Why, what is the commonest crime one sees? A sullen face. That is the truth of the matter.

"Now all my life I have believed that we are intended to be happy, that joy is of all gifts the most divine. And when I left London, abandoned my career, such as it was, I did so because I intended to devote my life to the cultivation of joy, and, by continuous and unsparing effort, to be happy. Among people, and in constant intercourse with others, I did not find it possible; there were too many distractions in towns and work-rooms, and also too much suffering. So I took one step backwards or forwards, as you may choose to put it, and went straight to Nature, to trees, birds, animals, to all those things which quite clearly pursue one aim only, which blindly follow the great native instinct to be happy without any care at all for morality, or human law or divine law. I wanted, you understand, to get all joy first-hand and unadulterated, and I think it scarcely exists among men; it is obsolete."

Darcy turned in his chair.

"Ah, but what makes birds and animals happy?" he asked. "Food, food and mating."

Frank laughed gently in the stillness.

"Do not think I became a sensualist," he said. "I did not make that mistake. For the sensualist carries his miseries pick-a-back, and round his feet is wound the shroud that shall soon enwrap him. I may be made, it is true, but I am not so stupid anyhow as to have tried that. No, what is it that makes puppies play with their own tails, that sends cats on their prowling ecstatic errands at night?"

He paused a moment.

"So I went to Nature," he said. "I sat down here in this New Forest, sat down fair and square, and looked. That was my first difficulty, to sit here quiet without being bored, to wait without being impatient, to be receptive and very alert, though for a long time nothing particular happened. The change in fact was slow in those early stages."

"Nothing happened?" asked Darcy rather impatiently, with the sturdy revolt against any new idea which to the English mind is synonymous with nonsense. "Why, what in the world should happen?"

Now Frank as he had known him was the most generous but most quick-tempered of mortal men; in other words his anger would flare to a prodigious beacon, under almost no provocation, only to be quenched again under a gust of no less impulsive kindliness. Thus the moment Darcy had spoken, an apology for his hasty question was halfway up his tongue. But there was no need for it to have traveled even so far, for Frank laughed again with kindly, genuine mirth.

"Oh, how I should have resented that a few years ago," he said. "Thank goodness that resentment is one of the things I have got rid of. I certainly wish that you should believe my story—in fact, you are going to—but that you at this moment should imply that you do not, does not concern me."

"Ah, your solitary sojournings have made you inhuman," said Darcy, still very English.

"No, human," said Frank. "Rather more human, at least rather less of an ape."

"Well, that was my first quest," he continued, after a moment, "the deliberate and unswerving pursuit of joy, and my method, the eager contemplation of Nature. As far as motive went, I daresay it was purely selfish, but as far as effect goes, it seems to me about the best thing one can do for one's fellow creatures, for happiness is more infectious than small-pox. So, as I said, I sat down and waited; I looked at happy things, zealously avoided the sight of anything unhappy, and by degrees a little trickle of the happiness of this blissful world began to filter into me. The trickle grew more abundant, and now, my dear fellow, if I could for a moment divert from me into you one half of the torrent of joy that pours through me day and night, you would throw the world, art, everything aside, and just live, exist. When man's body dies, it passes into trees and flowers. Well, that is what I have been trying to do with my soul before death."

The servant had brought into the pergola a table with siphons and spirits, and had set a lamp upon it. As Frank spoke he leaned forward towards the other, and Darcy for all his matter-of-fact common-sense could have sworn that his companion's face shone, was luminous in itself. His dark brown eyes glowed from within, the unconscious smile of a child irradiated and transformed his face. Darcy felt suddenly excited, exhilarated.

"Go on," he said. "Go on. I can feel you are somehow telling me sober truth. I daresay you are mad; but I don't see that matters."

Frank laughed again.

"Mad?" he said. "Yes, certainly, if you wish. But I prefer to call it sane. However, nothing matters less than what anybody chooses to call things. God never labels his gifts; He just puts them into our hands; just as He put animals in the garden of Eden, for Adam to name if he felt disposed.

"So by the continual observance and study of things that were happy," continued he, "I got happiness, I got joy. But seeking it, as I did, from

Nature, I got much more which I did not seek, but stumbled upon originally by accident. It is difficult to explain, but I will try.

"About three years ago I was sitting one morning in a place I will
show you tomorrow. It is down by the river brink, very green, dappled
with shade and sun, and the river passes there through some little clumps
of reeds. Well, as I sat there, doing nothing, but just looking and listening,
I heard the sound quite distinctly of some flute-like instrument playing a
strange unending melody. I thought at first it was some musical yokel on
the highway and did not pay much attention. But before long the strangeness and indescribable beauty of the tune struck me. It never repeated
itself, but it never came to an end, phrase after phrase ran its sweet course,
it worked gradually and inevitably up to a climax, and having attained it,
it went on; another climax was reached and another and another. Then
with a sudden gasp of wonder I localized where it came from. It came
from the reeds and from the sky and from the trees. It was everywhere,
it was the sound of life. It was, my dear Darcy, as the Greeks would have
said, it was Pan playing on his pipes, the voice of Nature. It was the life-
melody, the world-melody."

Darcy was far too interested to interrupt, though there was a question
he would have liked to ask, and Frank went on:

"Well, for the moment I was terrified, terrified with the impotent horror of nightmare, and I stopped my ears and just ran from the place and
got back to the house panting, trembling, literally in a panic. Unknow-
ingly, for at that time I only pursued joy, I had begun, since I drew my joy
from Nature, to get in touch with Nature. Nature, force, God, call it what
you will, had drawn across my face a little gossamer web of essential life.
I saw that when I emerged from my terror, and I went very humbly back
to where I had heard the Pan-pipes. But it was nearly six months before
I heard them again."

"Why was that?" asked Darcy.

"Surely because I had revolted, rebelled, and worst of all been frightened. For I believe that just as there is nothing in the world which so
injures one's body as fear, so there is nothing that so much shuts up the
soul. I was afraid, you see, of the one thing in the world which has real
existence. No wonder its manifestation was withdrawn."

"And after six months?"

"After six months one blessed morning I heard the piping again. I wasn't afraid that time. And since then it has grown louder, it has become more constant. I now hear it often, and I can put myself into such an attitude towards Nature that the pipes will almost certainly sound. And never yet have they played the same tune, it is always something new, something fuller, richer, more complete than before."

"What do you mean by 'such an attitude towards Nature'?" asked Darcy.

"I can't explain that; but by translating it into a bodily attitude it is this."

Frank sat up for a moment quite straight in his chair, then slowly sunk back with arms outspread and head drooped.

"That," he said, "an effortless attitude, but open, resting, receptive. It is just that which you must do with your soul."

Then he sat up again.

"One word more," he said, "and I will bore you no further. Nor unless you ask me questions shall I talk about it again. You will find me, in fact, quite sane in my mode of life. Birds and beasts you will see behaving somewhat intimately to me, like that moor-hen, but that is all. I will walk with you, ride with you, play golf with you, and talk with you on any subject you like. But I wanted you on the threshold to know what has happened to me. And one more thing will happen."

He paused again, and a slight look of fear crossed his eyes.

"There will be a final revelation," he said, "a complete and blinding stroke which will throw open to me, once and for all, the full knowledge, the full realization and comprehension that I am one, just as you are, with life. In reality there is no 'me,' no 'you,' no 'it.' Everything is part of the one and only thing which is life. I know that that is so, but the realization of it is not yet mine. But it will be, and on that day, so I take it, I shall see Pan. It may mean death, the death of my body, that is, but I don't care. It may mean immortal, eternal life lived here and now and forever. Then having gained that, ah, my dear Darcy, I shall preach such a gospel of joy, showing myself as the living proof of the truth, that Puritanism, the dismal religion of sour faces, shall vanish like a breath of smoke, and be dispersed and disappear in the sunlit air. But first the full knowledge must be mine."

Darcy watched his face narrowly.

"You are afraid of that moment," he said.

Frank smiled at him.

"Quite true; you are quick to have seen that. But when it comes I hope I shall not be afraid."

For some little time there was silence; then Darcy rose.

"You have bewitched me, you extraordinary boy," he said. "You have been telling me a fairy-story, and I find myself saying, 'Promise me it is true.'"

"I promise you that," said the other.

"And I know I shan't sleep," added Darcy.

Frank looked at him with a sort of mild wonder as if he scarcely understood.

"Well, what does that matter?" he said.

"I assure you it does. I am wretched unless I sleep."

"Of course I can make you sleep if I want," said Frank in a rather bored voice.

"Well, do."

"Very good; go to bed. I'll come upstairs in ten minutes."

Frank busied himself for a little after the other had gone, moving the table back under the awning of the veranda and quenching the lamp. Then he went with his quick silent tread upstairs and into Darcy's room. The latter was already in bed, but very wide-eyed and wakeful, and Frank with an amused smile of indulgence, as for a fretful child, sat down on the edge of the bed.

"Look at me," he said, and Darcy looked.

"The birds are sleeping in the brake," said Frank softly, "and the winds are asleep. The sea sleeps, and the tides are but the heaving of its breast. The stars swing low, rocked in the great cradle of the Heavens, and—"

He stopped suddenly, gently blew out Darcy's candle, and left him sleeping.

Morning brought to Darcy a flood of hard commonsense, as clear and crisp as the sunshine that filled his room. Slowly as he woke he gathered together the broken threads of the memories of the evening which had ended, so he told himself, in a trick of common hypnotism. That accounted for it all; the whole strange talk he had had was under a spell of suggestion from the extraordinary vivid boy who had once been a man; all his own excitement, his acceptance of the incredible had been merely the effect of a stronger, more potent will imposed on his own. How strong that will was, he guessed from his own instantaneous obedience to Frank's suggestion of sleep. And armed with impenetrable commonsense he came down to breakfast. Frank had already begun, and was consuming a large plateful of porridge and milk with the most prosaic and healthy appetite.

"Slept well?" he asked.

"Yes, of course. Where did you learn hypnotism?"

"By the side of the river."

"You talked an amazing quantity of nonsense last night," remarked Darcy, in a voice prickly with reason.

"Rather. I felt quite giddy. Look, I remembered to order a dreadful daily paper for you. You can read about money markets or politics or cricket matches."

Darcy looked at him closely. In the morning light Frank looked even fresher, younger, more vital than he had done the night before, and the sight of him somehow dinted Darcy's armor of commonsense.

"You are the most extraordinary fellow I ever saw," he said. "I want to ask you some more questions."

"Ask away," said Frank.

For the next day or two Darcy plied his friend with many questions, objections, and criticisms on the theory of life and gradually got out of him a coherent and complete account of his experience. In brief then, Frank believed that "by lying naked," as he put it, to the force which controls the passage of the stars, the breaking of a wave, the budding of a tree, the love of a youth and maiden, he had succeeded in a way hitherto undreamed of in possessing himself of the essential principle of life. Day by day, so he thought, he was getting nearer to, and in closer union with the great power itself which caused all life to be, the spirit of nature, of force, or the spirit of God. For himself, he confessed to what others would call paganism; it was sufficient for him that there existed a principle of life. He did not worship it, he did not pray to it, he did not praise it. Some of it existed in all human beings, just as it existed in trees and animals; to realize and make living to himself that fact that it was all one, was his sole aim and object.

Here perhaps Darcy would put in a word of warning.

"Take care," he said. "To see Pan meant death, did it not?"

Frank's eyebrows would rise at this.

"What does that matter?" he said. "True, the Greeks were always right, and they said so, but there is another possibility. For the nearer I get to it, the more living, the more vital and young I become."

"What then do you expect the final revelation will do for you?"

"I have told you," said he. "It will make me immortal."

But it was not so much from the speech and argument that Darcy grew to grasp his friend's conception, as from the ordinary conduct of his life. They were passing, for instance, one morning down the village street, when an old woman, very bent and decrepit, but with an extraordinary cheerfulness of face, hobbled out of her cottage. Frank instantly stopped when he saw her.

"You old darling! How goes it all?" he said.

But she did not answer, her dim old eyes were riveted on his face; she seemed to drink in like a thirsty creature the beautiful radiance which shone there. Suddenly she put her two withered old hands on his shoulders.

"You're just the sunshine itself," she said, and he kissed her and passed on.

But scarcely a hundred yards further a strange contradiction of such tenderness occurred. A child running along the path towards them fell on its face, and set up a dismal cry of fright and pain. A look of horror came into Frank's eyes, and, putting his fingers in his ears, he fled at full speed down the street, and did not pause till he was out of hearing. Darcy, having ascertained that the child was not really hurt, followed him in bewilderment.

"Are you without pity then?" he asked.

Frank shook his head impatiently.

"Can't you see?" he asked. "Can't you understand that that sort of thing, pain, anger, anything unlovely throws me back, retards the coming of the great hour! Perhaps when it comes I shall be able to piece that side of life on to the other, on to the true religion of joy. At present I can't."

"But the old woman. Was she not ugly?"

Frank's radiance gradually returned.

"Ah, no. She was like me. She longed for joy, and knew it when she saw it, the old darling."

Another question suggested itself.

"Then what about Christianity?" asked Darcy.

"I can't accept it. I can't believe in any creed of which the central doctrine is that God who is Joy should have had to suffer. Perhaps it was so; in some inscrutable way I believe it may have been so, but I don't understand how it was possible. So I leave it alone; my affair is joy."

They had come to the weir above the village, and the thunder of riotous cool water was heavy in the air. Trees dipped into the translucent stream with slender trailing branches, and the meadow where they stood was starred with midsummer blossomings. Larks shot up caroling into the crystal dome of blue, and a thousand voices of June sang round them. Frank, bare-headed as was his wont, with his coat slung over his arm and his shirt sleeves rolled up above the elbow, stood there like some beautiful wild animal with eyes half-shut and mouth half-open, drinking in the scented warmth of the air. Then suddenly he flung himself face downwards on the grass at the edge of the stream, burying his face in the daisies and cowslips, and lay stretched there in wide-armed ecstasy, with his long fingers pressing and stroking the dewy herbs of the field. Never before had Darcy seen him thus fully possessed by his idea; his caressing fingers, his half-buried face pressed close to the grass, even the clothed lines of his figure were indistinct with a vitality that somehow was different from that of other men. And some faint glow from it reached Darcy, some thrill, some vibration from that charged recumbent body passed to him, and for a moment he understood as he had not understood before, despite his persistent questions and the candid answers they received, how real, and how realized by Frank, his idea was.

Then suddenly the muscles in Frank's neck became stiff and alert, and he half-raised his head, whispering, "The Pan-pipes, the Pan-pipes. Close, oh, so close."

Very slowly, as if a sudden movement might interrupt that melody, he raised himself and leaned on the elbow of his bent arm. His eyes opened wider, the lower lids drooped as if he focused his eyes on something very far away, and the smile on his face broadened and quivered like sunlight on still water, till the exultance of its happiness was scarcely human. So he remained motionless and rapt for some minutes, then the look of listening died from his face, and he bowed his head satisfied.

"Ah, that was good," he said. "How is it possible you did not hear? Oh, you poor fellow! Did you really hear nothing?"

A week of this outdoor and stimulating life did wonders in restoring to Darcy the vigor and health which his weeks of fever had filched from him, and as his normal activity and higher pressure of vitality returned, he seemed to himself to fall even more under the spell which the miracle of Frank's youth cast over him. Twenty times a day he found himself saying to himself suddenly at the end of some ten minutes' silent resistance to the absurdity of Frank's idea: "But it isn't possible; it can't be possible," and from the fact of his having to assure himself so frequently of this, he knew that he was struggling and arguing with a conclusion which already had taken root in his mind. For in any case a visible living miracle confronted him, since it was equally impossible that this youth, this boy, trembling on the verge of manhood, was thirty-five. Yet such was the fact.

July was ushered in by a couple of days of blustering and fretful rain, and Darcy, unwilling to risk a chill, kept to the house. But to Frank this weeping change of weather seemed to have no bearing on the behavior of man, and he spent his days exactly as he did under the suns of June, lying in his hammock, stretched on the dripping grass, or making huge rambling excursions into the forest, the birds hopping from tree to tree after him, to return in the evening, drenched and soaked, but with the same unquenchable flame of joy burning within him.

"Catch cold?" he would ask, "I've forgotten how to do it, I think. I suppose it makes one's body more sensible always to sleep out-of-doors.

People who live indoors always remind me of something peeled and skinless."

"Do you mean to say you slept out-of-doors last night in that deluge?" asked Darcy. "And where, may I ask?"

Frank thought a moment.

"I slept in the hammock till nearly dawn," he said. "For I remember the light blinked in the east when I awoke. Then I went—where did I go?—oh, yes, to the meadow where the Pan-pipes sounded so close a week ago. You were with me, do you remember? But I always have a rug if it is wet."

And he went whistling upstairs.

Somehow that little touch, his obvious effort to recall where he had slept, brought strangely home to Darcy the wonderful romance of which he was the still half-incredulous beholder. Sleep till close on dawn in a hammock, then the tramp—or probably scamper—underneath the windy and weeping heavens to the remote and lonely meadow by the weir! The picture of other such nights rose before him; Frank sleeping perhaps by the bathing-place under the filtered twilight of the stars, or the white blaze of moonshine, a stir and awakening at some dead hour, perhaps a space of silent wide-eyed thought, and then a wandering through the hushed woods to some other dormitory, alone with his happiness, alone with the joy and the life that suffused and enveloped him, without other thought or desire or aim except the hourly and never-ceasing communion with the joy of nature.

They were in the middle of dinner that night, talking on indifferent subjects, when Darcy suddenly broke off in the middle of a sentence.

"I've got it," he said. "At last I've got it."

"Congratulate you," said Frank. "But what?"

"The radical unsoundness of your idea. It is this: All nature from highest to lowest is full, crammed full of suffering; every living organism in nature preys on another, yet in your aim to get close to, to be one with nature, you leave suffering altogether out; you run away from it, you refuse to recognize it. And you are waiting, you say, for the final revelation."

Frank's brow clouded slightly.

"Well?" he asked, rather wearily.

"Cannot you guess then when the final revelation will be? In joy you are supreme, I grant you that; I did not know a man could be so master of it. You have learned perhaps practically all that nature can teach. And if, as you think, the final revelation is coming to you, it will be the revelation of horror, suffering, death, pain in all its hideous forms. Suffering does exist; you hate it and fear it."

Frank held up his hand.

"Stop; let me think," he said.

There was silence for a long minute.

"That never struck me," he said at length. "It is possible that what you suggest is true. Does the sight of Pan mean that, do you think? Is it that nature, take it altogether, suffers horribly, suffers to a hideous inconceivable extent? Shall I be shown all the suffering?"

He got up and came round to where Darcy sat.

"If it is so, so be it," he said. "Because, my dear fellow, I am near, so splendidly near to the final revelation. Today the pipes have sounded almost without pause. I have even heard the rustle in the bushes, I believe, of Pan's coming. I have seen, yes, I saw today, the bushes pushed aside as if by a hand, and a piece of a face, not human, peered through. But I was not frightened, at least I did not run away this time."

He took a turn up to the window and back again.

"Yes, there is suffering all through," he said, "and I have left it all out of my search. Perhaps, as you say, the revelation will be that. And in that case, it will be good-bye. I have gone on one line. I shall have gone too far along one road, without having explored the other. But I can't go back now. I wouldn't if I could; not a step would I retrace! In any case, whatever the revelation is, it will be God. I'm sure of that."

The rainy weather soon passed, and with the return of the sun Darcy again joined Frank in long rambling days. It grew extraordinarily hotter, and with the fresh bursting of life, after the rain, Frank's vitality seemed to blaze higher and higher. Then, as is the habit of the English weather, one evening clouds began to bank themselves up in the west, the sun went down in a glare of coppery thunder-rack, and the whole earth broiling under an unspeakable oppression and sultriness paused and panted for the storm. After sunset the remote fires of lightning began to wink and flicker on the horizon, but when bed-time came the storm seemed to have moved no nearer, though a very low unceasing noise of thunder was audible. Weary and oppressed by the stress of the day, Darcy fell at once into a heavy uncomforting sleep.

He woke suddenly into full consciousness, with the din of some appalling explosion of thunder in his ears, and sat up in bed with racing heart. Then for a moment, as he recovered himself from the panic-land which lies between sleeping and waking, there was silence, except for the steady hissing of rain on the shrubs outside his window. But suddenly that silence was shattered and shredded into fragments by a scream from somewhere close at hand outside in the black garden, a scream of supreme and despairing terror. Again and once again it shrilled up, and then a babble of awful words was interjected. A quivering sobbing voice that he knew, said:

"My God, oh, my God; oh, Christ!"

And then followed a little mocking, bleating laugh. Then was silence again; only the rain hissed on the shrubs.

All this was but the affair of a moment, and without pause either to put on clothes or light a candle, Darcy was already fumbling at his door-handle. Even as he opened it he met a terror-stricken face outside, that of the man-servant who carried a light.

"Did you hear?" he asked.

The man's face was bleached to a dull shining whiteness.

"Yes, sir," he said. "It was the master's voice."

Together they hurried down the stairs, and through the dining-room where an orderly table for breakfast had already been laid, and out to the terrace. The rain for the moment had been utterly stayed, as if the tap of the heavens had been turned off, and under the lowering black sky, not quite dark, since the moon rode somewhere serene behind the conglomerated thunder-clouds, Darcy stumbled into the garden, followed by the servant with the candle. The monstrous leaping shadow of himself was cast before him on the lawn; lost and wandering odors of rose and lily and damp earth were thick about him, but more pungent was some sharp and acrid smell that suddenly reminded him of a certain chalet in which he had once taken refuge in the Alps. In the blackness of the hazy light from the sky, and the vague tossing of the candle behind him, he saw that the hammock in which Frank so often lay was tenanted. A gleam of white shirt was there, as if a man were sitting up in it, but across that there was an obscure dark shadow, and as he approached the acrid odor grew more intense.

He was now only some few yards away, when suddenly the black shadow seemed to jump into the air, then came down with tappings of hard hoofs on the brick path that ran down the pergola, and with frolicsome skippings galloped off into the bushes. When that was gone Darcy could see quite clearly that a shirted figure sat up in the hammock. For one moment, from sheer terror of the unseen, he hung on his step, and the servant joining him they walked together to the hammock.

It was Frank. He was in shirt and trousers only, and he sat up with braced arms. For one half-second he stared at them, his face a mask of horrible contorted terror. His upper lip was drawn back so that the gums of the teeth appeared, and his eyes were focused not on the two who approached him but on something quite close to him; his nostrils were widely expanded, as if he panted for breath, and terror incarnate and repulsion and deathly anguish ruled dreadful lines on his smooth cheeks and forehead. Then even as they looked the body sank backwards, and the ropes of the hammock wheezed and strained.

Darcy lifted him out and carried him indoors. Once he thought there was a faint convulsive stir of the limbs that lay with so dead a weight in his arms, but when they got inside, there was no trace of life. But the look of supreme terror and agony of fear had gone from his face, a boy tired with play but still smiling in his sleep was the burden he laid on the floor. His eyes had closed, and the beautiful mouth lay in smiling curves, even as when a few mornings ago, in the meadow by the weir, it had quivered to the music of the unheard melody of Pan's pipes. Then they looked further.

Frank had come back from his bath before dinner that night in his usual costume of shirt and trousers only. He had not dressed, and during dinner, so Darcy remembered, he had rolled up the sleeves of his shirt to above the elbow. Later, as they sat and talked after dinner on the close sultriness of the evening, he had unbuttoned the front of his shirt to let what little breath of wind there was play on his skin. The sleeves were rolled up now, the front of the shirt was unbuttoned, and on his arms and on the brown skin of his chest were strange discolorations which grew momentarily more clear and defined, till they saw that the marks were pointed prints, as if caused by the hoofs of some monstrous goat that had leaped and stamped upon him.

36

The Toll-House

By W. W. Jacobs

It's all nonsense," said Jack Barnes. "Of course people have died in the house; people die in every house. As for the noises—wind in the chimney and rats in the wainscot are very con-vincing to a nervous man. Give me another cup of tea, Meagle."

"Lester and White are first," said Meagle, who was presiding at the tea-table of the Three Feathers Inn. "You've had two."

Lester and White finished their cups with irritating slowness, paus-ing between sips to sniff the aroma, and to discover the sex and dates of arrival of the "strangers" which floated in some numbers in the beverage. Mr. Meagle served them to the brim, and then, turning to the grimly expectant Mr. Barnes, blandly requested him to ring for hot water.

"We'll try and keep your nerves in their present healthy condition," he remarked. "For my part I have a sort of half-and-half belief in the supernatural."

"All sensible people have," said Lester. "An aunt of mine saw a ghost once."

White nodded.

"I had an uncle that saw one," he said.

"It always is somebody else that sees them," said Barnes.

"Well, there is the house," said Meagle, "a large house at an absurdly low rent, and nobody will take it. It has taken toll of at least one life of every family that has lived there—however short the time—and since it has stood empty caretaker after caretaker has died there. The last care-taker died fifteen years ago."

"Exactly," said Barnes. "Long enough ago for legends to accumulate."

"I'll bet you a sovereign you won't spend the night there alone, for all your talk," said White suddenly.

"And I," said Lester.

"No," said Barnes slowly. "I don't believe in ghosts nor in any supernatural things whatever; all the same, I admit that I should not care to pass a night there alone."

"But why not?" inquired White.

"Wind in the chimney," said Meagle, with a grin.

"Rats in the wainscot," chimed in Lester.

"As you like," said Barnes, colouring.

"Suppose we all go?" said Meagle. "Start after supper, and get there about eleven? We have been walking for ten days now without an adventure—except Barnes's discovery that ditch-water smells longest. It will be a novelty, at any rate, and, if we break the spell by all surviving, the grateful owner ought to come down handsome."

"Let's see what the landlord has to say about it first," said Lester. "There is no fun in passing a night in an ordinary empty house. Let us make sure that it is haunted."

He rang the bell, and, sending for the landlord, appealed to him in the name of our common humanity not to let them waste a night watching in a house in which spectres and hobgoblins had no part. The reply was more than reassuring, and the landlord, after describing with considerable art the exact appearance of a head which had been seen hanging out of a window in the moonlight, wound up with a polite but urgent request that they would settle his bill before they went.

"It's all very well for you young gentlemen to have your fun," he said indulgently; "but, supposing as how you are all found dead in the morning, what about me? It ain't called the Toll-House for nothing, you know."

"Who died there last?" inquired Barnes, with an air of polite derision.

"A tramp," was the reply. "He went there for the sake of half-a-crown, and they found him next morning hanging from the balusters, dead."

"Suicide," said Barnes. "Unsound mind."

The landlord nodded. "That's what the jury brought it in," he said slowly; "but his mind was sound enough when he went in there. I'd known

462

him, off and on, for years. I'm a poor man, but I wouldn't spend the night in that house for a hundred pounds."

He repeated this remark as they started on their expedition a few hours later. They left as the inn was closing for the night; bolts shot noisily behind them, and, as the regular customers trudged slowly homewards, they set off at a brisk pace in the direction of the house. Most of the cottages were already in darkness, and lights in others went out as they passed.

"It seems rather hard that we have got to lose a night's rest in order to convince Barnes of the existence of ghosts," said White.

"It's in a good cause," said Meagle. "A most worthy object; and something seems to tell me that we shall succeed. You didn't forget the candles, Lester?"

"I have brought two," was the reply; "all the old man could spare."

There was but little moon, and the night was cloudy. The road between high hedges was dark, and in one place, where it ran through a wood, so black that they twice stumbled in the uneven ground at the side of it.

"Fancy leaving our comfortable beds for this!" said White again. "Let me see; this desirable residential sepulchre lies to the right, doesn't it?"

"Farther on," said Meagle.

They walked on for some time in silence, broken only by White's tribute to the softness, the cleanliness, and the comfort of the bed which was receding farther and farther into the distance. Under Meagle's guidance they turned off at last to the right, and, after a walk of a quarter of a mile, saw the gates of the house before them.

The lodge was almost hidden by over-grown shrubs and the drive was choked with rank growths. Meagle leading, they pushed through it until the dark pile of the house loomed above them.

"There is a window at the back where we can get in, so the landlord says," said Lester, as they stood before the hall door.

"Window?" said Meagle. "Nonsense. Let's do the thing properly. Where's the knocker?"

He felt for it in the darkness and gave a thundering rat-tat-tat at the door.

"Don't play the fool," said Barnes crossly.

"Ghostly servants are all asleep," said Meagle gravely, "but I'll wake them up before I've done with them. It's scandalous keeping us out here in the dark."

He plied the knocker again, and the noise volleyed in the emptiness beyond. Then with a sudden exclamation he put out his hands and stumbled forward.

"Why, it was open all the time," he said, with an odd catch in his voice. "Come on."

"I don't believe it was open," said Lester, hanging back. "Somebody is playing us a trick."

"Nonsense," said Meagle sharply. "Give me a candle. Thanks. Who's got a match?"

Barnes produced a box and struck one, and Meagle, shielding the candle with his hand, led the way forward to the foot of the stairs. "Shut the door, somebody," he said; "there's too much draught."

"It is shut," said White, glancing behind him.

Meagle fingered his chin. "Who shut it?" he inquired, looking from one to the other. "Who came in last?"

"I did," said Lester, "but I don't remember shutting it—perhaps I did, though."

Meagle, about to speak, thought better of it, and, still carefully guarding the flame, began to explore the house, with the others close behind. Shadows danced on the walls and lurked in the corners as they proceeded. At the end of the passage they found a second staircase, and ascending it slowly gained the first floor.

"Careful!" said Meagle, as they gained the landing.

He held the candle forward and showed where the balusters had broken away. Then he peered curiously into the void beneath.

"This is where the tramp hanged himself, I suppose," he said thoughtfully.

"You've got an unwholesome mind," said White, as they walked on. "This place is quite creepy enough without you remembering that. Now let's find a comfortable room and have a little nip of whisky apiece and a pipe. How will this do?"

He opened a door at the end of the passage and revealed a small square room. Meagle led the way with the candle, and, first melting a drop or two of tallow, stuck it on the mantelpiece. The others seated themselves on the floor and watched pleasantly as White drew from his pocket a small bottle of whisky and a tin cup.

"H'm! I've forgotten the water," he exclaimed.

"I'll soon get some," said Meagle.

He tugged violently at the bell-handle, and the rusty jangling of a bell sounded from a distant kitchen. He rang again.

"Don't play the fool," said Barnes roughly.

Meagle laughed. "I only wanted to convince you," he said kindly. "There ought to be, at any rate, one ghost in the servants' hall."

Barnes held up his hand for silence.

"Yes?" said Meagle, with a grin at the other two. "Is anybody coming?"

"Suppose we drop this game and go back," said Barnes suddenly. "I don't believe in spirits, but nerves are outside anybody's command. You may laugh as you like, but it really seemed to me that I heard a door open below and steps on the stairs."

His voice was drowned in a roar of laughter.

"He is coming round," said Meagle, with a smirk. "By the time I have done with him he will be a confirmed believer. Well, who will go and get some water? Will, you, Barnes?"

"No," was the reply.

"If there is any it might not be safe to drink after all these years," said Lester. "We must do without it."

Meagle nodded, and taking a seat on the floor held out his hand for the cup. Pipes were lit, and the clean, wholesome smell of tobacco filled the room. White produced a pack of cards; talk and laughter rang through the room and died away reluctantly in distant corridors.

"Empty rooms always delude me into the belief that I possess a deep voice," said Meagle. "Tomorrow I—"

He started up with a smothered exclamation as the light went out suddenly and something struck him on the head. The others sprang to their feet. Then Meagle laughed.

"It's the candle," he exclaimed. "I didn't stick it enough."

Barnes struck a match, and re-lighting the candle, stuck it on the mantelpiece, and sitting down took up his cards again.

"What was I going to say?" said Meagle. "Oh, I know; tomorrow I—"

"Listen!" said White, laying his hand on the other's sleeve. "Upon my word I really thought I heard a laugh."

"Look here!" said Barnes. "What do you say to going back? I've had enough of this. I keep fancying that I hear things too; sounds of something moving about in the passage outside. I know it's only fancy, but it's uncomfortable."

"You go if you want to," said Meagle, "and we will play dummy. Or you might ask the tramp to take your hand for you, as you go downstairs."

Barnes shivered and exclaimed angrily. He got up, and, walking to the half-closed door, listened.

"Go outside," said Meagle, winking at the other two. "I'll dare you to go down to the hall door and back by yourself."

Barnes came back, and, bending forward, lit his pipe at the candle.

"I am nervous, but rational," he said, blowing out a thin cloud of smoke. "My nerves tell me that there is something prowling up and down the long passage outside; my reason tells me that that is all nonsense. Where are my cards?"

He sat down again, and, taking up his hand, looked through it carefully and led.

"Your play, White," he said, after a pause.

White made no sign.

"Why, he is asleep," said Meagle. "Wake up, old man. Wake up and play."

Lester, who was sitting next to him, took the sleeping man by the arm and shook him, gently at first and then with some roughness but White, with his back against the wall and his head bowed, made no sign. Meagle bawled in his ear, and then turned a puzzled face to the others.

"He sleeps like the dead," he said, grimacing. "Well, there are still three of us to keep each other company."

"Yes," said Lester, nodding. "Unless—Good Lord! suppose—"

He broke off, and eyed them, trembling.

"Suppose what?" inquired Meagle.

"Nothing," stammered Lester. "Let's wake him. Try him again. White! WHITE!"

"It's no good," said Meagle seriously; "there's something wrong about that sleep."

"That's what I meant," said Lester; "and if he goes to sleep like that, why shouldn't—"

Meagle sprang to his feet. "Nonsense," he said roughly. "He's tired out; that's all. Still, let's take him up and clear out. You take his legs and Barnes will lead the way with the candle. Yes? Who's that?"

He looked up quickly towards the door. "Thought I heard somebody tap," he said, with a shamefaced laugh. "Now, Lester, up with him. One, two—Lester! Lester!"

He sprang forward too late; Lester, with his face buried in his arms, had rolled over on the floor fast asleep, and his utmost efforts failed to awake him.

"He—is—asleep," he stammered. "Asleep!"

Barnes, who had taken the candle from the mantelpiece, stood peering at the sleepers in silence and dropping tallow over the floor.

"We must get out of this," said Meagle. "Quick!"

Barnes hesitated. "We can't leave them here—" he began.

"We must," said Meagle, in strident tones. "If you go to sleep I shall go—Quick! Come!"

He seized the other by the arm and strove to drag him to the door. Barnes shook him off, and, putting the candle back on the mantelpiece, tried again to arouse the sleepers.

"It's no good," he said at last, and, turning from them, watched Meagle. "Don't you go to sleep," he said anxiously.

Meagle shook his head, and they stood for some time in uneasy silence. "May as well shut the door," said Barnes at last.

He crossed over and closed it gently. Then at a scuffling noise behind him he turned and saw Meagle in a heap on the hearthstone.

With a sharp catch in his breath he stood motionless. Inside the room the candle, fluttering in the draught, showed dimly the grotesque attitudes of the sleepers. Beyond the door there seemed to his overwrought imagination a strange and stealthy unrest. He tried to whistle, but his lips were parched, and in a mechanical fashion he stooped, and began to pick up the cards which littered the floor.

He stopped once or twice and stood with bent head listening. The unrest outside seemed to increase; a loud creaking sounded from the stairs.

"Who is there?" he cried loudly.

The creaking ceased. He crossed to the door, and, flinging it open, strode out into the corridor. As he walked his fears left him suddenly.

"Come on!" he cried, with a low laugh. "All of you! All of you! Show your faces—your infernal ugly faces! Don't skulk!"

He laughed again and walked on; and the heap in the fireplace put out its head tortoise fashion and listened in horror to the retreating footsteps. Not until they had become inaudible in the distance did the listener's features relax.

"Good Lord, Lester, we've driven him mad," he said, in a frightened whisper. "We must go after him."

There was no reply. Meagle sprang to his feet.

"Do you hear?" he cried. "Stop your fooling now; this is serious. White! Lester! Do you hear?"

He bent and surveyed them in angry bewilderment. "All right," he said, in a trembling voice. "You won't frighten me, you know."

He turned away and walked with exaggerated carelessness in the direction of the door. He even went outside and peeped through the crack, but the sleepers did not stir. He glanced into the blackness behind, and then came hastily into the room again.

He stood for a few seconds regarding them. The stillness in the house was horrible; he could not even hear them breathe. With a sudden resolution he snatched the candle from the mantelpiece and held the flame to White's finger. Then as he reeled back stupefied, the footsteps again became audible.

He stood with the candle in his shaking hand, listening. He heard them ascending the farther staircase, but they stopped suddenly as he went to the door. He walked a little way along the passage, and they went scurrying down the stairs and then at a jog-trot along the corridor below. He went back to the main staircase, and they ceased again.

For a time he hung over the balusters, listening and trying to pierce the blackness below; then slowly, step by step, he made his way downstairs, and, holding the candle above his head, peered about him.

"Barnes!" he called. "Where are you?"

Shaking with fright, he made his way along the passage, and summoning up all his courage, pushed open doors and gazed fearfully into empty rooms. Then, quite suddenly, he heard the footsteps in front of him.

He followed slowly for fear of extinguishing the candle, until they led him at last into a vast bare kitchen, with damp walls and a broken floor. In front of him a door leading into an inside room had just closed. He ran towards it and flung it open, and a cold air blew out the candle. He stood aghast.

"Barnes!" he cried again. "Don't be afraid! It is I—Meagle!"

There was no answer. He stood gazing into the darkness, and all the time the idea of something close at hand watching was upon him. Then suddenly the steps broke out overhead again.

He drew back hastily, and passing through the kitchen groped his way along the narrow passages. He could now see better in the darkness, and finding himself at last at the foot of the staircase, began to ascend it noiselessly. He reached the landing just in time to see a figure disappear round the angle of a wall. Still careful to make no noise, he followed the sound of the steps until they led him to the top floor, and he cornered the chase at the end of a short passage.

"Barnes!" he whispered. "Barnes!"

Something stirred in the darkness. A small circular window at the end of the passage just softened the blackness and revealed the dim outlines of a motionless figure. Meagle, in place of advancing, stood almost as still as a sudden horrible doubt took possession of him. With his eyes fixed on the shape in front he fell back slowly, and, as it advanced upon him, burst into a terrible cry.

"Barnes! For God's sake! Is it you?"

The echoes of his voice left the air quivering, but the figure before him paid no heed. For a moment he tried to brace his courage up to endure its approach, then with a smothered cry he turned and fled.

The passages wound like a maze, and he threaded them blindly in a vain search for the stairs. If he could get down and open the hall door—

He caught his breath in a sob; the steps had begun again. At a lumbering trot they clattered up and down the bare passages, in and out, up and down, as though in search of him. He stood appalled, and then as they drew near entered a small room and stood behind the door as they rushed by. He came out and ran swiftly and noiselessly in the other direction, and in a moment the steps were after him. He found the long corridor and raced along it at top speed. The stairs he knew were at the end, and with the steps close behind he descended them in blind haste. The steps gained on him, and he shrank to the side to let them pass, still continuing his headlong flight. Then suddenly he seemed to slip off the earth into space.

Lester awoke in the morning to find the sunshine streaming into the room, and White sitting up and regarding with some perplexity a badly blistered finger.

"Where are the others?" inquired Lester.

"Gone, I suppose," said White. "We must have been asleep."

Lester arose, and, stretching his stiffened limbs, dusted his clothes with his hands and went out into the corridor. White followed. At the noise of their approach a figure which had been lying asleep at the other end sat up and revealed the face of Barnes. "Why, I've been asleep," he said, in surprise. "I don't remember coming here. How did I get here?"

"Nice place to come for a nap," said Lester severely, as he pointed to the gap in the balusters. "Look there! Another yard and where would you have been?"

He walked carelessly to the edge and looked over. In response to his startled cry the others drew near, and all three stood staring at the dead man below.

About the Editor

BILL BOWERS IS A FREELANCE WRITER AND EDITOR WHO HAS LOVED ghost stories as long as he can remember. The tales collected here are among his all-time favorites. He lives with his wife in a small village in rural New England.